BREAKING FREE

THE BREAKING SERIES BOOK 1

JULIANA HAYGERT

COPYRIGHT

English - Portuguese

For a complete list of words used in the series <u>click here</u>!

Note that some words and expression don't have a perfect literal translation. The translation you see here is the one that fits the context of my novels.

Ai – ouch

Ainda bem – thank goodness

Até depois – see you later

Beijinho – a sweet made with condensed sweetened milk

Bem – fine, good, well

Boa noite – good night

Boa sorte – good luck

Boa tarde – good afternoon

Bom – well

Bom dia – good morning

Bomba – item to drink chimarrão with

Bombacha – typical pants used by gaúchos

Branquinho – same as Beijinho

Brigadeiro – a sweet made with condensed sweetened milk and cocoa powder

Café colonial – continental breakfast

Calma – calm down

Carreteiro – typical dish made of leftover steaks from barbecues

Chato – a name for someone who annoys you

Chimarrão – herb-based drink from the south of Brazil

Churrasco – Brazilian barbecue

Churrasqueira – a type of a grill where Brazilian barbecue is made

Claro – of course

Credo – jeez/damn

Cuia – kind of cup to drink chimarrão with

Dança folclórica gaúcha – typical dance from the south of Brazil

De nada – you're welcome

De novo – again

Delícia – delicious

Desculpa – sorry

Deus do céu – Lord above/Oh my God

Droga – crap

E aí – what's up?

É assim – this way

Eita – whoa

Então – so?

Eu não vou me atrasar – I won't be late

Eu te amo – I love you

Eu vou te matar – I'll kill you

Feijoada – dish made with black beans

Feliz Páscoa – Happy Easter

Filha da puta (daughter of a bitch), mimada (spoiled), china (it's like *prenda*, but in a bad way), rapariga sem vergonha (girl without shame), invejosa (jealous) – insulting names for women/girls

Filho duma puta – son of a bitch

Gaúcho(a) – people from the south of Brazil

Graças a Deus – thank God, thank goodness

Grande coisa – whatever

Guria – girl

Idiota – idiot

Irmã – sister

Irmãzinha – little sister

Mãe – mother

Me dá – give it to me

Me deixa em paz – leave me alone

Merda – shit

Meu Deus – my God

Morena – brunette, but in Brazil this term is used in a caring way, like darling or sweetie

Não – no

Negrinho – same as Brigadeiro

Nossa – wow/whoa

O que – what?

O que é isso – what is this?

Obrigado (a) – thanks

Oi – hi/hello

Ótimo – great

Pai – father

Pão de queijo – cheese bread

Parabéns - congratulations

Peão/Peões –cowboys in Brazil

Perfeita(o) – perfect

Pois então – well/you see

Por favor – please

Por que/por quê – why

Porque – because

Porcaria – crap/jeez/damn/shit/bad stuff

Porra – fuck/shit

Prazer – Pleasure, a short way of saying "nice to meet you"

Prenda – just like a gaúcha

Presta atenção – pay attention

Preta – black

Puta merda – fuck/shit/bullshit

Puta que pariu – goddamn it, holy shit, fuck

Que droga – crap/jeez/damn/this sucks

Que foi – what?

Que mentira – what a lie

Que nada – nonsense

Que porcaria é essa – what the hell is this?

Querida – dear

Rio Grande do Sul – southernmost state in Brazil

Sem rodeios – without rodeos, means without dillydallying

Senhorita – miss

Sério – really

Sete de Setembro – Brazil's Independence Day

Sim – yes

Tá bom/bem – okay

Tá tudo bem – it's okay

Também – too/also

Tchau – bye

Tche – common expression used by gaúchos – it can mean many things. A salutation, an exasperated exclamation, or even addressing someone

Te amo – I love you

Te comporta – behave

Tia – aunt

Tio – uncle

Tudo bem/Tudo bom – how are you?

Um minuto – one minute

Vai com – go with

Veado – deer. In Brazil, it's a nickname for homosexuals. Between friends, it's used as a friendly, teasing name.

Vestibular – an extensive and hard test Brazilians take to enter college – each college has its own vestibular test and if the student doesn't pass it, he/she doesn't enter that particular college.

Você – you

 Created with Vellum

AUTHOR'S NOTE

I hope you enjoy reading *Breaking Free*!

WARNING!
This book contains scenes of domestic violence, and sexual content (but no rape!), and mentions of animal cruelty.

Don't forget to sign up for my Newsletter to find out about new releases, cover reveals, give-aways, and more!

If you want to see exclusive teasers, help me

decide on covers, read excerpts, talk about books, etc, join my reader group on Facebook: Juliana's Club!

EIGHT MONTHS EARLIER

I CRANKED THE VOLUME ON THE STEREO AND SANG along to an old track from Lady Antebellum while driving away from my grandma's ranch. She insisted I stay since it was almost midnight and drive back to campus in the morning, but she knew I wouldn't change my mind. I didn't mind driving at night. Actually, I preferred it. Besides, I knew these roads by heart.

The aroma of cookies filling the inside of my car made me smile, and I inhaled deeply. She always baked something whenever I came to spend the weekend with her—which was often—and made me a huge container of whatever it was so I could take it back to campus. The bad side was that I had to share it with my roommate. Although we weren't close by any means, she loved my grandma's cooking.

I guess *everyone* loved my grandma's cooking.

I glanced at the cookies on the passenger seat. Mmm, too tempting. I reached for one and my eyes shifted over my tote beside it. It was open, and my big economics book, along with all the notes I'd stuck in it, was missing. Crap. I'd taken it out to study while grandma baked the cookies. Maybe it was still in her kitchen.

The bright blue light from the clock on the dashboard indicated it was past midnight. I was already close to town, but I had to go back. I would need my notes for my morning class. Great. What was supposed to be a twenty-minute drive had just turned into an hour-long one, if I counted going back to the ranch, then back to campus.

Cursing, I pulled over and turned around.

Thirteen minutes into my drive back, my cell phone rang, playing one of Tim McGraw's best songs.

"I thought you would be sleeping by now," I said.

"Hannah, where are you?" Eric asked. "I thought you were supposed to be on campus by now. I'm waiting for you to call me from your room, when you're safe and sound in your bed, so I can go to sleep too."

"Sorry, change of plans."

"What do you mean?"

"I'm going back 'cause I forgot my book and my notes at the ranch." For a second or two, he said nothing. "Eric, are you there?"

"Baby, you shouldn't worry about your book. It's late and you're probably tired. I would feel better if you didn't drive back and forth so much."

I smiled. He always cared so much about me. "Don't worry. I'm sure grandma will convince me to sleep over and drive back in the morning. She suggested it earlier anyway."

"Even so. You'll be tired in the morning."

He had a point, but it was too late now. "Eric, I'm almost there."

"Baby—"

"Why don't you tell me about your trip while I drive the last six miles?" I drove by the Thompson ranch. Not too far to go now. "It'll help pass the time."

"I already told you about it. We won."

"Yeah, but I'm sure there's more to it. Like, how was the other team? How was the hotel? Was the food good, and did Tomas fall off his horse this time?"

"It was all good. And no, Tomas didn't fall. Though, Justin's pony was limping by the end of the match. She'll be checked out by the vet tomorrow."

"Oh, I hope Irina is okay."

"I do too. Justin is too attached to that damn horse. If she's ill, he'll have a breakdown."

"And that's not good," I said. "Oh, speaking of not good, guess who showed up at the ranch this afternoon?"

He sighed. "No idea."

"Mr. Nash. Damn, sometimes I want to punch him for grandma. When is he going to learn she won't sell the ranch to him? Or to anyone? The man doesn't get it. Worse, when grandma refused to keep discussing it, he started yelling and threatening her. It was creepy."

"See? One more reason not to go there so much. What if this guy turns violent?"

"Ah, Eric. He's like a dog. All bark, no bite."

I turned left onto a smaller road and approached the ranch gates. Everything was supposed to be dark, except for a few lights around the stables and the house.

But the dark night was tinged by orange.

"Eric," I whispered. "Something's wrong."

The road to grandma's house and the stables

was a long one, but it suddenly seemed infinite. And the orange on the horizon seemed far away.

"What is it?"

The phone fell from my hands as I slammed on the brakes at the end of the road, causing the car to skid.

The main stable was completely engulfed in fire.

THE COFFEE MAKER BEEPED AND I REACHED FOR IT. If Eric saw me making a new pot in the afternoon, or any time of the day, he would dump it on the sink. Thankfully, he was at a meeting with his team at the polo club, so my coffee was safe.

I gripped my mug with both hands and inhaled deeply. Ah, the perfect comforting smell. And even more perfect mixed with the house's permanent vanilla scent. My grandma used it in everything—perfume, candles, fabric softener. After eight months, her home still smelled like it.

I looked around the kitchen and, as always, my eyes settled on the largest portrait on the wall. It was a 24-by-18 frame of grandma, Hercules, and me in front of the old stable a couple of weeks before the fire. Grandma and I were smiling, and Hercules had his muzzle on my neck. Damn, how I missed them.

My gaze fell on Hercules, my beautiful, happy horse. He was very different from the one in my stable right now.

My cell phone rang.

I glanced at the screen before answering and groaned. "Hi, Mom."

"Good afternoon, Hannah," she said, her tone flat. "I'm just calling to make sure you remember our dinner party tonight." She didn't wait for me to answer before continuing, "Do you have plans to come early and spend a few minutes with your parents?"

I sighed. "I'll try."

"You will try," she muttered.

"Mom, today is Jimmy's day off, and I have tons of stuff to do around here."

"Hannah, you're a Taylor. You can do anything you want to. If that means hiring more employees so you have more time for your family, you do it. But as a Taylor, you're never late to your appointments and events. Never."

I gritted my teeth. Typical, playing the you-are-a-Taylor card. It didn't matter to them that I spent most of my time as a student at the University of

California in Santa Barbara, or that I lived on a ranch by myself.

No. To them I was Hannah Taylor, one of the two heiresses to an equestrian empire, and girl-friend of the best polo player in the world.

I closed my eyes. "I'll be there about an hour before the party starts, Mom."

"Good," she said, sounding triumphant. "I'll see you and Eric in a few hours, then."

A loud cracking noise came from the stable, and I snapped my head to the window.

"Yeah, sure," I said, my mind on what that noise could be. "Mom, I gotta go. Bye."

Barely thinking, I turned off the phone, let go of my coffee, ran to the foyer, pulled on my boots, and ran out of the house.

The sun peeked out of heavy clouds, unable to dry the grass and dirt road from the morning rain. The trees and the flowers' scent drifted around me, accentuated by the dampness in the air.

I dashed down the stone path, careful not to slip, and reached the new stable as thunder rolled in the sky. Apparently, the rain wasn't over yet. The odd thing was it rarely rained over this region.

All the horses were quiet in the stable, except for Argus.

I'd barely seen this horse since Jimmy convinced me to bring him. Four days ago, I was arriving home after I had finished my last final for the spring semester, when Jimmy, my grandma's right hand, came running from the arena. "Miss Taylor."

I stepped out of my car and headed for the house. "Hi, Jimmy."

I entered the house but Jimmy halted by the door and took off his hat. "Michael, the animal control officer, rescued a horse this morning. He wants to bring him here."

"What? Why?"

"Your grandmother was the one who took care of them ..."

"Well, she isn't here anymore."

"But he thought you would like to have the horse." He scratched his thin mustache. "He mentioned putting him down if you don't accept him."

I crossed my arms. "That's a big pressure on me. You know I'm not my grandmother, Jimmy. I can't do what she did."

"But, besides me, you were the one who spent more time with her around this ranch. You may have never healed a horse by yourself, but you've seen your grandmother do it."

I had seen her doing it, yes, but that didn't mean I knew how to do it by myself. This would be the first time I would work on a damaged horse without her. It would only serve to make things more real, to remind me she wasn't here anymore and never would be again. That my own horse wasn't here anymore and never would be again.

The ranch had plenty of horses, but I didn't feel like they were mine. I hadn't cared for them the same way I cared for Hercules. I hadn't picked them like I had picked Hercules. Still, they had been my grandma's horses, and now I was taking care of them. Leaving her ranch to me was her wish.

Since she died, I had not taken or bought any new horses. It just didn't feel right. And accepting this one, even if for a short period of time, felt like I was betraying Hercules. Like I had found a substitute for him.

However, I couldn't let animal control put the horse down. Who was I kidding? Even if remembering Hercules hurt, I couldn't deny help to a horse.

"All right," I finally said.

Ugh, I had underestimated my preparedness to "cure" a horse by myself, and the pain I felt at thinking about taking care of any horse other than Hercules.

For now, I allowed Jimmy to take care of him.

But this Saturday being his day off, I was alone at the ranch.

The white horse jerked around in his stall, kicking and bumping his body against the wooden walls.

I approached his door. "Hey, boy," I whispered. "Easy, easy."

But he didn't go easy. He turned to me and, when his eyes met mine, he nickered loud and clear. Then, all the other horses complained and joined him, their screams ringing in my ears. I couldn't afford to have him disturb them. It would cause a ruckus, and I wouldn't be able to control them all.

Breaking the stare, Argus used his hind legs to kick at the door, and I retreated on instinct.

"Argus, please, look at me."

He kicked at the door. That was where the noise I heard from inside the house came from. The wood of the door was cracking and he knew it.

I glanced behind me to the shelf on the wall where the extra syringes and sedatives were. I could use that, but I had no idea how I would get close enough without being stomped on. There was another solution I could try.

I ran to the tack room and searched for something I could use to block the door. Either that or I could put him in another stall, but then he would just break it again. My best choice was to calm him down, if I could. Or give him sedatives like Jimmy had been doing whenever he became agitated.

Crap. Why had I allowed Jimmy to bring him in? I knew the answer without having to think about it. The poor animal was found beaten and frightened. I couldn't leave him alone or put him down without at least trying to save him.

Another crack, louder this time, startled me. I grabbed the first pair of bridle and reins I saw and dashed to Argus's stall just as he was about to jump over the broken door.

He halted and looked at me. I froze, afraid that if I moved he would gallop away.

"Argus, boy, come here." I hid my hands behind my back. "I've got carrots and apples here. Want some? Come and get it."

The horse was either too smart or too wary. He snorted at me before racing out of the stable.

I grabbed a syringe and a sedative from the shelf and scurried after him.

I would never be able to catch up with him, but I had to try. I put my hand inside my pocket to pick up my phone and realized I had dropped it when I was putting on my boots. I cursed myself and considered racing to the house and grabbing the phone, but if I didn't go after him, I would lose him. And if I lost sight of him now, I might never find him again.

He trotted down the path leading away from the property as if he savored freedom. Thunder echoed through the sky. Startled, the horse nickered and sped up.

"Argus!" I yelled, running after him.

Great! Now I would spend the afternoon racing after this damn horse instead of doing my chores and getting ready for the party. I hoped I solved this situation fast, otherwise I would be late for the damn dinner party, and my mother wouldn't care about explanations.

Speaking of my mother, if she saw me like this —in short jeans, a pink tank, and red cowboy boots, now covered in mud—she would have an anxiety attack and faint, at the very least. Thank goodness, she lived one hour away.

The horse left the ranch and turned on the main road. Keeping up with a horse was impossible, and soon I'd have to stop chasing him. Hopefully, the Thompsons would be outside their barn, and I would be able to holler for help.

"Argus, stop!"

He slowed when he reached a turn in the road.

Tall trees reached up and entangled their leaves together, creating a beautiful green tunnel.

Something moved in the bushes behind him, and Argus halted, watching it. Damn, I hoped it wasn't a mountain lion. I tried not thinking about it as I used the horse's distraction to get near him.

A few seconds later, a squirrel climbed a tree.

Argus snorted and darted away from it, crossing the lanes.

An SUV appeared on the road from under the tree tunnel. Moving too fast.

My heart stopped.

Argus jumped high, super high. High enough that the SUV missed his hind legs by a few inches.

The horse tumbled on the grass. The SUV skidded to a halt. I ran to Argus but stopped before I got too close and scared him even more. I fell to my knees by the side of the road, feeling like jelly. My heart pumped against my chest, and I couldn't control my breathing.

A guy got out the SUV. "*Meu Deus!*" He looked from me to Argus and back again, visibly lost. "What happened?"

His brown eyes huge, Argus remained on the ground, shaking against a tree surround by beautiful purple Douglas Iris flowers. If this wasn't a bad situation, I would have admired this place.

Though they grew all over the Central California coast and were common, I loved these flowers.

The guy walked toward him, but I raised my hand.

"No. You'll scare him away."

"It's okay. I know how to deal with horses," he said, a heavy musical accent dripping from his words.

He knelt on the grass, several feet away from Argus, spread his hands on the ground, and spoke stupid but sweet things to the horse. Like a mother talking nonsense to her baby. And several of the words were in another language.

I just watched it. And ... noticed him for the first time. He appeared to be my age, maybe a year older, at most. Even crouched, he was tall, with chin-length, layered, light brown hair, tanned skin, a strong jaw, thin nose, and full lips. His shoulders and arms seemed constricted under his white T-shirt, and the same went for the dark jeans covering his thighs. To top it all, he wore brown cowboy boots. All designer pieces. A Tommy Hilfiger cowboy.

He was ... handsome.

And a stranger.

I thought I knew all the ranches or horse-related people in the region.

Without taking his eyes from Argus, the guy scooted toward me and grabbed the halter and reins from my hands.

"Do you have any rope?" he asked, his voice low. I shook my head. "What's his name?"

"Argus."

He tucked the reins into his back pocket and raised his hands. "Hey, Argus, I'm going to get closer. But it's okay. I want to help you."

I held my breath.

He crawled toward the horse, whispering soothing words. Almost imperceptible, Argus shook less and less. The guy reached over and touched Argus's foot. The horse neighed, but the guy didn't take his hand away. He left it there, as if waiting for Argus's permission to do more.

And I stood as still as I could.

"Good horsey," he cooed. "See, I'm a good guy too."

Slowly, he groped for the reins.

Then another stupid squirrel came down the tree. Argus shot up, kicked the guy back, and dashed in the opposite direction the squirrel went.

I was undecided for a second. Should I go after Argus or help the guy, who was curled up in the grass, his hand on his stomach?

The Good Samaritan in me spoke louder, and I

scooted over to him. "Are you okay? Did he hurt you?"

With his eyes closed, the guy shook his head. "Not really." Then why was he making a face? "I'll be fine." He took a long breath and sat up, opened his eyes, and looked at me.

My breath caught. His eyes were green-blue, clear like water, and shiny as light.

Amazing.

I willed myself to move and rose to my feet. "Well, if you're fine, I'm going after my horse."

"Wait." The guy stood, gaining a good nine or ten inches on me. He still had his hand on his belly and made another painful face. His nose was kind of cute when scrunched up. Oh, what was I thinking? "He's too far away already. We can catch up with him in my car." The guy gestured to the black Grand Cherokee.

"Hmm." I closed my mouth, unsure of what to say. I shouldn't have looked at him, noticed him, much less ride in the same car as him. "I'm sure I can find him later," I lied, walking away.

Lightning crisscrossed the sky, followed by deafening thunder. I wouldn't make it home before getting drenched. However, I was more worried about Argus than me. He was the one who didn't like storms, howling winds, and loud thunder. He was the one with past phantoms to overcome.

The first drops hit my face and I mentally cursed, adding a jacket to the list of things I should have picked up before rushing out of the house.

The SUV stopped by my side, and the window rolled down.

"Come on," the guy said, leaning over and opening the door from the inside. He showed me the halter and reins. "Besides, you have to get these."

Was he trying to trick me? A psycho luring a woman in before raping and killing her? Oh no. He could keep the halter and the reins. I had about two dozens of those back at the ranch.

I continued walking. "I'm fine."

The rain intensified.

The guy drove the SUV to my side again and propped the door wide open. "Listen, I'm no crazy man, okay? I'm just trying to help." He picked up his cell phone from his pocket and extended it toward me. "Here, you can keep this. If you think I'm crossing the line even for half a second, you're welcome to call for help."

I eyed the cell phone. What game was he playing?

"Oh, there's this too." He leaned over the backseat and grabbed a baseball bat. "Here. You can use it to hit me before calling for help."

I laughed.

He smiled.

My breath caught again. Holy shit, the guy was too handsome. For that alone, I shouldn't get in his car.

"Come on," he urged. "You're getting all wet."

Yes, I was, but I would also avoid a lot of trouble if I got wet instead of getting in his car.

I glanced from side to side. Nobody was here. Nobody would know. All he had to do was drive me home, and then it would be as if nothing ever happened.

Feeling like a teenager lying to her parents about a sleepover turned into going out, I got into the car, and he handed me a towel. Was there anything his car didn't carry?

"Thanks," I said, taking the towel and keeping myself as far away from him as the seats allowed.

"You're welcome." He started driving in the direction Argus had gone. "My name is Leo, by the way."

"I'm Hannah."

"Nice to meet you."

"You too."

"So, hmm, does your horse run away a lot?"

"Argus isn't technically mine. And no, this is the first time."

Leo frowned. "I saw Argus's scars. What happened to him?"

I sighed. "He was mistreated by his previous owner. His owner beat him and even let his dogs bite him. The Santa Barbara County Animal Control Unit took him away and brought him to me."

"Sorry to ask, but why to you?"

I glanced at him, wondering if he was just trying to keep the small talk going or genuinely interested. It didn't really matter. "It was my grandma's job. Besides running a riding and training ranch, she also recovered traumatized horses."

"Was?"

I looked out the window. The rain had picked up to a steady downpour, making it difficult to see much farther than the road. It would be impossible to find Argus like this.

"She died eight months ago."

"Oh, I'm sorry." He peered at me with a small smile, and my heart fluttered.

"It's okay." I busied myself by picking up the syringe and the ampoule from my pocket. "Maybe we should use this."

Leo glanced at my hands. "Sedative? Not my

preferred method of dealing with horses, but it may help. Prepare it, just in case."

I broke the top of the ampoule and filled the syringe with the yellowish liquid. I recapped the syringe and returned it to my pocket.

As we passed through some trees along the road, I spotted a white dot among them. "There," I yelled.

He pulled the car over a short distance from the trees, so as not to scare Argus away before we got close enough. If I thought Argus was shaking before, it had been nothing compared to now.

Leo grabbed the halter and reins. "Any plans?"

"Not really, but just know he will be extra frightened. He seems to hate rain and thunder."

"Duly noted." Leo grabbed a leather jacket from the backseat and offered it to me.

I stared at it, then shook my head. "I'm not made of sugar."

His gaze locked with mine, and a shiver ran down my spine. "Maybe, but it would be better if you didn't get a cold."

"What about you?"

He smiled. "I never get sick."

He jumped out of the car, and I felt paralyzed for a second. What had just happened?

I left his jacket on his seat and turned to leave

the car, then saw him tiptoeing to where Argus was hidden. His wet white T-shirt became translucent and clung to his body, the muscles on his back contracting with each movement.

I swallowed, ashamed for noticing such things. Yes, I had a boyfriend, but I wasn't blind. I tried not looking, but it was hard.

Hiding the reins in his pocket again, Leo halted several feet from Argus, arms outstretched to the sides. He was saying something, but with the rain, I couldn't hear what.

What was I doing inside the car when I should be helping him?

Upset with myself, I shot out of the SUV and tiptoed closer, but not too close. For some reason, I thought Argus was starting to prefer the stranger to me.

Leo took a step forward. The horse nickered loudly and retreated farther into the trees. It seemed that he would have blended with the bushes and Douglas Iris flowers if he could. So Leo changed tactics.

He turned to me, grabbed the syringe from my pocket, and whispered, "Don't move."

Following his own advice, Leo knelt on the grass, his hands visible at his sides. He stayed like that without saying a word, his eyes on Argus, and his breathing quietly controlled.

After ten minutes, Argus stopped trying to blend in with the trees and flowers. After twenty minutes, Argus took a step forward. After thirty minutes, he took another step closer.

By then, we were all soaked and shivering.

I was about to give up, to tell Leo it wasn't worth it, and to try and just grab the horse and inject him with the sedative somehow. Then thunder rang through the sky and Argus neighed, lifting his front legs. Leo jumped up and charged, putting his arms around Argus's neck. The horse fought against it, but Leo was quick and strong, and pricked him with the syringe. The horse neighed once more, but Leo didn't let go. He even got the halter on Argus in no time. The horse stumbled; the sedative was already working. Leo pushed him against one of the trees and pressed his body to Argus's. The horse didn't like it, but Leo said something and ran his hand along Argus's neck. The horse quieted some.

After a few minutes, Argus slumped to the ground, his breathing slower and his eyes heavy.

Leo looked at me over his shoulder. "Now what?"

2

———

"THERE," LEO SAID, CLOSING THE STALL DOOR.

Back at the road, he had tied Argus to a tree, then drove me to the ranch, where I'd gotten the truck and the trailer. He left his SUV at the ranch and drove with me to pick up Argus. It was hard, but we'd made the horse stand up and take a few steps by himself and into the trailer. Afterward, we'd driven the trailer back to the ranch and put Argus into a new stall in the stable.

"Thank you," I said, giving him a cup of coffee and a towel I'd brought from inside the house. I sipped from my mug and pulled my towel tight over my shoulders.

"*Obrigado*," he said, putting the towel around himself. Thank God, because I couldn't take staring at that wet shirt over his muscles any longer. "If I were you, I would reinforce the door of the stall he's in." He looked around, closing a fist on the edge of the towel and tugging it tighter, and I noticed the thin black band on his right ring finger. Interesting. "Maybe even the walls."

I glanced at drunken Argus over the stall door. Even like this, he didn't look peaceful. "For a horse in his condition, he sure is strong."

Leo leaned against the wall. "And beautiful. At least, he appears to be, without all the scars and cuts."

If it depended on me, the bastard who'd done this would rot in the filthiest prison in this country. Ugh, I couldn't think about what he'd done. It hurt too much to know Argus probably wasn't the only animal being mistreated out there.

Taking a big swallow of my coffee, I focused on something else. I dared spying over my mug at this stranger, who was being way too nice to Argus and me. His wet hair clung to his face, adorning his perfect features, and the dampness on his skin glistened.

Poor me and my weak will. I shouldn't start any small talk. I should keep my mouth shut and send him away. I should get ready for the damn party I was already late to, but I couldn't help it.

"So, where are you from?"

Leo smiled. "Brazil. My family and I just moved to the O'Connor ranch. I was on my way there when I almost ran into Argus."

I winced, trying to keep away the threatening images. Just thinking of what could have happened made me nauseous.

Worse than that was looking at the horse and seeing his wounds. Most were scabbed over, but some would take months or even years to fully heal. The more visible ones were the stitches on his left hind leg, his left shoulder, his chest, and the left side of his neck. And he still had bandages on his right front cannon.

"My turn," Leo said. "Do you live here? Alone?"

And just like that my defensive wall sprouted right back up. "Why do you ask?"

"Just curious. I didn't see anyone else. I can't imagine living all alone at such a big place." He put his empty mug over the short wall of an empty stall. "And your parents? Do they help?"

"No. My father has a horse breeding farm and he doesn't approve of this ranch."

"May I ask why you have it, then?"

"The ranch was my grandma's. She left it to me, but everyone keeps telling me I should sell it."

"Why?"

"My father wants me to take over the family business once I graduate from college." It was the truth, but not all of it. I avoided telling him about what Eric thought. Bad me.

"College, huh? What major?"

I squinted. "Are we playing twenty questions or something?"

He averted his eyes. "No, sorry. I didn't mean to pry. It's just ... you seem so independent and, well, you're caring for this horse, so that's something. I'm intrigued, I guess."

I watched him as he turned to peek at Argus. I was intrigued too. Way more than I should have been.

I sighed. "Economics. Next fall I start my sophomore year."

"You don't sound happy about it."

"It was my father's choice, not mine. He wants me to enroll in an MBA after. It's not bad, and yes, I want to take over the family business, but I'll say no if that means selling this ranch." My honesty surprised me. Not that it was a secret. My father—and Eric—knew my opinion on the matter, but I'd never told a stranger.

He looked at me, and once more, the green-blue of his eyes amazed me. "This place means a lot to you."

"It does," I whispered, without taking my eyes from his.

He brushed a strand of wet hair from my face, his fingers grazing my cheek, lingering on my skin. His gaze fell on my mouth, and I licked my lips without meaning to. He rested his hand on my cheek, and a shiver rolled down my body.

Why did I feel like this—and I wouldn't name it because it would only make everything worse—about this stranger? Yes, he was handsome, but so was Eric. Maybe it was just my body reacting to something equally attractive but in a different way. Besides, Eric probably looked at other girls too— just appreciating the view—and remained faithful and loving to me. I could look at the guys around me and appreciate their good looks, couldn't I?

Still, I didn't like it.

I stepped backward, releasing myself from his touch.

"Thank you for helping me with Argus. I don't know what I'd have done if you hadn't shown up. So thank you." I took his empty mug from the wall. "But, if you don't mind, I've got someplace to be."

His brows knitted together. "*Sim*, sure. I understand." He removed the towel from around his shoulder, and I fought the urge to look at his white shirt. More specifically, at the chest and shoulders under the shirt. "Thank you. For the coffee and the towel."

I didn't wait for him to go. I *shouldn't* wait for him to go. Because I could change my mind and start a new conversation before he reached his SUV, or I could just gape at his behind and make a fool of myself.

I nodded and dashed out of the stable and into the house without looking back.

I stopped my car in front of the gates and pressed the button to slip my window down. I leaned over the door and punched in the numbers. A second later, the gates slid sideways, allowing me to pass.

I drove down the long, winding road, admiring the familiar view. On the right were lush green lawns, trees on the horizon, and hidden behind it, a lake. I sighed and turned my head to the left. More green lawn, followed by a huge stable topping a hill, where my parents' prized horses stayed. Behind it, there were other stables, simpler though, and extensive fields.

Right at the end of the path, a white four-story house presented itself.

To many, it would be a dream house. To me, it meant control and seriousness. Not that growing up here had been bad. Far from it. It was just that, when I visited my grandma, which had been often, I experienced how caring and warm and open a person could be, and I missed that.

I stopped the car by the front steps, and a valet opened the door for me.

"Eric called to let us know he would be arriving late," my father said as I climbed up the front stairs. He looked impeccable in his brown suit. I had his green eyes and his straight, dark brown hair, though his was cut short with every strand in the right place.

"How nice of him," I said with a smile. Used to the fakeness of the society they lived in, my parents didn't notice the sarcasm dripping from my words.

"You're late," my mother said. Her tone wasn't disapproving or accusing. Though it was almost uncaring.

I could try to explain what happened, but I doubted she would care. So I ignored her comment and kissed her cheek. "You look beautiful, Mom."

She looked down at herself, pretending to be demure. "Thanks, dear." Her indigo cocktail dress accentuated her blue eyes, and her blond hair was pulled back into a fancy bun. I had inherited her short height, five-four, and delicate form, nothing more. "You look dashing too."

"Thanks."

My father put his hand on my back and led me in. "How's school?"

"Four days ago was my last final. The semester is over."

We heard the engine of a car approaching the house. My father patted my shoulder. "If you'll excuse us, we'll greet our guests."

"Sure."

They turned back to the front door, and I glanced around the foyer. Imposing and too white. At the top of the rounded stairs, my sister watched me.

"Hi, Hilary," I said, offering a smile.

She didn't smile back. "Hi."

She flipped her blond hair and walked down the stairs like a Miss America contestant. Though she was already a little taller than me at sixteen, she was exactly like our mother. Fair, perfect skin, rosy lips, green eyes—the only thing she didn't get from our mother—and a complete snob. She didn't pretend to be demure as our mother did.

"Is school over yet?" I asked, attempting to initiate some kind of conversation with her.

She looked at her pink nails as if bored. "Two more weeks."

We walked together to the living room. A waiter offered us drinks, and I grabbed a glass of sparkling water. "Any big plans for the summer?"

Hilary took a glass of some pink cocktail. Hopefully, it wasn't alcoholic. "Not really."

This wasn't going well. She had to give me more, or I wouldn't be able to keep this conversation going by myself.

My parents and their guests entered the living room moments later and, as good hosts, they kept everyone entertained and talking.

My parents loved hosting fancy dinners where they could show people how rich and elegant they were, how beautiful their daughters were, how impeccable their house was, and how exquisite their horses were.

I hated all of it.

What I wouldn't give to go back to my ranch, light the fireplace—even in the summer—and curl up on my sofa with a book and a glass of whiskey on the rocks. With Eric massaging my feet, of course. Not that he would ever do that. He hated that ranch. Unfortunately, he was more like my parents, loving fancy and rich things.

At some point, tired of listening to the women talking about the new dresses they'd bought or the latest resort they'd gone too, I went into the kitchen. The waiters widened their eyes at me, until the cook hugged me.

"Hello, Miss Taylor," Rosa said. "Long time no see."

"True." I pulled back and smiled at my mother's cook. She had been with the family since I was a kid and she knew I loved hiding in the kitchen—and tasting whatever she was cooking—during these dinners.

She held my hand between hers. "How have you been?"

Ah, the golden question. "I'm good." I reached to the counter behind her and served myself some whiskey. The waiters seemed confused, which in turn was almost entertaining. "So, what goodies do you have here?"

Rosa smiled and showed me a tray with what looked like homemade Swiss bonbons. Dessert before dinner, one of the many reasons I loved the kitchen.

"Hannah." My father's voice came from the

door, and I almost choked on my bonbon. "Can I talk to you for a second?"

With my glass in hand, and trying to swallow the rest of the bonbon, I followed my father to his office. He closed the door behind me and showed me to the seat before his thick mahogany desk.

"What is it?" I asked, a little worried.

He clasped his hands on the desk. "We haven't talked business lately, and well, it has been eight months since you inherited the ranch. We should talk about your plans for it."

"Should I have any plans? I mean, I thought about running it like grandma did. Offering riding lessons, accepting a horse for boarding every now and then."

"Once you graduate, you will sell it, won't you?"

"What? Of course not." My grandma, his mom, had left the ranch to me because she knew I'd take care of it. If she wanted to have it sold, she'd have left it to him. But she didn't. I wouldn't betray her like that.

He frowned. "Excuse me? You have to forget about this idea and sell it. Or incorporate it into our lands and business."

"Dad, I don't like talking about this. You're still

young and will be the head of the company for a long time."

"I'm fifty-eight, and I'd like to retire before I'm too old to truly enjoy what my money can buy."

He'd been telling me that since I was five years old. That one day I would run the entire farm and he would be able to retire. When I was a kid, I felt proud because that meant he trusted me. Now, I was torn. I loved horses and wanted to keep his farm. But it wouldn't be at the expense of grandma's ranch.

"I would prefer keeping both businesses. Her ranch and your breeding farm."

"I don't think you'll be able to keep up with both. And, if we analyze this situation, you will see that the breeding business is the best choice."

"I don't need to do this alone. I have Jimmy. And Hilary could help me with your farm."

My father laughed out loud. "Hilary? Have you seen her around horses? No, I don't think so. She doesn't like them. She doesn't even look in the stables' direction."

Yeah, I remembered, but I thought she would grow out of that phase. "Dad, I need more time to think."

"There's nothing to think about. You have to

sell the ranch. And the sooner you do it, the better."

"But I don't—"

A knock on the door shut me up.

Eric peeked inside. "Am I interrupting something?"

A huge smile appeared on my father's face. "Eric! Come in. Hannah and I were just talking business."

My boyfriend strode into the room, sporting a big grin. His hands were inside the pockets of his gray suit, which emphasized his dark blue eyes. With short black hair and his fair skin, he looked amazing.

"Well, whatever you say, sir. I'm on your side."

My father laughed. "That's why I like you."

Eric winked at me, enjoying the good points he had scored with my father over the years. I would never understand what he'd done to earn my father's blind approval. It was like that with almost everyone. Eric would smile their way and win them over.

With that same pretty smile, he offered me his hand. "Hello, baby."

I took it and he pulled me up. Even though I had on four-inch heels, he was still a couple of inches taller than me. "Hi."

He kissed my cheek and whispered, "You look beautiful."

My father walked around the desk and patted Eric's back. "Good to see you, my boy. You might like to know Hannah and I were discussing selling the ranch."

Eric's brows shot up. "Really?"

Since the day the lawyer told me that everything my grandma had owned belonged to me, Eric had been trying to convince me to get rid of it. It wouldn't be good for me to hold on to the past so much, he'd said.

"No," I said. "Father, like always, suggested it and I negated it."

"You really should think about it," Eric said. "Your father and I have been telling you that since day one. Don't you think you should listen to us?"

"Good point," my father said. "We have experience with business ownership, Hannah, and we agree that you should sell that ranch."

I knew I had no arguing point here anymore. So, to change the subject, I lied. "I'll think about it."

"Good." My father walked to the door and held it open for us. "How about we go back to the party? We shouldn't leave our guests unattended."

Eric and I followed my father out of his office,

but before we could walk into the living room, Eric held me back.

"You really look beautiful," he said before kissing me.

My hands slid around his shoulders as I opened my mouth to him. His kiss was hungry, demanding, and forceful. His fingers dug into my hips, and he pulled me to him. Knowing we had been together for a little over two years and I still had this effect on him took my breath away. He'd first shown interest in me when I'd been a teenager, and being five years older than me, he'd been a man already running his family business. I couldn't believe he truly wanted anything with me.

His lips trailed down my jaw, and his hot breath on my skin sent a shiver rolling down my spine.

"We better stop now," he whispered.

Smiling, I pulled back. "What? Can't lose control, Mr. Bennett?"

He rested his forehead on mine. "Not here, no, I can't."

I laughed and slipped my hand in his. "So, tell me, how was the meeting?"

"Not too good. The French team we were negotiating with doesn't want to lend us a player anymore."

"Oh, I'm sorry."

"It's okay," he said, turning to the archway leading into the living room. His arm snaked around my waist, and he positioned me beside him, my left shoulder in front of the right side of his body. "Let's go."

He loved that. Showing us off. The beautiful heiress to the equestrian empire and the best polo player in the world. What a couple, everyone said. You two belong on the cover of magazines, I'd heard before.

Sometimes I thought he had chosen to date me just because of my father's business, because of our money. But he was filthy rich too, so that wasn't right. Maybe he wanted to keep his family status. Though when he looked at me, his eyes gleaming with desire and possessiveness, as if I were only his and he was damn happy about it. I knew that status and money didn't really matter to him.

The room went quiet when we walked in.

"Good evening," Eric said with a diplomatic smile, and the people exploded into grins and salutes and compliments.

Five seconds later, we were engulfed by the guests, talking about polo matches and horses. Every now and then, someone would tell us how good we looked, what a fortunate couple we were, and what a great player Eric was. It was annoying, really.

One of my father's associates approached us. "Hi, I'm Scott O'Neill."

Eric shook his hand. "Hello, Mr. O'Neill. I'm Eric Bennett. I assume you're doing business with Mr. Taylor."

"That's right," the man said. He looked younger than most of the men my father did business with, around thirty-five, and his black suit complemented his gray eyes. "And you're the famous polo player."

Eric smiled. "That, and I also run my family's farm."

"Oh, really? A breeding farm as well?"

"Not exactly. My business is a regular horse and cattle farm."

"I see." Mr. O'Neill's eyes found me and he smiled. "And you must be Hannah Taylor, famous for your beauty. The rumors don't lie."

My cheeks heated, and Eric's grip on my waist tightened. "That's a new one," I said, smiling politely, though all I wanted to do was to walk away from him.

Scott nodded to Eric. "You're a lucky man."

"I know," Eric said, the amusement in his tone gone.

Relief colored Eric's face when the butler came in, announcing dinner was ready.

The food was delicious, and dinner would have been bearable if it wasn't for Mr. O'Neill's constant stare and Eric's tight grip on my thigh under the table. Each time the man smiled at me, Eric's fingers dug into my skin and I pressed my lips together, willing the scream to stay in my throat.

"What do you do, Miss Taylor?" Mr. O'Neill asked from across the table.

"I'm attending college in Santa Barbara and I run a riding ranch."

His brows arched up. "Really? That's interesting."

One of my mom's friends asked, "But the town is almost ninety minutes away. You live on campus?"

"No, I—"

"Ah," she interrupted me. "That's good. I have only heard bad things about college residency."

"Where do you live, then?" Mr. O'Neill asked.

Right then, Eric's grip became agonizing and I jerked free. He was probably imagining the man's throat instead. That didn't excuse him for hurting me.

I opened my mouth to answer, but Eric spoke first. "The club might hire a French player to add to my team," he announced.

I frowned. He had just told me it wasn't going well, and now he was announcing it to the entire table as if it were a done deal. But he succeeded in what he planned as everyone shot him questions about it, including Mr. O'Neill.

3

―――――

THE FOLLOWING MORNING I TOLD JIMMY WHAT happened with Argus—though I had to alter the story to leave Leo out of it—and asked him to nail more wood around Argus's stall.

Thankfully, we only had a familiar group scheduled for today, and they could ride around the property without any guides. I helped them saddle the horses and sent them on their way before sinking to the ground. I pressed my back against the wall, and my eyes fixed on Argus's door.

I had no idea what to do with him. My first error had been to allow him to come here. I wasn't my grandma. I couldn't "cure" a horse like she could. Even though she denied it, we all called her a horse whisperer. She was *that* good. And I certainly wasn't.

"Just looking at him won't fix him," Jimmy said as he walked into the stable.

"I shouldn't have agreed to this," I told him.

He sat on the bench beside me. "You wouldn't have forgiven yourself if he'd been put down instead."

True. But that didn't do anything to help the horse. Poor animal. I wasn't much different than his owner. I saw him suffering and did nothing. The only thing we did so far was call the vet in to treat his visible wounds.

I sat on the bench. "I want you to get started with him."

"Me? I can only ride horses, nothing more. You're the one with your grandmother's blood."

"As if being able to help a damaged horse was some kind of genetic trait."

"Maybe not that, but your personality. Your character. You're just like her."

I looked at him. To my grandma, Jimmy had been like a son. She had taken care of him, helped raise him, and had given him a job. Growing up, he had been like an uncle to me.

I wondered why my grandma had left only a couple of horses and a tiny house on the property to him if she considered him a son. Didn't she love him enough to give him more? I certainly didn't need all of this, not with my family's money. At least I'd given him a fat raise.

"I'm not like her," I finally said. "She was determined, contagiously happy, and decided. She knew what she was doing. I don't."

"Sure you do. You just have to trust your instincts."

He would never understand. "I can't," I whispered.

He took my hands into his callused ones. "How long since you last rode a horse?"

"What does that have to do with helping Argus?"

"Just answer."

"No."

"Well, good thing I know then. Since that day. Since your grandmother and Hercules died."

I pulled my hand from his and shot up. "I still don't know why that matters."

Jimmy stood and looked into my eyes. "'Cause you're afraid. You're afraid of caring for this poor animal as much as you cared for Hercules."

"What? That's nonsense."

"Is it? Then explain to me why you haven't touched other horses? And I don't mean to saddle them up for our customers. I mean to pet them. To ride. To jump. You loved jumping. You were great at it."

"I'm too old to pursue a career in jumping, and someone has to run this place. And my father's place too, someday."

"I'm not talking about being professional anymore. You could do it as a hobby."

"I'm out of shape."

"Another excuse."

I groaned. "What do you want from me?"

"I want you to admit the truth to yourself. Deep down you know it." He put his hands on my shoulders and squeezed. "You can see yourself falling for Argus and you're afraid of it. Just because your horse is gone, it doesn't mean you'll stop caring for him. You won't. Ever. Think of it like this. Even if you meet new people and make new friends, you won't forget your grandmother, right? You will love her forever, right? Same for the horse. You don't need to feel guilty for helping another horse, for caring for him. You can love more than one horse at a time, you know."

Actually, I didn't know. And I didn't *want* to know.

Hand in hand, Eric and I walked from the parking lot to the club's main house.

"I'm glad your classes are over for now," he said, squeezing my hand. "Otherwise, I would have had to come here alone."

I smiled, not amused. He would never be alone. First, he had his teammates: Tomas, David, and Justin. Second, he knew everyone at the club and everyone adored him. He just wanted to please me, and I loved him for that.

However, I was glad my classes were over for now too. I needed more time at the ranch and I liked coming to his games, even exhibition-only like this one. Granted, I hated everything else about the club and the people here.

As soon as we stepped into the main house, we were surrounded. Friends of my parents, Eric and my father's business partners, horse-loving people, and the ladies from high society welcomed us into the club, as if we hadn't been here in ages, when, in fact, Eric had been here yesterday, and I was here two weeks ago.

"Oh my goodness." Sandra, a friend of my mother's, looked me up and down. "You look so beautiful."

I knew these people complimented everyone in here like that, as if the money in the bank account decided who was beautiful and who wasn't.

"Thank you." I kept smiling.

She looped her arm with mine. "Megan is here. She'll be happy to see you." She tugged me forward and I glanced at Eric. He smiled, encouraging me to go mingle, and let go of my hand. I let the woman lead me wherever she wanted. "How is Joyce?" she asked.

"Mother is good. She should be here tomorrow afternoon."

"That's great. I need to talk to her about our latest trip, and the one we're going on next month."

We stepped onto one of the porches, where several tables with white linen and silver plates and high-back chairs took over the place, overlooking the tennis courts.

Sandra led me to her daughter. Megan was seated at a table close to the ledge with Blaire and Andrea.

"Hannah!" Megan said, standing up to greet me. She hugged me tight. "Ohmygosh, it's so good to see you."

Growing up, Megan had been my best friend. It was right before our debutante ball, the one I was forced to attend, that I noticed we were too different. We didn't like the same things; we didn't do the same things. With time, we grew apart, especially after I started dating Eric and spent all my free time with him.

"You too," I said.

As we sat down, her mother leaned against the rail and looked over at the courts.

After greeting Blaire and Andrea, who I wasn't too close with, we ordered tea as the conversation continued. They talked about shoes and the latest Roberto Cavalli creations. I spoke a bit here and there, though I would have preferred talking about Country Outfitter instead. Suddenly, the subject changed to trips. Carmel, Aspen, Paris, Rome, and other fancy places.

And I was bored.

My gaze drifted from side to side, and I noticed Sandra had left, but I wasn't really looking for anything.

Until I found him.

The first thought on my mind was, what the heck was he doing here? The second, damn, he looked good. The third, I shouldn't be thinking that.

Dressed completely inappropriate for a polo club—in jeans, a blue T-shirt, and cowboy boots— Leo walked up the path to the right of the tennis courts, flanked by three guys and a girl. They talked animatedly, smiling and touching each other's arms or shoulders occasionally. A few feet behind them, a couple holding hands followed. By their similarities, I would bet they were all related.

The girls kept talking and giggling about whatever, but their voices were a buzz in my ears as I strained to catch anything, any word, from Leo and the ones with them. They were too distant, and even the few words I heard were spoken in fast Portuguese.

A few steps from the main house, Leo looked at the courts, following the game closest to him for a couple of seconds, before his gaze continued on.

Until he found me.

His eyes wide, Leo stopped in his tracks, and the man behind him bumped into him.

"Hey," the man said, taking off his baseball cap and sunglasses. He looked familiar, somehow.

"Why is that guy staring at our table?" Megan asked, giggling.

I averted my eyes and pretended I didn't know what she was talking about.

"What guy?" Blaire asked, turning in her chair. "Oh, he's cute. All four of them are."

"Look at them," Andrea said. I didn't, but from her eyes, I noticed they were moving again. "They must be the team playing against the Knight House."

I knew Eric was going to play against an international team, but in all his dealings with France, it never occurred to me the team could be from somewhere else.

Could it be? Eric was playing against Leo? And why did I care? Leo was nobody.

"Oh yeah," Megan said. "Ohmygosh, I've seen one of them here before. He was an exchange player, with a team from Florida."

Really? So that was why one of them looked familiar. Or it could be because they all looked like each other, and I'd taken my time observing Leo the other day. The urge to peek in his direction was strong, but I avoided it at all costs.

"True," Blaire said with a big smile. "What's his name again? Oh, Ricardo Fernandes. He was swoon-worthy. I bet he still is."

The girls giggled, and I forced a smile so they didn't notice how disturbed I was.

"Maybe we should go welcome them to the club," Megan suggested, wiggling her eyebrows. Then she patted my hand. "Lucky you. Practically married to a gorgeous man while we have to chase potential dates around here."

I *was* lucky, wasn't I? Eric was handsome, educated, generous, kind, and a great polo player. He was a little too jealous for my taste, but I reminded myself that was because he loved me so much. What else could I need?

Andrea stood. "I like this idea."

Blaire shot up beside her. "Maybe not welcome them, but, you know, hang in the lobby with them, until they notice us and come talk."

"Oh, great idea," Megan said, joining the others. She looked down at me. "Aren't you coming?"

"Oh no. Being practically married, I'll mess up your plans." I hoped she didn't notice the sarcasm in my tone. "I'll stay here for a little bit and finish my tea."

"Okay. See you later," Megan said.

Looking like teenagers, they disappeared into the main house and I relaxed, letting my shoulders sag and my back slide down in my chair. My pretty summer dress would get all wrinkled, but who cared?

Not long ago, I lived my perfect life as a Taylor heiress: just going to college, loving my boyfriend, and attending his games. Then it all changed when my grandma died, and I tried to figure out how to juggle college, the ranch, and learn about my father's business, as well as enjoy my boyfriend's success.

As if that wasn't enough, more trouble found me, and everything changed a second time. A broken horse had been thrown into my arms, and some guy came strutting into my life and messed with my feelings. It was too much of a coincidence meeting him on the road and having him move in next door. And now he would be playing at Eric's club.

I hoped he would go back to Brazil soon.

4

"THERE YOU ARE," ERIC SAID AS SOON AS I STEPPED out of the restroom.

After finishing my tea and still feeling jittery, I needed to splash some cold water on my face. It helped calm me down a little. The problem was having to apply makeup all over again.

"Sorry, I was retouching." I showed him the lipstick still in my hand, and notice he was wearing his uniform: a white and red polo shirt, white pants, and brown boots.

He took the lipstick, put it inside my purse, and entwined his fingers with mine, pulling me close. "It's almost time," he whispered against my mouth. "And I'll need my good luck kiss before the game."

I smiled, trying to shut down the thoughts that Leo would be at the field, watching, and the fact that it bothered *me*.

Eric planted a light kiss on my lips before pulling me out of the main house.

The clouds were gone, and the sun warmed us as we strolled down the path to the field. Instead of leading me to where Megan and company were seated on large chairs to the right side of the field, Eric took me to the left, where his teammates stood with their horses, waiting for the game to start.

The guys greeted me, polite as always. They knew how jealous Eric could be, and tried to keep their distance from me. It was odd, the way they avoided looking at me, even when I was right in front of them or talking to them.

Eric looked over my shoulder and tensed.

I didn't have to look to know who approached, but it was hard not to.

Willing my face to appear nonchalant, I let my gaze wander to the forthcoming group. Leo and his teammates pulled their horses to the field. The name of their team, Montenegro, was written in white on their dark blue polo shirts. White pants and black boots completed the rest of their uniform. The older couple and the girl were with them.

Leo's eyes met mine.

A horse nickered and I jumped, noticing I'd been staring.

Focusing my attention on the small white mark on the pony's forehead, I patted his muzzle.

"This will be easy," David said, mounting his horse.

"As usual," said Justin.

Eric nodded. "Boys, we're not supposed to gloat. Not before the game anyway." The men laughed at his joke. "Besides, this is an exhibition. We're here to have fun."

"As if that would make you any less competitive," Tomas said.

"True." Eric grinned before turning to me. His arms encircled my waist, and he pulled me to him.

"Good luck," I whispered, before kissing his cheek.

Not satisfied with his good luck kiss, Eric placed a hand on my nape and guided my mouth to his. He held me there, pressed tight against him, as his tongue invaded my mouth, demanding and provocative, as usual.

Finally, he let me go. Dizzy, I stumbled back as

he mounted his horse, a big grin stamped on his features.

I turned away, but not before glancing up and seeing Leo frowning at me. Heat took over my cheeks, and I didn't understand exactly why. Eric always kissed me before each game. Why did I feel embarrassed about it this time? Of course, I knew the answer but I wouldn't admit it.

I walked down the path leading to the other side of the field and sat beside Megan and her friends.

She smiled at me, a genuine and rare smile. "I envy the way Eric idolizes you. It's so romantic. I want to find a man who looks at me that way. Actually, if I found a man who looks at me *half* the way Eric looks at you, I'd be in heaven."

The game started, saving me from commenting.

Eric didn't go easy. He never did. Two seconds in and he had the ball, his pony weaving away from the others, and his mallet pushing the ball forward.

Then, fifteen seconds in, Leo brought his pony across Eric's, swung his mallet right in front of the horse's nose, and stole the ball.

It took Eric another ten seconds to recover

from the shock and go after Leo and his teammates.

"They're good," a man standing behind us said.

"I heard they are the best in South America," another one said.

If that were true, why had I never seen their team up here? After the girls mentioned it, I remembered seeing Ricardo at a couple of tournaments during the last two years. But what about the others? They hadn't just started playing last week and then came here, to the most prestigious polo club in the country, for an exhibition game with the best polo team in North America. Usually, players became professional around eighteen.

"Yes, they are," a third man said. "Did you know three of them are brothers? Ricardo, Pedro, and Leonardo. The fourth one, Guilherme, is their cousin."

"Really? That's interesting."

"It gets more interesting," the man continued. "Their father is the coach. His name is João Pedro Fernandes. During his younger years, he was the best polo player in the world."

"I take it the woman standing beside him is his wife?"

"Precisely. And the young girl is Beatriz, twin of Leonardo."

"Oh."

"They own a big ranch in Brazil. They breed polo ponies, have a polo school, and polo teams by levels."

"This family is something."

At that moment, Leo weaved out of Eric's way and scored the first goal. The crowd cheered, even the ones I knew were die-hard fans of the Knight House.

"They sure are," the man said.

Leo pulled the reins of his horse, making him turn to the center of the field. His face angled toward the crowd, but with the dark goggles on, I couldn't make out where exactly he was looking. However, I could feel his heavy green-blue gaze on me, and that weight pressed against my chest, making it hard to breathe.

"I need some water," I said, standing up.

Megan's hand clasped gently around my wrist. "Where are you going? Ask a waiter."

"No, it's okay. I need to go to the restroom too," I lied, then dashed away before she could question me further.

I weaved my way out of the crowd watching the game and plopped down on a barstool.

"Sparkling water, please," I told the bartender.

"*Oi.*"

I turned to the voice carrying a lyrical accent and found a girl smiling at me. She had the same green-blue eyes as her brother, and the same light brown hair, though hers was long and full of waves. Her skin was not as tanned as Leo's, and she wasn't as tall.

She sat on the stool beside mine. "I'm Beatriz."

"I know."

Her eyebrows shot up. "You do?"

The waiter handed me my water, and Beatriz ordered an iced tea.

"Well, the men were talking about your brothers' team and someone mentioned your name."

She smiled. Damn, she was pretty. "Ah, *sim.* Ugh, horny men from polo club. Almost as bad as a country club. Or golf clubs." I laughed and her smile widened. "*Bom*, let me introduce myself properly. I'm Beatriz Fernandes, daughter of João Pedro and Agnes, sister to Ricardo, Pedro, and Leonardo. My friends call me Bia. I'm here 'cause my brothers' careers control every aspect of the Fernandeses' lives and I have no choice. Good enough?"

I laughed again. "I guess so." I extended my hand to hers. "I'm Hannah Taylor."

The waiter brought her iced tea over.

"I know."

My turn to arch my brows. "You do?"

"I didn't know your last name, or that Eric Bennett is your boyfriend, but I've heard about you."

"Really?"

"Leo told me about helping you with your horse the other day."

"What?" My eyes widened and I glanced from side to side, scared anyone would hear her.

"Leo is my twin. We're very close." She sipped from her drink. "That day, he got home later than we expected him, wet and dirty. We were worried, but he was smiling, which is rare for him. Too rare. When we were alone, he told me he had just met the most amazing girl."

Heat flooded my cheeks and I stood up. "I have to go back to the game."

Beatriz stepped in my way. "The thing is, I can see by your reaction"—she pointed to my cheeks —"and by what he told me that day, that you're not unaffected."

"I'm unaffected," I said, more to convince myself than her. I stared down at my feet and whispered, "I have to be."

I placed a fifty on the bar, and walked away from her before she could say anything else and make the uncomfortable pressure in my chest any more painful.

5

AFTER THE FIRST GOAL, LEO'S TEAM DIDN'T GET much action. Full of energy, Eric dominated the game. There were a lot of times when I admired his competitiveness and how he could turn a game around. There was nothing he couldn't do. There was nothing he *wouldn't* do. That was always inspiring.

But not today. This time, I could see the almost sick smile on his lips and—if he hadn't been using goggles—I was sure his eyes would have had that same gleam. He was driven by fury, by the will to win, to prove he was still the best and nobody could take that away from him.

If I hadn't known he was an entirely different

person with me, seeing him like that would have put fear in me.

Two hours later, he left the field with a huge smile, his demeanor not competitive anymore, but proud and happy.

Unable to resist, I smiled too. But when he embraced me, drenching my pretty dress in sweat, I cringed. That enticed him, of course, and he pulled me closer, showering me with small kisses.

I giggled and scrunched my nose. "Stop, stop! God, you reek!"

He let go of me and sniffed his shirt. "It's not that bad."

I laughed. "Ha. As if."

He made to embrace me again, but I turned and dashed away. And bumped into Leo.

I began falling back, but his hands on my elbows steadied me.

"Careful," he said, his eyes on mine. It took my breath away. He wasn't wearing the hat or the goggles anymore, and his hair was glued to his face, reminding me of our afternoon together.

Aware of his skin scorching mine—and Eric standing a couple of feet behind us—I pulled away. "Thanks."

Eric's arm draped around my waist as he came

to stand by my side. Smiling, he extended his other hand to Leo. "Mr. Fernandes, great game."

"Call me Leo," he said, shaking Eric's hand briefly. "I agree. It was a great game."

"Yes, you and your brothers form quite the team," Eric said. Leo's eyes flickered to me, and Eric followed it, never losing his smile. "Where are my manners? Leo, this is Hannah Taylor, my girlfriend."

As if we had never met, Leo offered me his hand. "Nice to meet you, Miss Taylor."

"Likewise," I whispered, once more aware of him and how well my hand fit in his.

Leo never took his eyes from me. "I take it you two have been together for a long time."

"Two years," Eric said. "Hopefully, she'll accept my marriage proposal soon and we'll start counting decades then."

Without meaning to, I looked from one to another, and noticed Leo was about two inches taller and a couple of inches wider than Eric. The lines on his face were sharper, his jaw harder, and his lower lip was a little fuller. *Damn, wake up, girl!*

Finally, Leo glanced at my boyfriend. "You're a lucky man."

Eric lost the smile, and his grip around my waist tightened. "I know."

Then Leo's gaze returned to me.

"Excuse us," Eric said, veering us away from Leo. With his death grip around me and large strides, he led me away from the field.

I almost tripped on one of the stones in the path. "I'm wearing heels. Can you please slow down?"

His arms slid from my waist, his hand clasped around my arm, and he pulled me harder, like what I had just said enticed him.

He was jealous. I knew he would be. The moment Leo caught me, I knew Eric would feel as if he were losing me.

"Eric," I called, willing my voice to sound gentle, though I wanted to scream at him to let me go. I wouldn't be surprised if a purple mark appeared on my arm from the force he was holding me. "Eric, please."

But he didn't let go, nor did he stop.

A couple of minutes later, we reached the parking lot and he threw me against his car. I bumped my back hard and gasped for air. He put his hands on either side of me and leaned in, a feral expression on his face.

"That guy thinks I'm lucky," he said through gritted teeth.

Trying to come up with something to say that

wouldn't get me in more trouble, I rubbed where he'd held my arm. It was already red. "It's not the first time you heard that."

"But it's the first time a guy stared at you this openly, right under my nose."

"What?"

"During the entire game. And the intervals. And after." He punched the car and I winced. "I should go back there and break his face."

He turned around, but I pulled him back. "No, Eric, please. Stay with me," I whispered as tears filled my eyes. "Let that guy go. He doesn't matter." I held his shoulders and whirled him to me. "You and me. That's what matters."

I buried my head in his chest and put my arms around him, holding him tight. I didn't know if I did it to comfort me or to avoid him going after Leo. And I didn't care.

"Stay with me," I whispered again.

Slowly, the tension left his body and he looked down at me. His eyes weren't full of rage or jealousy anymore. "I'm sorry. I don't know what came over me. I hate when men look at you as if you're a model standing there to be admired. Which is stupid since you are too beautiful and people will look at you anyway."

I didn't add the fact that he loved showing me off, causing everyone to look at me, wanted or not.

"It's okay. I know you don't mean to."

He kissed my forehead. "You're the best thing that ever came into my life. I have no idea what I'd do without you."

I smiled. "I love you, Eric. You have nothing to worry about."

He pulled my mouth to his. "I love you too, baby."

***

"MORE WINE, DEAR?"

I shook my head. "No, Mrs. Bennett, I shouldn't."

The woman smiled at me. "After two years of dating my boy, you still call me that. It's Chloe."

"I know. It's just ..." I looked around. The Bennett house was even bigger than my parents'. The living room we were in, one of the five sitting areas of the house, had vaulted ceilings and heavy crystal chandeliers hanging from the corners, Persian rugs, leather love seats, velvet armchairs, antique wooden tables, supposedly famous paintings on the walls, and draped curtains hiding large windows under them. It was beautiful but too much. Being here, having dinner with my boyfriend and his mother, and feeling as if I was at a debutante ball instead was too much. "It's fine. Okay then, Chloe, I'll take more of the wine."

Still smiling, she gestured to the waiter at the back of the room, and he rushed to my side to re-fill my glass. All the while, she looked like the queen of England, though younger and less powerful. Her dark hair was pulled into a short braid that fell over her right shoulder, hiding the long scar on the side of her neck, and she wore a beige cocktail dress and lots of jewelry. I'd dressed up all right, knowing what it was like each time Eric brought me here, which was more often than I would like, but I always felt underdressed next to her.

Seated beside me and wearing a designer suit, Eric held my hand in his. "And how was your day, Mother?"

"It was good," she said. "I visited your father and your brother."

Eric squeezed my hand, and I tried to melt into the love seat and disappear.

I hated it when they talked about Nolan and Ian Bennett. They had died in a car accident four years ago, the same accident that gave Chloe the scars on her neck and her back, and left her in an almost permanent state of depression.

Thankfully, Eric had practice that day and wasn't in the car with them. The fact that Eric had to step into the man-of-the-house position, deal with his father's and older brother's death, and deal with his mother's depression made me sad, and I loved him a whole lot for turning out so great.

Visiting them meant she went to the cemetery, to their magnificent mausoleum.

The butler came into the living room. "Dinner is served," he announced.

Eric exhaled a heavy sigh and stood up, pulling me along with him.

In the dining room, the subject changed to an all too familiar one.

"How is school, dear?" Chloe asked from across the table.

I smiled. "Good. The semester is over and I've decided not to take any summer classes, so I can spend more time at the ranch to learn everything I still don't know, and to sort out whatever needs sorting out."

She frowned at me. "Oh, so you're keeping the ranch?"

Why the hell did everyone ask me if I would sell it? "Yes, I plan on keeping the ranch."

"Even though everyone wants you to sell it," Eric said from his place at the head of the table, his tone nonchalant and his eyes on his plate.

What was wrong with keeping the damn ranch? I'd explained it a thousand times, but nobody understood me. Sometimes I thought they pretended they didn't understand me.

I chose not to say anything and stuffed my mouth with food. Clueless of my change in mood, Mrs. Bennett continued, "But the ranch doesn't make a lot of money, does it? I bet it gives you a lot of work. In the end, you're probably not making any profit."

Eric raised his eyebrows at me. "See? Everyone knows that, baby. Even my mother, who has no business background." I shook my head, willing the bad words to stay under my tongue. However, Eric continued, "And you wouldn't have to go looking for a buyer. Mr. Nash is still interested in buying the ranch, isn't he?"

I brought my hands under the table where no one could see them clenching and unclenching. "You know I hate the man. Even if I considered selling the ranch, which I'm not, I would never sell it to him."

"Baby." Eric dropped his silverware and reached for my hand, but I pulled it away, glaring at him. Whatever he was going to say was quickly forgotten.

He pursed his lips and stiffened his back. He was mad at me? Why? I was the one that should be mad here.

Thankfully, the dinner went by without any more significant conversation. Dessert was brought, then coffee. We retreated to the living room, but soon Mrs. Bennett bid us goodnight, saying she had a headache and wanted to lie down.

I wished she had stayed longer because I wasn't in the mood to deal with what was coming.

"Hannah."

"No, Eric. Don't." We sat on the love seat, and I scooted away from him as much as I could. "I don't want to talk about it."

"But, baby, you have to listen to reason."

I glared at him. "Reason? Why do you think you're the right one here?"

He rested his arm over the back of the seat, his hand reaching for my shoulder, but I didn't let him touch me. "If you forget the sentimental part and add up the facts, you'll see the logical solution."

Forget the sentimental part? As if I could erase

my grandma and Hercules from my mind. As if I wanted to.

"Please, Eric, drop it. I don't want to argue."

He turned his body to face me, one of his legs folded over the love seat. "Then don't argue with me. Sell the ranch. You'll have peace of mind then."

"Please, don't say it."

"I will say it because I want to."

"The thousandth time you say it won't be the charm."

He continued as if I hadn't said anything. "You should drop college. We should get married, buy a new house, and you should run our place. You should let me run your father's business when it's time. Baby, can't you see? It would be our happily ever after."

I took a deep breath, thinking of how to answer him without making things worse. I really didn't want to argue. "Eric, I'm only twenty years old. We have plenty of time to get married."

"We don't have to wait."

I sighed and tried another approach. "We'll only live our happily ever after if you let me do what I want to do."

"I don't see why this can't be a decision we make in conjunction."

"Will you consult with me before you make any decision about your business and your polo career?"

"What? Of course not."

"Then I don't see why I need to consult with you before deciding what I want to do with my life."

"That's nonsense! My polo career and my farm won't affect our life together. Your ranch and your father's business, though, affect our relationship. Because of them, you barely have time to relax with me anymore."

"I don't have time? Eric, you're the one running up and down all day, with practice and meetings all the time, even on weekends."

Again, he chose not to hear me. "And there's also college. Thank God, you don't live on campus anymore. Not that the ranch is safe. The police never found out who started that fire after all."

He didn't even notice as I winced and squeezed my eyes shut. If I stopped to think that whoever killed my grandma and Hercules and the other horses was out there, I wouldn't relax. I would go nuts and try to find the murderer myself.

"I'm not afraid," I said, willing my tone to stay calm.

"But I am! I would prefer having you near me,

knowing you're safe." The desperate and frustrated shine in his blue eyes melted my will a little. "I love you, Hannah, and—"

"This isn't a matter of loving or not, Eric."

"—all I want is to make you happy. Let me make you happy." He leaned closer to me, and I realized I would lose this battle if I didn't focus on something else.

I stood up, intending to walk around the coffee table and talk to him from there, far away and safe from his charms, but his hand on my arm pulled me back down.

"Eric—" My protest died when his lips crashed on mine.

On its own volition, my mouth parted and welcomed his urgent caress. His arm slid around my waist, and his fingers splayed over my lower back. He lifted himself up, while using his hand to lay me over the love seat, under him. His body pressed against mine, and a longing sigh escaped my mouth.

His kiss intensified as his hand cupped my butt and pulled my hips closer to his. He was already hard and ready, and I groaned in anticipation.

"I want you," he whispered in my ear, his breathing hot on my skin, sending shivers down my spine.

He wanted me. He wanted a lot of things, which included telling me what to do.

What the hell? We had been arguing a couple of seconds ago, and now we were hot and all over each other?

With my hands on his chest, I pushed him away. "Stop." He didn't move and didn't stop either. "Eric, stop."

He nibbled on my ear. "Why? You like it."

I pushed against his chest again, but he still didn't move. "Because we were arguing. You can't just charm me and think you won the discussion."

"Wanna bet?" He grounded his hips against me and I gasped. "See."

I twisted my body, trying to escape him. "Eric, please."

He pulled back a little but didn't release. "Baby, look at me." When I did, he continued, "We're not going anywhere, right? Even arguing, we still love each other, right? So, why not enjoy the moment? We can continue arguing tomorrow."

"That doesn't make any sense." It actually did, but I wasn't about to award him any points.

Eric stood up and extended his hand to me. A little wary, I took it. He pulled me to my feet and led me upstairs to his suite. He closed the door as I sat on his king-size bed and turned on one of the bedside lamps.

He leaned against the wall, his serious eyes on me. "I love you, Hannah, too much. Even when we argue or disagree, I don't plan on going anywhere. We'll work this out. Our differences. We'll work them out." He walked to the bed and gripped the thick wooden footboard. "We haven't spent too many nights together lately, and I would love to take advantage of this one."

My heart constricted. He was right. Our nights together had been limited between college, the ranch, and his tournaments, and if we spent them arguing, we would only end up tired and sad.

I hated giving in so easily, but we could argue some other time.

Sighing, I patted the spot on the bed beside me. A large smile took over Eric's face, but he didn't sit on the bed. Oh no. He threw himself over me, knocking the air out of my lungs. His mouth found mine as I fell back on the bed, his body over mine.

"Let me make you happy," he whispered against my lips.

Well, he could definitely try.

6

THE LAST RIDING GROUP OF THE DAY LEFT, AND I SET out to clean their mess, relieved the rush was over. Sunday afternoons were the ranch's busiest day of the week, and I didn't blame them. The horses were beautiful and amicable, and the view around the ranch was breathtaking. Plus, they all stopped at the waterfall to take a dip.

Happy as that made me, I felt exhausted.

Jimmy brought in the saddles and whips and halters scattered around by our guests, and left them on the floor of the stable, while I stored them in the tack room. Each saddle weighed a ton, and I knew I would have back problems if I continued with this heavy work. Of course, I could always hire someone else to help, but my grandma had done all of this with only Jimmy's help. The riding instructor, Paul, didn't count, and grandma had always complained he was the exact opposite of helpful, leaving everything a complete mess after each lesson. If she could do it at her age, so could I. Besides, letting a stranger mess with her stuff seemed like I didn't care for them.

"*Oi.*"

The saddle I'd been holding fell on top of my foot. I shut my mouth and screamed on the inside as pain spread throughout my foot.

"*Desculpa,*" Leo said, rushing to my side. "I didn't mean to scare you."

He pushed the saddle aside and knelt in front of me. His hand found my boot, and he attempted to take it off, but I limped away before he could get a good grip on it.

I splayed my hand on a wall and tried to balance myself. "What are you doing here?" My tone sounded as frustrated as I felt.

He frowned. "Hello to you too."

As he stood, his gray shirt stretched over his chest and shoulders, and the jeans didn't hide his form either. I forced my gaze to my hurt foot.

"You didn't answer my question."

He picked up the saddle from the floor and put

it in its place along with the others. "And you didn't say hi."

I put my foot on the floor and tested it. Each time I pressed down on it, pain shot up from my toes to my ankle. "Damn it."

I limped to the bench in the center of the room and sat down with a heavy sigh. Pain won and I took off my boot. A big red welt stained the top of my foot.

"*Desculpa*, really," Leo said, sitting beside me.

I made the mistake of looking into his mesmerizing eyes. A girl could easily get lost in those. "It's okay. Nothing some ice won't fix." I returned my attention to my foot. "Seriously, what are you doing here?"

He pulled a purple Douglas Iris from behind him and offered it to me.

My heart stopped, and all I could do was gape at it.

He reached up and slid the flower behind my ear. "This flower reminds me of the other day, when we met." He averted his eyes. "I just ..."

Jimmy walked into the tack room, holding a bunch of reins and halters. He halted a few steps away and stared at my foot. "Everything okay, Miss Taylor?"

"I'll be fine."

"Hi, Jimmy," Leo said, confusing me.

Jimmy nodded to him. "Hello, Mr. Fernandes. Good to see you again."

"Again?" I asked. "How do you two know each other?"

Jimmy began putting the stuff he carried in the right place. "Mr. Fernandes showed up here last evening looking for you, and I told him you were at Eric's." He made a face, showing me exactly what he felt for my boyfriend. "But he stayed for a bit and we talked horses."

Unbelievable. "You don't say?"

Leo busied himself by helping Jimmy with his load and didn't say anything.

When done, Jimmy turned to me. "I'll feed the horses now, then I'm off."

That reminded me. "Has Argus eaten anything?"

Jimmy sighed. "Yes, but not enough. That horse is going to pass out soon, and he ain't gonna wake up again."

"Try to feed him some more now, please," I said. "I'll check on him later."

"All right." Jimmy tipped his hat toward Leo and me. "Good night."

"Good night," Leo and I answered together.

Jimmy left and an awkward silence filled the room.

Without looking at me, Leo leaned against a free spot on the wall, his arms crossed. I didn't know what to say to him, what to do. Just looking at him awakened something in me. All these unwelcome but inciting feelings swirled inside me, confusing me.

"You came here yesterday?"

His eyes finally met mine, and the wariness there hurt me. "Yes. A couple of hours after the game. I had ..."

When he didn't say anything, I prodded, "What?"

"I had to talk to you. To ask you something."

"Okay."

"Why didn't you tell me you have a boyfriend?"

I swallowed hard. A good question I didn't have an answer for. "I don't know. It's not like people walk around holding signs showing if they're single or not. The subject never came up."

"Still. I thought I'd seen something. As if you found me as intriguing as I found you."

He hadn't imagined it. I did find him intriguing. But I couldn't tell him that, could I? "I'm sorry I gave you the wrong impression."

"Me too." He pushed away from the wall and started for the door.

I sighed, relieved I didn't have to send him away myself, although my chest tightened when he walked out without saying goodbye. For some reason, I felt like crying. What a stupid thing.

I focused on the pain in my foot, blaming that for the tears in my eyes. Better that than being sad over something that wasn't and would never be.

I closed my eyes and took a deep breath. It wasn't the first time I'd noticed other guys. After all, I wasn't blind, and some of my classes had some good-looking men in them. But to look at them, to notice them, was one thing. To instigate it, to talk to a guy and let him believe I was single and interested was another. If hell existed, I would die young and go straight there because of my impure thoughts.

This would pass. I was sure it would. Leo would go back to Brazil, and he would be out of sight and out of mind soon enough. For now, I just had to avoid him, and the club, as much as possible. Eric would be pissed if I didn't go to the games, but it was for the best. I could lie about having something urgent to take care of here. He would understand, everything would go back to normal, and I would be able to focus on Eric again.

I groaned when I stood. More like a scream, but who cared? I was alone in the stable and only the horses could hear me. I bet they didn't care about my outbursts.

I tested my foot and grumbled again. I couldn't put too much weight on it yet, but at least I could limp to Argus's stall before heading to the house and sinking into my bathtub, filled to the brim with hot water—with my foot hanging out, enveloped in ice. I was in desperate need of a relaxing bath.

Leo walked into the room and, startled, I jumped back, lost my balance, and fell on my butt.

"Ouch," I yelled.

"*Meu Deus, desculpa!*"

I shut my eyes, fighting back tears of pain and frustration and embarrassment. I felt arms slipping under me and then I was being lifted from the floor. My eyes snapped open. Leo gazed at me, and I noticed how close his face was to mine, how bright his eyes shone, how the muscles in his arms popped, how wide his shoulders were, how ...

I shook my head and looked away. "What are you doing?"

"Helping you," he said as he sat me back on the bench.

I scooted away from him. "I thought you'd left."

He stared at me. It was hard not to feel anything when his blue-green eyes locked on mine like that. "I was going to, but then I saw Jimmy putting the horses' rations away and helped him."

"Why?"

He shrugged. "They looked heavy and I have nothing better to do at home."

"That's not what I meant."

"I know," he said, still looking at me. "*Desculpa*, for making you fall." The corners of his lips tilted up. "I had no idea you were this jumpy."

"Try living alone on a ranch that was set on fire under suspicious circumstances." The words were out of my mouth before I could stop them.

His eyes widened. "What?" I looked away, but only for a moment, because when his hand clasped around my arm, I couldn't help but gaze at him again. "What happened?"

"Nobody knows for sure. Someone started a fire at the stable, on purpose. In seconds, it was all destroyed."

He looked around. "This one is new?"

"Yes. It was built a couple of months after. An exact replica of the old one."

"And the horses?"

An anguished pang rushed through my chest. "The fire took all the horses in here, including mine, Hercules. And my grandma."

"*Droga.* I'm so sorry. I had no idea she died like that. When you mentioned it, I thought it was of old age."

I swallowed, finding it difficult to talk about this, though I wanted to. "Nope. Someone killed her. Why? I'll never know." I held back the tears. I didn't want to break down in front of him.

"That's ... horrible."

"The worst part is that the police never found whoever did it. They just told me it wasn't accidental and, after a couple of months without any results, they dropped the case." A sob wracked my chest. "I was here half an hour before. If I'd stayed, I could have saved her."

"You don't know that. For all I know, you could have died too."

It had been ages since I'd spoken about the fire. I thought about it all the time, but I never said anything. Eric didn't want to hear about it; he didn't want to know anything related to my grandma and the ranch, so I closed up. I bottled all the feelings and forgot about them, knowing they would explode someday.

I just never thought today would be that day. Here I was, baring my soul to a stranger. Another sob found its way through me, and I wiped the tears away. Leo pulled me to him, and I couldn't find the strength to protest. Quite the opposite. I buried my face in his chest as his arms tightened around me, pulling me close, toward safety. He rocked me like a child, and I felt myself entranced in that, as if he were singing a lullaby and I was drifting to sleep, confident only good dreams would find me.

After a few moments, my sobs calmed down. His scent filled my nose, and it was delicious. A mix of wood, spices, and something unique to him. I turned my head up to his neck and inhaled deeply, taking in as much as I could, relishing in the feel of his hot skin on my face. I could die here, in his arms, breathing him, feeling him.

He shivered, and realization fell over me like a kick to my gut. I stiffened and slowly lifted my eyes to his, finding his face tilted down toward mine. The shine in his eyes was pure longing. Desire. It made my heart flutter. His gaze lowered to my lips, and I realized his were only inches away.

I snapped out of it.

Blushing, I pushed away from him and looked to my solitary boot on the floor. "I'm sorry."

"It's okay. You miss your grandmother and your horse. I understand."

That wasn't what I meant and I thought he knew that. Still, I was grateful he didn't say anything about what almost happened. The feel of his arms around me and the sensation of his scent in my lungs were still too vivid in my mind, and I shivered. Damn it, this wasn't happening.

Afraid of any more pain, physical and emotional, I stood slowly. My shoulders relaxed when I attested that my butt didn't hurt anymore and my foot was a tiny bit better. Tension built up again in my body when Leo stood beside me.

"Hmm, I need to go check on Argus," I said, limping past him. I hoped he took that as a good-bye, go away, and don't ever come back.

"I can help you."

Perhaps I needed to be more specific. "It's okay. I got it."

I limped to the main hallway of the stable and to the far back, where the biggest stall was. Where Argus was safely tucked away. The sun was setting, filling the place with a few orange rays and dark shadows. I turned on some lights and Argus neighed, kicking at the walls.

"Shh," I whispered. "It's okay. It's only me."

He snorted, circled the stall, and bumped against the wood.

"Poor animal," Leo said from right behind me, and I jumped. "*Desculpa.*"

For all I knew, he was doing that on purpose. "I thought you were leaving."

"Well, I'm not." He leaned against the rail, looking at the horse. "How is he doing?"

"Not well." I grabbed one of the empty buckets along the wall. "He isn't eating enough. He's too thin and has a lot of healing to do. The vet was here this afternoon—"

"The vet comes in on Sundays?"

"Dr. Bohm was a close friend of my grandma, and he lives nearby. He simply comes over sometimes to check on the horses."

Leo glanced around the stable. "All of these horses, they are all new?"

"Nope." I looked through a window and pointed toward a hill. For a moment, I was lost in the view. Tall and lush trees, big blue skies, orange sun descending and being engulfed by the perfect green lawn. It was a pity I couldn't see the waterfall from here. "There's another stable on the other side of that hill. These horses were there during the fire."

"And your horse was here?"

"Yes." Pursing my lips, I filled half the bucket with grain. I tried to pick it back up, but it was too heavy. I couldn't limp and hold it at the same time.

"*Me dá.*" He reached for the bucket. "Hmm, sorry. Portuguese keeps slipping in here and there."

I smiled. I kind of liked his accent. A lot. "It's okay. It's similar to Spanish, so I understand it most of the time."

He smiled and took the bucket from me, causing my cheeks to heat up. "My sister, Beatriz, flips every time someone asks if we speak Spanish. Or if Buenos Aires is the capital of Brazil."

We walked to the stall and I opened the door. I grabbed a handful of grain and extended it toward Argus. "Here, boy. I have something for you." With his back to me, Argus snorted, not caring one bit. "Come on, boy. If you eat just a little, I'll grab an apple for you. Deal?" He didn't move, and I decided to take a step forward. "Argus?"

The horse bucked, kicking his hinder legs high. I retreated as fast as I could, which wasn't much with my hurt foot. I saw the legs coming down, right at me. I stumbled back and fell, but I didn't hit the ground. Leo wrapped his arms around my waist and pulled me out of the way just as Argus's legs fell right on the spot I'd been. Leo closed the door and leaned against it, holding me close to him, while I shook.

I should have pushed away, but I couldn't. I folded my arms around him and pulled tighter. I needed the comfort, the understanding. Argus nickered, and a strong tremble coursed through me.

Leo cradled me, his head lowered toward me. "It's okay," he whispered in my ear, his breath warm on my neck. I shivered. This time it wasn't because of Argus.

Trying to find the self-respect I'd lost along the way, I pushed away from him. "I shouldn't have let them bring him here."

"Why not?"

"The animal control officers think I can perform the same miracles my grandma could, so they pushed it, and I ended up accepting. You should have seen him when they brought him in. So thin and fragile and terribly scared. Worse than now, if you can imagine that. It broke my heart. But the officers are mistaken. I'm not my grandmother. I just ... couldn't let them put him down, you know? I had to try." I sighed. "But I can't. I tried. He doesn't respond to me."

Leo stared at me, serious. "I think what you're

trying to do is noble. I hope you don't give up. Not yet."

"I can't get near him without him freaking out. How am I going to fix him?"

With a small tug of his lips, Leo reached for the bucket and got a handful of grain. He opened the stall door and stayed there, frozen in place, his arm extended forward.

A few minutes passed before Argus turned his head and peeked at Leo. He snorted but turned a little more. Curious, I approached the stall and leaned on the rail, trying to see exactly what he was doing.

A few more minutes went by, and Argus moved a couple of inches toward Leo, who remained with his face calm and relaxed, his eyes fixed on Argus's, his open hand forward. It was a game of patience, and I was tired from only watching.

Almost fifteen minutes passed before Argus took an entire step toward Leo. Another ten passed before he touched his nose to Leo's hand. He smelled it and retreated a step. I was about to sigh loudly when Leo crouched, his hand still in front of him, and Argus gave half a step to him. The patience battle continued for over forty minutes, until Argus reached over and ate what Leo had in his hand.

I smiled.

Without changing his expression or moving too much, Leo dipped his hand into the bucket and left it there. Argus followed Leo's hand and dunked his nose on the grain. And he ate.

I wiggled my butt and moved my arms in a circle as a small victory dance, and blushed big time when Leo stood up and watched me, a wide smile on his face and a warm shine in his eyes.

Embarrassed to my bones, I stood still. "Thank you."

He chuckled. "You're welcome."

7

———————

"HERE YOU GO." I HELD THE TEN-YEAR-OLD GIRL BY the waist, helped her sit on the horse, and handed her the reins.

"Thanks," she said, with a huge, nervous smile.

I patted the horse's side. His coat was shiny and silky, much like Hercules's had been. "Don't worry. Paul here will take good care of you," I told her.

Over his own pinto horse, Paul tipped his cowboy hat at us. "Come on now," he called the group of kids. "Let's ride out of here."

The kids pulled on their reins and turned their horses, following Paul to the fenced arena near the main stable. Smiling, I watched them go. At age ten, I'd already participated in local jumping tournaments. And won.

But that belonged to my past.

I readjusted the pink hat on my head and set
out back to the stable, hoping to avoid Jimmy and
his philosophical questions. "Why aren't you on a
horse? You know, this is a ranch. A riding ranch.
And you ain't riding." He knew the answers, so
why ask? He wanted to make me think about it.
Which I did. All the time.

I walked around the stable, checking if the remaining horses had enough water. It was only
early June, and the heat was already picking up
too much for my taste.

I wiped my forehead with my arm and decided
to ditch the hat. It was cute and it helped when I
was under the sun, but it suffocated me when I
was under a roof.

In his secluded stall, Argus was unsettled.
When I leaned over the rail, he neighed, making
me jump back in surprise. Stupid horse. Leo may
have gotten him to eat, but one meal wasn't
enough to keep him standing. Only one way to
help him. I filled a bucket with grain and opened
the door to his stall. I waited as he circled the area,
nickering and snorting.

Patience. Lots of patience.

A couple of minutes passed, and he finally stopped in the back corner. He peered at me and I offered him my hand, the grain on my palm. He snorted and turned away. Of course, he wouldn't make it easy. Doing like Leo did, I knelt down, my arm still extended, and tried to put a blank mask over my face, as if nothing in this world bothered me.

After an eternity, Argus walked closer, but not close enough. A frustrated scream lodged in my throat. Damn, this horse was messing with me. Determined to make this work, to feed him and heal him somehow, I dragged my knees forward a few inches and leaned closer, hoping the grain's scent would reach his nose.

Wrong move. He reared and neighed, the fear and shock clear in his dark eyes.

The grain fell from my hand and I crawled back. Breathing heavily, I slammed the door closed and rushed away from him.

Stupid. Stupid. Stupid.

In the tack room, I took a deep breath and forced my mind to think of something else. Anything else. I wouldn't let a horse bring me down.

I stared at the schedule attached to the message board on the wall. Two more classes and Monday would be done. And it was only three in the afternoon. I rolled my shoulders, forgetting about Argus, and dreamed about my bathtub, some quiet music, and my glass of whiskey.

Thinking about drinking made me thirsty. What a shame it was too early in the day for an alcoholic beverage. I could settle for coffee, though, and I had made a pot after lunch. It would have to do.

After taking off my red boots and leaving them on the porch, I entered the house and headed to the kitchen at the back. I turned on the speakers with my iPod and swayed to the rhythm of Taylor Swift while the coffee heated.

Like a ritual, I glanced at the picture on the wall and my heart squeezed. I wondered if it would ever stop hurting.

The sound of a car coming down the road caught my attention, and I leaned over the kitchen window. It was Eric. I looked at the clock on the wall. Only 2:20. He was supposed to be practicing at the club. Who cared? It was always nice to get an unexpected visit from him.

I smiled. For three seconds. The memories of the previous evening invaded my mind and I pursed my lips, my cheeks heating. Leo and I hadn't done anything wrong, per se, but Eric would throw a fit if he found out Leo had been here.

Embarrassed of my bad behavior, I inhaled and focused on calming down and keeping my expression neutral. Eric wouldn't find out if I didn't tell him. All I had to do was keep calm.

To please him, I put the kettle on and brought the tea selection to the island. He would scowl at my coffee, since he hated it, but at least he would have something to drink and would leave my coffee and me alone. Hopefully.

The front door rattled when Eric barged in.

"Hi," I chimed, all too happy as I made my way to the doorway to greet him. Still in his practice uniform, he pushed past me, glowering and puffing. "What happened?"

"They happened," he yelled.

I cringed but managed to turn him to me. "You're gonna have to be more specific," I said, my tone soothing.

At his sides, his fists clenched and unclenched. "Those Brazilian parasites. They happened. They came here for a few exhibition games, but they're going to stay."

I froze. "What?"

"See, even you're appalled. Can you believe it? I almost jumped at Ronny's throat when he told me this morning that he offered them a six-month contract. And they accepted it."

"But why?"

He shrugged. "Who knows? I didn't let him explain. I just left. We still had at least one more hour of practice left, but I couldn't stay. I just left the club and came right over here."

I hugged him. "Everything will be all right. Ronny will explain and it'll be fine again. You're overreacting."

He pushed me away, and I bumped my back against the island. "Overreacting? They are trying to steal my club and my spotlight, and *I'm* overreacting?"

I gritted my teeth, suppressing the pain spreading through my back, and walked to the stove. "I'm sorry. I didn't mean it that way. I just know there must be a good explanation for it."

"There is!" he shouted. "Ronny always talked about adding another top-notch team to the club. He hasn't found one until now. Ah, if I knew this would happen, I wouldn't have agreed to this damned exhibition game in the first place."

I took the kettle from the stovetop and poured boiling water into a mug. Acting as if we were talking about the weather was better than worrying about the odd way he was behaving. "You don't know that. Maybe it would have happened one way or another."

"I don't care!" He punched the island and I jumped back, startled. "It's my club, my games, my career!"

"Eric, please ..."

"You know what's worse? If they do well, the contract can be extended."

"Maybe they deserve it?"

"Deserve it? Latin scum do not deserve anything!"

"I'm sure they aren't scum. In fact, I heard they're pretty rich in Brazil."

Squinting, Eric walked to me, each step more menacing than the other. "You heard it? Are you interested in their life now?"

I took a step back. "Don't be ridiculous. You know how the people at the club gossip. I just heard some men talking about them." I sat down on a stool, refusing to let his actions affect me. "Here"—I pushed the tea box toward him—"choose one and sit down with me."

"I don't want tea! I want them gone." With a growl, he swept his arm over the island, throwing the box, the mugs, and the kettle on the floor. I jumped from the stool, my eyes wide and my hands shaking, as cracking and breaking filled the kitchen.

In complete shock, I stared at him while he repeatedly punched the island. He would break either his hand or the granite counter.

I eyed the doorway. It wasn't too far away and I probably could inch my way around him. He seemed focused on his own rage, but I wasn't sure leaving him alone was a good idea. He'd come here for a reason. To be consoled by me.

Filling my lungs with air and my mind with courage, I went to him and held his arms. Gently at first, but as he thrashed against me, I tightened my grip and pulled his fists away from the island. I pressed his hands together.

"Eric, please, calm down."

He twisted his arms around mine and caught hold of my wrists. "Are you on their side? Because you wouldn't ask me to calm down if you weren't. If you were on my side, you would understand."

"I do understand," I choked, fighting the panic rising in my chest. I tried pulling away, but his grip tightened.

He leaned over me, his teeth bared. "No, you don't," he hissed.

He pushed me back, and I stumbled into the counter once more, then he spun around, punched the picture on the wall. The glass broke into a million pieces, and the frame jiggled on its hook before falling to the floor and breaking too.

However, Eric didn't see that. He marched out of the house as I knelt beside the picture. With shaking hands, I swept the broken glass aside and picked up the photo. It was ripped, right between grandma and Hercules and me, separating me from them both.

I held it to my chest and cried.

WHEN JIMMY RUSHED INTO THE HOUSE, TELLING ME Officer Michael was in the stable, I almost dropped my coffee mug. What was he doing here so early? I mean, it had been a couple of weeks since he brought Argus, but it took more than that to help a mistreated horse.

Between Eric's freak out last evening, crying, and barely sleeping during the night, my nerves were on high alert, especially with the obscene amount of coffee I had been drinking all day long to keep me going.

I had planned on taking a nap after lunch, but Officer Michael had just spoiled that.

With Jimmy by my side, I entered the stable

and found the man standing in front of Argus's stall.

"Officer Michael, good afternoon," I greeted him.

He spared me a quick glance. "Good afternoon, Miss Taylor."

With his gaze on Argus, he took a step toward the stall. That simple act alarmed the horse, and Argus bumped into the door with his body, neighing, his hooves stomping the ground, his eyes enraged. Officer Michael jumped back.

I came to stand between them, knowing all too well that this horse could break down the door and advance on us if he wanted to. "Calm down, boy," I whispered, my hands raised, palms turned to him.

Behind me, Officer Michael sighed. "He doesn't seem much better."

I retreated a step and stood beside him. "It has been only two weeks or so. With his history, he'll need much more than that."

He nodded. "I know, but there are rules, Miss Taylor. If we don't see progress within the month, even if small, we'll have to put him down."

What? Only a month?

I stared at Argus. He paced from side to side inside his stall, snorting and shaking his head.

"A month won't be enough," I said.

"I know. But any progress is progress. Show me he doesn't jump at visitors or lets you pet him or eats better. Anything. That will be enough to buy him more time."

For whatever reason, Officer Michael approached the stall once more. I wanted to say no and pull him back, but he was the officer here. Argus halted, his head down. He snorted and spied through his mane. He was waiting. Waiting for the man to come closer to do only God knew what.

"I'm thinking he still associates me with the place I found him. I took him away from there, but in his mind, I was there anyway."

I didn't know what to say. Perhaps? Could be? Then why don't you just leave? Those didn't seem like appropriate responses.

Jimmy saved us from the awkward moment. "Don't worry, officer. We'll make sure he progresses."

Officer Michael snapped out of it and turned to us with a tight smile. "Good. Because I really don't like putting animals down." He walked past us. "I should stop by again in about a month or so. If anything happens before then, give me a call."

"Yes, sure," I said. "Thanks, officer."

"Have a good day," he said before exiting the stable.

I sagged against the wall across from Argus's stall, feeling as if someone had dropped a huge rock on my chest.

Jimmy put his hand on my shoulder. "You can do this, Miss Taylor. I know you can."

"I'm not so sure," I said, watching Argus. He was now standing in a corner inside the stall, his back to us, his head down.

"You know I'll help you. Tell me what to do."

The sad, frustrated feeling left in me from last night grew and pressured me. I felt as if the walls were closing in on me.

I sighed. "I don't know."

8

THE NEXT AFTERNOON, I TRIED TO GET OUT OF going to the club with my mother. She'd made arrangements with her friends to bring their daughters, have tea, and a nice chat. Have a pleasant afternoon, as she'd said it.

Yeah, right.

I squirmed in my seat each time Megan mentioned the dresses she had bought for the upcoming parties and ball. I lost count on her twelfth. Meanwhile, her mother complained about the club's employees.

"The quality hasn't been the same," she said.

Of course, my mother agreed, and promptly they came up with a plan to write to the club's president about how he should better the service before they canceled their membership.

One hour of this and I stood up. "Excuse me," I said, retreating from the table. I weaved my way to the restroom, but once in the hallway, I turned in the opposite direction, passed an empty dining room, and exited to the porch.

I leaned against a pillar and let out a long sigh, feeling bad for not enjoying their company the way they wanted me to, and for not being interested in the same things they were. I was the only woman here interested in horses and my family's farm. The others were just interested in the money the farms provided, which was exactly what Eric wanted from me.

Ugh, Eric. I was still mad at him. Frustrated. Disappointed.

Last night, I'd stared at my phone for hours, thinking he would call and apologize any minute. But he didn't, and that made me even more upset.

All right, time out was over. I had to go back before they came looking for me.

I stepped toward the big French doors when I heard a shout and stopped. I looked around, trying to find the source, but didn't see anyone. Letting my curiosity win, I descended the porch steps and followed the short stone path around a tall wall. Perhaps I shouldn't spy, but I was concerned it could be someone who'd been riding and fell or something.

What I didn't expect was to find Leo arguing with his father. In Portuguese.

I should have left. I should have retreated, pretended I never saw anything, and gone back inside the main house and back to my mother and her friends.

But I caught a few words and sentences whispered in fast, harsh tones. Disappointment. Make me proud. Grow up. Work hard and stop playing.

My curiosity piqued, making me stay glued to my spot in the corner.

"*Me deixa em paz, tche!*" Leo shouted, turning his back to his father and stalking away.

I stepped back and hid behind the wall, hoping for all that was holy that he hadn't seen me. My hopes went down the drain when he stepped around the corner three seconds later, his hard eyes on mine.

"I'm sorry," I whispered. "I didn't mean to."

His jaw tightened, and he crossed his arms over his blue T-shirt. The color emphasized his bright eyes, and the fabric clung to him, especially over his stomach, where a dark blotch of sweat showed off his hard abs. His goddamn white practice pants and the sweat-damp hair didn't help either.

"How much did you hear?" he asked.

I swallowed, forcing my mind to push back images of his god-like body. "Not much. But I only understood a couple of words here and there." I shifted my weight, uncomfortable under his gaze, and not only because I'd seen and heard something I wasn't supposed to. *Keep your mouth shut, Hannah. Keep your damned mouth sh...* "Want to talk about it?"

The shine in his eyes changed, and the tension in his neck seemed to lessen. He shook his head. "Don't worry. It's just the usual banter."

Usual? I didn't like the sound of that. His family seemed so perfect, so warm, so close, so happy. His sister had said he rarely smiled, which seemed odd since I had seen him smiling before. I was dying to know why he and his father usually argued.

Instead, I started a new subject. "I heard you're staying."

He nodded. "It was the plan all along."

"Really?"

"*Sim.* Polo in Brazil isn't that strong. Here, though, is another story."

"I see." I looked from side to side. "Do you and

your brothers plan on staying for … long?" I pressed my lips together, chiding myself for almost saying forever.

"We don't know. Perhaps, if all goes well." He took a step closer, his eyes still on mine, making me slightly breathless. His body loomed closer, the difference in our heights and widths almost hilarious, if it wasn't for the fact it turned me on. Crap. "I hope we do." A shiver rolled down my spine. "How is Argus doing?" he asked.

The change in subject surprised me. "The same," I muttered. "Barely eating. Jumping with each click and crack around him. Neighing and bothering the other horses. Shooing me from his stall."

His lip turned into a lopsided grin. "Maybe I should stop by again. To check on him."

"That's not neces—" I pressed my lips tight. An idea brought hope and I felt instantly excited. "You know, that's not a bad idea."

His eyes widened. "Really?"

"Yes. In fact, I may need more than just a quick check on him." It pained me to admit it, but I had to. "The officer who rescued him thinks I'm not doing a good job … and I agree with him. But I don't know what to do. However, you seem to be able to reach him."

A frown appeared between his brows. "And ...?"

I took a deep breath. "You need to help me. I mean, I need your help. I know you're probably busy with practice, but if you could stop by every now and then and—"

"Yes," he said.

I gaped. "Yes?"

"Yeah, I'll help you."

A big smile exploded on my lips. "That's ... great. Thanks!"

He nodded. "Sure. When should I come by? Tonight?"

"No," I said quickly. I didn't know what was going on in Eric's mind or when he would show up, but I was sure it wouldn't be tomorrow night when he had a business dinner with some men. Stuff for his family's business. "Tomorrow evening."

His eyes sunk into mine and my breath caught. "I'll be there."

"Thanks," I muttered again. "I've gotta go now."

I marched away without giving him time to respond or saying bye, and guilt settled low in my stomach. Guilt for listening to his argument with his father. Guilt for asking for his help and knowing I wouldn't tell Eric about it. Guilt for having feelings for him I couldn't seem to control.

I sped up the steps and, upon opening the French doors leading inside the main house, practically ran into Beatriz.

"*Eita!*" She grabbed my shoulders to steady me. "Where's the fire?"

I winced. God, if only she knew about the real fire that took everything I loved the most away from me, she wouldn't make jokes like that.

"I should get back to—"

"There you are." My mother's voice carried her permanently flat tone. She stood on the other side of the room, looking as unaffected as always. "You were taking so long I thought you had fainted in the restroom."

I glanced from her to Beatriz and back. "Well, I ran into Beatriz here and I thought she could join us. She's a member of this club, after all."

My mother's perfect brows rose up, but she smiled. "Of course. We would love if she joined us."

Beatriz glared at me, but I ignored the warning in it and held her arm, tugging her into walking with me. "Come on," I said loud enough so my mother would hear. "I'll introduce you to my friends."

Thankfully, Beatriz let me take her to our table. I introduced her to everyone while the waiters arranged a place for her beside me. The ladies around the large table looked at her with mild interest. Crap, I was bringing her into the snake nest and she had no clue.

Too late to regret it.

We sat down and Megan didn't waste time. "So, how is it to live with four hot guys?"

"Ew," Beatriz said and made a face. I pressed my lips tight, holding back my laughter.

Oh, God, this should be fun. She turned those blue-green eyes to me again, something like anger shining from them. "*Eu vou te matar*," she whispered, before flashing a fake smile to Megan and engaging in her conversation like a pro.

Off the hook for a while, I sighed and relaxed a little.

THE AFTERNOON HADN'T BEEN ALL BAD AFTER ALL. As I drove home, I smiled, remembering how much better I'd felt around the club's ladies after Beatriz had joined us. I even laughed, and at some point, she stopped glaring at me, though she said that if I tried putting her through that again, she would punch me in the face. And I believed her.

I entered the ranch's private road, and my smile died when I saw Eric's car in my driveway.

I parked my car beside his and counted to ten. I hadn't heard from or seen him in almost forty-eight hours, and it worried me. He never went more than five hours without calling me to tell me he loved or that he missed me. I seriously hoped he wasn't here to argue more, because I wasn't in the mood.

I found the house's front door open, and when I stepped in, a spicy aroma hit my nose. I inhaled deeply and sighed.

"Hello?" I called, taking off my sandals and leaving them beside the stairs. I followed the scent into the kitchen and found Eric in front of the stove, wearing an apron that read *Polo players do it better*. He wore a cooking mitten on one of his hands. "What are you doing?" Even I could hear the wariness in my voice.

"Surprise." He smiled, showing me to the table. It had my grandma's best tablecloth on it, a white crocheted one passed on to her by her grandmother, porcelain plates, crystal goblets, and a bottle of expensive red wine.

I crossed my arms and frowned at him. "What are you doing?"

His smile faltered for a quick second. He turned off one of the stove's burners and pointed to something behind me.

Still feeling guarded, I turned and gasped. The photo was back on the wall, with a new frame, and even though I could see where it had been ripped, I couldn't help but feel relieved it was in its place once more.

"I'm sorry," he whispered, right behind me.

I didn't turn. "You lost it. You broke my mugs and my picture. You freaked me out."

His hands rested on my upper arms. I jerked them, but his grip tightened. "I'm so sorry, baby. I know I lost it, and that it scared you. I scared myself too. It's just …" He took a long breath. "I'm very competitive and I let it get the best of me. I overreacted and I'm so sorry I frightened you."

"We've been together for two years. I know you're competitive. But why have I never seen this side of you before?"

"I didn't think that you ever would. I guess my temper acts up sometimes, and I thought I could control it enough around you." He turned me around to face him. "I still think I can. You know I would never, ever hurt you."

But it did hurt. He scared the hell out of me, and apparently, he didn't trust me enough to tell me about his problems. "Why didn't you tell me about this before? About your temper?"

"I didn't want you to worry about it. Besides, I swear I'm okay now."

Was he really? Because he'd seemed perfectly fine before the freak out too.

He brushed his fingers over my cheek, and his gaze fell on my lips. "Tell me you forgive me. Please."

"I want to say that I forgive you, but the truth is you really scared me."

His arms wound around me, pulling me tight against him. "I know, baby, I know. I'm so sorry." He kissed my forehead. "I love you so much. I can't bear the way you're looking at me right now."

It wasn't as if I could control it. Worse was the thought blooming in the back of my mind: what kind of woman would I be if I just stepped out of his life in a moment like this, a moment where maybe all he needed was a little understanding and comforting? Besides, the two years we had together had been almost perfect, and this was just a small hiccup. I could live with it. I could help him with it.

I embraced him back and felt his muscles relax

under my hands. "It's okay," I whispered. "We'll be okay."

I rested my head on his shoulder, and he squeezed me tighter. "I was so worried you would tell me you don't love me anymore and send me away."

Before I could say—or think—anything about it, the oven dinged.

Eric gently pushed me into a chair, smiling. "Dinner is ready."

9

ERIC LEFT LATE LAST NIGHT, AFTER PAMPERING ME with a delicious dinner, good wine, and conversation. He told me all about the upcoming tournament in Florida and how he was preparing for it. Thank God, he didn't try to stay the night or sleep with me before leaving, because I wasn't completely over his scene yet. In fact, I had stayed awake in bed for hours, thinking about his freak out and what I could do to help him never have one again.

Sleeping only a little resulted in a tired me the next day. I dragged myself up and down the ranch, going from chore to chore, barely thinking. Jimmy asked me several times if I was okay and suggested I give in and go take a nap.

When Paul was done with his last class, he helped me put away the saddles and bridles for once. I think even he noticed how tired I was. However, he left before I could try to have him help me with more chores. Jimmy, on the other hand, helped me past his usual work hours.

"I'm going to the stable in the back. Need to feed the horses there."

"Good idea," I said.

He walked out of the stable, and I turned to Argus's stall.

I'd debated taking him out of there and putting him in the stable in the back, but I'd figured keeping him that distant, with fewer horses, would be worse. He had to get used to lots of noise, the other horses, and to the children who came in here all too eager to ride the ponies. For now, he remained in the largest—and recently reinforced —stall in this stable.

I spied inside his stall. He was standing in the back, against the wall, his side glued to the wood, muzzle down, and his bucket still full. Damn, I hoped Leo would get to him once he arrived.

Speaking of which. I pulled my phone out of my pocket and checked the time. Almost seven. As far as I knew, practice went until five. Two hours to get here? The club was only half an hour from here, and his ranch was not ten miles away. That didn't sound right, but I tried not to worry. If Leo wanted, he would come. Besides, he had no obligation to come and help me, even though he said he would.

I debated what to do.

I knew only a little about training horses and I felt bad about that method. My father had trainers working all year long on his horses, and they called their method "breaking the horse." It was brutal. They made the horse afraid of stepping in the wrong direction.

My grandma, however, had her own method, which I knew even less. I had seen her training horses in a much gentler way, but I had never actually learned it. I always thought I had more time with her and eventually, after I graduated from college most likely, I would be able to learn her method.

Now she was gone and I had a damaged horse on my hands. At this point, he didn't need training, he needed fixing, and the only thing I knew about that was to stand still, with patience, and wait for the horse to come to me in his own time. But what if the horse didn't want to?

Sure, I could hire someone to come help me, like a true horse whisperer or natural trainer. But, hmm, that would certainly wound my pride. Not that asking Leo for help hadn't been the same thing.

Sighing, I turned to finish things around the stable and go to the house, but stopped when I heard a car entering the property. With deliberate steps, I walked to the doorway and saw Leo parking his SUV beside my car. He was jumping out of his car when his eyes met mine, and he smiled.

My breath caught.

How he could rock jeans, a striped white and green polo shirt, black boots, and a black hat, I would never know. I didn't *want* to know.

Whatever I told myself to keep my heart from beating faster, didn't work, because crap, every time I laid eyes on Leo, I was reminded he looked too handsome to be real.

Swallowing, I trained my face to remain emotionless, which I bet was a failure.

"Sorry I'm late," he said, walking toward me.

"It's okay," I replied, feeling suddenly shy. It was not okay. It was late, I was famished and tired, and I had plans of crashing on my bed early. I could go on with the planned session, but in truth, I wanted him to leave so I could crawl into my house. "I was actually thinking we shouldn't—"

"Work Argus out tonight?" he continued for me. My eyes widened. Then why was he here? "We should just stay with him, make him used to our presence."

"Oh," I muttered.

He walked past me, into the stable, and toward Argus's stall.

"How about we take him out to the arena and stay there with him?"

The idea wasn't bad.

I ended up nodding and his smile broadened, if that was possible. I averted my eyes before I was sucked into his magic. Seriously, I was in a perfectly happy relationship with a great guy. If the man before me made me feel this way, I could only guess the single girls melted in love puddles at his feet.

Shaking my head, I closed the entrance to the stable and opened the back gate, which led to the fenced arena. I made sure all other possible exits were sealed before Leo unlocked Argus's stall. Argus remained still.

"Come," I muttered to Leo, before dashing out. I ran across the arena and sat on top of the fence. Leo followed me out and sat beside me.

And we waited.

Argus would come eventually. I knew he

would. We just had to be patient, which wasn't my most honorable trait.

It took him over twenty minutes to poke his muzzle through the back gate, but once he did, his eyes widened, and he neighed and dashed into a beautiful run. He galloped close to the fence, as if looking for a way out. When he approached us, he stepped away, leaving a wide berth between us, then continued his surveillance. I shook my head.

The horse circled the arena six times before he stopped. Far away from us, of course.

Meanwhile, I couldn't help but be aware of Leo beside me. He seemed relaxed and focused, his eyes on Argus. I dared spy him from the corner of my eyes. His chin was high, showing off his perfectly sculpted jaw. His hair curled around his neck, and I wondered if it was on purpose or if he was just too lazy to get a trim. Either way, it looked so damn fine on him.

Crap, I had to stop thinking of him like that. He was just someone—not even a friend—who was here to help me with Argus. That was it. No beauty, hotness, or breathtaking stares involved.

"After we left the club yesterday," Leo started, "Beatriz complained that you made her sit through a tea or whatever it was. She was furious, in a funny kinda way."

I smiled, remembering her mortal glare. "I told her I was sorry about that, but I don't regret it. In fact, the whole thing became more bearable with her there."

He frowned. "*Sim*, she said something about it."

"About what?"

"How you looked uncomfortable there, and how you barely talked to any of the women, even though they wouldn't shut up. Bia was pretty impressed actually, because she hates pompous people, and apparently you do too. So, let's say you're ranking better on her meter now than you were yesterday morning." I laughed, but he didn't. "Can I ask you a question?"

"It depends on the subject," I said.

"About what Bia said."

"Go on."

"Why were you so uncomfortable there? I mean, you were raised among them, weren't you? You are supposed to be like ... What's her name again?"

"Who?"

"The girl with blond hair and brown eyes. She's always with her mother, and they look like Xerox copies of one another, though, you know, minus the wrinkles."

I laughed. He was cute when he babbled as well. "Megan."

"*Sim*, that one. She's one annoying girl, huh? She keeps inventing excuses to follow my brothers and me everywhere around the club."

"Yes, that would be Megan."

"*Bom*, like I was saying, you're not like her. I can't imagine a girl like Megan wearing this." He gestured to my clothes as his eyes raked down my body.

Suppressing a shiver, I looked at my clothes. Cutoff jean shorts, a dark orange tank top, brown cowboy boots, and my hat was hanging around here somewhere. Yeah, no way Megan would ever wear this.

"So," he prompted.

I glanced into his eyes, and it took me a minute to focus on the question again. I shrugged. "I don't know."

He frowned. "*Desculpa*. Sorry. I shouldn't be prying."

"It's okay." I sighed. "I used to be more comfortable among them. It's just ... I don't know. My grandma was a simple woman. After my grandpa made our family money, she didn't change. They ended up divorcing because of that. Anyway, being with her on this ranch was my favorite thing to do, my favorite place to be. I guess her simplicity in-fluenced me a little."

"That's good," he said.

"And what's your story?" I asked, surprising even myself. But then curiosity took hold of me and I really wanted to know. "I mean, you're filthy rich too, I think, but you go to the club in jeans and a T-shirt. I don't know how they haven't ex-pelled you from there yet."

A hint of a smile—a mischievous one, good Lord—appeared on his lips. "We're simple too. We spent most of our lives on ranches, helping, taking care of horses and cattle, dealing with *peões*." His nose scrunched. "Hmm, don't know how to trans-late this word. It's like cowboys, but it's for the men who work at the ranch."

I grinned like a silly teenage girl. "I get it."

"Anyway, we really don't mind getting dirty in mud or cow poop. Besides, suits and ties are nice for balls once in a while, but I'm more of jeans-and-boots kind of guy."

Oh, I could see that. And that style looked too damn good on him.

To push back those dangerous thoughts, I broke his burning stare and searched for Argus.

Leo jumped off the fence and turned to me, offering me his hand. I stared at him, breathless. Crap.

"Come on," he said. "He won't get used to us if we stay far from him."

He was right, of course.

For some childish reason, I ignored his hand and jumped off the fence by myself. I didn't want to look like a proud brat, but I was already confused and I was afraid of what touching him would cause within me.

As if nothing had happened, Leo and I approached Argus with slow steps.

I glanced up. The sun was setting, and I could see the faded moon on the other side of the sky, ready to take over. The lights outside the stable were already on, but once the sun was gone, they wouldn't do much to illuminate the arena. That didn't bother me, but it could bother Argus.

I lowered my eyes and once again my gaze fell on Leo, who was two steps ahead of me. He looked so intent and serious, focused on Argus.

"Why are you helping me with Argus?" I didn't mean to ask that out loud, but the words were out before I could filter them through my brain.

Abruptly, Leo turned around and looked at me. I skidded to a stop, almost bumping into him. His brows hunched together, and a pained look haunted his sea-like eyes. "Because ... my father put down a horse before, many years ago, a horse I was growing attached to."

My heart clenched in sympathy. "I'm sorry. I shouldn't have asked."

"No. It's okay." He reached with his thumb to his ring finger and began turning his black band. I could see it was an unconscious act. "It had to be done. At the time, I didn't understand that. I was too young and believed any horse, any animal, could be saved. But now I do understand. That poor horse had to be put down." Sighing, he glanced over his shoulder to where Argus stood. "Argus will need lots of work and patience, but he can be saved." His eyes returned to mine. "And I want to help you save him."

My eyes watered. I knew firsthand how much it hurt to lose a horse. Leo had lost one too. And, even though it probably pained him to be near Argus, as it did me, here he was, fighting his own demons to help this broken horse.

"Thank you," I whispered.

He nodded and turned to Argus. I took in a big swallow of air, willing my heart to calm down. *He's here for Argus. Nothing more. Just Argus.* Maybe if I repeated those words for three days nonstop, I would actually believe them.

The horse had his head down as if he hadn't seen us, but he had and he was aware of every movement we made. He looked ready to bolt.

Apparently knowing this, Leo raised his arm to his side, right in my path. I almost bumped into it. I wouldn't have minded, but again, I was afraid of what it might do to me.

I cursed myself.

"Just ... stand there," Leo whispered.

I didn't dare move a muscle. We just stood there, like he said. And Argus didn't move either. His head was down, his muzzle on the grass, but it was obvious he wasn't actually munching anything. He was observing us like we were observing him. Poor animal. His defenses were constantly up, and he seemed exhausted and still scared. I wanted to reach to him and tell him that we wouldn't hurt him.

Which led me to wonder what method Leo used for training horses. Well, he had trained horses before, hadn't he?

Leo stepped forward in a bold attempt to get closer to Argus.

I leaned closer and asked, "You're not adept at breaking horses, are you?"

Leo stopped mid-step and his head whipped to face me, his expression confused. "What?"

"If you're adept at breaking horses to train him, I will take back my request and ask you to leave."

It took him a moment to catch up with my busy mind and me. "I'm seriously opposed to anything that goes against the horse's nature, and that includes breaking him. That ... is just brutal."

"I think so too, but there are a lot of people out there who still use those methods."

"I think the large majority still use and prefer breaking the horse." He shook his head. "I wish I could put those people through one session like that. They would never do that to their horses again."

Noticing we were lost in conversation, Argus took a few steps in the opposite direction, gaining some distance from us. Leo sighed.

"I'm sorry," I muttered.

"It's okay. We wouldn't be able to get close to him anyway. I was just testing it." He played with his ring again, his eyes on mine. "I'm a fan of the Buck Brannaman and late Ray Hunt's way." Those names weren't strange to me, but I couldn't pinpoint them. "They are horse trainers and practitioners of natural horsemanship, which is working with the horse, not against it."

That rang a bell and I remembered grandma talking about them. "Horse whisperers."

"Exactly. The real ones. According to their philosophy, the horse is a friend, not a slave. The animal doesn't need to live in fear of being punished if he doesn't do the right thing. He should *want* to do the right thing; he should *want* to learn and be your friend."

"Now that you say that, I remember grandma saying that the horse can make mistakes, like anyone else, but it's wrong when he starts dreading mistakes because he's afraid of being punished."

"Yup. And I believe that wholeheartedly."

I grinned on the inside. So good to know we were on the same page here. "Perfect."

He leaned closer, his stare more intense, and I sucked in a breath. "Indeed," he said in a low tone.

When he looked at me this way, I felt like I was about to lose it. Somewhere in me, there was this thing called respect—for Eric, for Leo, for me—and I searched for it. When I found it, I grabbed it with both hands and sunk my nails in it, so it would hurt if it tried to escape me again.

I retreated and turned to where Argus stood.

For the next thirty minutes or so, Leo and I walked around the arena, chasing Argus—in silence. Every time we approached him, he dashed away. This way, he would be forced to be close to us, even if only for a few seconds, and I had hopes that later, when we stopped, he would be tired and hungry.

When the sun was gone, Leo and I came at Argus from opposite sides, giving him only one option of where to go. He trotted to the stable and into his stall.

Leo closed the back gate while I checked on Argus's water and food. Ignoring me and the grain, Argus turned his back to me, his head low.

I sighed.

"Patience," Leo said, standing by my side.

"I know. I just don't want to see him die of malnutrition."

"He won't."

I turned my head to Leo and found him too close, looking at me with those mesmerizing eyes. My heart sped up.

How could he be sure? I wanted to ask him, but I was afraid of starting more conversation I wasn't supposed to be having.

I averted my eyes. "Well, thank you."

"*De nada*," he said. "Though, we barely started. I'll be back tomorrow evening."

"No!" I shrieked. God, no. Eric would probably be here tomorrow evening, and if he saw Leo here, he would think the worst thing possible and would never let me explain. Eric would kick Leo's ass and argue with me. I wanted to avoid all that. I cleared my throat and tried again. "No. I can't."

His brow knitted together, and I was sure he knew why I couldn't.

Leo played with the band on his finger. "My practice doesn't start until 10 a.m. tomorrow. If you're up for it, I can come early."

I looked back at him. "Early?"

"Yeah, what time do you usually get up?"

I couldn't help the grin that spread on my lips. I was about to burst his bubble. "6 a.m."

"All right. I'll be here at six-thirty," he said, dead serious.

My face fell. "Are you sure?"

"I'm sure." He tipped his hat to me. "Good night."

And just like that, he walked past me and out of the stable.

10

I WAS UP AND READY AT 5:20 A.M. THE TRUTH WAS I barely slept all night. My mind went on and on about several things, including the fact that Eric had no idea Leo was helping me with Argus, and that was bad. Really bad. First, because it seemed like I had something to hide, and I didn't. Second, because Eric would be jealous and possibly mad about it. He would consider it a betrayal, which prompted me to think hiding Leo's help was better. But it wasn't. Or was it?

Confused, I finally gave up sleeping and prepared a strong coffee for me, while pretending I wasn't thinking too much about which clothes to wear. In the end, I shoved on one of my usual cutoff jeans shorts, a tank top, and my boots, and I pulled my hair up in a ponytail since the day promised to be hot. *It sure would.*

Crap. *Get your head out of the gutter, Hannah!*

The day would be hot, as in the weather. Not because Leo would be here. No. Not at all.

Yeah, keep telling yourself that.

At 5:50, I entered the stable and almost had a heart attack.

"What are you doing here?"

Leo stood in front of Argus's stall, a bucket of grain in his hands. "*Bom dia,*" he said, without looking at me.

I retreated two steps and spied out. Sure enough, his Grand Cherokee was parked beside my car. How did I miss that?

I returned my gaze to him. He put the bucket into the lazy Susan on the wood wall of Argus's stall, then closed it. Leo watched Argus intently, but if the horse noticed our presence and the fact that he was given food, he hid it well.

And, while Leo observed Argus, I observed Leo. He was wearing jeans, a black polo shirt, and cowboy boots. He wore the same style of clothes I always saw him in, but the fact that he looked so damn good in them, that his black polo hugged his large shoulders and looked a little too snug around his biceps and triceps, that the jeans weren't too tight but still fitted enough so I could see the contours of his perfect, round butt, and that the black cowboy boots were a nice touch showed me he was truly a horse guy, not just someone who liked horses.

My eyes wandered to his face, to the way his jaw, chin, and cheekbones seemed chiseled to perfection, and how his longish light brown hair curled around his neck, and the way his blue-green eyes shone with something I couldn't define when they turned to me.

Crap. I shook my head and cleared my thoughts.

"You're early," I said, crossing my arms.

"I know." He turned to Belle's stall. "I couldn't sleep, so I thought I could compensate for being late yesterday."

He opened the lazy Susan on Belle's stall and filled her bucket with grain.

"You don't have to do that," I said.

"I know."

I didn't understand him. Who in any good sense would come to a stranger's ranch before six in the morning and start doing chores?

After serving Belle, he walked to Chip's stall.

Frowning, he looked at me. "*Tche*, are you going to watch or are you going to help me?"

I shook my head once more. "Sorry." I walked up to where the buckets were lined on the floor along the wall. I grabbed a bucket for Black Jack because I knew his lazy Susan wouldn't have one. He liked to chew on his buckets, and we avoided leaving them in his stall longer than necessary. "I was ... caught off guard. Besides Jimmy, I don't have help around here."

Leo closed Chip's lazy Susan and turned to me. "Only you and Jimmy for the entire ranch?" I nodded, and he continued, "I can't imagine taking care of a ranch like that. In Brazil, our ranch is big, but it has at least twenty employees, and here we have about seven. And looking at it, your ranch is about the same size as ours."

I inserted the bucket into Black Jack's lazy Susan. "Yours has forty-three acres more."

One corner of his lips tugged up. "I forget you probably know that ranch better than we do."

I closed the lazy Susan. "I wouldn't say I know it better, but the O'Connors were good friends with my grandma. I spent a lot of time there during my childhood."

"How do you do it? I mean, taking care of the ranch by yourself?"

I shrugged. "I don't know. Grandma did it with only Jimmy's help. I guess I can do it too."

"But you have college too. And your father's business, right?"

I nodded. All right, this conversation was going to a place I didn't want it to go. Time to get back to the matter at hand. "So, what's the plan today?"

He stared at me for a few seconds, as if noticing I was changing the subject on purpose and wondering why. "I'm not sure," he finally said, walking up to the next horse's stall. "What time is the first riding class?"

"At seven." I spied into the tack room and glanced at the clock on the wall. It was 6:20 a.m.

He served breakfast to the horse. "That's early."

"Yes. This class is older, people between thirty-five and fifty-five years old. They wanted the class to be before work hours. Then, the other class is at eight. A children's class." I smiled. "Seven to ten years old. They started about a month ago, two times a week. They didn't know anything until then, and they are doing so well."

He tilted his head at me. "You sound proud."

Noticing I had been smiling, I closed my expression again. "I guess I am, though Paul is the instructor and he's the one that should be proud."

He nodded but didn't say anything.

In silence, we checked on the horses' water.

The stalls had an automated water supply, but even so, I was neurotic that they could stop working and leave the horses without anything to drink for hours. In this heat, that wouldn't be a good thing.

A few minutes later, Jimmy arrived.

"Mr. Fernandes. Good to see you here," Jimmy said with a big smile.

"*Bom dia*, Jimmy," Leo said.

"Morning." Jimmy tipped his hat at me. "Miss Taylor."

"Hello, Jimmy," I said.

"Don't tell me Miss Taylor finally gave up being Super Woman and hired you to help us out," Jimmy said, still sporting a wide smile.

"What?" I squeaked.

Leo chuckled. "No. She's still Super Woman, but she asked me to help with Argus."

"Oh, that's nice."

I cleared my throat. "How about we get the horses ready for the first class?"

"Right," Jimmy muttered.

Leo and I entered the tack room, grabbed saddles, halters, and reins, and headed out to the arena while Jimmy brought the horses over.

Jimmy held the horses, Leo saddled them, and I put on their halters. It was so synchronized I could hear the song our movements composed. If someone walked in on us right now, he or she would think we had been doing this together for a long time. I was not sure if the two men noticed, and I wouldn't be the one to bring that up.

Leo was saddling Black Jack, the last horse, when Paul came in. I introduced Paul to Leo and vice versa.

"So nice to get here and have all the horses set," Paul said in his perpetual teasing tone. "Miss Taylor, I say you hire this young man and let him do that every day. I would certainly appreciate it."

I rolled my eyes.

"Sorry," Leo started. "My schedule is already too busy. I can't have two jobs without totally screwing one."

"Darn it!" Paul flung his arms into the air, pretending to be hurt.

Soon, the students arrived and the minutes flew by as they greeted everyone, got ready, chose their horses, and set out with Paul.

"It ain't barely seven and I'm already spent." Jimmy sighed. "Miss Taylor, I'm gonna check on the other stable, if that's all right?"

"It sure is," I said.

Leo and I watched Jimmy as he crossed the

small gate at the arena and walked up the hill to the stable in the back.

Then, Leo pointed over my shoulder. "I see you have a round pen."

I nodded without looking toward it. The covered round pen was connected by fences to the arena. It had not been used in ages.

"We should take Argus there," Leo said. "It'll be a smaller place for him to run from us. Unless you have more stuff to do around here."

"No, it's fine. Argus is the priority. I can do whatever I have to do later."

"I don't mind helping."

"I know."

He didn't mind helping. I could see that. I could *feel* that. And it hurt. It hurt because a total stranger wanted to help me while my boyfriend ran from this place when he could.

Taking a deep breath, I stepped around him, toward the stable. "Any idea of how we take him there?"

Leo followed me inside. "Not really."

We stopped before Argus's stall. The horse had not moved at all since I had first seen him this morning, over an hour ago. If it weren't for the slow up and down of his ribs, I would think he was dead.

Or maybe he was sick.

Panic rose in me, and I opened the stall door.

Leo's hand on my arm stopped me. "What are you doing?"

"He hasn't moved yet. I'm worried."

Leo closed the stall door and pulled me back. "He's testing you. Don't let him win."

I turned my face to him and I found him too close to me. I inhaled sharply. "Checking on him is letting him win?"

"It is when he's playing a game, yes."

I sighed. Leo was right, as I was finding out he usually was. As much as I didn't want to play any games, Argus was playing one. A serious one. And I had to be careful of any move I made.

"What then?"

He beckoned me to follow him into the tack room.

There, he grabbed some halters and reins from the wall. "You'll distract him, somehow."

"Somehow?"

"Yeah, make some noise, call him, threaten to enter and get close to him, but don't really do that."

"Okay ..." I said, sounding doubtful even to my ears.

"I'll try to sneak in and put the halter around him, and then we can pull him to the round pen."

I stared at him. "And you really think he'll just let us pull him across the arena and into the round pen?"

"Any other great ideas?" he asked, and I shook my head. "Then let's try it."

We walked over to Argus's stall. He was in the same position, but I noticed he was alert. His ears were slightly perked and his body seemed a little tense. Crap, he really was playing.

I went to the leftmost corner of the stall, while Leo was on the right.

"Argus, boy, come here," I said, feeling lame about it. I tapped on the wood railing. "Boy, I have something to show you. Come on." His ears moved a little, but other than that, nothing. I leaned over the rail. "Look at me, boy." Using my hands and arms, I pulled myself over the rail.

"No," Leo muttered.

"I won't go in," I whispered. "I'll sit over the rail. If he comes at me, I jump down."

Even though Leo didn't seem satisfied with my answer, he nodded.

I sat over the rail, keeping one leg in and one leg out, just in case. "Look, Argus." The horse turned his head toward me, and I almost smiled. "Come here."

It took him a few minutes, but with lots of cajoling, the horse finally turned his whole self to me, though he was still on the other side of the stall, with Leo in his peripheral sight.

My stomach was in knots with anticipation. "Come on, boy." I ended up swinging the second leg over the rail and into the stall. Leo shot me a warning look, but I ignored him. "Come on, Argus."

He gave one big step toward me, probably putting Leo out of his line of sight.

Then, as Leo climbed over the rail, I talked nonstop, so Argus wouldn't hear him. "Come on, boy. You can do it. One more step. Here. See? You can do it. I'll show you something. Come on." Leo stood directly behind him, a few steps to the side. Still, my heart bumped hard against my chest. If Argus decided to kick his hind legs, he would hit Leo and that would be bad. Very bad. "You can do it, boy. I won't hurt you." Argus gave another step in my direction, and I sighed in relief. Still not good enough, but better. "Come on. Just one more step. I believe in you."

Leo jumped forward, and in one fluid motion, put the halter over Argus's face. He pulled back through the reins, causing the bridle to fall into place when Argus wiggled. The horse neighed and reared, and Leo stepped to the side, holding the reins firmly. The horse pulled back, Leo pulled forward, and I sat with my heart in my throat, afraid Argus would stomp over Leo.

"Get out," I yelled.

Leo slid his hand to the end of the rope connected to the reins and retreated to the door, while Argus jerked from side to side, neighing loudly.

I jumped out and opened the door for him. He stepped out and I closed it. It was better to keep the horse in there until he calmed down a little than to try to pull him like that across the arena.

Leo held on to the reins with firm hands.

"What now?"

"We wait."

We did wait. For over twenty minutes. By then, Leo's arms had to be hurting.

"I'm sorry," I whispered.

He glanced at me. "For?"

"For this." I gestured to everything around us. "I'm sorry it's so difficult."

He chuckled. "You thought it would be easy?"

"Not really. But I guess I never stopped to consider how difficult this can be."

"I know what you mean," he whispered, and I

wondered if we were talking about the same thing, which brought on my curiosity with full force.

I looked at Argus. He was quieting down, but not as much as I wanted him to.

"You know a lot about me. Now it's your turn. Tell me about you," I said, still looking at Argus.

Leo let out a loud sigh. "There's not much to tell."

"I'm sure there is. How was life in Brazil? Do you miss it?"

"I miss it, but not as much as I thought I would. I miss our farm, for sure, but the one here is almost as good. I miss some of the horses that we didn't bring; I miss some of my friends. The worst part is knowing that, if we go back, those friendships won't be the same."

I turned to look at him. "Why?"

"I don't know. I've barely spoken to them since we came here. I know they will always have my back, but it's not the same thing. Before, we spoke every day, several times a day, and talked about any crap that popped into our minds. Now, I have no idea what they are doing, what they are up to. If we go back, I have my doubts things will go back to the way they were before."

"Do you plan on going back?"

A lopsided grin took over his lips. "Our plan

right now is to stay for the next six months, and hopefully get a new contract in a couple of weeks to stay a whole year. After that, we don't know. I would like to stay," he said in a low voice that made butterflies zoom in my stomach. "Brazil isn't that big on polo and the U.S. is. We have much to offer and some of the clubs here are among the best in the world."

The butterflies melted away. "Oh."

Leo nudged me in the ribs with his elbow, and I almost jumped. "Look, he's calm."

I turned toward Argus. He was calm. Still tense and alert, but he was just standing there, not fighting anymore.

"Ready?" I asked, reaching for the door.

Leo nodded and I opened the door. I grabbed a whip from the shelf along one of the walls and rushed to stand on the way, so the horse wouldn't be able to come from the opposite direction.

Surprising both of us, Argus followed Leo's tugs and pulls, and followed him to the arena without any problems. I followed them out and closed the back gate, just in case.

Right in the center of the arena, Argus reared, neighed, and pulled back. Leo couldn't hold on to the rope without falling or being stomped over, so Argus trotted away from him.

I dashed to Leo. "Are you okay?"

"Yes." He glanced at his palms. They were red from trying to hold on to the ropes.

"That doesn't look good." I reached over and placed my hands under his. The warmth of his skin seeped into mine and I realized what I had done.

He tensed. I felt it in his hands. I shouldn't have, but I looked up and found him watching me. He was close, his eyes intense.

"It's not that bad," he said, pulling his hands away.

Clearing my throat and probably blushing, I looked around for Argus. He was on the north most side of the arena, trotting from side to side, kicking and rearing and neighing and snorting nonstop.

"Should we just let him be again?"

"I don't think so. We can't let him win."

"But we can't force him into anything either."

"Think of this like parenting. Parents want to be friends with their children, but before being a friend, you have to be a parent. You can be firm and impose things without actually demanding it and applying fear into the horse."

I returned my eyes to Leo. How did he know so

much about this? It was incredible. I couldn't imagine doing this on my own.

I was about to say thank you, but he spoke first.

"Do you have a rope? I mean, not the ones from the reins. I mean a longer rope. Over thirty feet long."

"Yeah, inside the tack room. Do you want it?"

"Yeah. Oh, and gloves," he added. "Can I borrow them?"

I frowned. "Okay, I'll go grab them."

He nodded and I ran into the stable, grabbed the long rope and gloves from the closet, and ran out again. Argus was still thrashing close to the fence, and Leo had walked a bit closer to him. His stance was firm, and yet not tense, as if he was studying Argus, his guard up, but he wasn't afraid. Not at all.

I handed the rope and gloves to him just as the cars of a few parents bringing their children for the next class arrived. They parked their cars, and the kids came running to the arena.

"Don't enter," I said. "That horse is misbehaving, and I need you to stay outside, okay?"

The kids nodded, an eager and fascinated look on their faces.

Paul came back with his first class. Noticing

Argus wasn't in good shape, he told his students to wait outside the arena too.

Meanwhile, Leo put on the gloves and worked on the rope. His hands moved fast, pulling here and there, tying knots and whatnots. I was dizzy from watching.

"What ...?"

With a winning smile, he held up a lasso to me. "You'll see." He gently touched my hand. "Can you please step back a little?"

I didn't say anything; I just retreated.

And he started.

Leo flung the lasso above his head and began circling it. Swoosh, swoosh, I heard, each time the rope made a complete circle. He walked closer to Argus, only to have the horse trot away. Still holding a smile, Leo shook his head and threw the lasso. When he saw the lasso, Argus skidded to a stop, missing being captured by inches.

The kids cheered and I smiled.

What a sight. Leo with a lasso, chasing after an enraged Argus. Who knew he could do this? It was incredible how he kept on surprising me.

Leo pulled the lasso back and started again as Argus, now knowing what was happening, galloped the perimeter of the arena.

"Get out, Hannah," Leo said, his eyes following

Argus around, and the horse was getting close to where I was standing.

I didn't really want to, but I got out. Sort of. I climbed the fence and sat on top of it, close to the children.

Leo tried tricking Argus. He whirled the lasso above his head, his back to the horse, and pretended he was going to throw the lasso to one side, but threw it to the other side instead. This time, he missed Argus by an inch. Or less.

The kids yelled, sounding excited, and the horse neighed, irritated.

Even if Leo caught him, I wasn't sure we would be able to do more with him today. He was already too distressed, and it wasn't even eight in the morning.

Leo swung the lasso over his head and began spinning it. He spun and spun it while Argus galloped and galloped. I knew what he was doing. The patience game. I would have lost already.

"Won't he throw the lasso?" Lisa, an eight-year-old girl, asked me.

"He will," I said. "As you guys can see, Argus isn't in great shape. With a horse like him, you have to be patient."

"What happened to him?" Billy, a ten-year-old boy, asked.

"His previous owner didn't take care of him."

"And how did he end up with you?" Morgan, a seven-year-old girl, asked.

"Kids," Morgan's mother began. "It's not nice to ask so many questions."

I smiled at her and mouthed, "Thank you."

As much as I would love to tell them all about mistreating a horse, or any other animal, and how not nice that was and such, I wanted to pay attention to Leo and his work. I could lecture the kids about this another time.

I returned my focus to Leo and Argus. They were still playing the patience game. Leo whipped that lasso like a boss, marching slowly with squared shoulders and straight back, and Argus ran from him, trotting like a mad horse.

Then, Leo stopped walking but kept the lasso going. Noticing something had changed, Argus slowed down to a trot, but he didn't stop. Leo didn't even turn to face Argus anymore, but when Argus came around him, I noticed the tiny shift in Leo's stance.

He threw the lasso and caught Argus. The kids boomed beside me and I smiled.

Leo knelt down, pulling on the rope, while Argus jerked around, fighting Leo. I jumped down from the fence and ran to him.

"Need help?" I asked.

He shook his head, too focused on the amount of force he had to channel to hold on while the horse pulled. Leo angled the rope toward the ground and put his knee over it to give him a stronger base, forcing Argus to turn his head slightly down. Gritting his teeth, Leo held on.

Argus thrashed against the lasso, as much as he could.

Leo extended one arm along the rope as far as he could, entwined his hand on it, and pulled it. Argus fought, but he didn't have a choice. He advanced toward Leo until he reared and pulled back at it, causing Leo to lose his grip. He wobbled, and I thought he would face-plant into the ground, but he recovered and tightened the grip around the rope before all of it was gone.

He reapplied the force.

"I might need that help, after all," he muttered, and I noticed he was a little out of breath.

"Tell me what to do."

"Hold the rope and help me pull it when I tell you too." He dared a glance at me. "Oh, you don't have gloves. Then no."

"Here," Paul yelled. I turned my head to him. He was taking off his gloves.

I waited for Argus to trot to the other side to

dash closer. Paul threw them at me. I caught them and slipped them on as I ran back to Leo.

I grabbed the rope behind him. "I'm ready."

"Okay, let's do this. Now," he said. We pulled on the rope, and I instantly felt the struggle when Argus worked against it.

"Holy shit," I muttered.

Leo chuckled.

This wasn't a game.

We knelt down again, but this time Leo didn't use his knees as help since I was with him. He inclined the rope toward the ground, and did the same thing as before. He stretched his arm along the rope and clasped it in his hand.

"One more time. Ready?"

"Yes."

"Now," he said. We pulled the rope. Argus yanked against it, but we kept pulling. I was sure I was now gritting my teeth too. "Again," Leo said. We applied more force, and Leo brought more of the rope in. "Again."

This time, when we were done bringing the rope in and holding it there, Argus fell to his knees.

The kids cheered. I thought I heard Paul cheering too.

Smiling, Leo stood up. "You can let go now."

With a loud sigh, I dropped the rope. My arms were killing me.

Keeping the rope stretched, Leo walked closer to Argus. When he was about five feet from the horse, Leo tugged on the rope gently. I could see the battle in their eyes. It was as if they were having an entire argument without words. Argus resisted at first but then stood up with Leo. As a sign of trust, Leo relaxed the rope.

Leo glanced at me. "Unfortunately, I don't think he'll do much more today. How about I take him back to the stable?"

I nodded.

Leo directed Argus back to his stall. The horse tested him a few times by stopping, but Leo just needed to tug a little more firmly on the rope and Argus began walking again.

"Wait there, kids," I said. "Let me help that class." I pointed to Paul and the students with him. "Then we'll get to yours, okay?"

They didn't seem enthusiastic about it, but there wasn't much they could do.

Paul opened the gate and let his students come into the arena. Jimmy entered with them—I just now noticed him here. Immediately, he started helping Paul's class with dismounting and putting things away.

I was about to help them when Leo came back to the arena, the rope still in his hands.

"I must say, I'm impressed."

He offered me a huge smile. My heart skipped a beat. "Oh yeah?"

"I didn't know you could do that. How did you learn that?"

He shrugged. "I'm not sure. It was something so natural when growing up on a farm where cattle are raised." His proud smile changed to a naughty one. "But let me show you something I learned when I was about ten years old." He retreated a few steps from the crowd. "Let the kids in. They will like this."

"This?" I asked. My curiosity corroded my insides.

"You'll like it too."

"How can you be so sure?"

"Come on, *morena*, do it."

"*Morena*?"

Laughing, he turned to the children. "Come inside, kids. While you wait for your class, you might want to see this."

The kids all but lost their legs on the fence and gate, climbing and rushing through it. They closed in around Leo, but he asked them to stand back a little, and they did so. I stood with them.

Leo swung the lasso over his head. Then he turned it sideways. Then to the other side. Then in front of him. Then on his back.

He was doing tricks with the rope. A trick roper.

Oh my God.

Next, he circled the rope close to the ground and jumped in the middle. The kids clapped, cheered, laughed, and smiled. It was contagious.

Leo drove the rope around his body, from his feet up to his head, and he never stopped whirling the damn rope. He brought the rope to his front and played with it, making figure eights and pushing the rope in on itself. I was expecting it to knot, but it never did. After a few minutes showing off those tricks, Leo turned the rope sideways again, close to his body, and he jumped through it.

The kids went wild and I laughed.

I glanced over my shoulder. Paul, Jimmy, the students, and the kids' parents were all watching, with huge eyes and smiles.

Leo did the side jump again, and once more, the kids screamed. Then his eyes settled on me, and I knew what was coming a millisecond before it happened. He threw the rope at me and caught me.

The kids laughed out loud.

"Very funny," I said, trying to sound mad, but I was laughing too.

"It actually is," he said, pulling me closer to him.

The kids took that as a cue, and they stood around Leo and me.

"Can you do that again?"

"How do you do that?"

"Are you a magician?"

"Can you teach me?"

And the questions went on.

Leo tried answering as much and as fast as he could, but kids were kids, and he couldn't keep up with eleven of them.

He was saved when Paul and Jimmy called them to get ready. They didn't want to go, but Paul said he would bring Leo another day if they came quickly. So they did.

I tried making a mad face at Leo again. "Can you please let me go?"

"Maybe," he said, a hint of a smile on his lips.

I stared at him. "You were right. I liked that."

The smile stopped hiding and shone in his face. "I knew you would."

11

After the kids had gone to their classes, Jimmy went back to his chores, and since Argus was probably done for the day, I invited Leo for a snack. After all, I had breakfast three hours ago and I was already green with hunger.

I made us coffee and we sat on the swing on the front porch.

"So, what are the other secrets you hold?"

He almost spat his coffee. "Me? No secrets. You get what you see."

"Hmm, I see a famous polo player, ranked number six in the world, and—"

"Number four."

"But ... I was sure it was six."

"It went up two weeks ago and it'll probably go

up again next week or so. I know because I've been counting my points."

"Oh ... okay then. Number four in the world ranking, a skilled trick roper, and on the way to becoming a horse whisperer. With a nice family, at least that's what it seems."

"*Sim*. It is pretty nice." He sipped from his mug. "Bia, Gui, Pedro, and Ri are my best friends."

I pulled my feet up on the swing and wrapped my arms around my legs, laying my cheek on my knees, careful not to spill coffee from my mug. "How old are they? I mean, I can guess, but ... I'm curious."

"Ri is twenty-five, Pedro is twenty-three, Gui is twenty-one, and Bia and I will be twenty-one in August."

"Hmm, your birthday is getting close." I tilted my head up, resting my chin on my knees. "How about Gui's parents? They just let him come with you guys?"

"Yeah. Gui is a great player, and if he didn't come, his talent would be wasted. His father was supportive, but his mother was heartbroken. She calls several times per day."

"Is he an only child?"

"No, he has a younger sister. Gabriela is seventeen."

Another girl among four guys. I bet they gave Beatriz and Gabriela a hard time. Which brought to mind the next question.

"What about girlfriends and boyfriends?" I asked. He gave me a quizzical look, and I felt the heat spreading on my cheeks. "I mean, it's normal for people to date. I can't believe not one of you had a serious relationship before moving here."

"True. Ri has a girlfriend, Joana. They talk daily and she spent a weekend here two weeks ago. Now he's talking about going down there for a weekend soon. He plans on proposing to her, then after the visa and all that crap is done, bringing her to live here."

"That's romantic."

"Yes and no. Can you imagine being newly-weds and living with the in-laws? And it's not only my parents. There's another four of us. I'm not sure she'll like that idea," he explained.

"You're right. That wouldn't be good."

"Because of that, Ri is trying to convince Dad to build another house on the property. However, we don't know if we're staying, so Dad doesn't want to do that just yet."

"I guess that also makes sense."

"As for Pedro, he had an on-and-off relationship with a girl from our school, Paula. They put a real end to it when he was about to leave. Gui was never the serious type, and Bia hid her boyfriends from us, so I'm not sure if she was dating someone when we moved here."

I laughed. "I understand why she hid them from you guys."

He didn't laugh. In fact, he was too serious. "That's not funny."

"It is, actually." I poked him in the ribs with my elbow. "What about you?"

He averted his eyes. Uh-oh. "In truth, I was much like Gui. Not the serious type."

Something inside of me deflated. "Oh."

He brought his gaze back to me. "But I think I met a girl —"

His cell phone rang, and I realized I was tense. Too tense.

He pulled the phone from his pocket. "*Merda*," he muttered, looking at the screen and frowning. "*Oi.*" He answered the phone sounding way too curt. "*Sim. Sim. Eu não vou me atrasar, tche. Tá bom.*" He turned it off and shook his head. "Sorry. It was my father."

I bit the inside of my cheek. It was not the first time I saw him tense because of his father, and I wondered what was there that I didn't know. I wanted to ask him but I was afraid to.

He sighed. "You can ask about it."

"What?"

"I can see the questions in your eyes. Ask about it."

"I don't mean to pry," I whispered.

"I know. If I don't want to answer, I won't. But you'll never know until you ask me."

I held my breath and formulated what I thought was the right question in my mind. "What happened between you and your father to make you this upset?"

He looked out at the stable, and I thought he wouldn't answer it. "A couple of years ago, my father and I had a big argument," he finally said. His thumb poked the black ring on his finger. "We didn't speak to each for almost two years. Unfortunately, things never went back to normal between us. I guess this is the new normal."

Wow. Two years without talking to his father? I couldn't imagine that. Well, maybe if my father sold the ranch behind my back or something. Even so, I guess I would try to let my anger dissipate and solve things. Or not. It was hard to gauge how I would act. Besides, I had no idea what the cause of Leo's and his father's argument was and, feeling he didn't like this subject, I wasn't about to ask. Not yet.

"I'm sorry."

"Me too." He stood up. "*Bom*, I think I should be going. I still have to stop home before heading to the club."

"Oh, okay."

He placed the mug on top of the porch rail and looked at me. "When should I be back?"

I wish it would be this evening, but I was sure Eric would come after practice.

"I don't know," I confessed, looking down at my mug.

"I need to know one thing. Eric doesn't know I'm helping you, does he?" Still not looking at him, I shook my head. He groaned. "And you don't want him to know?" I shook my head once more. "*Certo.* Then why don't you write down my number and call me when you want me to come?"

Hmm, having Leo written in my contacts wouldn't be a good idea, but I could program his number with another name. Not the best of ideas, but it was the only one I could think of.

He told me his number, I programmed it on my phone, and then I called him so he would have mine.

"Good. Okay." He looked at me, and I thought I would faint with the potency of his eyes. "Have a great weekend."

He ran down the stairs and rushed along the path to his SUV.

I watched him as he drove away and I replayed the morning in my head. Though we hadn't had any progress with Argus, it felt like a productive morning, in some way. I just didn't know which.

"Good morning, baby."

I rolled to my side and found Eric sitting on my bed, wearing his silk pajama set, a tray with breakfast on the nightstand by his side.

The heavy sleep-fog slowly faded away, and I realized it was Saturday morning. Eric had come last night for dinner as I had predicted, and he stayed for the night. We talked a lot, mostly about his trip to Florida the next day for a big tournament, which he was sure he would win.

"Good morning," I muttered, hugging my pillow and closing my eyes again.

"No, no." He nudged my shoulder. "Wake up, baby. I made you breakfast."

"Hmm, five more minutes."

He laughed. "It's almost nine in the morning, and I've gotta go soon, so please, can you wake up and have a nice breakfast with me?"

I opened my eyes. "You gotta go?"

"Yes." He ran a hand over my hair. "I had to schedule a meeting for this morning before leaving for my trip. They didn't want to wait until I'm back, and I'm not willing to lose this business. Sorry, baby."

I sat up. What was *this* business exactly? I was sure it was something to do with his family's farm, though he never talked about it, and I wasn't sure why since I had my nose in horse farms since I was born.

"I understand."

He smiled. "Great. Now, get ready for a delicious breakfast." He popped open the tray's legs and placed it over me.

It looked nice and smelled good. Toast, scrambled eggs, cheese, and a big mug of coffee. Coffee?

I stared at him. "You made coffee?"

"I knew you wanted it."

"But that implies touching my coffee maker and my mugs, and you always say you can't touch them because they disgust you."

He chuckled. "Of course you would remember stuff like that, wouldn't you? Yes, I say that, but it's mostly because I want to tease you. Though I do hate coffee." He glanced at my mug and made a bleh face.

I smiled and reached for his hand. "This is sweet. Thank you."

He held my hand up to his lips and kissed my palm. "You're welcome."

Then he was up and running and taking a shower and getting dressed while I ate my breakfast in bed.

Once he was ready, he knelt onto the bed and leaned over the tray. "This meeting is going to take a long time." He made a bored face and I smiled. "But I should be back by five, maybe 6 p.m., and I'll take you out for dinner in Santa Barbara. What do you think?"

I liked going into town, especially if we could get into a waterfront restaurant. "I would like that."

"It's settled, then." Eric closed the distance between us and placed a quick peck on my lips. "I'll see you later."

"Have a good meeting."

He scooted away from my bed. "Thanks. Bye."

"Bye."

He walked out of the bedroom, and it took me a second to stop fighting the thought pushing against all others since Eric announced he would spend the day away.

I grabbed my phone from the nightstand, and waited until I heard the wheels of Eric's car crunching gravel as he left the property to send Leo a message.

We have until 4 p.m. to work on Argus.

A full minute went by without any answer, and I started panicking he was ignoring me on purpose. Then I quickly added.

If you can, of course. If you have other plans, please don't change them. I totally understand.

Did I sound like a lame teenager or what? Crap.

Once more, the minutes went by and no answer. I could stay in bed all morning, staring at my phone, willing it to beep with a new message, or I could get up and do something with my day.

Feeling like an idiot, I pushed the tray to the side and hopped out of bed and into the shower. After, I put on white jean shorts, a sleeveless checkered shirt, and my red boots.

I headed down and out to the stable. Jimmy was taking Chip to the arena to exercise when I entered.

"Morning," he said.

"Morning." I took a set of bridle and reins from the shelf. I opened Belle's stall, put the halter on her, and pulled her out to the arena with Chip. "What time is Paul's first class?" I asked. It was hard keeping track of the summer schedule. No two weeks were the same.

Jimmy took the halter off Chip and patted his side. The horse trotted away. "One class at three."

"And riding groups?"

"One at noon, and another one at four-thirty."

I pulled the halter off Belle. "Calm day." Compared to the others, this day would be easy.

"It seems like that."

We worked around the stable in silence. We let Chip and Belle run around and around for over thirty minutes, then switched them with Back Jack and Duchess. We cleaned a couple of stalls. Jimmy brushed them while I checked their shoes—and replaced them when necessary.

All the while, I ignored the itching to reach out to my phone and check my messages. I would hear the phone shimming if Leo sent one.

It was almost ten when Jimmy brought Black Jack and Duchess in. He was about to take two more, but I told him to hold it. I couldn't delay anymore, otherwise the day would be gone in a flash, and I would be mad at myself later for not doing anything.

"I'll try to take Argus to the round pen first, then you can use the arena for two other horses."

He frowned. "Are you sure?"

I took another set of bridle and reins from the pins on the wall. "I am."

"Miss Taylor, I don't thi—"

"I have to do this, Jimmy." I halted in front of Argus's stall. The horse was on his feet, but in his usual corner, his left side facing me. "He's not progressing fast enough, and if I don't do this, Officer Michael will take him from us and put him down. I don't want him to be put down."

Jimmy didn't say anything else, but he didn't leave either. He stood at the end of the main hallway, by the back gate, watching.

I closed my eyes and took a deep breath. I wasn't sure what to do or how to do it, but I had to try something. Perhaps the best way for me would be to try to reach Argus and go from there. One step at a time. Much better than none at all.

"Hey, boy," I said, opening my eyes. "Do you want to go for a walk? You need to stretch those muscles, you know." Argus turned his head to me for a second, and then went back to staring at the ground.

Under the wounds and scars, his coat was so incredibly white, and his whitish mane was growing, proving to me he was truly beautiful. It was a shame that he was too thin and that his pretty, big brown eyes held this perpetual sad and terrified shine. I sort of understood why he was so jumpy and reared every time we got too close. He needed that to defend himself where he came from, to survive. Even though it didn't seem to have worked many times, otherwise he wouldn't have so many scars. To think this animal had to *defend* himself hurt. Why would a horse have to defend himself? They were supposed to be our friends.

Hercules had been my friend. Paul and grandma had trained him, but it was easy to train a horse that was born on a caring ranch, where he was treated right and lived with other horses that were already used to the daily activities. The jumping part though, Hercules and I learned together. We were a great duo, and I missed it desperately.

I shook my head, trying to bring myself to the present.

Argus was the focus now. I wasn't sure I could make a friend out of him—if Leo could—but I sure would try. Hopefully, someday, he would be a good friend to someone.

"You must be tired of being in here for so long, aren't you?" I reached for the door. His eyes were intent on me. "If you promise to be a good boy, we can arrange for you to do more. Run in the arena a little. I bet you would like that." He gave two steps toward me. I smiled. "I know you'll like that."

He took a couple more steps in my direction. Until the sound of hooves stomping on the front path echoed through the stable, and he retreated again.

"What the ...?"

A magnificent black horse entered the stable, with an equally magnificent rider.

Leo.

For the love of all holy things in this life, he was dressed in some sort of strange cowboy attire, but holy crap, he looked fantastic. He wore baggy white pants, a red and black sash, a black shirt, black boots, a black hat, and spurs.

His eyes found mine and he smiled.

My heart skipped a few beats.

He jumped off the horse and took the reins in his hand.

"He's stunning," I said, shifting my focus to the horse. His gleaming black coat reminded me of Hercules. "What's his name?"

"Minuano."

I frowned at Leo. "That's an odd name."

"Minuano is the name of a cold wind that blows across the south of Brazil. It even makes a howling sound sometimes."

My frown grew deeper. "You're kidding."

He raised his free hand as if in a promise. "I'm not."

"How old is he?"

"Four years, eight months." He walked past me, pulling the horse behind him. "His father is one of my father's prized horses."

"You brought a horse from Brazil?"

"We brought several horses from Brazil. Unfortunately, we didn't bring our dogs. But we brought a lot of things from Brazil."

That answer sparked another question. "When did you learn English? I mean, I don't think that's something every Brazilian knows."

"No, not every Brazilian knows. During school, we're required to take a second language class. Usually, it's Spanish or English. But lots of teenagers also take private English classes, because with globalization, English is becoming almost a requirement."

"You took private English classes, then?"

"Yes. Everyone in my family did. Since my father had an international career and knew how important it was, he wanted us to learn. And when it became clear we would have careers of our own, the classes become more frequent and harder."

"Oh." My eyes wandered down to his odd pants.

He noticed it and smiled. "These are called *bombacha*. It's our cowboy pants, if you will."

"It looks … strange."

"For you. In the south of Brazil, it's very common." He glanced at me over his shoulder. "Do you mind if I put Minuano in an empty stall?"

"Not at all."

I looked around, trying to remember what I was doing before Leo came in like a hurricane and messed up my thoughts.

Oh, Argus. Yeah.

I turned to his stall and noticed Jimmy wasn't where I had last seen him. I ran my eyes around the place, and he was gone. I felt my cheeks becoming hot at the thought that Jimmy probably left me alone with Leo on purpose.

"Why are you blushing?" Leo asked, standing right by my side.

"Nothing," I muttered.

He stepped in front of me and reached to my face. I froze. He brushed my hair back and placed a Douglas Iris over my right ear.

I looked into his eyes and held his intense stare. I couldn't distinguish what I saw in his eyes, but I knew it was something I should stay away from.

The heat on my cheeks increased, and I stepped back. "What's that for?"

He shrugged. "Sorry I didn't reply to your message. My father was grilling me, and by the time I got free from him, I rushed here."

"You didn't need to come."

"I want to," he whispered.

His gaze shifted for half a second only, but it was enough for me to see it went to my mouth and back to my eyes. I held my breath.

I walked around him and stood before Argus's stall. The horse was still on his feet, and he observed us and every little move we made.

"I was about to take him out."

"By yourself?" Leo's voice came from directly behind me.

"You say that as if I couldn't."

He stood by my side. "I say that as someone who would prefer you to be careful with Argus."

The things he said ... I shook my head. "So, any ideas on how to take him to the round pen? Hopefully, in an easier way than yesterday."

"Dangle a carrot in front of his head and hope he follows it."

I nudged his elbow with mine, and he laughed. Oh, the *things* he said ... "I'm serious."

"I know." He seemed to focus for a moment. "Remember how he followed me after I lassoed him yesterday? Maybe I should do the same thing now. Just lasso him from here and lead him to the round pen like that."

"Try it."

He looked around. "Where's the rope?"

I dashed into the tack room, grabbed the rope, and brought it to Leo. "Here."

"*Obrigado.*" He took it from me and did his thing on it, tying the ends and whatnots. Once he was done, he picked up a pair of gloves from the shelf behind him and put them on. "All right, here were go."

I stood back, trying to relax my corded muscles. Why was I so wound up? We would take the horse out, one way or another, and then train him, work *with* him. Nothing to it.

After taking a deep breath, Leo flung the rope and Argus didn't even flinch. He let Leo catch him.

Carefully, Leo opened the stall door and tugged the rope. "Come on, boy."

Argus turned his head to Leo. They stood there for a long moment, staring at each other. I could see Leo was speaking to Argus with his eyes, and I wondered how he did it. Not that I thought he was magical and could actually speak to the horse, but there was something about him, something that made horses get him, something that made *me* get him.

My mouth fell open when Argus went with him. With a step every minute, but he did go with Leo.

Leo shot me a big smile, and I couldn't help but smile back.

12

———

WE CROSSED THE ARENA, AND EVERY STEP OF THE way, I expected something to happen. Like, Argus rearing and galloping away, or advancing on Leo, or simply stopping and not moving at all. But nothing happened and I was completely dumbfounded.

Holding the halter and whip Leo had asked me to bring, I rushed around them—not too fast though, so I wouldn't disturb Argus's collaborative attitude—and opened the gate to the round pen. Besides the high, open roof and the pillars holding it, the round pen looked like the arena, but on a smaller scale and proportionally round. It was the ideal place to train difficult horses or mistreated ones.

Leo took him inside, and I stepped in with them and closed the gate. I rested my back against the gate while Leo approached Argus with controlled and slow movements.

"I'm just going to take the lasso, okay?" Leo said, his voice calm and reassuring. He reached for the knot on the rope and Argus winced. "It's okay," Leo whispered. He loosened the knot and pulled the rope up and out from around Argus's neck. The second he was free, Argus trotted away. "Whoa."

Leo stepped to the side as Argus advanced toward him. The horse flew past him and began trotting from side to side.

"He's distraught again," I said as Leo halted by my side.

"Yes. We gotta control him now before he gets worse and we can't do anything else with him." He took the whip from my hand. "I'm gonna show you what I think is going to work, but you gotta do it, okay?"

"Why me?"

"He's your horse. You should be the one training him."

"He's not my horse," I said too quickly.

Leo frowned. "At the moment, he is your horse."

I felt like a shovel had hit me in the head. What? No, no. Argus wasn't my horse. He was ... nobody's horse? I didn't know. What I did know though was that I was helping Officer Michael with this case while he searched for a new home for Argus. At least, that's what I thought I knew.

Could I be wrong?

Leo walked toward Argus, his arms open to his sides, the whip in his right hand. Argus didn't stop pacing and stomping, but he watched Leo.

"It's okay, boy," Leo said. "I'm not gonna hurt you." Leo extended the whip toward Argus. "This won't hurt you."

Distrusting, Argus snorted and dashed farther away from Leo. With a calm stance, Leo simply turned and followed him. They played the cat and mouse game for several minutes.

During one turn, Argus trotted my way, and I didn't know what came over me but I didn't move. The horse snorted and whirled around, ending up face-to-face with Leo, who had trailed him there.

Leo didn't waste time. "This won't hurt you," he repeated his earlier statement, and extended the whip toward Argus. He brushed the tip of the whip over Argus's back. The horse flinched, and I jumped back, afraid he would do more. "See." Leo brought the whip to his neck. "It doesn't hurt if used properly."

Argus snorted again as if telling Leo that he wasn't quite sure yet.

Leo gestured to the halter in my hand. I rushed to his side and helped him put the halter on Argus. The horse complained but didn't fight it. Then Leo tied the rope to the end of the reins.

"Now, stand back please, and I'll show you what to do," he said. I took several steps back and observed, probably as wary as Argus was. "Buck Brannaman once said," Leo started. He held the rope in his right hand, and the whip in his left. "Everything you do with a horse is a dance." Keeping his arms spread out, he tugged on the rope. "We're about to go dancing."

Argus gave one short step toward the tug. Leo jerked the rope again, and Argus took one more step toward it. When Argus took too long to keep up with the yank, Leo used the whip. He didn't hit the horse. No. He brushed its tip against his hind legs, making the horse wince with the contact and move.

For the next few minutes, Argus followed Leo's pulls as if they were dancing. To the right. To the right. To the left. To the right. To the right. To the left. The pulls weren't perfectly to the side, but diagonal, which caused them to have to keep circling the round pen. Like they were dancing in a ballroom.

I couldn't understand how Leo did it. How he was able to calm that horse down and have the animal do whatever he wanted it to. I was starting to believe he was a better horse whisperer than my grandma. What he could do ... that was a true gift.

"Your turn, *morena*," Leo said.

That word again. I forgot to look up what that meant.

"Is that like a nickname?"

"Sort of."

"What does it mean?"

He stood in the middle of the round pen, his side to me. Even so, I could see the big smile on his lips. "Just come here."

I walked to him, tensing with each step I took. "I shouldn't do this," I said from right behind him. "You have a gift for doing this. Not me. I'll probably make his issues worse."

"*Que nada.* I told you. He's your horse. You should train him."

"But—"

He turned his chin to me and looked into my eyes. "I'll be here, don't worry. I won't leave you alone with him, okay?"

Those eyes ... they were like two hypnotizing blue-green stones. They had to be.

"Okay," I whispered.

Leo raised his arm and passed it over me, putting his chest against my back. I held my breath before I fainted with the sweetness of his scent. He handed me the rope and the whip, but held my wrist.

"This is how you do it." He pulled my arm back, causing the rope to pull on Argus. The horse didn't come. I was about to open my mouth and say a lot of curses when Leo's hands rested on my shoulders. "Relax," Leo whispered in my ear. His breath washed over my neck, and I shivered. His hands moved slightly, massaging my tense muscles, and I sagged against him. "You're too uptight and worried. He can sense it and becomes uptight and worried too." He pressed on a sweet spot under my shoulder blades, and I almost moaned. "Just ... relax."

If I relaxed more than this, I would be doing things I wasn't even supposed to be thinking. Half-thinking, half-dreaming, I tilted my head back. His chin touched my cheek. I heard Leo's sharp inhale and felt his hand freezing, his body stiffening.

"*Merda.*" He took several steps back.

The heat of embarrassment flooded my

cheeks, and I stared at the ground, mortified. Crap, what had I done?

I thought about throwing the rope and whip to the ground, running, and hiding in my house, but I wasn't a child. Whatever. I felt like one right now.

"Relax, Hannah," Leo said from behind me, though this time he wasn't close. And what happened to *morena*? "Relax and do as I showed you."

Shaking my shoulders, I took a deep breath and focused on the here and now. My eyes found Argus's. "Hey, boy. Everything is all right. We're just playing, okay?"

Argus didn't snort or neigh, so I took that as a good sign and pulled on the rope.

"Too gentle," Leo said. He sounded a little disappointed. Because I had been gentle to the rope? "Pull a little harder. He's a big horse. You won't hurt him, don't worry."

I didn't like it, but I trusted Leo, so I did as I was told. I yanked the rope harder. The halter tugged and Argus's head jerked with it. One second later, he took a step in the right direction.

"Good job," Leo said.

I smiled.

Copying Leo, I pulled Argus twice to the right and once to the left, twice to the right and once to the left. The horse followed my commands without blinking.

"Don't forget to let the rope loose right after the tug," Leo said. "The horse has to know, to feel, that you trust him as much as he trusts you."

I nodded and tried to remember that detail.

We kept going. After a couple of minutes, I pulled Argus to the left, but he stepped to the right instead.

"The other side, boy," I said, tugging him to the left again. He took another step to the right, which made him closer to me since he stepped in a diagonal path. "Argus, what is it?" I pulled the rope to the left, and he once more went to the right. Then I realized he was within my arm's reach. My heart sped up. My fingers itched. "Argus?"

"*Morena*," Leo whispered from somewhere along the fence. "Be careful."

How could I resist this? It was like Argus was asking me to touch him. Me! To *touch* him. He hadn't let anyone touch him willingly. I extended my arm and—

A honk blared through the air, followed by the sound of tires crushing gravel. Argus neighed and reared. I jumped back as Leo wrapped his arm around my waist, and pulled me back. We both hit the fence hard. Neighing, Argus trotted to the opposite side of the round pen.

"Are you okay?" Leo asked, setting me straight before him.

"Yes, I think so." I turned to the fence and looked through the wood railing to the car entering the property. "What the hell?"

Leo pushed away from the fence. "What?"

Mr. Nash stepped out of the silver Ford Escalade. He straightened out his suit and smiled at me.

Ever since watching the Disney version of *The Princess and the Frog*, I thought Mr. Nash could be an exact copy of Eli "Big Daddy" LaBouff. Tall, with a large belly, brownish hair and mustache, and always wearing fancy suits. However, while Big Daddy was a nice man, Mr. Nash was a pain in my ass.

I groaned and marched out of the round pen.

"Hannah, who is that man?" Leo asked.

"My irritation in person," I mumbled.

Mr. Nash stepped on the grass and didn't look too happy about it. I walked in his direction. My eye caught movement to my left, and I saw Jimmy coming from the other stable. He probably saw Mr. Nash arriving and wanted to be here to stop me from jumping down his throat.

"Miss Taylor, lovely morning, isn't it?" He made a point of looking up to the sky, his hand over the jacket of his suit.

I halted a few yards from him. "What are you doing here?"

He turned his conniving brown eyes to me. "Didn't your parents teach you any manners, girl? It isn't nice to be rude to visitors."

"You're not welcome here, thus you're not a visitor."

His gaze shifted past me. He was probably checking Jimmy and Leo out. "Is Mr. Bennett here?"

"Why do you want to know about Eric?"

"I want to talk business with him." An evil smile spread through his entire face. "I want to ask him to show me around the ranch."

"What?" I clenched my fists.

He looked around. "This place looks miserable, Miss Taylor, even more than when your grandmother was alive." He tsked. What did he just say? "I know you're in college and your father wants you to work with him. You don't have time to care for this place."

"Don't—"

"Name a price. I'll pay it and you'll be free of this burden."

I closed my eyes and counted to ten. I was about to explode. Until Leo's hand rested on my arm.

"Take a deep breath," Leo whispered. "That's exactly what he wants. To upset you. Don't let him."

I almost rolled my eyes. "It isn't that easy."

Mr. Nash didn't miss a beat, and his curious gaze took everything in. From the guy he didn't know to the fact he was holding me. I could bet the conclusions his mind drew weren't pretty.

Jimmy stood by my side. "Mr. Nash, I'm going to have to ask you to leave."

Mr. Nash didn't move for several seconds. He only looked at us, the three of us, as if calculating his next move, thinking of his next words.

He ran his hand over the front of his jacket. "All right." He settled his eyes on me. "If you change your mind, Miss Taylor, you know where to find me."

On instinct, I took a step forward, as if my figure could scare Big Daddy away. Leo held me back though.

The three of us stood in silence, watching Mr. Nash as he drove away.

Once his truck was out of sight, I exhaled loudly.

"Are you okay, Miss Taylor?" Jimmy asked.

I laughed—it sounded almost hysterical. "Not really."

"Mr. Fernandes is right," Jimmy continued. "Mr. Nash wants to upset you. To annoy you. And you're letting him."

"I don't want to feel this way," I said, my voice louder than usual. Harsher. "But just the thought of him drives me nuts. I hate him. I truly hate him."

Leo turned me around to face him. "Take a deep breath." I scoffed. "Come on, Hannah. You're looking as stubborn as Argus now."

Argus. Horses always calmed me down. Hercules always had. Maybe working on Argus would help me.

I brushed Leo and Jimmy aside and walked to the round pen.

Inside, Argus was more agitated than before.

"Hannah, don't go in there," Leo said.

Shaking my head, I entered the round pen. Argus stopped moving immediately. That made me feel a tiny bit better. It showed me he was responding to me.

I closed my eyes and let his presence charge my senses. I loved this place. I would never sell it. I loved horses, even if I didn't ride them anymore. I loved seeing people riding horses, making connections with them, making friends. I loved being here, in the outdoors, under the sun, with my boots and hat, sometimes even barefoot so I could feel the grass tickling my skin. Those things. I had to focus on those things and forget about how mad Mr. Nash made me feel.

Mr. Nash. Ugh.

I opened my eyes. My anger and frustration weren't gone, but I felt more in control.

"*Morena*," Leo called me. I looked at him over my shoulder. He was inside the round pen, but close to the fence, while Jimmy stood outside. "Let's take a break."

"I'm fine."

"Miss Taylor, please take a break," Jimmy requested.

If I gave in and went on a break, I would explode. I would remember all the reasons I hated Mr. Nash, all of his unwanted visits, all of his words and the meaning between the lines; I would feel the anger and frustration again, and I would explode.

I didn't want to spend the rest of my day in a bad mood. No. I could get around this. I really could. I had to focus on the things I liked about this place, why I loved it so much, and I would be okay.

I turned on a big smile. "I'm fine. Really." Argus stopped moving from side to side like a crazy horse the moment I picked the whip up from the ground. "It's okay, boy." I opened my arms to my sides as Leo had done before. "We'll keep doing the previous exercise, okay?" Argus snorted and took one step back. "Come on, boy. You want to get back to it, don't you? We want you to get better too, but you gotta help us."

I dared to move in his direction. I expected him to go in the opposite direction, but he didn't. So I dared going closer. Again he didn't move. With my eyes on his, I slowly leaned forward and grabbed the rope tied to his reins.

There, I did it.

A loud sigh escaped through my lips. "All right, boy, you know what to do, don't you?"

I pulled the rope to the right, but Argus didn't go with it. I tugged it again, a little harder, and he still didn't budge. I tried pulling the rope to the left. Nothing.

"I think he's still feeling your distress," Leo said.

"I'm better now."

"I know. I can see it. But you're not totally relaxed either, and he can feel that."

How the hell could he feel it? I was in control of my emotions, and my distraught was locked up deep inside me right now. Argus couldn't possibly feel it.

My cell phone chimed and Argus snorted, jerking his head against the rope.

"Crap," I muttered. I let go of the whip and reached for my phone before it dinged again.

It was a message from Eric.

Mr. Nash called me saying you shooed him from the ranch, threatening to pull your grandmother's rifle on him. Want to tell me what the hell that was that about?

"What?" I shrieked, my rage erupting from every one of my pores. "That jackass, son of a bitch, asshat—"

"Hannah!" Leo yelled.

I glanced at him and he was running toward me, his eyes over my head. Like I was in a slow-motion movie, I turned to Argus and saw him kicking his hind legs high. Then he came at me. I raised my left hand as if it could stop a thousand-pound animal. I screamed as his teeth closed around my hand. Then the movie fast-forwarded. My flower fell from my hair and Argus stomped on it. Leo took the whip and used it to force Argus back, while his arms went around my waist, and he hauled me back to the fence.

In shock, I barely saw as Leo dragged me out of the round pen, sat me on the grass, and he and Jimmy knelt in front of me.

"She was lucky. He could have bitten her whole hand off."

"*Sim*, but she's going to need stitches anyway."

Stitches? I looked down at my left hand. A red crescent moon stained my fair skin, right between my little finger and my wrist. Blood oozed from it.

That was when the pain started. Tears sprung to my eyes, from pain and frustration, and I suppressed a scream.

Leo took off his black shirt—he had a black tee under it. Wasn't he hot in this weather?—and pressed it against my wound. With his other hand, he cupped my face and brought my eyes to his. It was harder to fight the tears this way.

"Hannah, I know it's hurting, but hang in there. I'm gonna take you to the hospital now, okay?"

"Hospital? No." I tried scooting away, but he slid his hands down to my shoulders and held me there. "There's a first aid kit in the tack room. We can use that."

"No, Hannah. Some of his teeth tore through

your flesh. You need stitches."

Jimmy's hand touched my arm. "Listen to him, Miss Taylor."

But ... what if someone I knew saw me there with Leo? What would stop them from telling Eric? I knew Eric would be upset that Argus bit me. Add Leo's presence to that, and I didn't know if I could handle it.

"I would prefer not," I whispered.

"It's not open to discussion," Leo said, his eyes hard. "You need to go to the hospital. Right now."

I knew he was right. I knew it. Damn it. A tear rolled down my face and I nodded.

Jimmy and Leo helped me up, and my gaze went straight to the round pen, more specifically to Argus inside the round pen. I thought I saw him leaning against the fence, his whole body trembling.

"What about him?" I asked.

Leo followed my gaze. "Leave him alone for now. We can take care of him later." Leo put his arm around my waist and helped me walk to my car. "Come on."

I looked up at him. "I'm sorry about the flower."

"Don't worry." He squeezed my side. "I can get you another one."

13

I PRESSED LEO'S SHIRT AROUND THE BITE, HOPING IT would diminish the throbbing pain. A nurse had taken us to a small partition within the ER, separated from other beds by blue curtains, and then disappeared, saying she would be back soon. Leo stood along the wall beside the bed, and I was seated on the edge of the bed, avoiding his gaze at all costs.

The pain escalated considerably on the way to the hospital, as did my shame. Leo and I barely talked since leaving the ranch, other than his questions if I was still okay.

"I'm sorry," I whispered.

Leo approached me. "Actually, I'm sorry." I raised my eyes to his. "I knew you were angry or frustrated or whatever, and I didn't stop you from going to Argus. I should have stopped you."

"It isn't your fault. I would have pushed you away and continued being stubborn about it."

Leo's lips twisted in a small smile. "I know. But I would have done my part."

I reached to him and took his hand in mine. "It's just a small bite. I'm okay."

Suddenly stiff, Leo stared at our hands together for a moment. Then he cleared his throat and gave a step back, letting go of my hold. "It's not a small bite. He could have bitten your hand off. He is strong enough for that."

I didn't let the fact that he purposely distanced himself affect me.

"I know." I sighed. "Poor Argus. I hope he isn't more traumatized by this."

"I don't think so. He was going through the motions. You know, another thing Buck Brannaman said is that the horse is a mirror to your soul. Your anger got the best of you, and it snuck into Argus."

"I'm so stupid," I muttered, looking down at my hand.

The nurse came in and asked me to follow her for an X-ray. They wanted to make sure Argus hadn't broken any of my bones. Fifteen minutes later, I was back in the small partition.

I felt bad about being in a hospital and not telling anyone. I felt like I should tell my parents and Eric, even if this was a small thing.

Playing with his black ring, Leo sat on the other side of the bed. "Are you going to tell me what happened there with that man?"

I shrugged. "If you don't mind my anger coming back."

A new shine took over his eyes. "I won't bite you for that." My breath hitched and he became serious again. "Sorry. Bad joke."

Oh no. I wasn't breathless because I thought it was a bad joke. No. And I certainly wouldn't think of the real reason I was breathless, because it would only make everything worse.

I focused on his question. "Mr. Nash owns the ranches around mine. To the northeast, it actually borders yours b—"

"Really?"

"Yes, but only for a quarter of a mile or so. The rest is Mr. Nash's, and he has been on a mission to buy the ranch since I was, I don't know, fourteen years old? That's when I first remember him bothering my grandma. And did he bother her. He was a prick. Well, he *is* a prick. He would go to the ranch once a week to try to convince her to sell it to him. But she didn't budge. The day she died, he came to the ranch earlier. He was there that afternoon and he threatened her. He seriously threatened her. He almost came at her, and I thought he was going to hit her. He seemed possessed that day, I don't know. He told her he would have the ranch one way or another. My grandma was shaking with so much anger. At some point, Jimmy was able to convince him to leave, but not before telling Mr. Nash we would call the police. Then, that night, the stable was set on fire."

Leo frowned. "You think it was him."

"Does it matter? The police said they investigated him, but Mr. Nash has a good alibi and everyone knows him around here. Everyone thought I was crazy for even suggesting it." I shook my head. The anger was gone, replaced by exhaustion and a powerful feeling of uselessness. "He came to me during her funeral. He wanted to make me an offer on the ranch. Can you believe that? He was so rude. His words are always perfectly thought out to hurt in the place he wants them to."

Leo's jaw ticked. "What a jerk. I wish I had known this. I would have punched him square in the face."

A tiny smile reached my lips. "That would have been nice. In theory. His lawyers would come at you like sharks in less than a minute."

Leo opened his mouth to say something, but the nurse came back. She told us one of my bones —metacarpus—had been nicked and, after stitching the cuts, I would need to wear a splint for a few weeks. Great.

The nurse gave me some pills for pain and a tetanus shot. "These pain meds are strong. You might feel sleepy soon." She finished the stitches and helped me put on the splint. "Don't grab anything with this hand, and don't support any weight on this arm."

I almost argued with her that I lived on a ranch, where there was a ton of manual work to be done, and I didn't have time for this, but decided it wouldn't make a difference and shut my mouth.

When the doctor came in, he examined everything, handed me a prescription for pain meds, and told me to be back in about ten days to get the stitches out and take another X-ray to check if I needed more time with the splint or not.

When they let me go, I stood up, the world spun, and I sat down on the bed again.

"It's the pain meds," the doctor said. "They will

make you groggy. You should go home and take a nice nap."

Leo helped me up, holding tight around my waist. "Thank you."

"Of course." The doctor nodded. "Make sure your girlfriend gets plenty of rest and doesn't move her hand for a couple of days."

Leo's face grew red. "No. She's not ... I mean ..." The doctor gave him a quizzical look. I wanted to help Leo explain, but I was too dizzy to form any coherent sentences. "Okay," Leo said, sounding defeated. "I'll make sure of it."

He led me out of the hospital and to my car. I put on the seat belt and turned sideways so I could snuggle on the seat. Leo hopped behind the wheel, watching me.

"Thank you," I said.

He watched me. "No problem."

Moments later, he turned the engine on, put on a rock ballad on the stereo, and drove off. The last thing I remembered before drifting into sleep was how handsome he looked when worried about me.

14

"Hannah," someone called me. Heavy fog surrounded me, and I didn't feel like escaping it. "Hannah." Something touched my shoulder and shook me.

The fog dissipated and I opened my eyes. "Eric." Panic rose in me. He was here. I looked around. In my room. How the hell was I in my room? "What are you doing here?"

He frowned. "I told I would come pick you up for dinner."

I grabbed my cell phone from the nightstand. Crap, it was past six, which meant I had fallen asleep in my car, and Leo had brought me to my bed and left. So, Eric probably didn't see him. The panic was replaced by something that resembled yearning.

Eric touched my arm. "What happened?"

"What?" I followed his gaze down my arm and saw the splint around my hand. I had already forgotten about that. "Oh ... an accident here at the ranch. Nothing big."

"Nothing big? You have a cast on."

"It's not a cast. It's a splint."

"Did you break something?"

"No. Just nicked a bone."

Eric looked extremely worried. "*Just* nicked a bone? Hannah, tell me what happened."

Shaking my head, I stood from the bed. "Don't worry about it. You wanted to go out for dinner, right? Can I take a quick shower and change first?"

Eric stood in front of me. He ran his hands over my arms. "You shouldn't use your arm, right? Maybe we should stay in. I'll even cook. How about that?"

I nodded. "Sounds good."

He stared at me with worried eyes. "Tell me what happened, baby. Please."

My shoulders sagged. "I was training Argus when Mr. Nash arrived. We argued and he pissed me off. I should have taken a break, but I was so pissed that I decided to push through the training.

Argus felt my mood and he ended up biting my hand."

His eyes went wide. "He bit you?" I nodded. "But—"

"I've got about nineteen stitches under the splint."

"WHAT?" He took my hand and stared at it as if it were the most precious thing he had ever seen. "You went to the hospital and didn't call me?"

"Jimmy drove me there," I lied. "I was in shock."

"Of course you were. Oh my God, that horse could have bitten your hand off."

"I know, but he didn't. We're fine now."

"No, baby, you're not fine. You won't be until that horse is gone. Don't you see? He's dangerous. He *bit* you. Next time he'll stomp over you."

"Nonsense. He reacted that way because I was stressed. I'll be more careful now and I won't go near him when I'm not one hundred percent well."

He cupped my cheek. "Baby, you're not listening to me. Most of the time, mistreated horses can't be saved, and I want you to consider that this might be the case." He shook his head. "Sorry, I can't believe that he bit you and you're okay with it."

"It's not that I'm okay with it, but I know why it

happened." I stepped around him, to get away from his almost-convincing words. "We've been raised around horses, Eric. We know they are heavy, big, powerful animals, and that one tiny thing can lead to a kick or a stomp the wrong way and we're done for. We have always known that. Argus bit me. He did what he was supposed to do. The horse is terrified of anything that moves, and I screamed in rage right in front of him. Of course he reacted. It's not his fault."

"Maybe it isn't, but this horse is gone, baby. He's too dangerous. I'm telling you. He bit you once. He'll bite you a second time. I hope it's not worse than the first one."

I looked into Eric's eyes, and the worry stamped on them made me shiver. "I'm fine, Eric. Don't worry about it."

"How can you say that, Hannah? I love you. Of course I worry about you." He tsked. "This horse has to go. You need to call the officer who dropped him off here to come put him down."

"You can't be serious," I whispered.

"Of course I am serious!"

I headed to the bathroom. "I'm not having this conversation with you."

"Hannah, don't walk out on me! We're not done here!"

I entered the bathroom and closed the door behind me. I didn't lock it, because I would probably have to swallow my pride and ask for his help during my shower. Ugh. I would probably have to ask for his help now, since I wouldn't be able to get off my clothes without moving my arm.

Cursing, I sat down on the toilet's lid.

Why was he so damn against the horse? I was the one to blame for Argus's reaction. He bit me because I wasn't careful.

It wouldn't happen again. There was no reason to think about quitting and putting him down. I shuddered. Crap. I couldn't even imagine Officer Michael coming in to take Argus away.

I sighed. "Eric."

After three seconds, he opened the door and stuck his head in. "What?"

I pointed to the splint. "I need help."

Without any words, he helped me.

WHILE IN THE SHOWER, MY HAND STARTED HURTING, so I took my pain meds, which made me groggy, and I barely made it through dinner. On Sunday, I slept until noon, when Eric woke me up to give me a quick goodbye kiss because he was leaving for Florida.

After he left, I reluctantly got up because my stomach was growling, ate something, and went back to bed. I woke up around midnight in pain, took more meds, and slept like a drunken teenager until Jimmy banged on my door Monday morning to check on me.

By then, I was feeling a little better and was able to switch to the slightly less drowsing pain pills.

It took me about forty minutes to get dressed instead of my usual three, and that counted combing my hair and putting it up in a ponytail, which I didn't do since I couldn't move my arm.

It was well after ten when I entered the stable.

"No, no, no." Jimmy stepped out of the tack room. "Mr. Fernandes told me what the doctor and the nurse said. You have to rest, and you need to keep that arm quiet as much as you can."

"I can't. You know me. I can't stay quiet for too long, and I've been sleeping since Saturday afternoon. That's way too much rest."

"Miss Taylor, you—"

"I won't do anything, Jimmy. I'll just hang around here. Better than staying inside the house looking at the walls."

He didn't seem convinced. "If you say so."

I didn't tell him the real reason I was out though. I wanted to see Argus. I hadn't seen him since the incident, and I wanted to make sure he wasn't traumatized.

He was standing in the right corner, as usual.

"Argus," I called, and to my surprise, he turned to me at once. "Hi, boy, how are you doing?"

He looked at me as if he had never seen me before. It was a little ... scary.

Jimmy walked behind me. "Be careful, Miss Taylor. You should probably give him time."

"I know." I sighed. I probably needed time from him too. "You brought him back from the round pen that day?"

"No. Mr. Fernandes did. He brought you back from the hospital, left you in your bed, and went back to the round pen. He stayed there for at least an hour with Argus. Then he brought the horse in, helped me put some stuff away, and left."

I blinked. What? Why? I mean, he had no obligation to help me with Argus and yet he looked like he wanted to. Maybe it was because of that horse his father had to put down when he was younger, but that wasn't a big reason, was it?

I shook my head.

I felt like a child in the naughty corner for not

being able to help Jimmy while he walked back and forth, picking this up, hanging that up, stashing this away, and cleaning that.

At 11:30 a.m., Paul brought his class back. Almost all of the students asked me what happened with my hand. I tried not lying, but I wasn't comfortable telling them the truth. I was afraid people would assume Argus was dangerous, like Eric did, and advise me to give him back.

Soon, they all left, including Paul.

Jimmy turned to me. "I can help you with lunch, Miss Taylor. Heat up or cook something. It's up to you."

I smiled. "No, Jimmy, I'm fine. My right arm can handle grabbing a plate from the fridge and putting it in the microwave. Don't worry."

"Are you sure?"

I waved him off. "I am."

With a disbelieving mien, Jimmy tipped his hat at me and left.

I waited for fifteen minutes to make sure Jimmy was truly gone and to check the arena. All gates were closed. I walked back into the stable and, being careful with my left hand, I closed the gate at the entrance.

I opened Argus's stall and stepped aside. "I thought you might like to stretch your legs a little."

He didn't move. "Don't worry. I'm not going to try to train you. I just want you to exercise a little while I'm around, okay?"

He still didn't move, so I walked out to the arena, hoping he would soon follow me like the other day.

It didn't take long. I leaned against a fence and watched as he trotted around the arena, always keeping his distance from me.

But I wasn't going to make it easy for him. My plan was to tire this horse, to make him run like he never did, until he fell to the ground and could only get up after drinking tons of water and eating at least an entire bucket of rations.

I marched to him. As I expected, he trotted away. Good.

I raced after him, realizing this would be an exercise for me too—one that I should not have been doing.

He halted at some point, but as I got nearer, he moved again.

I jogged to where he was, but he surprised me, trotting in a circle and coming from behind me, nickering loudly, kicking his hind legs into the air, his muscles trembling.

I didn't think I was afraid of him. Maybe hesitant, careful. But not truly afraid.

As he came toward me, his nostrils flared and his eyes widened, shining with terror. *He* was scared and he wanted to do something to keep me away at that moment.

I began retreating to the fence, then stopped. What the hell was I doing? What the hell would my grandma do?

I closed my eyes, inhaled deeply, and stood there. I held my breath when I felt the air whooshing past me as his legs came down inches from my face. His hooves hit the ground right next to my feet. I fought an involuntary flinch, trying not to imagine what could have happened if he had been a tiny bit closer. Instead, I puffed my chest.

I won't move. I won't move.

Argus snorted and began circling me in a quick trot. He kept that up for a few minutes while I slowly breathed in and out to keep my nerves in check. Finally, he halted.

I opened my eyes and found him right there, a couple of feet away, watching me. There was a shine in his eyes, like a desperate feeling, a silent wish, a deep longing mixed with fear.

My heart squeezed. Poor pony. He had suffered so much, being so unloved. I couldn't begin to understand that. And I didn't care that he wasn't a person. He still had feelings.

Without breaking his stare, I took a step forward. He didn't retreat. Good. Now was his turn. I waited there for a long, long time, shaking a little with anticipation. Honestly, I doubted he would move, but I had to try. I had to begin somewhere. He had already let me get close. If he didn't come to me today, that was okay. We could try this again tomorrow, and the day after that, and the day after that.

My heart skipped a beat when Argus did move. He took a tiny step in my direction. Then, my heart raced as he raised his muzzle, shortening the distance between us even more.

He's going to touch me! He's going to touch me!

The sound of a car approaching surprised us both. With renewed suspicion, Argus snorted, retreating a few steps, then he neighed and reared before trotting away.

My shoulders sagged. Shit! We were about to have a breakthrough. Now it was all gone, and I was sure it would take even longer to bridge the gap next time.

I whirled and squinted at the SUV coming to a stop in the parking lot.

"Are you okay?" Leo asked, climbing out of his

vehicle and walking toward the arena. He was wearing a dark T-shirt and jeans—both fitted—and cowboy boots. His hair fell over his face, and once again, the realization that he was too handsome hit me, taking my breath away.

Clearing my throat, I approached the fence as he did. "Yes. Actually, I think we were making some kind of progress. Until you showed up."

"Really? When I saw you both, I thought he was coming at you, to hurt you again."

"Nope. He was coming *to* me, lowering his walls."

He ran a hand over his head, pulling his hair back, just to have it flop back in place. "*Merda*. I'm sorry about that."

I sighed. "I'll try again tomorrow." He leaned against the fence, and I leaned away. His eyes locked onto mine, and breathing became a hard thing to accomplish. "I thought you were in Florida."

"My ride leaves for the airport in an hour."

"Then what are you doing here?"

His brows drew together. The sunlight illuminated one side of his face, and shadows played with the other, making his jaw and his chin look even more angular. "I ... I wanted to know how you're doing. Shouldn't you be resting?"

I averted my eyes, suddenly too conscious of his intense gaze. "I'm fine. Thanks, by the way, for the other day."

"My pleasure." He nodded his chin past me. "How is he doing?

"I just want him to eat. I brought him out to tire him. I hoped he would eat after exercising." I peered over my shoulder. Argus was trotting across the arena. "Well, I gotta take him back inside before Jimmy comes back. Bye."

I turned to leave but his voice stopped me. "Wait." He jumped over the fence and caught up with me. "I can help."

"You really don't have too. I'm—"

"I want to."

I opened my mouth to argue. Who was I kidding? I wanted him to help me, and with my hurt hand, it was good that someone helped me. Afraid of what would come through my lips if I decided to talk again, I just nodded.

We walked to the stable, side by side, without another word. The only sound was the crunch of the grass under our boots. A breeze blew, whipping my hair. I snapped my head to push my hair back and caught sight of his silhouette in the sun.

He was ... perfect. Tall, powerful, strong with

the right amount of manly hunk, gentleman and boyish demeanor.

I sighed.

This wasn't right. I had to send him away. Like right now.

"You—"

"I don't see him anywhere," Leo said.

I stopped and looked around the arena. "Argus!" Leo was right. He wasn't out there. I entered the stable. "Argus, where are you, boy?"

Leo walked past me and glanced inside Argus's stall. "Did you see him come in here?"

"Not really. I saw him coming in this direction, though."

"Where could he be?" He dashed back to the gate, and I watched him.

What was his deal? Why did he care about Argus so much? Why did he come here so often? Oh, I was thrilled about it. About *all* of it. But I shouldn't be. I was happy with Eric. Well, with non-freaking-out Eric, but I was sure that was something we could work on. We had been together for two years. Two happy years. That didn't go away like that, right?

This situation was ridiculous and it had to stop.

Leo came back inside and checked the open

stalls, gently calling for Argus. For a second, while watching the way his T-shirt stretched around his shoulders, the way his muscles popped whenever he moved even if just barely, I faltered.

Shaking my head, I walked up to him. "I don't understand. What are you doing?"

He turned to me with a funny are-you-blind expression. "Searching for Argus."

"No, not that." I took a deep breath, gathering courage. "You know what I mean. Why are you helping me? Why do you come here?"

A knot of his own appeared between his brows. "I told you. I had a horse put down and I want to avoid it happening to Argus if I can."

"That's not a strong enough reason. I mean, you can't save every horse out there, why bother with this one?"

"You're serious?"

"About?"

"You really don't know why I come here."

I shrugged, feeling heat spread over my cheeks. "I thought I did. I mean, I'm not stupid. A guy usually doesn't just appear at a girl's house for no reason."

"Exactly."

"But—"

"What?"

"*You* can't be serious." I snorted. "Shit, that's it, right? Is this some kind of Brazilian joke or something? To come after a girl and pretend you're interested. Let me tell you, it's not funny."

"What?" He laughed, but it wasn't an amused tone. "First, no, it's not a joke, not a Brazilian one. Where I come from, men take pride in being masculine, strong, and honest. Well, perhaps there are a few who play with girls, but those exist in any culture. I'm not that kind of guy, though."

"But ... I don't get it." I walked around him, intent on finding Argus. "This is ridiculous," I whispered.

I was asking this guy why he was here, or better implying if he was here because of me, and, at the same time, I hoped he said no. My heart fluttered when I imagined him saying yes. Ridiculous and impossible. Besides, I could be wrong. He could be here because of his previous horse, like he said. Or because he was bored, maybe? Anyway, I wasn't going to put myself out there more than I already had.

As I leaned to spy inside a stall, Leo came to stand in front of me. "Apparently you need to have it spelled out. Why am I here? Because of you." He stared at me, his eyes serious and his powerful body looming over mine. "Yes, it's also because of my late horse, but it's mostly because I'm attracted to you. Is that a good enough reason?"

I gasped and retreated a couple of steps. His confession both thrilled me and frightened me. "This is wrong. You do know I have a boyfriend, and I'm not the kind of girl who cheats. Sorry if I gave you that impression." I gulped. "If all you're looking for is a good lay, you know where the town is. Usually, there are parties every night somewhere on the university campus, and I'm sure you'll find several girls to suit your needs."

Shut up, shut up, shut up! I was making everything worse.

He shook his head. "Nope. No other girls right now. I'm sure I'm pretty attracted to you."

I gaped. "But ... why?" He raised a brow, and I felt the heat over my face again. "I mean, aren't people in relationships off-limits? I mean, when I was single, the guys dating were off the radar. I never, ever looked at them."

He looked away, his jaw clenched. When his eyes returned to me, it was with a pained expression. "I can't help it. Believe me, I tried."

"It doesn't make sense."

He advanced three feet. "Since that first day out in the rain, you flipped a switch I thought was broken. You intrigue me way too much. A beautiful girl standing up to her father, standing up to some jerk who insists on buying her property, taking care of a broken horse, not afraid of living alone at this ranch—"

"I never said I'm not afraid of living here alone."

Leo took a sharp inhale. His jaw ticked, and I fought a sudden, unwelcome urge to lick it. "You can't say stuff like that to me."

"Like what?"

He took another step in my direction, and I retreated, my back hitting a stall's door. "Like you're afraid of being here alone."

"Why?" My voice came out raspy, low.

"Because it makes it harder to stay in control." He advanced, grabbing the low door behind me, his palms over the wood, inches from my waist. His body hovered over me, his compelling eyes on mine, something dangerous gleaming in them, something that made me feel like it was one hundred and fifty degrees in here. "I'm not a good guy, Hannah. In fact, I'm a bad guy trying to act like a good one for once. However, my good side is losing right now."

I gulped. On their own, my eyes flicked to his mouth.

He groaned and closed the distance between

us. His body crushed mine with a force that made all the air escape my lungs. His lips brushed against mine, gentle and tentative. A shiver raked through me, and as I opened my mouth to him, a loud neigh and stomping hooves froze me. Froze *us*.

Argus exited the tack room and trotted in our direction. Leo caught my good hand and was about to pull me out of the way, when Argus turned around, neighed again, then proceeded to an empty stall on his own.

Returning to my senses, I quickly pulled my hand out of Leo's and walked to Argus. Shame consumed me, but I tried to keep it under control as I locked the stall the horse was in. To hell if this one wasn't reinforced. I wasn't about to move him now.

Shaking, I walked past Leo and reached for the entrance gate. I unlocked the gate and pushed the leaves open, thinking of what to say to him, of how to tell him he should go.

"*Morena*," he whispered. For a fraction of a second, I cursed myself for not looking up what that word meant, but decided it didn't matter right now. I started walking out, but he caught up with me. "I'm sor ... you know what? I'm not sorry. I *am* sorry you have a boyfriend. I'm sorry I can't seem to respect your relationship. I'm sorry you don't have the same feelings I have for you, but I'm not sorry for wanting you. Because, *droga*, I really want you."

I turned to him and he stopped, watching me with his mesmerizing blue-green eyes. Crap, I didn't need this.

"Thank you for the help you've given me with Argus, and with me." I raised my arm and gestured toward the splint. "But I can't have you helping me anymore. Please, if you care about me as you *think* you do, then don't come back here."

I ran to the main house with my tears brimming in my eyes and my heart splitting in two.

15

ONE OF MY MOTHER'S MAIDS OPENED THE FRONT door for me and pointed to the sunroom at the back of the house. In there, my mother was seated on a regal armchair, reading a magazine and enjoying the warm sunlight trickling in through the thin shades. As usual, Hilary was nowhere to be seen. She would probably emerge from her room when Rosa called for lunch, and then grumble about being bored throughout the meal, like she always did whenever my parents scheduled these Sunday gatherings.

"Good morning," I said, sitting down on the love seat across the coffee table.

"Good morning," my mother answered

without taking her eyes from the magazine. "How are you?"

"Good," I lied. "Where's Dad?"

"Outside." She beckoned to the door leading to the outside porch. My father paced on the porch, yelling into the phone. "He's been arguing with Mr. O'Neill for over forty minutes."

"Mr. O'Neill? Isn't he the man who came to one of your dinner parties a few weeks ago?"

"Exactly. Their business together is falling through, and Mr. O'Neill has been upset about it. Yesterday, he called, threatening to bring your father's company down somehow."

What was with everyone and threatening? Couldn't people actually talk and solve their problems? I thought of Mr. Nash and me. No. No talking there. I wanted to get a shovel and hit his head.

"How is Eric?" she asked.

"Good. He is up to the championship match this afternoon."

"That's good," she said, sounding disinterested.

"Hannah," my father said, entering the sunroom. He had the phone tight in his hands. "How are you?"

How was I? Honestly, I wasn't sure. Two weeks had passed since I told Leo to stay away from me, and he'd done like I told him. However, deep inside I hoped part of that was because he was still in Florida. To make things worse, I researched what *morena* meant. Apparently, it was a sweet nickname for a loved one, and it certainly didn't help my cause. I couldn't stop thinking about him and how I wanted him to ignore what I'd said. But I knew, oh, how I knew, that this was for the best. He had to stay away from me, and I had to find a way to forget him too. I felt so lost.

I was also feeling alone, as if I were fighting a huge war by myself with no ray of hope. Argus and I made no progress. In fact, I was pretty sure we had gone back to zero. The stupid horse didn't want to eat much, he wouldn't let me get close anymore, and when I released him into the arena, he just stood there, watching the fence as if it would disappear under his gaze. The vet said his physical health was a little better. He needed to gain more weight; there were a few scars that would never completely heal. Still, I was losing hope.

Since he freaked out in my kitchen, Eric had been nice and loving, extremely careful with his words and actions. Even now, while in Florida, he called me at least four times a day and asked me what I was up to, how I was feeling, and told me he loved me. It was all nice in theory, but I couldn't shake the feeling that things weren't the same as before. Our relationship hadn't been the same since my grandmother died, and there was nothing I could do to change it.

"Good," I lied, followed by an automatic smile.

He sat in an armchair beside my mother. "Good." He gestured to my arm. "What happened?"

"Just ... a horse. He hurt me without meaning to, but I'm good." Jimmy took me to the hospital two days ago. The doctor said I couldn't take off the splint yet, because the bone wasn't one hundred percent. He told me to come back in a week. My father frowned. "I should take this thing off soon. And how are things around here?"

"Same old, same old." My father clasped his hands together and stared at me. "Don't change the subject, Hannah," he said. His cold tone told me everything.

I closed my eyes for a second. "Father, please, let's not talk business today. Please."

"But we have to," he said. "You have been so busy with the ranch that we barely see you anymore. And now you tell me a horse hurt you. You know how dangerous they can be." He shook his head. "We need to talk."

I sighed. I couldn't win this. "Okay. Talk."

He sat up straighter and smoothed his polo shirt. "Eric has been talking about marriage since you two began dating. Last week, before he left for Florida, he came to ask my permission to marry you."

"What?" Wait. I thought I was going to get a lecture on the ranch and Argus, and why I should sell it right now.

"I don't think he plans on asking you soon, but I think he's getting everything ready."

"Why are you telling me this?"

"Because I want you to think about it. Your mother and I are afraid that you might say no because Eric's plans don't always match yours."

"Like dropping college and becoming his trophy wife?" I slapped my hand over my mouth. The weight of my mother's gaze fell over me, and I found the pattern of the ceramic floor interesting.

"Eric wouldn't want you for a trophy wife. You're too smart for that," my father said, oblivious to my mother's hurt expression. "I told him you shouldn't quit college because I want you to run my business, but he insisted he can do it."

"And?"

"I know he can do it. Even though I consider Eric family, this is *our* business. I would like a

Taylor running it, even if a Bennett helps out. I want you in charge."

"I want that too," I whispered.

"That's good to hear. Eric is a good man, Hannah. He'll see reason and understand your wishes with time. Don't say no and waste the great future you two can have together because of his stubbornness."

If my father had told me that about a month ago, I would have agreed. Though, if Eric asked too soon, I still wouldn't accept his proposal. We were too young, and I couldn't see myself getting married before I was twenty-five. Maybe even twenty-eight. Still, I should be glad he loved me that much; I should be glad he was serious about our future together. Now ... now I wasn't sure about anything.

"I think the big problem between us right now is the ranch," I confessed.

"All right. You're quite adamant about keeping the ranch. I want to know why and how you plan on running it, keep up with college, and learn the family business."

Finally, he would listen to me! I just hoped he would also understand. "I don't really know how else to say it other than the ranch is part of me, Dad. I grew up there as much as I grew up here.

Grandma was more than a grandma. She raised me too. Her scent is forever imprinted in that place. My horse was born and raised there. He also died there. I learned how to jump there." Though I'd thought about it a lot, I'd never said it out loud, and that made all the difference. A sense of pride filled me as I said, "The ranch is my home."

"I see." He nodded. "But it's not a safe place, Hannah. Even if I can't convince you to sell it, I'm not okay with you living there alone."

"Jimmy's house is close, and the Thompsons are just across the main road."

"Well, that didn't stop some crazy bastard from setting the stable on fire, did it?"

I flinched. God, how I hated when people talked about that night as if it was something that happened eons ago.

"I'm okay, Dad. Jimmy is always checking on me, and there are always people around. Paul, Dr. Bohm, and the students."

"That's how it was with my mother too, and look what ha—"

"Can we please change subjects?" my mother asked, her tone clipped. "This is supposed to be a fun family get-together, for God's sake."

Fun? When did she learn what fun was?

Hilary must have read Mother's mind, because

she entered the sunroom, her bored mien in place. "Is lunch ready yet?"

"Hello to you too," I said, standing up to greet her.

She hugged me back, the same way she would hug a contagious gorilla or something. "Where's your man? I thought he didn't let you go anywhere without him."

I suppressed the urge to roll my eyes at her. "He's my boyfriend, not my owner."

"It doesn't always look like it."

"What?"

Rosa saved Hilary from losing her tongue when she stepped into the sunroom and announced lunch was served in the dining room.

"Come on, girls," my father said, ushering us through the door. "Let's have a nice time as a family."

***

THE RAIN CASTIGATED THE RANCH DURING THE night. The wind whistled outside the windows, and thunder flashed bright and loud.

And Argus cried the entire time.

I tried ignoring it, putting my pillow over my head and pretending I didn't hear him or the other horses that had started complaining with him, but at three in the morning, he won. With my pillow under one arm, a blanket under the other, and a raincoat over my head, I ran to the stable. Who cared if my splint got wet? Argus certainly didn't.

As soon as I stepped in and turned on the tack room light, Argus stopped. He stood still until I faced him over his stall's door. "Happy now?"

He didn't do anything other than look at me with huge eyes.

I placed the blanket on the floor and the pillow against the wall, and slid down, doing my best to pull the edges of the blanket tight around me. It was summer, but rainy nights spent in the stable could be chilly.

He lay down close to the door, and I saw one of his eyes through the cracks between the wooden boards. He stared at me, and that made me feel as if I could reach to him again. Not now, I would probably scare him more, but another day. I could do it, and he would let me.

Moments later, I was shaken awake. "Hannah, dear."

My eyes shot open, and the first thing I registered was my father, in dress slacks and shirt, kneeling beside me. The second thing was the weak sunlight fighting to come out from behind the clouds. It was morning already. The third was that my whole body hurt.

"Dad." I ran my good hand over my messy hair and reached for my cell phone. It was freaking seven in the morning! "What are you doing here?"

"What are you doing *here*?" He gestured around us.

"Well," I began, trying to think of a lie. Ugh, why lie? "Argus has many problems, and one of them is rain and thunder. He was going nuts last night, so I came down to try and calm him. I didn't think it would work. The funny thing is, it did." He looked at me with such a foreign expression and a small smile on his lips. "What?"

"I never thought you were this devoted to the place."

I stood up. "I thought I made that clear, many times."

"Yes, well, until now I'd thought it was an exaggeration." He walked to Argus's stall and watched as the horse slept. "What happened to him?"

"His previous owner was a bastard. He hit Argus, made him pull heavy stuff, much heavier than he should be able to, and he put his dogs on Argus when he thought the horse was misbehaving. They bit him, Dad. They almost killed him once, and that's when animal control found him."

"And they brought him here, of course. My mother could heal any horse."

"They brought him in not long ago, actually."

He squinted at me. "You're the one healing him?"

"Not really. I'm trying, but ... I don't know. I can't seem to reach him." And I wasn't sure how to break through my own walls to do so.

"Are you a horse whisperer too?"

I laughed. "No, I'll never be like grandma. I think animal control brought him here because they had no place else. Or perhaps they thought I had inherited grandma's talent? But so far, it's been hard. He's barely eaten."

"He did that?" He pointed to my hand.

I nodded. "It was my fault. I was stressed and angry, and tried to reach him even so."

"Horses are intuitive animals. They feel what we feel." His gaze went back to Argus. "He's a beautiful animal. Under the wounds, I mean. He does need a few pounds, but it's easy to see how beautiful he can be."

I leaned over the door and stared at the sleeping horse too. His white coat was shiny and smooth, but he was still too thin. "Yes, he's beautiful." Silence filled the air until I gathered the courage to ask him, "Dad, what are you doing here? And so early?"

He took a deep breath. "The things you said about the ranch yesterday, about growing up here, about seeing your horse being born and learning to jump here. All of that happened to me too, many years ago. I loved this place so much. Until we moved to a bigger house, and I learned to love that place more. I don't know. Maybe because I was young and easily impressed back then. The new house was not only bigger, it was fancier. I forgot this place so easily after we moved, and I never understood why your grandma insisted on keeping it. After they divorced, she sold the other house to come back here. I thought she was crazy. Who wanted to live and take care of such a hole when you could have a mansion?" He looked around, to the bridles and blankets and boots along the walls, to the stalls and the horses. "You made me remember why yesterday."

My eyes filled with tears. "What are you saying?"

"I'm saying that I understand why you want to keep this place, why you want to live here and preserve your grandma's memory. She was such a wonderful woman. I miss her too, you know." I flung my arms around his neck, ignoring the pain shooting through my hand, and he hugged me tight. "You're turning out to be just as wonderful as she was. I'm so proud of you."

A sob raked through me. "Thanks."

"We'll figure out how to keep this place and our breeding farm running together if that's what you want."

"That's what I want." I kissed his cheek like I hadn't done since I was eight years old. "Thank you."

"No. Thank you." He disentangled himself from me. "Now, I need to get going or I'll be late for another stressful meeting with Mr. O'Neill."

"Oh, Mom told me you're having problems with him."

"The word *problems* doesn't even begin to cover it. He's acting crazy since our business fell through. We're trying to fix it, but I'm not sure I want to do business with him anymore."

"I understand."

He leaned in and kissed my forehead. "Have a great day, Hannah."

"You too, Dad."

16

______

THE NEXT DAY, PAUL'S LAST CLASS ENDED AT FOUR-thirty in the afternoon, and Jimmy was done with his chores a little after five. Good thing too, because Eric would be back from Florida and in for dinner around six.

I quickly took a shower and began preparing the meal. Usually, he liked the sophisticated stuff like lobster or complicated duck sauces or whatever, but he never complained about eating my lasagna or ravioli or stroganoff.

Like the apology dinner he'd made me a couple of weeks ago, I was trying to cook him a let's-solve-whatever-the-problem-is-and-go-back-to-normal dinner. It was time for me to really put Leo out of my mind, and to remember I had always been crazy about Eric. Besides, after my father's support and understanding, there was little that could put off my mood.

For the occasion, I'd put on a flowery summer dress and high-heeled sandals, and I'd blown dry my hair, pulling every strand into a perfectly straight line, the way he liked it. I thought about taking off the splint from my hand because it disrupted my look, but I wanted to heal fast and for that I needed to stay with this crap.

I smiled when I heard the engine of his car driving down the road toward the ranch, and ran to the porch to greet him. He parked his car beside mine and slid out, wearing slacks and a polo shirt. I watched him, ashamed for having forgotten how handsome he was, how good he looked when dressed up, and also how proud I was of being his girlfriend.

He raced to the porch, smiling, and barely slowed down as he put his arms around me and lowered his face to mine. His lips were hard and demanding, his hands on my back rough and greedy. He pushed me back toward the door, probably with intentions of going upstairs, but I pushed him away.

"No, no," I said, catching my breath. I held his

hand and beckoned him inside. "I'm making dinner. Come on."

He followed me to the kitchen, but then his demeanor changed. He frowned at the stove. "I was going to invite you to go out with me, to a nice restaurant."

"Oh." By nice, he meant fancy, with dishes that cost well over a hundred dollars, and drinks over five hundred. "I thought after your trip you would like to stay in with me."

"No reason why." He turned off the burners and I stared. "I want to treat you to a nice meal and a good glass of wine. You deserve it."

I crossed my arms, not buying it. "Eric, what is it?"

He sighed, turning puppy eyes toward me. "Sorry, baby, but I don't like it here, you know that. I want to take you out for dinner, then to my house."

Frustration surged in me and I shook my head. "You've gotta get used to this place because it's not going anywhere." He offered me a confused look. "I've talked to my dad. If I want to keep the ranch, I have his support."

"What?" He squared his shoulder and grew taller somehow, as if his curt tone of voice made him more intimidating. "No. I talked to him before my trip. We are on the same page. He wants you to sell this place as much as I do."

"Not anymore. He understands me and my reasons for wanting it. He agrees with me and supports me. I'm sorry, Eric, but I'm not selling the ranch. Ever."

Grunting, he turned his back to me. I tensed, praying to not witness a repetition of his tantrum when he broke the picture. But it didn't come. Instead, he took several long breaths and his shoulders sagged. A couple of seconds later, he peered at me over his shoulder. "I'm sorry."

I let out a relieved breath. For a moment there, I'd been worried he was going to freak out again, and then ... and then I didn't know what would happen.

"It's okay. I'm glad you're okay."

"Me too." He approached me, a little wary. "Let's get out of here and not talk about this place tonight. For me. Please?"

What good would it do? I wouldn't change my mind, and apparently neither would he. But perhaps this was the best way of dealing with Eric's newly revealed explosive temper. I had to deal with things one at a time, taking *everything* slowly. I could do that. I could at least try to do that.

I nodded and let him take my good hand and drag me out of my home.

<hr>

ORDER A NEW SADDLE: CHECK. RUN TO THE pharmacy and grab my pills: Check. Stop by the university bookstore and sell books from previous semester: Check. Retrieve parcel from post office: Check.

I stepped out of the building carrying the small but sort of heavy box and squinted at the sun. What I most loved about Santa Barbara was its weather, though the day was warming up too fast for my taste.

The second thing I liked most about Santa Barbara was downtown. Spanish mission-style buildings, white and off-white facades, and mosaic-like sidewalks. It was quaint and beautiful. It was a nice place to walk around, with no certain destination. Maybe that was just what I needed.

"Hannah."

I heard my name called in a sensual woman's voice. My heart lurched as I stopped and saw Beatriz walking toward me. With tight jeans, flat ballet slippers, and a polo shirt, she looked incredible. I bet she could rock any look and I kind of hated her for that.

"Hey." My eyes scanned behind her, searching for her twin, even when I knew I shouldn't. He wasn't with her.

She halted a couple of steps from me. "Odd running into you here." I was thinking the same thing. "How are you?"

"Good. And you?"

"How do you say it? Hmm, same old, same old?"

"Yup, that's right."

"I haven't seen you lately," she said. "Are you avoiding the club because of my brother?" She winked with a knowing grin on her pretty face.

My jaw fell open. Wow, the girl was direct.

I shut my mouth and pretended ignorance. "Why would I avoid the club because of him? I just haven't fel—"

"*Que mentira*! You think I don't know Leo has been to your ranch a couple of times, and that you two are attracted to each other?"

My eyes widened, darting around us. "No, no. I'm not attracted to him."

"*Guria*, you're only lying to yourself."

I opened my mouth to retort, but I didn't really know what to say. "Beatriz ..."

"Bia."

"What?"

"You can call me Bia."

I shook my head. Crap, this girl was confusing. "Bia, I don't know what you're talking about."

She rolled her eyes. "Anyway, thanks very much for not showing up. Those crazy women have dragged me to those damn teas, and you're not there to make me feel at least a little bit better."

I laughed, imagining her among my mother and the other snobs. "Sorry."

She narrowed her eyes and offered me a teasing smile. "The thing is, I don't think you are."

"You're right. I'm not. Damn, how I wish I could have seen you alone with them."

She smiled. "Oh, it was super fun. Ha." Her smile fell a little. "You can't avoid us forever, you know. We're staying for at least six months, and the next tournament is going to be here. I bet your boyfriend will want you there."

Crap, she was right. I'd totally forgotten about the coming tournament. "I'll deal with it one day at a time." Like everything else lately, it seemed.

"Won't you ask me how Leo is doing?"

Again, I couldn't help but look around,

searching for people who could overhear us and ruin my life.

Of course I wanted to know how Leo was. I was dying to. But I shouldn't ask.

The ringing of my cell phone saved me from answering her.

I frowned upon seeing "mother" flashing on the screen. "Hi, Mom."

"Hannah." She said my name like a prayer, and that deepened the furrow between my brows. "Your father is in the hospital."

17

I PACED THE SMALL WAITING ROOM WHILE MY mother stared at the wall, deep inside her own mind, and my sister texted on her phone. We'd been at the hospital for three hours and had seen no sign of the doctor to tell us how my father was doing.

Several times I'd thought about going to the cafeteria downstairs, just to have something to occupy my mind, but I gave up on the idea a second later. What if the doctor came when I wasn't there?

I flopped down in the chair beside my mother.

"I don't understand," I whispered.

My mother reached over the armrests and held my good hand. I stared at our fingers laced together. She *never* did that.

"There isn't much to understand," she said. "We won't know the details until he can tell us."

But when would that be? We had no idea when he would wake up. *If* he would wake up.

My father had gone to Santa Barbara for a meeting with his lawyer. While walking back to his car in the underground garage after the meeting finished, he was assaulted. One of the security guards heard the gunshots and found him unconscious and bleeding beside his car, his assailant—or assailants—long gone. However, his wallet, cell phone, expensive wristwatch, and his important documents hadn't been stolen. And that was all everyone knew.

The lawyer told my mother they were discussing arrangements for Mr. O'Neill and his threats, which led me to consider that Mr. O'Neill had been the one behind my father's incident.

Two more hours went by. At least Hilary, who didn't seem too affected, had gone to the cafeteria and brought gallons of coffee and stuff to eat. I ate without tasting anything. My nerves were uncontrollable, and the uncertainty made me feel like I would pass out at any moment.

Jimmy had called once to check on me, and Eric had called twice, telling me he was finishing up some business that couldn't wait and would be over soon. I wanted to be mad at him for not being here yet, but I understood that sometimes he had to work around other people's schedules.

Finally, almost six hours after having arrived at the hospital, the doctor came to see us.

My mother stood, looking pale. "How is he?"

"Stable," the doctor said, his eyes hard and jaw tight. "But he isn't out of risk yet. Two of the six bullets were close to his heart, and a third one perforated his left lung."

Six bullets? I locked my knees before they buckled. "What does that mean?" I asked. "Will he be okay?"

"At this point, we can't predict that," he said. "Rest assured we're doing whatever we can to save him."

"When can we see him?" my mother asked.

The doctor shook his head. "He just got out of one surgery, and we'll take him into another one soon. I don't think you'll be able to see him before tomorrow morning." I checked my phone, totally lost in time. It was 5:20 in the afternoon. "I suggest you all go home and try to rest a little. We'll call if anything changes."

He left as I was about to tell him to go to hell. Go home and rest when my father was undergoing delicate surgery? Yeah, right.

"I'm going home," Hilary said, finally putting her phone down. "Mom, are you coming with me?"

"No." Our mother sat back down on the firm chair.

I couldn't hold my tongue. "Really? You're going home? I know you're a spoiled brat, but I didn't think you were this unaffected."

"What?" Hilary turned to me, appalled. "Of course I'm affected. He's my father too, you know. But we've been here for hours, and the doctor said the situation won't change any time soon. And I'm tired."

"And we aren't?"

"I'm sorry I'm not as noble as you are."

"What does that even mean?"

"Girls," my mother said, her commanding tone on. "Stop bickering this instant."

Hilary sighed. "I don't think I'll be able to sleep, but I need my bed right now."

"Go, dear," Mom said. "Go home and rest. We'll call you if anything changes."

"All right." Hilary kissed Mom's cheek.

Mom showed her a tight smile. "Be careful, okay?"

Without looking at me, Hilary paused at the door and nodded.

She left and I sat down beside my mother. Once again, she grabbed my right hand and squeezed it.

More time passed, and I drifted in unwelcome sleep until my phone rang. I reached for it without looking at the screen, certain it was Eric calling to tell me he was still busy.

"Hello."

"Hannah." It was Leo. My heart skipped a couple of beats. "How are you? Wait. Hmm, what a stupid question. Sorry."

I stood, walked out of the waiting room, and dashed across the hallway, afraid somebody would hear me.

I stepped through the double doors and entered a busy, loud lobby. "Why are you calling?"

"Bia told me she was with you when you found out about your father. I've been dialing your number and then giving up for over four hours." He paused, and instantly, I missed his voice, his accent.

Tears surged up, strong and sure, and rolled down my cheeks. The urge to have him here, comforting me like he'd done many times, overwhelmed me. I knew it was wrong, but crap, I wanted it. "I'm glad you called," I confessed.

I heard a sharp inhale. "Me too," he muttered. "How is he?"

"I'm not sure. Some time ago the doctor said he was stable, but still in critical condition." I wiped a few of my tears away just as a new sob shook me. "Someone shot him. Six times. I don't know if I've ever heard of someone surviving that many bullets."

"*O que*? Six shots? That's crazy. Did they catch whoever did this?"

"No. The police don't know if it was one guy or thirty, or why it was done so viciously."

"There are robbers in any part of the world. Unfortunately, Brazil has quite a few of them."

"But they didn't steal anything."

"What?"

"My father was found with all his belongings still on him. His wallet was in the pocket of his jacket, his wristwatch still on his wrist, his cell phone and his briefcase with several important papers on the ground." I pressed my eyes closed. "Whoever did this wanted to kill him."

"*Que merda*," he muttered. "Maybe I shouldn't say this but, damn, I wish I was there with you, *morena*."

"Me too," I said before I could think it through. Oh crap.

There was a long pause. "Say the word and I'm there. Please ... say it."

At that moment, besides hearing from the doctor that my father wasn't at risk anymore and would be all right, what I wanted the most was Leo here with me. But it wasn't fair.

My thoughts traveled to the my-own-boyfriend-isn't-here-yet-but-there's-a-perfectly-fine-guy-wanting-to-be land one too many times.

"I can't," I whispered, feeling like a coward. "Leo, I won't lie, okay. Not today. Whatever I feel for you, it shouldn't be there. Yes, I want you here to hold me more than anything, but ... it's not right."

"It could be."

I shook my head as new tears flooded my eyes. "It isn't that simple."

"You do know people are the ones that complicate things, right?"

I smiled through my tears. "It's easier when we're not seeing each other."

"Easier for whom?"

Good question. Not for me, and apparently not for him.

But I owed it to Eric. We had over two years together, two great years. I owed him to at least try to make things work again as well as it had before. I couldn't just throw everything we had away.

"My statement still stands," I said. "If you like me as much as you think you do, please, stay away."

"Hannah, I don't *think* I like you. I know I do. And I'll confess it's getting harder and harder to honor that wish of yours."

I know. "Please."

He grunted. "Don't do that, *morena*."

"I have to." I took a deep breath. "Thanks for your concern about my father's health."

"I'm concerned about you too."

I closed my eyes tight and gathered my strength. It was hard when he kept saying stuff like that. "Goodbye," I whispered.

Afraid I would be weak and call him back and tell him to come and be here with me, I turned off my cell phone and walked back into the waiting room.

It really was going to be a long night.

18

"You look beautiful," Eric said, watching me from behind the wheel.

I squirmed in my seat and smoothed my dress. I donned a one-shoulder, going from hot pink on the top to white on the bottom, with a tight waist and flared skirt. A few vertical lines of translucent sequins added a little bit of sparkle. My long dark hair was pulled up in an intricate ponytail adorned by braids. Silver stilettos and silver jewelry completed my look. Thank goodness, I had taken the splint off a couple of days ago, because it didn't go well with my outfit. Yes, I guess I looked beautiful, but I felt uncomfortable in such an updo while my father was still in the hospital.

I'd begged Eric to leave me out of this one, to

go to this damn ball alone. After all, it had been only nine days since my father was gravely shot, but he insisted, saying that fresh air and friendly faces would be good for me. I guess he wasn't entirely wrong, but knowing my father's condition was still critical didn't make it any easier to relax.

However, I knew this was an important night for Eric. It was the opening ceremony of one of the most important tournaments of the year, one based at his club, and one that he had to do great at if he wanted to keep his spot as number one in the world.

I offered him a small smile. "Thank you."

At the Polo and Racquet Club, the valet opened the door for me, then drove the car away as Eric held my hand and walked into the ballroom with me. The place was heavily decorated with different kinds of yellow flowers, thick golden candles, heavy beige tablecloths, and delicate silverware. The curtains had been tied to the sides, exposing the large double doors leading outside. The crystal chandelier sparkled, and the floor had been polished to resemble pearl.

Like a magnet, my eyes found Leo almost instantly. He was across the room, near the bar, with Bia and one of his brothers. And his eyes were on me. My breath caught in my throat. He looked gorgeous in a black tuxedo and dark green tie. His usually unkempt hair had apparently met a comb. The bangs were pulled back, giving him an older and more sophisticated air. He drank from the glass in his hand—was that soda?—still holding my gaze. I noticed everyone around him had a flute of champagne or a glass of whiskey, but he was drinking a soda. An almost twenty-one-year-old guy *not* drinking alcohol?

A little pressure on my lower back woke me from the daze, and I quickly turned to Eric, ashamed of my weakness. He guided me through the ballroom, always keeping me a half step in front of him, as if I were some big prize he needed to show off to everyone. People greeted us, told us we looked gorgeous, and sent their best wishes to my father and good luck to Eric during the tournament.

I looked around. These people were too judgmental. What were they thinking of me right now? The uncaring daughter who danced over her father's not-so-ready grave? Gosh, how I didn't want to be here.

Finally, Eric showed me to the table we would share with his teammates and their girlfriends or spouses. Soon after, the speeches began. The president of the club spoke first, welcoming everyone and officially opening the tournament. The organizer of the event spoke, followed by a few other important people, one of them was Eric.

The end of his speech surprised me. "I would like to invite everyone to send good vibes to Mr. Charles Taylor, one of the most illustrious members of this club and my girlfriend's father." He gestured to me, and I wanted to crawl under the table as all eyes fell on me. "Thank you for letting me bring you here tonight when I know you wanted to be at the hospital with your father instead."

I nodded while everyone applauded. Eric said thanks and walked off the stage, toward me. People redirected their attention as dinner was served a minute later. At our table, the guys talked about the upcoming games. The first one was the next afternoon, against a team from Chile. Meanwhile, I did my job of small talking with the women.

Then the band began playing, and, without asking, Eric caught my hand and steered me onto the dance floor. A slow song played and he held me close, swaying to the rhythm.

"I meant it," he said, looking into my eyes. "Thank you for being here with me."

At moments like this, when he said things like

that and stared into my eyes with adoration, I knew we could work things out and make our relationship strong and solid again. I just knew it.

I rested my cheek on his shoulder. "You're welcome."

My eyes found Leo's, and the urge to run to him assaulted me. Damn, why couldn't there be at least one thing that was simple in my life? Just one. Was it asking too much?

Apparently, it was.

Leo danced with Bia a few feet from me, and his gaze never wavered the entire time, except for the quick seconds when he spun his sister around and had his back to me. But then it was Bia's turn to have her knowing eyes on me. She wore a dark green gown that matched Leo's tie, and her long hair was curled to perfection, flowing like a smooth wave down her back. Did they know how good they looked? How *wonderful* they looked?

"Are you okay?" Eric asked, and I almost jerked in his arms. "You seem tense."

I wonder why. "I'm fine," I lied. Why was it getting easier and easier to lie? I'd never lied to him, or anyone else before. Now it had become a part of my life.

"How about I get us a drink?"

"Sure."

Hand in hand, Eric and I weaved through the crowd to our table, but our flutes were gone.

He scanned the room for a waiter. There were quite a few, but they were incredibly busy.

"Why don't you sit here while I go to the bar?" he asked, pulling my chair back.

I nodded and sat down. He leaned in, gave me a peck on the cheek, and then left me alone at the empty table.

Without meaning to, I glanced around, telling myself I wasn't looking for Leo. The dance floor was too crowded, and I couldn't find Leo and Bia anywhere. However, I saw Megan, Blaire, and Andrea ambling toward me, legs twisting, heels tripping, champagne flutes swishing.

I stood up to greet them, and the beer and whiskey smell enveloped me before I even embraced them.

"Enjoying the party?" I asked.

"Ohmygosh, tonight is the night," Megan said, wiggling her eyebrows.

"For?"

"Attacking," she whispered, and the other girls giggled. She must have noticed my quizzical look, because she continued, "We've been on the hunt for a couple of weeks now, and tonight is the night to attack. Blaire will have Pedro Fernandes, Andrea will have Guilherme, and I'll have Leonardo!"

My mouth hung open. "What?"

"Well," Blaire butted in. "They don't know it yet, but we have an infallible plan. They won't be able to resist our charms."

"Want to know our plan?" Andrea asked.

"Of course she wants to know," Megan said, before taking a long sip of her champagne.

No, I didn't.

"Let me tell her," Blaire said.

The three of them started bickering about who was going to tell me what. Megan reached around me to hold Blaire's flapping hands, and her champagne splashed down my arm.

"Oh shoot," she said. "I'm so sorry."

Andrea grabbed a cloth napkin from the table. "Here."

"Thanks." I dabbed the liquid from my skin, thankful it hadn't spilled onto my dress.

"There. All gone." Megan placed her empty flute on the table. "Where were we? Oh, the plan. So—"

"Sorry, girls," I interrupted her. "My skin feels sticky. I need to wash it off. Be right back."

I whirled on my heel and dashed to the restroom, relieved at having found a way out of the conversation. Holy crap, what were those girls up to? Megan would try to seduce Leo? Damn, I so didn't need to know that.

I turned into the short hallway where the restrooms were located, and a sick feeling settled in my stomach. Inside, I avoided looking in the mirror as I splashed a little water down my arm, afraid of seeing what reflected back in it as I tried not to think about Leo.

But it was too hard, especially when I was alone with a mirror in front of me. I raised my head and stared at my eyes. There it was. The agony of loving Eric and desiring Leo. *Because I still love Eric.* Nobody just stopped loving like that. Right?

As for Leo and my desire for him, it was a fleeting thing, I was sure. He had a pretty face— a *gorgeous* face and a damn hot body—and happened to be around while my boyfriend and I were experiencing a few bumps in the road. My feelings for Leo were an infatuation that would die out with time. I wished time passed faster. It would help if I didn't see him during that time. But how could I not if he was part of the club? Beatriz was right. I wouldn't be able to avoid them forever. However, I could avoid the club.

A couple of minutes later, I stepped out of the

restroom and ran into someone.

"*Guria*, we so gotta stop meeting like this," Beatriz said.

"Agreed." I looked over her shoulder and found Leo leaning against the wall across the hallway, his eyes on me and his thumb on his black ring. So much for avoiding him.

Bia followed my gaze and grinned. "Do you know Mr. Owens?"

I frowned at her. "Yes."

"That creep has been following me around the club like an old tiger on the prowl since we moved here. So, I assigned Leo as my chaperon tonight. He's not thrilled about it, but I'm not giving Mr. Owens a chance to dance with me."

I nodded. "Yes, that would be Mr. Owens. Don't worry, though. He'll get the hint soon and will move on to another girl."

"Good to know." She moved past me. "Excuse me."

She winked and entered the restroom, leaving me alone with Leo in a five-by-eight corridor. Not the wisest of actions. But then, I thought that she was rooting for me to dump Eric and take on her brother, so why not?

Because it was wrong. So, so wrong.

I lowered my head and started walking past

him, but something inside stopped me. I faced him with the same intensity he looked at me with. His gaze left me breathless while I was sure my eyes showed him how annoyed I was.

"Megan plans on sleeping with you tonight," I said.

"What?" He frowned and half-laughed. "Where is this coming from?"

"She just told me, rather proudly, that you wouldn't be able to resist her charms tonight."

He pushed away from the wall, shortening the distance between us. "You're jealous." I opened my mouth to retort, but nothing came out. Taking advantage of my momentary blank, Leo leaned toward me. "You *are* jealous."

I raised my chin in defiance, regretting it the moment I did as it put my face even closer to his. "I have no right to be jealous."

"Neither do I, but how do you think I feel when I see you with *him*? Dancing with him? His hands on your back? You leaving with him? I can't even think of what you two do when you're alone. I might kill someone if I do."

"I haven't slept with him in over a month." I put my hand over my mouth as soon as the words flew out, ashamed of confessing something so private. I had to put some restraints on my tongue around him. Not only for the words it might utter ...

Crap.

Slowly, Leo closed his hand over my wrist and pulled my hand away from my mouth, and me closer to him. "What? More importantly, why?"

I averted my gaze. There were several reasons. We had been busy, and I hadn't seen much of him. Besides, I've been worried about my father and I couldn't relax enough to let it happen.

However, it certainly had nothing to do with Leo being in my mind all the time.

Nope. Nothing at all.

He groaned. "*Morena*, you're killing me," he whispered in my ear. His breath teased the skin on my neck, sending a delicious shiver rolling down my body. I turned my head ever so slightly toward him, and his scent flooded my senses. I inhaled deeply, savoring this forbidden moment. "Say it. Tell me what you feel for me, and I'll whisk you away from here, in front of everyone. I'll even punch him if he gets in our way. Please, tell me, 'cause I can't let you go now." His hands snaked around my waist, and he pressed my body against his hard frame. I gasped. "Please, *morena*, say it."

Nothing felt more right than this moment, than me in his arms, our breaths mingled, our heartbeats in accelerated synchrony. But I found some leftover courage and, with my hands on his chest—damn, I could feel his muscles under the two layers of fabric—I pushed him back.

"This isn't right."

"It feels way too right."

I retreated a couple of steps, hoping to get out of reach. "This is just an attraction. Lust. Even if I surrendered to it, you would be over it by tomorrow. I can't throw a strong two-year relationship out the window for someone I don't even know how I really feel about."

Holding my stare, he tilted his head to the side. "Are you sure you don't know how you feel?"

I shook my head. "I think it's only lust, and maybe a little excitement over a challenge, an adventure. But it's just that."

He crossed his arms over his chest, his chin high and jaw tight. "You're lying."

I'd just gone over this inside my head in the restroom, and I wasn't in the mood to explain every detail to him.

"Have a good night," I said in my best robotic voice. I turned and hurried back to the ballroom.

Before I crossed the archway, and music blasted my ears, I heard Leo calling me one more time. *"Morena!"*

19

"THERE YOU ARE," ERIC SAID AS I APPROACHED THE table.

He was seated on his chair, two flutes of champagne on the table in front of him. Across the table, Tomas and his girlfriend were having dessert, but Megan, Blaire, and Andrea weren't there anymore. Without meaning to, I glanced around, looking for them.

My stomach tightened in knots when I saw the girls dancing in a circle right beside where Ricardo, Pedro, and Guilherme were standing, talking among themselves, with drinks in their hands.

I slumped down onto my chair.

"Are you okay?" Eric asked, caressing my cheek with the back of his hand.

"I'm fine," I blurted, turning my attention to him. "Sorry. I had to go to the restroom."

"Yes, Megan told me she spilled her drink on you. Did it stain your dress?" The concern in his expression made me feel ashamed. He was worried about me. He loved me. I wondered if he ever had doubts about us, if he ever had desired another woman while dating me. Ugh, at the same time, I didn't want to know. I guess finding out he had cheated on me would be the death of my self-esteem and pride. And that made me feel even worse, because I had considered, even if only for one-tenth of a second, cheating on him. How could I even think of doing something to him that I didn't want him to do to me?

Once more, shame consumed me.

"No. Thankfully, it only spilled on my arm."

"Good." He smiled and handed me a champagne flute. Desperate for an outlet, I drank all the contents in two long gulps. "Whoa. Looks like someone is ready to party hard."

I set down my flute, and saw Leo and Bia entering the ballroom. I couldn't help but look at Megan. She was searching the room, probably for him. Her eyes and her smile widened once she found him heading their way—or actually, his brothers' and cousin's way. She elbowed the other girls and they all giggled.

I reached for Eric's flute and downed it.

"Go slow, baby. I don't even remember the last time you drank this much."

My head spun. "I can handle it. Let's get more."

I stood, but Eric tugged my wrist and made me sit again. "I'll get it for you."

He was back in a blur, holding two new flutes.

"Thanks," I said, reaching for one, but he placed them on the table and held my hand instead.

"Let's dance a little, then we can come back and drink more." He hoisted me up from my seat. "I'll even call Pete and ask him to drive us home, so we can drink all we want."

Pete was Eric's chauffer—though he acted more like a bodyguard most of the time. Well, that did sound like a good plan.

"Then you won't mind if I take one more sip before hitting the dance floor." I batted my eyelashes, hoping it looked as charming as I thought it did.

Eric chuckled. "All right." He handed me a flute and I drank half of it.

The liquid was chilled with only a hint of

sweetness, and it went down smooth. Right now I felt okay, but champagne was a bitch. When least expected, it would drag me down, and I would fall like gelatin. Lord, help me, but I so just wanted to blackout and wake up when all the mess was solved, when Leo and his family were back in Brazil, when Eric and I were back to what we were before, when my father was awake and well.

Eric guided me to the center of the dance floor, and we danced along with the pop beat the band was playing. Soon, some friends and known faces stopped by us, shimmed a little, and then moved to other circles. When I could keep my mind in the moment, in dancing with the man who loved me, in wearing a beautiful gown to a fancy ball, and nothing else, I felt good.

It was fun. It was ... easy.

Three songs later, the band started playing a slower classic song.

With a grin, Eric grabbed my hands, placing them on his shoulders, then slid his hand to my waist and moved us along with the rhythm.

"I don't remember telling you how incredible you look tonight," Eric said.

"I do," I said. "But thanks. It's nice hearing it."

"I'm indeed lucky. You're beautiful, kind,

strong, and everything a man could ever want in a woman. I love you so much, baby."

"I lo—"

Someone bumped into us, and I tripped on my heels. Eric held me still as Leo and Megan stopped dancing and turned to us.

I went rigid and my eyes widened.

"I'm sorry," Megan said, her smile shining almost as much as all the chandeliers in the ballroom.

"It's okay," I said, trying and failing not to glance at Leo. Staring at me, he placed his hand on her back. I did my best not to glare at them.

Eric offered an acknowledgment nod to Leo. "How is it going?"

"*Bem,*" Leo said. His accent was pronounced. "How about you?"

"Never better." Eric smiled, and I instantly recognize which kind it was. A challenging smile. "Ready for the tournament?"

"Absolutely."

"Careful, Eric," Megan said, leaning into Leo. "Soon, Leonardo is going to steal your spotlight."

Eric's hand tightened on my waist. "We'll see about that."

"Hmm, we should get together some time," Megan said. "Like a double date."

Something like surprise flashed in Leo's eyes.

"I didn't know you two were dating," Eric said.

"Me neither," Leo muttered.

I pressed my lips together to suppress the laugh bubbling up.

Apparently, Eric hadn't heard him either. "With the games the next couple of weeks, it'll be hard to find a free spot on the calendar. Perhaps after the tournament."

"I guess that would be all right." Megan turned her face to Leo and pouted. If she had been sober, it would have been sort of sexy. Right now, it looked like she was ready to slobber all over. "I guess the two of us will be busy too."

A knot adorned Leo's forehead. He was dancing with her of his own free will. If it bothered him, he wouldn't have asked her to dance, or accepted it. So why the hell was he frowning?

The next song began, and it was another pop beat.

I turned to Eric. "How about we go home now?"

He kissed my cheek and whispered, "As you wish." Then he straightened and nodded to Megan and Leo. "Good seeing you both. Together. Leonardo, good luck with the games. Good night."

"Good night," Megan and I said together.

"*Boa noite,*" Leo said, his eyes on mine, a gleam I didn't quite understand in them.

With his hand still firm on my waist, Eric steered me off the dance floor. We stopped by our table, and I drank the rest of the champagne. It went down smooth, and the soft buzz in the back of my mind spiked for a few moments, instantly calming my nerves.

On our way out, we bid goodnight to everyone we knew, which accounted for ninety-five percent of the two hundred guests.

In the end, Eric hadn't drunk that much and he ended up calling Pete and canceling the ride. As he drove us out of the club and toward his house, my mind went back to the ball.

I couldn't stop thinking about Leo and Megan. Dancing. Touching. Kissing? Oh damn. They would sleep together, and next time I went to the club, she would want to tell me all about it. I bet she would even mention their upcoming wedding.

Leo was right. I *was* jealous. Insanely so. And that was completely crazy. Like I'd told him, I had no right to be jealous.

Shutting those thoughts out of my head, I brought one leg under me and turned my body to Eric. He was staring at the road intently.

I took a deep breath and drank him in. I observed how charming his profile looked in the dark, how his skin was smooth, his face freshly shaved, and his cologne just strong enough that I could get a faint sniff from here. Hmm, it smelled good. It smelled familiar. He looked dashing and strong in his tuxedo, and if he posed beside his fancy car, he would look like an international model or a famous actor girls swoon over. Then why wasn't I swooning anymore?

I closed my eyes, ignoring the buzzing inside my head, and remembered many of our good times. I was twelve and Eric was seventeen when we were first introduced to each other. To him, I was a baby, but to me, he was the guy of my dreams. What twelve-year-old wouldn't be crazy in love with a hot polo player who had the most charming smile in the entire world?

Then I grew up, and he started doing business with my father. By then, he was talking to me, bumping into me, and I waited for those moments with bated breath. Soon after, he asked me out. He was my first kiss, my first time, and my only on both accounts. I was crazy about him, even more because he was crazy about me. My father was thrilled when we told him we were dating. It felt like Christmas, and I was so proud for choosing someone he liked. We traveled together to Paris,

Milan, Venice, Rome, London, Cancun, Vancouver, and so many other places. We went riding together. We talked business, and he was adamant I shouldn't worry about it. At the time, I'd thought it was flattering, that he wanted to take care of me. It still was, in some way. He took good care of me, gave me gifts every now and then, even when there was no special occasion. He stole kisses and squeezed my hand, and was at my side whenever I needed him.

Of course, like every relationship, there were the not-so-good times. Like when I'd told Eric I was going to live on campus, or the time I'd told him I was moving from campus to the ranch after my grandma died. Or when I insisted on keeping the ranch. But that was normal. No relationship was perfect. We were too different people. Having disagreements was a given. Having disagreements and working them out was what made a relationship strong. I was sure we could do it.

I opened my eyes as Eric glanced at me. "Why are you smiling?"

"I'm smiling?"

"Yes."

I leaned my head on the headrest. "I'm thinking about us."

He reached out to me and rested his hand on my leg. "Good things, I hope."

"Uh-huh," I mumbled, sleepy and wanting to surrender to the lull of the car.

He squeezed my leg, and the next thing I knew I was being carried into his house.

"Go back to sleep," he whispered, shutting the front door behind us with his foot. "I'll take care of you."

I didn't fall back to sleep right away, but I felt too heavy to try and help him as he took off my shoes and dress, put on my nightgown, slipped the covers over me, and tucked me into his bed.

"Thank you," I whispered, eyes still closed.

The mattress dipped as he lay beside me. He kissed my temple. "I love you, baby."

I wanted to answer him, to tell him I loved him too, but sleep had already taken me.

ERIC LET ME SLEEP UNTIL ELEVEN THE NEXT morning. I wanted to go home and change before going back to the club, but he insisted that I stayed, since I had everything I needed here.

"I'm going to visit my father at the hospital," I protested.

"Baby, he's probably still under an induced coma. You won't be able to talk to him. I know you want to be there, but it won't make much difference right now. Why don't you call your mother? She'll let you know how he is."

So I called her, and she said exactly what Eric had predicted. There hadn't been any progress, and my mother sounded exhausted, yawning every two words. She probably stayed there all day and night, staring at the walls and waiting for something to happen. But nothing would happen. Not today at least. Still, guilt filled me for not being there with her. I promised I would spend most of the next day at the hospital, even if all we did was stare at the walls.

Afterward, Eric went to talk to his mother, and I took a shower and dove into Eric's closet. Lucky for me, I had a good amount of outfits here. I chose a red and white dress with a tight waist and a slightly flared skirt that went just below my knees. It matched my red pumps and white hat. Unfortunately, it wasn't a cowboy hat, but it was game day and everyone was required to dress their best.

It was nearly two in the afternoon when Eric pulled the car into the club parking lot. The opening game was at three, and it was the Knight House against a team from South Carolina. Their best player was ranked eleventh in the world. According to Eric, it would be an easy win for his team.

Inside the club, Eric met with his teammates while I made my way outside. The chairs and bleachers around the field were filling up quickly, especially the spots with shade and umbrellas. I entered the reserved VIP area, a fenced square right next to the field, with cushioned armchairs, side tables, a retractable shade, and waiters.

Sandra and a couple of other elite members were already there. We greeted each other, and I endured a few minutes of boring conversation before I was able to retreat and sit in an armchair as far away from them as I could.

It was only when I saw Megan coming from the main house that I realized my insides were a tight bundle of nerves. Oh crap. I so didn't want to hear what she had to say, because I knew she would want to tell me all about her night with Leo. On the other hand, I couldn't help but want to know.

Megan was stopped by Mr. Owens and one of his not-so-direct friends, Mr. Smith. I smirked as she tried to withdraw gracefully from their conversation, which clearly steered into not-so-comfortable zones. Not safe to talk with old perv men, at least.

I was still grinning when something caught the corner of my eye. Squinting, I turned toward it. Leo and Bia walked past the VIP area, their eyes never wavering from mine. She wore a pretty but not too formal blue dress, and—I held my breath —he was dressed in jeans and a fitted white shirt with long sleeves rolled up to his elbows. How the hell did they let him in dressed like that? Not that it was bad.

Not at all. Not by a long shot.

In fact, it looked utterly sexy on him. But there were rules and one of them was clear: no jeans on the premises.

Bia waved and Leo just stared, his blue-green eyes blank, his expression neutral. Even so, it was as if he was overcrowding me, overwhelming me. Still holding my breath, I nodded in acknowledgment. Instantly, I imagined Leo and Megan together, and I almost gagged.

They sat with their family on chairs right beside the VIP area. The game had not even started yet, and I was already wishing for its end.

To distract myself, I called Jimmy.

"How's everything going?"

"Fine," he said. "Paul is getting ready for his next class. I set a few horses out to exercise, and Dr. Bohm dropped by a couple of hours ago."

"Did he check on Argus?"

"He did." Jimmy sighed. "It's like you said. On the outside, the horse is healing, though a few of those scars won't ever disappear. The inside is the problem, and Dr. Bohm can't help with that."

"I know," I whispered.

"Argus was more frightened this morning than I've seen him since his first days here."

"What else is new? That horse is moodier than a one-year-old without a nap."

Jimmy laughed. "Well, I agree, but Dr. Bohm is worried. He'll have to report Argus's progress to animal control soon ... and it isn't looking good for him."

"What does that mean?"

"That they might come and take him since there has been no real progress."

I gasped. "That again! Where will they take him? I mean, there's no one around that would welcome him."

A slow panic crawled up to my chest. They couldn't take him. Not yet.

"Well, if the horse can't be cured, then he'll be put to sleep."

I took a deep breath. "This isn't the time and place to be discussing it." My attention had to be here, on the forthcoming game, otherwise I knew I would bolt and disappoint Eric. "Tomorrow morning. We'll talk about Argus and his situation, then come up with a plan."

"That's more like it," Jimmy said, not disguising his smiley tone.

Megan began walking to the VIP area.

"Jimmy, I gotta go." We said goodbye and I put my phone away.

Megan waved to me as she approached her mother, and I sat on my hands before I bit my nails in anticipation. And nervousness. And jealousy. And guilt.

I glanced over my shoulder at her. She was engrossed in a conversation with her mother and friends. She would come over to sit with me at some point, wouldn't she?

As I whipped my head back to the field, my eyes skimmed over where the Fernandes family sat and met with green-blue eyes. My heart skipped a beat. He was staring at me. A slow lopsided grin stole over his perfect lips as he pulled his gaze from mine. For the first time, he was the one to break the stare. His smirk angered me to no end.

Megan plopped down by my side, and I jumped in my seat, my heart racing.

"Oh, sorry," she said, smoothing the skirt of her teal dress over her knees. "I forgot how jumpy you are." She looked at me with something like regret glinting in her eyes. "I guess that's what happens when two friends become distant, huh? They forget about silly things like that." She paused and

I remained quiet, unsure what to say. "So, the ball was great, right?"

"Right," I said, hiding all the sarcasm that wanted to slip out with my words.

"You and Eric left early, though. The fun really began later," she said, smiling.

Control yourself, Hannah. Control yourself.

If I tilted my head an inch to the side while turned to Megan, I could see Leo, watching me. Or was he watching Megan?

"Oh, really?"

"Really." She leaned back in her chair, allowing me a full view of Leo. And he *was* watching me. Or her. Or the both of us. Oh damn! "All right. Not even Blaire and Andrea know about this yet, because I didn't talk to them since we got separated near the end of the ball," she dragged on, and I was about to explode. "And they will kill me for telling you first, but ohmygosh, I can't—"

"Just tell me," I said, surlier than I wanted to.

"Okay, okay." She giggled. "So, Leonardo asked me to dance and, after you and Eric left, we went to the bar and talked a lot. Have you ever talked to him?" I opened my mouth, unsure of how to answer, but she didn't give me time to answer as she kept on. "He has the sexiest accent. And his eyes? Have you seen his eyes up close? Of course not."

She giggled again, and I clasped my hands before I strangled her. "He has the most incredible pair of eyes I have ever seen."

"What happened next?"

"Oh yeah, sorry. I get caught up in his goodness too easily." She laughed, putting her hand over her mouth for a second. "Okay, so he asked if I wanted to walk around the club with him. I told him it probably wasn't allowed because it was too late, but he insisted, and well, you know about my plan, right? He was falling right into it. Then, when we were walking around the tennis courts, he—"

"Hannah." Eric's voice made me jump and I shot up, alarmed and ashamed for all that brewed inside of me.

He leaned against the VIP fence, clad in his uniform, helmet and goggles in his hand. I walked to him, focusing on the moment, on him, his game, his confident smile, and his loving eyes on me.

"Hi," I whispered.

"I want my good luck kiss," he said, reaching for me over the fence.

I let him pull me to him. I let him snake his hand around my neck. I let him kiss me. Concentrating, I shut my mind to all else and really kissed him back, like I hadn't done since the early stages of our relationship, when the hunger for each other was still something we had no control over. My tongue teased his, and I ended the kiss, sucking on his lower lip. I wanted to drown in him. I wanted to forget everything else, *anyone* else.

"For Pete's sake, baby," he whispered, still holding me close and breathing hard. "That was sexy as hell. Damn, this game." He glanced over his shoulder. His team was waiting for him. "We're going to pick this up tonight."

I nodded and he smiled.

I didn't move as he dashed to where his teammates stood with their horse on the side of the field. When I did, I whirled on my heels, and my eyes, acting on their own, swept over Leo. Once more, he was watching me, but this time he was frowning, his arms crossed and his jaw ticking.

Catching my breath, I sat beside Megan once more.

"Ohmygosh, I thought you two were going to eat each other's face right in front of everyone," Megan said. "You're one lucky girl."

Was I? My intention had been to kiss Eric as if there were no tomorrow, to drown in him, to forget everything else. I wanted it to ignite our dying flame once again. The kiss had ended and he seemed worked up and excited. But I wasn't. I hadn't felt that kiss as deeply as he had, as deeply as I'd once felt. Shouldn't I love him blindly as I once did? I wanted to say I did, to pretend I did, but deep down I knew.

I didn't.

21

My eyes were on the game, but my mind was far away. Well, not that far away, actually. It was right outside the VIP area, where a certain Brazilian was seated.

A bomb had fallen on me, exploding realization around me.

I loved Eric, but I wasn't *in love* with him anymore. I hadn't been for the longest time. Our relationship started when I was still a starstruck girl who had just scored the hottest guy around.

However, looking back at the two-plus years, I saw myself changing. I spent less time with Megan, I became more distant from Hilary, I didn't go to the ranch as much, I didn't get close to any of my classmates in college, I spent less time learning the family business, I jumped less, I rode Hercules less. Without meaning to, without realizing, I had been living life according to Eric's wants and needs.

Everything changed when grandma started calling me more, insisting on me spending a couple of weekends with her on the ranch, which led to me enjoying more of Hercules. It was like she knew she didn't have much time left and wanted to spend it with me. Then she was gone, Hercules was gone, and the ranch was handed to me. Because of grandma, I'd begun thinking for myself again, wanting things for myself once more. Eric disagreed with all of it, and with that came his jealousy, which had always been an issue, but now it felt asphyxiating.

To top it all, Argus was brought into my life. And then Leo.

I took a deep breath, but it wasn't enough. There wasn't enough air to calm me down. This realization was too big, too nerve-racking. It was like I forgot to sweep one single strand of hay from the ground two years ago, and now I was buried under a huge haystack, suffocating, being squashed, with no strength or idea on how to get out.

"Are you all right?" Megan asked as the game started.

"Of course," I said. "Never better."

She grinned. "Good, because I need to finish telling you about last night."

I raised my index finger to her. "Give me a minute."

I closed my eyes for a moment. Freaking out here wouldn't do any good. I had to calm down and wait. Once Eric took me home, I would tell him I wasn't feeling good or something, and hope he took the hint and left. After all, he was winning this game and had others coming. He wouldn't want to risk getting sick from me right now. So, he would leave me alone and I would think. Just ... think. All night and during the entire next day if that was what it took for me to figure out ...

Everything.

My present.

My future.

Myself.

The cheer from a score boomed around the field, and I knocked a glass from the end table beside me. A waiter picked it up with a smile as I counted to twenty and inhaled deeply again. The umpire called the end of a chukka, and almost instantly, chatting voices carried away with the breeze.

Open your eyes, Hannah. Damn it, just open and do your thing.

Holding my breath, I looked across the field to where Eric was with his teammates, waiting for the game to resume. He was staring at me, his expression concerned. He was probably wondering why I wasn't watching his game. Watching him.

Then it hit me. He was insecure. Incredibly insecure. That was where his jealousy came from. I hadn't noticed that until now.

His eyes flickered to my side, distant enough that I knew he wasn't looking at anyone inside the VIP area. Three seconds later, his gaze was on me again, hard and dubious. Damn, he couldn't have put two and two together just like that, could he?

With gritted teeth, Eric returned to the game. The change in his game from one chukka to the next was noticeable. He always had a hint of aggression and competitiveness, but he had transformed into an animal. He threw his pony over the players from the other team, making them stray from their paths. He stole the ball by linking his mallet to his adversary's mallet and pushing it out of the way. He was just short of hitting them in the face with his mallet. All master moves too, because the umpires never saw any of it. He argued about every fault, every move, every point.

And I watched him as if I were seeing him for the first time.

No, but it wasn't the first time. This attitude had been there all along. I'd just been purposefully blind to it. He *always* argued during games, he was *always* aggressive, but I always put a cover over it and pretended it was his game plan. Moreover, I'd seen him losing it before, not long ago.

I shuddered, remembering that awful day. He had totally freaked me out.

I considered leaving the club. Getting up and leaving. But I knew that would only anger him more. Instead, I remained seated, quiet, my eyes on him.

Until Megan spoke again. "So, Leonardo kissed me."

My heart stopped. "What?"

"He did," she said, her smile from ear to ear. "We didn't go further, but ohmygosh, kissing him was heaven."

My stomach twisted into knots. "Oh, I thought your plan was to take him to bed."

"It was, but well, he didn't make any moves, and for some reason, I didn't want to push him.

Maybe it's best. I mean, this could become serious and I don't want to be the easy girl, you know."

I nodded, feeling too sick to reply.

She launched into a detailed description of the rest of her night. How they walked around the tennis courts, how they held hands, how he pulled her to him, how he took the lead and kissed her.

Oh, Lord, I wanted to run now more than ever.

Instead, I held my ground, pressed my lips together, and kept my eyes on Eric until the game ended. The Knight House won, and I hoped it helped in abating his anger.

After greeting everyone who came toward him with a smile, which was a good sign, Eric came to me, took my hand, and led me out of the VIP area and away from the field. He was quiet and his grip tight.

"Congratulations," I said.

He didn't reply.

With rigid moves, he opened the door of his car for me, and then closed it once I slipped inside. He slid into the driver's side and drove out of the club, in silence.

"Eric, if you don't mind, I want to go home. It's the middle of the week, and I have tons of stuff to do."

His knuckles turned white around the steering

wheel. My heart beat faster, concerned he would drag me to his house and ignore my wishes. Surprising me, he took the road that led to the ranch and I relaxed. Now I just had to put my plan into action.

By the time we got to the ranch, the sun was beginning its slow descent and the colors, green from the grass, blue from the sky, yellow and pink from the flowers, and red from the barn, looked more vibrant because of the sun's orange glow.

We walked to the house in silence. I glanced at the barn and noticed that Jimmy and Paul were already gone.

When I closed the front door behind us, Eric turned to me with fresh anger in his eyes.

"What the fuck was that?"

"Excuse me?" I asked, taking a step back.

"That Latin scum, he was eating you with his eyes. What is going on?"

"Eric, what are you talking about?"

"You know!" he shouted, clenching his fists at his sides. "Leonardo Fernandes has been staring at you, nonstop, since the day he set foot in the club. Only a blind person wouldn't see it."

"But you saw it last night, Megan and him together. She said they kissed," I told him, and I saw the surprise flash through his eyes for a second.

"No, no," he hissed. "The way he was looking at you today. No. He's playing with Megan. Or he's trying to make *you* jealous."

If that was the case, Leo was succeeding, but I kept that to myself and played my part. "What? Eric, that's nonsense."

He towered over me, the shine in his eyes menacing. "Is it? Because he looks at you like he loves you, and how can you love someone if you don't know them?"

"Eric," I muttered. My mind raced as fast as my heart, trying to find a good answer. What could I say that would calm him down? "Seriously, he was probably looking at Megan, not me."

Shaking his head, Eric held my upper arms glued against my sides. "Oh, baby, how innocent you are." I didn't want to have him freak out, I didn't want to anger him more, so I didn't jerk or try to wiggle free from his grasp. I did step back, though, but hit my back against the stair railing. I felt the corner of the console table against the wall brushing my leg. His body came against me, his face a couple of inches from mine. "Each time I see that Latin scum looking at you, I want to jump at his throat and strangle him." He said it in a low, deep voice, and with a shine in his eyes, as if he would have enjoyed it.

"You're scaring me," I whispered.

His fingers sunk into my skin, and I suppressed a whimper. "You're mine, Hannah, and only mine. Nobody, no other man will lay hands on you. You hear me?" He pressed his mouth to my ear. "You're mine."

He licked the flesh under my ear and made his way down my neck, to my shoulder. My eyes watered, and I turned my head away from his. I closed my eyes for a second, trying to shake the shock from my system, but it felt like my movements were in slow motion, too drugged and confused to act normal.

When he thrust his hips against mine and I felt how hard he was, I shoved him back.

"Stop it," I said, my tone brusque. How could he be turned on when we were fighting?

"Excuse me?"

"You're ... not yourself, and I'm not gonna let you touch me when you're like this."

He growled and pushed at me again, but this time he didn't stop by pinning my body with his or holding down my arms. No. This time, he raised his hand and punched the console table. I stepped out of the way as the table fell on the floor. A lamp, picture frames, and the glass decorations broke, spreading pieces and scraps all over the floor.

Eric kicked the broken pieces out of the way and stood before me, his expression murderous. Fear crawled up my spine as I realized Eric was turning not only obsessively jealous, but also violent.

"You're being a bad girl, baby," he said, pinning my wrist on the wall, right beside my head. "A very bad girl. And bad girls have to be punished." He leaned closer, and his eyes held a new light, an excited and crazy light. "You should behave, baby."

"Eric, let me go." I struggled against him. "Let me go!"

"Hannah, behave."

"Let me go. Now!"

Eric probably saw the desperation in me. He released me and stepped back. He paced the living room for several minutes, and I wondered what would happen next.

Surprising me, he came to stand by me, the anger gone from his eyes.

"Baby, I'm so sorry. I'm so, so sorry." He reached for me, but I slapped his hand away. "Please, baby. Try to understand." I didn't dare to speak, because I would probably yell at him and he would be angry again. "I can't stand it when men look at you like that. I just ... I lose it."

He knelt before me and hugged my legs, his

face against my thighs. And he cried. I could hear his sobs, but it was hard to believe.

My first instinct was to kick him and dash away. I wasn't that kind of person though. I was the kind of person who tried to see the best in everyone, and that included Eric. And, when he could control his freak-outs and jealousy attacks, Eric was a great man. He was kind and caring, he was a great polo player, he took care of his mother, he managed his father's business, and he took good care of me and loved me. There was more good than bad in him.

I looked down at him. If I were in his situation, where I couldn't control my temper, I would probably want help from loved ones, even if I never admitted it out loud. How could I turn my back on him now? Besides, I knew this was hard for him. He didn't like confessing he had weaknesses even to himself, and now I was seeing them too.

He needed professional help, but knowing him, I knew he wouldn't accept it easily. I had to be here for him, to show him he needed to seek aid, and then take him there. Small steps. Always small steps.

I touched his shoulders and urged him to stand.

He wiped his tears with the back of his hand and stared at me, with big wary eyes.

"Please forgive me?"

Nodding, I pulled him into an embrace. "I forgive you."

He sighed into my hair and held me tight. "I'll make it up to you. I promise."

22

I woke up to a beautiful breakfast table, with a huge bouquet of pink roses and an I'm-sorry card. Eric did all he could to compensate for the previous evening. He pulled out my chair for me, he served my food, he cleaned the kitchen, and he even made coffee.

After breakfast, we stopped by the hospital to see my father. As expected, he was still unconscious, and my mother was still seated in the same armchair I had last seen her. Hilary came a lot but didn't stay every minute of every hour like my mother did.

Eric and I had lunch at a fancy restaurant downtown. This new loving Eric was kind of fun, but I had to hold my tongue several times. I wanted to talk to him about his problem, but I knew that he was focused on the tournament and I would ruin it if I brought up that subject now. I had to stay by his side and wait until the tournament was over.

Around two in the afternoon, Eric drove us to the club for his next game.

Again, I sat in the VIP area while Eric went to meet with his teammates. I struggled against my good sense and lost. I scanned the area but didn't see Leo anywhere. In fact, I didn't see any of his family members yet.

That was ... strange.

Megan showed up with Blaire and Andrea. They sat beside me and included me in their gossip about the newest divorce—a known couple in the club. I pretended to care, so as not to be rude, but I couldn't look at Megan and not think of Leo. Crap, I would be sick if they were actually going out together.

In the first ten minutes of the game, Eric scored two goals, showing everyone this would be an easy match.

After the game, he took me to his house to celebrate. He opened a bottle of champagne and we had a nice dinner with his mother. As usual, she excused herself right after dessert and went to her bedroom.

And Eric took me to his.

He closed the door and turned to me, pulling me to him and kissing me.

Since my big revelation, I felt so bad for kissing him. I tried remembering I still loved him, because even if I wasn't in love with him, I did love him. He was a big part of my life, always would be. And because of his problems, I could see he would be for a long time, because I couldn't just drop him like that. It wasn't right. I wouldn't want someone I loved dropping me when I needed him the most.

But, as much as kissing was tolerable, I couldn't go further.

He started working on my dress's zipper, and I pushed him away.

"What's wrong?"

I walked to the other side of the bed. "I can't."

He looked at me as if I were speaking Mandarin. "What?"

"I can't, Eric."

He put a knee over the bed. "I don't understand." I groaned. Please, I didn't want to spell it out. Instead, I shook my head. "What's the matter, baby? Why not?" I sighed. At least he had understood my message. Again, I didn't say anything. "Talk to me, baby."

I sat on the bed. "I'm sorry, but I'm not in the mood. With everything that is going on—"

"Was," he said. "Everything that *was* going on. I told you, baby. I'm working on it. I'll be better from now on."

"I know, but I can't simply close my eyes and pretend nothing happened. I'm sorry." I traced the pattern of the comforter with my finger. "I don't mean to upset you but I can't. I need more time."

He sat on his side of the bed. "You said you forgave me."

"I did. I forgave you, but that doesn't mean I forgot."

He reached across the bed and touched my hand. "I never meant for this to happen. I never meant for you to distrust me. I'm so sorry. I'll fix this, baby."

I turned my hand to his and let him weave his fingers with mine. "I know."

He offered me a hopeful smile. "Will you let me hold you tonight, at least?"

I didn't want to hesitate, but I did. My first thought was to say no, but after all, I had mulled over the last twenty-four hours, I couldn't say no.

I nodded.

SUNDAY MORNING, I PUT ON JEANS, A CHECKERED shirt, and my red boots, and went to the stable with a few special treats. Thank goodness, there weren't any riding groups scheduled until two in the afternoon, which gave me a Jimmy-free environment until at least noon.

Keeping my mind blank, I fed the horses. Who was I kidding? I couldn't stop thinking about Eric and his strange behavior and what I would do about it.

I hadn't seen him since yesterday morning, when he drove me here from his house, saying he was going to spend the day at the club, watching the matches and socializing with other players and teams. He didn't even invite me to go with him, and I thought that was because I had been tense while he held me in bed. I was sure he felt it.

I shook my head. How? How had our relationship taken a turn for the worst, and why couldn't I seem to find the right route?

Eric had a big game this afternoon—I remembered that much—and it kind of hurt that he didn't invite me to go with him.

Sighing, I turned to the stall I had left for last.

Argus was in the corner of his stall, his body

curled as much as a long, powerful horse's body could, his head down, but his ears alert. He'd been keeping tabs on me since I had come in.

"Hey, boy," I whispered. "Want some food?" He didn't move. Cautiously, I open the door to his stall and stepped inside. I closed the door behind me and leaned against it. "I've got something for you."

He moved his muzzle two inches toward me so that he could look at me.

I smiled and showed him my hands, both filled with strawberries. "I know it's not the usual carrot or apple, but these are my favorite fruit and I hoped you would want to taste them."

I took a leap and knelt on the ground. Two seconds later, Argus was on his feet, still in the corner, but on his feet.

Remembering the night we'd made a little progress—which felt like eons ago—I took a deep breath and waited.

And waited.

And waited.

Ten minutes went by and my extended arms burned. I sang a Taylor Swift song in my mind, trying to ignore the pain and numbing sensation, because my muscles screamed more and more by the second.

He turned to face me, his eyes locked on mine,

looking like bottomless brown pools. I couldn't tell what mood he was in, but just the fact that he was staring at me gave me a new burst of energy; I held on.

A couple more minutes rolled by before he finally gave a step in my direction. I pressed my lips together, lest he saw the smile trying to creep out and change his mind.

Six minutes later, I couldn't take the pain in my muscles anymore and lowered my arms to my lap.

Then he walked all the way to me.

Son of a bit—

"Hannah."

I froze, dropping all the strawberries on the ground. Argus snorted, retreating all the way back into the corner again.

"Baby, where are you?" Eric asked again, his voice closer. I straightened, peering over the stall door, but remained in place. As if he were the most loving boyfriend in the world, he smiled wide, with Mr. Nash by his side. "There you are."

They walked up to me. "Hannah, you remember Mr. Nash, don't you?"

Anger pooled in my chest. "What is he doing here?"

"Hannah, baby, please, be nice to our friend."

I gaped. "Friend?"

Mr. Nash extended his hand to me. "Hello, Miss Taylor. It's nice to see you again."

I ignored his hand. "I can't say the same."

Eric leaned over the stall door and put his hand over my arm. "Mr. Nash is still interested in buying the ranch, you know. You should consider his offer, baby. It's very generous."

His words were like a horse kick in my stomach. "What?"

"I know you'll like it." Eric's gaze locked on mine, and once more, I was struck by how much I didn't really know him. "I'll show him around, okay, baby?"

He gently squeezed my arm, then turned to Mr. Nash and guided him through the stable, while I stood in the same place, in shock and perfectly still. What the hell was he doing? Hadn't I told him I would not sell this ranch? I couldn't understand why he ignored my wishes like that.

My body shook with fury, and I fought the urge to argue with him. But I pushed it back and told it to wait. I would let the anger out, but not in front of others. Mr. Nash had to leave at some point, and I would confront Eric. Bringing a buyer to the ranch, which wasn't and would never be for sale. What was he thinking?

I heard hooves crunching hay and whirled to

find Argus still in the corner. However, the strawberries were gone.

23

Eric left when Mr. Nash did, and without talking to me again. Which was good. Sort of.

But he did message me right after his car was out of sight.

I've got a game soon. I'll be back later.

I erased the message, wishing that I could erase the memories from my mind with a simple button too.

Soon, Jimmy showed up and we talked about Argus while we prepared the horses for the up-coming riding group.

"You ain't gonna give up, are you?" he asked, hauling Black Jack and Chip out to the arena.

I grabbed Dakota's and Belle's reins and guided them out too. "I don't want to, but I'm lost. I don't really know what to do other than be patient with him. However, being patient means time, and we don't have it."

"I don't think waiting for him to come around is wasted time."

"Me too, but still, it's precious time," I said. We tied the horses' reins to the fence. "What other options do we have?"

He turned to me, a don't-kill-me-please expression over his battered face. "Call Mr. Fernandes and ask him to keep helping you?"

I sighed. "I can't do that."

Jimmy tsked. "Then hire another experienced horse whisperer? Or send Argus to one?"

Surprisingly, my heart squeezed and I frowned. "I don't know." One corner of Jimmy's lips turned up. "What?"

"With all the effort you made to stay away from every other horse, I thought it would take longer for you to care about this one."

"I care for all horses," I said too quickly, busying myself by checking on Belle's saddle.

Jimmy nodded. "Well, it's not that kind of caring I'm talking about."

"He's a mistreated horse, and I'm just helping him."

"Once he's fixed, what are you going to do with him?"

My hands froze over the stirrups, realizing I had never thought about it. What would I do with Argus once he was well? Put him up for adoption? Return him to animal control so they could find him a new home? I guess I never really envisioned Argus leaving the ranch and that was ... disturbing.

Images of Hercules, so beautiful and powerful in his exuberant black form, flashed in my mind: running around this arena, riding with me to the waterfall, jumping with me in tournaments, lying on the ground under the shade of a tree and wanting me to lie over him, to take a nap after a tiring day.

My heart tugged. I still loved him way too much, and there was no room in my heart for another horse.

Once Argus was well again, I would find him a new home.

I opened my mouth to tell Jimmy that when cars drove up the road, their engines too loud for my taste, and parked beside the stable. The riding group had arrived, and I was allowed to keep my troubled feelings to myself.

Jimmy and I helped them settle on their

horses, and once they left, I straightened up the stable in silence, while Jimmy fed the remaining horses. He opened the lazy Susan feeder from Argus's stall and the horse neighed. I put away the bridle I had been holding and observed them.

Argus was in the same corner, snorting and hitting the ground with his right hoof. He was agitated and I wondered why. There were no loud noises, no rain or thunder, no danger.

"Calm down, boy," Jimmy said, one of his hands raised, the other holding a bucket of grain. He placed the bucket on the lazy Susan and closed it.

Once more, Argus neighed.

I went to stand beside Jimmy. VIP seating to one of Argus's inexplicable tantrums. Perhaps Jimmy was right. Maybe I should try to find a real horse whisperer to help Argus.

Argus and his agitated state kept going for at least another thirty minutes, and, as expected, he didn't eat anything.

The group came back after almost two hours out. They helped Jimmy and I take the equipment off the horses, take the horses to their stalls, and put everything away in the tack room.

After everyone left, including Jimmy, I went inside the main house and dashed to my bathroom. I wanted to take a quick shower, change, and go to the hospital. I had been talking to my mother often, but it wasn't the same. I wanted to be there for her and my father. I wanted to hear news from the doctor, even if it was only to tell me my father was still in bad shape.

I opted for jeans and another checkered shirt and boots. Why should I dress up to go to the hospital and just sit there? Besides, other than cutoff shorts and tank tops, this was my preferred outfit.

I stepped out of the house and found Leo's SUV in the parking lot. He slipped out of the car, wearing his official Montenegro uniform, his wet hair framing his perfect face. Apparently, he had come from a game. And he came here without showering? I didn't get it.

He walked up to me but remained down the porch steps.

"What are you doing here?"

His thumb twisted the black band on his ring finger. "You always go to all of his games, but you weren't there this afternoon and I was worried. As soon as the match was over, I rushed here."

My heart lurched. He still worried about me. I shook my head. "You had a game against Eric?"

"Yes."

Oh crap. I was afraid of asking who won.

I climbed down the steps and started walking past him. "You shouldn't have come."

Leo groaned. "Can I be worried about you?" I shook my head but didn't stop my path to my car. "And how about Argus? Can I be worried about him? I want to know how he is doing."

I paused to dig my car keys from my purse. "He's fine."

"That sounds like bullshit."

I turned to glare at him. "Did you come here to accuse me of something?"

He approached me, his eyes doleful. "You know why I'm here, *morena*." He reached to me, and I was about to step away when I saw the purple Douglas Iris in his hand. He placed it behind my ear, his fingertips lingering on my face.

I crossed my arms and tilted my chin up. "What about Megan? She was very excited to tell me about you two."

His hand dropped to his side. "*Porcaria*. Okay. Listen to me." He ran a hand over his hair. "I'm sorry about that. I was upset, I was frustrated, and I wanted to get back at you. I knew she would tell you right away, and at that moment, I wanted you to hurt as much as I hurt when I see you with that jackass." He closed his mouth, and his jaw popped.

"Leo—"

"Wait, let me finish," he interrupted me. "I thought I could pretend to date her for a couple of weeks, but I don't like her. At all. You know that. I haven't talked to her since that night." He tilted his head. "I hope you don't think I'm a jerk."

My gaze flicked to his mouth, but I forced myself to focus and stared into his eyes. I could see the longing in there, mingling with hope and desire. I wondered what mine told him. I bet he could see straight through me and see my desire.

"A little," I teased, but in truth, relief coursed through me. "Seriously, though. You shouldn't have come."

As if to prove me right, Eric's car entered the property. He zipped down the road and parked his car beside mine in record time.

My heart beating unevenly, I distanced myself from Leo.

Eric exited his car with eyes clouded by rage. Like Leo, he was sweaty and dirty and smelly, and still wearing his team uniform.

He marched toward us. "Mr. Fernandes, what a surprise seeing you here." He placed his arms over my shoulders.

"Mr. Fernandes came to check on Argus. He heard the horse was having problems and thought he could give me some advice."

"Really?" Eric asked, through gritted teeth. "That's generous of you, Mr. Fernandes, but we've got it covered. If Hannah needs any advice about that horse, she asks me."

Touching the black band on his finger, Leo frowned. "Of course. I guess I was too focused on helping an abused horse that I forgot you have a lot of experience with horses too."

"Exactly." Eric squeezed my shoulder.

Leo's eyes met mine briefly, but enough for Eric's fingers to dig into my skin.

"Thanks, Mr. Fernandes," I said, trying to fix this situation before Eric jumped at Leo's throat. "I'm sorry for your wasted trip here, though. Like Eric said, we've got it covered."

"I see," Leo said, his jaw popping in and out. "Good evening."

He simply whirled around and hopped into his SUV without waiting for a reply.

Eric's fingers on my shoulder stirred me to the house. We heard Leo driving away as I opened the front door.

Sensing his anger, I wiggled free from Eric's hold once we stepped inside, and rushed to the other side of the living room.

Eric banged the door closed and puffed, his rage pouring from him.

Clenching his fists, he growled and launched at me. What the ...? Fear crawled up my spine. I snapped out of it and ran across the hallway, and into the kitchen, but he caught up with me half a second later. His arms hooked around my waist and pulled me to him. I yelled, jerking as much as I could, but he was too strong. With my back glued to his chest, he held my wrists across my stomach.

"What was that Latin scum doing here?" he asked. I whimpered and that encouraged him to yell, "What was he doing here?" I yanked from side to side, trying to break free of him. "Stop fighting," he whispered in my ear, and I flinched. "Stop. Fighting."

I did. I knew I wouldn't win right now, and I didn't want to waste all my energy on futile escape attempts. Tears welled in my eyes.

"Good girl." His grip on my wrists loosened a tiny bit. "What was he doing here?"

I took a deep breath, willing my nerves to calm down. "What he told you. He found out about Argus and wanted to help."

Eric scoffed. "And you believed him? You aren't that blind, baby. You know why he was here."

I shook my head. "No, Eric. That's the only reason I know."

With fast movements, he spun me around and

pinned me to the wall. "You know what pisses me off the most? I was just at a game with him, and he rushed here the second it was over. I didn't know where he was going, of course, but I saw him running off the field. And while I was having a pep talk with my team, he was here, flirting with you!"

"No, no," I muttered. "Not flirting."

Eric pulled my hair back and I yelled in pain. "Do you know why I was having a pep talk with my team? Because I lost," he said through gritted teeth. "I'm out of one of the most important tournaments in the country because of that Latin scum. I LOST!" He punched the wall, missing my face by mere inches. I winced, letting out a sob. "Do you know how hard I worked to get where I am? How many sacrifices I had to make? How many ...?" He shook his head. "Mark my words, I'm going to wipe the winning grin off their faces one way or another." He growled before resting his forehead on mine. One of his hands curled around my waist, painfully, while the other traveled up to my neck.

For a moment, he seemed to focus on me, and his anger abated.

And that was my cue.

I kneed him in the groin. Surprised, he crouched, and I ran to the back door.

My hands were shaking, and it took me a couple of precious seconds to finally unlock the door and run out. I had reached the steps off the back porch when I was yanked back—one of Eric's hands on my upper arm, the other in my hair—and dragged into the house.

"Eric, let me go! Let me go." I yelled and jerked and tried to kick him again, but this time he was prepared. He held me tighter each time I tried to get away, or he deflected it whenever I tried to hurt him.

He pulled one of the kitchen's chairs from under the table and pushed me down on it.

"What the hell are you doing? Eric, what the—?"

My head whipped to the side. Pain exploded on my cheek. My vision darkened. The chair wobbled. I was sure the blow had hurt not only my face but my neck too. I pressed my eyes and lips closed, trying to swallow the pain and tears.

Oh good gracious, what the hell had just happened? Because I was certain that what I thought ensued couldn't have actually occurred.

It just couldn't.

I pressed my hand to my face, as if it would stop the pain, and noticed my cheek was wet. I was crying.

And just like that, a sob shook through me.

And another.

And another.

His hand curled over my chin, his fingers digging into my stinging skin, and he pulled my face to his. "You *are* going to be a good girl. You're going to behave. You're going to do whatever I tell you. And right now I'm telling you: SHUT UP!"

I whimpered.

Eric released me and paced the kitchen, his fists clenched, his shoulders tense, and his eyes radiating anger.

Who was this man and what had he done with my boyfriend? I was watching him and, besides the physical resemblance, there was nothing else familiar about him.

Nothing.

With a sudden movement, Eric knelt beside me. He ran his fingers up my arm and caressed my neck. "I love you, baby, and I know what's best for you. I want to take care of you. Let me take care of you." I gaped, sure I heard him wrong. "I love you, baby. So much." He traced his fingertips over my cheek, where he had slapped me. "I'm so sorry."

I couldn't respond to that. My mind was blank, completely in shock.

He looked at me with remorseful eyes. "I'm so,

so sorry, baby. I didn't mean for it to get out of hand, but you made me angry. I ..." He sighed. "I'm sorry." He kissed my forehead, and I jerked back. Pretending he hadn't noticed my reaction, he retreated a step. "To show you how much I love you and how sorry I am, I'll make us a romantic dinner."

A tear rolled down my cheek. My life was falling apart, and I had no idea how to fix it.

I stayed in the chair, wallowing in my pain and sorrow, while Eric fixed us dinner.

I squinted at him as he broke a few eggs into the frying pan.

What happened to the man who had just laid a hand on my face? He was gone, replaced by the same loving Eric I knew, the one who looked at me with dopey eyes and did everything to please me.

Just like that, he looked more like a dream than a nightmare. In appearance, he was still handsome, with his perfectly cut dark hair and blue eyes, fair skin and strong build. In addition, he had a killer smile and loads of charm that no one could resist.

I didn't resist him.

Not at first.

Eric turned off the stove and approached me. "Come on," he said, turning my chair to the table.

He brought the frying pan and the plates to the table. "I added lots of pepper, the way you like it." He smiled and sat beside me.

I stared at my plate, unsure of what to do.

He gently caressed the back of my hand with his fingertips. "Baby, try it. I'm sure you'll like it. Please."

A new tear fell down my face. I took the fork and grabbed a forkful of omelet. Perhaps, if I pretended nothing had happened ten minutes ago, it wouldn't be true. It wouldn't happen again.

I hoped.

24

ERIC BARELY LEFT MY SIDE FOR THE REST OF THE week. Fortunately, he didn't hit me anymore. But he still hurt me. With his strong grip when pulling, pushing, squeezing, or simply touching, his harsh words, his gestures, his looks, and his threats.

Mostly the threats.

The worst moment was when he caught me trying to feed Argus one evening.

"Strawberries for the broken horse? Are you crazy?"

I placed the handful of strawberries on the stall's lazy Susan and turned to Eric. "I think he likes them."

"Who cares?" He stared at Argus. "You

shouldn't have brought this animal here in the first place."

"I didn't bring him here. Animal control did." He should have known this, because I had told him before, but apparently, lunatics were self-centered.

"Same thing." His face twisted in disgust. "Look at him. All those wounds and scars. Atrocious."

Obviously agitated with Eric's surly tone and posture, Argus neighed and reared.

"Easy boy," I whispered, holding my hands high, palms facing him.

"I want him out of here."

I whirled to Eric. "What?"

"You heard me. I'm leaving in two days for the tournament in Switzerland. When I get back, I want this horse gone."

"You can't be serious."

Fists clenched, he towered over me, making me lean my back over the stall door. "Do I look like I'm joking? We are selling this place, you will quit college, you will accept my marriage proposal, and we'll be married by the end of the year."

"You can't make me."

"Watch me. I've indulged you long enough. It's time you get your priorities straight."

"You're cra—" The words died on my tongue when he gritted his teeth and raised his fist.

I sucked in air, preparing myself for the punch. Instead, a hard bump from my back rattled Eric and me, causing Eric to lose his footing and lower his arm. Argus neighed and kicked at the door again.

"What the fuck?" Eric shouted.

After that, I spent a long time calming down both animals.

The only relief to my troubled mind was the fact that Eric hadn't tried to sleep with me. Shudders broke through my body each time I thought he would try something. I couldn't bear the thought of him touching me like that and I was dying inside thinking it was only a matter of time until he came on to me.

How would I defend myself then?

On a Friday afternoon, Eric went to the club to watch the last game of the tournament—according to him, he needed to know who won the championship—and I took advantage of the quiet time to spy on Argus.

Jimmy was putting everything away after the last riding class when I entered the stable.

He halted in front of the tack room's door, holding a couple of bridles. "Everything all right?"

I buried my hands in the pocket of my jeans and averted my gaze. "Sure."

"Hmm, it doesn't look like it," he said. "Mr. Bennett has been around more than usual this past week, and you've been way too quiet and reclusive. It ain't your style."

"I'm ... worried about my father, that's all."

He nodded then disappeared into the tack room. I ended up helping him finish things up, and after trying to make me talk again, he went home.

And I turned my attention to Argus.

He stood in the center of his stall, head down, white coat dull, muscles slim, and his scars and wounds too apparent.

A pang assaulted my heart. Poor horse. He deserved much better than what I was offering him. He could be beautiful, he could be strong, and he could be healthy, if he had the right caretaker. Definitely, I wasn't it.

I stepped into his stall and placed a few strawberries on the bucket over the closed lazy Susan. "You like these, don't you?" His ears shot up. I smiled, but it was a sad, defeated smile.

I pulled my phone out of my pocket and searched for animal control's number. I knew I had it somewhere in there. Argus turned to me as I pressed the call button. This was the right thing to do. I would tell Officer Michael that it wasn't working and that Argus could remain here until they found some other horse whisperer to send him to. I could help with the search if it would help make things go faster. He deserved better than me. I would convince Officer Michael to give him to someone else. I just ... I couldn't deal with this anymore.

Someone answered the call.

"Hi, I'm Han—"

"Hannah!" Eric's voice boomed from the stable's entrance, and I recoiled, dropping my phone. He marched to me, his eyes raging, his teeth gritted, one of his hands in a tight fist, and the other brandishing a magazine in the air. "Look at this!"

He shoved the magazine in my face. It was *The Polo World,* and Leo was on the cover, sitting on a fake throne, holding a big smile. The headline read: *The new number one in the world.*

Oh.

Shit.

With a growl, Eric threw the magazine across Argus's stall, causing the horse to flinch and neigh. I scurried out of there before he could hurt me without meaning to. Not that it did any good, because the rage shining in Eric's eyes told me I would be hurt out here too.

He paced in front of me. "Who does he think he is? He can't waltz in here and mess with my life. Everything was going so well until he showed up. He charms the people in my club, stares at my woman like a creep, wins our match, and steals my title. What's next? He's gonna come in here and steal you too?"

I gaped, unsure what to say. I didn't want to comfort him or tell him he was exaggerating, because, well, I didn't want to comfort him ever again. Honestly, I was hoping someone, not necessarily Leo, would come in here and save me.

My dream went as far as hoping that I could trust this someone, so the rest of the world wouldn't know what had occurred here.

Eric held my arm and pulled me close. "Aren't you going to say something?"

"I'm sorry?"

The force of his grasp increased. "Are you? I don't think you are. I think you want that Latin scum to be your Prince Charming, coming to your rescue on a white horse."

"What?"

"Don't play games with me. I know you've been flirting with him."

"*What?*"

He tossed my back into the stall's wood paneling. "You think I'm stupid? You think I don't see you staring back at him?"

"I ... I don't kn—"

His fist met my face.

I cried as pain burst in my cheek, my brain rattling inside my skull. My legs gave out, but Eric held me up, clasping both my elbows, his fingers sinking into my skin. "Bitch. That's what you are." He pulled his fist back, and I sucked in a sharp breath.

Argus kicked the stall door I hadn't locked, pushing it open, and trotted to us.

"What the ...?"

Argus reared, his front legs aiming at Eric. With wide eyes and open mouth, Eric let go of me and retreated a few steps.

Snorting, Argus kept advancing toward Eric, who kept retreating.

"Stupid horse," Eric shouted. He caught a whip from the wall and swatted it in the air, trying to keep Argus distant.

Argus came at him again, and Eric wacked the whip on his neck.

"No!" I cried.

With renewed rage, Argus trotted forward and

raised his legs on Eric, who smacked the whip across the horse's legs.

Argus whined when his hooves hit the ground, and he crumbled to the ground.

"God, no," I whispered.

Eric looked at me, his eyes filled with rage. "I'm going, but just because I need to. I'm leaving for the tournament tomorrow."

Growling, he turned and stalked away.

I sagged to the ground.

My face throbbed, the pounding spread down my neck. I grunted, wishing I had enough strength to get the first aid kit and check on Argus, and then crawl to the house, grab an ice bag, and loads of ibuprofen.

I tried to wrap my mind around what had just happened, but all thoughts escaped me when Argus inched back to me and lay beside me, whining. Thin red lines adorned his neck and his legs. He didn't touch me, but we were only a couple of inches apart, which showed me how much he cared. Crap, he had been my white horse and saved me. Who needed Prince Charming?

"Thank you," I whispered.

He was broken.

I was broken.

But perhaps we only needed to give in to each other to be saved.

My phone rang from inside Argus's stall, and I let it. It was probably Eric, and I couldn't bear to *think* of him right now.

I needed this. Argus and me. Quiet, side by side, just ... here.

The phone kept ringing and ringing and ringing.

Eric wouldn't be this insistent. Or would he? Hmm, what if it was my mother calling from the hospital? Fighting the pain that sparked all over my face and neck and shoulders, I crawled into Argus's stall, grabbed my phone, and answered it.

"Miss Taylor? This is Officer Michael. I recognized your number. Anything wrong with Argus?"

I stared into Argus's eyes. For a second, I considered telling him Argus was injured but shoved that idea out of my head.

"No, officer. I was actually calling you to let you know we're making progress."

"That's great!" he exclaimed.

When I ended the call, I saw there was a brand new message.

You better behave while I'm away. I won't tolerate any wrong moves from you. If you think I'm bad now, you are mistaken. I can be much, much worse and I don't think you want to see that. Love, Eric.

This man, this creep, bastard, sicko that had hit me wasn't my boyfriend. No, I didn't know this man. Once he was back from his trip, I would break things off with him, even if he broke my entire body.

"COME ON, BOY." I LEANED OVER THE RAIL AND spied into the bucket on the lazy Susan. The strawberries were still there. "You have to eat something."

Jimmy came back from his lunch break and stared at me. "I thought you were going to stay in bed all day."

"Me too," I muttered.

I did spend all Sunday and Monday in bed, with an ice pack on my face and ibuprofen in my system. The only time I left my bed was to check on Argus in the evening after all riding groups and classes were gone. The horse had been in the same position he was now: standing in the right back corner of his stall, his head down, his back to me.

This morning, Jimmy knocked on my door

until I scrambled out of bed, but I told him I wasn't feeling well.

"You haven't been feeling well often lately. Is there anything wrong, Miss Taylor?" he asked.

I told him I was tired and closed the door before he could take a good look at my face. Thankfully, the black bruise on my cheek was mostly gone now, and I could conceal it with makeup.

Jimmy walked up to me and stood by my side, his eyes on Argus. "When I got here yesterday morning he was in that exact position. I closed the front gate and opened his stall, taunting him to go stretch his legs in the arena, but he didn't move." He turned to me, frowning. "I did notice he has a new bruise on his neck, though. What happened, Miss Taylor?"

I shook my head, not sure what to say. I almost told him I had done that, but I didn't want Jimmy thinking I was now being violent toward Argus. So, I went with my next idea.

"I was working on him on Saturday, and he advanced on me. Eric was here and used the whip to defend me. If he hadn't done that, Argus would have stomped on me." My stomach churned with disgust. I hated lying to him.

"Oh." Jimmy's face fell. "I'm glad Mr. Bennett

was here to save you, but unfortunately, Argus is more withdrawn now."

"I know." I sighed. "I don't know what to do, Jimmy. I can't let Officer Michael come and take him."

Jimmy put his arm around my shoulders. "You know what I think, right?"

I groaned, letting my head fall on his shoulder. "I know."

"Whatever happened between the two of you was so bad that you can't ask Mr. Fernandes for help again?"

With wide eyes, I pushed away from him, my heart racing. "Who said anything happened between us?"

Jimmy chuckled. "Even if you're too blind to see it, I saw it, Miss Taylor. And I think Mr. Fernandes saw it too. The connection between you two. The way you two worked together. Even the chemistry."

Heat spread through my cheeks. "Jimmy!"

"What? I'm an old man now, but I was young once, and I know what those gooey eyes meant."

"Gooey eyes?" I snorted. "Jimmy, stop it. You're saying that only because you never really liked Eric."

He shrugged, with a you-know-it grin. "Perhaps."

"See? I knew it."

Then he was serious again. "I can imagine what happened that made you push him away, Miss Taylor," he said, causing the heat on my cheeks to increase. "But you should think of Argus and push your pride away for a while. Argus needs Mr. Fernandes's help."

I glanced at Argus. He was so still, so thin, he looked like a corpse. I shuddered. "Even if I gave in and agreed to ask for his help again, he's probably in Switzerland for a tournament. And usually these tournaments go on for two weeks or longer."

"Oh. That ain't good."

I shook my head, suddenly wishing there wasn't a tournament at the moment. "Nope. It isn't."

LATER THAT AFTERNOON, I HEADED TO THE hospital. I hadn't been here since my father was transferred to a private room.

I held my breath as I entered the room.

My father was sleeping, an IV needle pushed into his arm, a couple of other wires around his bicep and on his chest. According to our last phone conversation, my mother said he was out of the danger zone, but not completely out of the woods. He was still unconscious most of the time.

I approached his bed. He was thin as a stick. His skin was chalky white, his hair and beard overgrown. He looked ... old and weak. I ran my fingertips over the back of his hand, wishing I could give him an IV of pure strength.

Quietly, I sat on the love seat next to my mother, who was also sleeping on a sort of comfortable looking reclining armchair. Poor woman. I bet she never left his side other than to go home, take a shower, and eat something.

Hilary stepped into the room, carrying a tray with two cups of coffee and some pastries. Her blond hair was tied into a braid, and she wore a cute orange summer dress.

"Oh, hi," she said in hushed tones, placing the tray over a table. "I didn't know you were coming or I would have asked for another coffee."

"That's okay," I whispered. She took her cup and sat beside me. "How are things over here?"

She stared at me, her expression closed. "Where have you been?"

I frowned and considered lying. Then, I realized I didn't need to lie about everything. "Eric and I are having problems."

"And your owner didn't let you come visit your father?"

I flinched at the word owner. He wasn't my owner. He was my abuser. Tears filled my eyes. "I hate that you call him that."

"Well, it does look like it."

"Hil, please, I don't want to argue with you too. I'm tired of arguing."

She shifted her gaze to our father. "He's ... better, I guess. At least he's out of the rabbit hole. The doctor said that he'll probably need another surgery. Something about fixing his lung or whatever, but other than that, it's a waiting game."

"I wish we could do more."

"Me too." She sipped from her cup thoughtfully, then faced me. "Mr. Clarkson asked about you yesterday." Joel Clarkson was my father's right hand. He had been working with my father on the breeding farm for over fifteen years. "He's going to call you, I think."

"Oh. What for?"

"You're supposed to take care of the farm when Father isn't able to, and ... Mr. Clarkson wants you to go there and do your job."

As if my list of things to do wasn't already long enough. "What about you?"

She raised her eyebrow. "What about me?"

"Can't you help?"

She snorted, looking down at her cup. "Smelly horses and reeking stables aren't my thing."

I watched her profile. She was still young but she was already too beautiful. "What *is* your thing?"

Her head whipped so fast, I thought she might have hurt her neck. And that reminded me of my own head whipping back, hurting my neck, and other things I wished I could wipe away. I rested my hand over my neck, willing the memories away, and focused on Hilary.

She stared at me as if I were a stranger. "Why the sudden interest?"

"Jeez, are you going to keep answering my questions with more questions?"

She smiled. "Apparently."

I gently bumped my shoulder on hers. "Tell me."

She reached to her purse, fished out a notebook, and handed it to me. "I like fashion design."

I opened the notebook and my mouth fell open: a drawing of an elegant woman clad in a gorgeous blue gown took over the first page. I flipped to the next page, and a slightly different model wore slacks and a fancy lace cami. On the next page, the model wore jeans and a one-shoulder orange blouse. The details, the shadows, the textures ... all incredible.

"You drew these?"

"I did."

I gazed up at her. "I had no idea."

"It's not a big deal." She shrugged and stood, avoiding my eyes. "I'm gonna grab more coffee. Want some?"

I frowned. "Yeah, sure."

She zipped out of the room, and I returned my attention to the pages of the notebook. Incredible. No other word could express the drawings. The clothes varied from ball gowns to everyday casual to swimwear and gym clothes. She had everything in here. Even jewelry and watches and purses and shoes. Most were too fancy for my taste, but I was sure it would please a lot of women.

Crap, I had no idea what Hilary wanted to do in the future. Did she plan to go to college or fashion school?

The fact that this five-minute exchange had been the deepest in our lives saddened me. I had to fix it. I had to reach out to her and be her friend, even if we were too different. After all, she was my baby sister, and no bond *should* be stronger.

My cell phone dinged and I quickly muted it. I didn't want to wake up my mother. I went to the new messages and found one from an unknown number.

Unknown caller: *How are you doing?*

Me: *Who is it?*

Unknown caller: *It's me, guria.*

Me: *Bia?*

Bia: *Who else? So, how are you?*

Me: *I'm fine.*

Bia: *And your father?*

Me: *He's stable. Still unconscious.*

Before she could type another answer, I asked: *Why the interest?*

Bia: *Guess? My brother is over my shoul—*

The message came incomplete, and I wondered if I should keep the conversation going or ignore her. And him.

Five minutes later, my phone vibrated.

Bia: *Sorry. Leo grabbed my phone.*

Me: *Wait. You're texting me from Switzerland?*

Bia: *No. The team decided to sit this one out.*

Oh. My. God. It was like the stars had aligned. Before I could recover, Bia texted again.

Bia: *Leo wants to know how Argus is doing.*

Me: *The same.*

Bia: *Meu Deus, Leo asked me to type a book. Sorry, I'm not gonna keep relaying his messages. I'm out. Tchau!*

Me: *Bye.*

I stared at my phone for a few more seconds.

Leo was worried about Argus. He wasn't in Switzerland. Eric was in Switzerland and would stay there for two weeks or more. There was no other explanation. The stars *had* aligned.

25

I stopped my car on the road, a few feet from the gate of the O'Connor ranch—I tried to calculate the time right and hoped they were home, since I had given them one hour after the regular practice time—and questioned my sanity for the umpteenth time since confirming they stayed in the country.

What the hell? I wasn't a chicken. Leo had helped me before. He could help me again.

I pulled down the sun visor and checked my makeup in the vanity mirror. If it had depended on me, I would have come here yesterday, after exchanging messages with Bia, but because I wanted to make sure the bruises were gone, I waited. Now, they were gone and nobody would ever know.

Swallowing my fear, I hit the accelerator and entered the property. It looked like any property around here. A long, winding road that led up to the main house, which was a large, white, spectacle, three-story house with a wraparound porch. To the side, the main stable, usually painted red, was dark green. A large arena was behind it, leading up to a second stable. My ranch had a waterfall; this one had a small artificial lake. And both had lots and lots of land covered in brown grasses.

Their cars—five of them, including Leo's Grand Cherokee—were in the big parking area to the side of the house. I parked my car among them, grabbed my cell phone from the console, and stepped out.

As I approached the house, his parents opened the door and stepped onto the porch.

His mother, Agnes, had her hair pulled into a loose ponytail and wore a green cotton sundress with a flowing skirt. His father, João Pedro, wore a brown *bombacha*, a blue sash around his waist, white shirt, and suede cowboy boots. He was holding something like a wooden cone ... with a silver straw?

"*Boa tarde*," he said, his accent heavy, then

shook his head. "Sorry, force of habit. Good afternoon, Miss Taylor."

"Hello, Mr. Fernandes, Mrs. Fernandes."

"*Por favor,* call us by our first names," Agnes said, waving her hand at me. "We almost never call someone by their last name in Brazil." She ushered me inside the house, and I smiled.

I couldn't help looking around. When the O'Connors still lived here, this house was as grandiose on the inside as the outside, with imposing neutral-toned furniture, priceless paintings and decor pieces, Persian rugs, and crystal chandeliers. Now, the furniture and decoration had changed, giving place to more rustic, more friendly tones. Large, reclining sofas, with several mismatching pillows thrown everywhere, including the floor, and there were no rugs, almost no paintings, and lots of family portraits. It was warm and inviting and comforting.

We crossed the large hallway leading to the kitchen, and I glanced over the portraits on the walls. All about polo. All of them, including João Pedro, playing polo. No ceremony awards, no championship podiums. Just them, on their horses, running around with big smiles.

In the kitchen, Agnes went directly to the island and resumed chopping onions. João Pedro leaned on the counter beside her.

He took a sip of whatever he was drinking out of that odd ... cup, then turned his smile to me. "What do we owe your lovely visit?"

I inhaled sharply, then burst out, "I'm having trouble with a mistreated horse and I wanted to ask Leonardo for help."

"Ah yes, he's good with horses," Agnes said. "He told us a little about your horse, about what happened to him. Such a shame, poor animal."

Leonardo had talked about Argus—about me—to his parents? Crap.

João Pedro reached over to a thermal bottle, squeezed hot water from it to the thing he had in hand, then passed it to Agnes. He caught my gaze and laughed. "This is called *chimarrão*. It's a typical drink from the south of Brazil. It's like tea."

"But it's not sweet," Agnes added, before sipping from the silver straw. "This"—she pointed to the cup—"is called *cuia*, and this"—she pointed to the straw—"is called *bomba*."

When she was done with the *chimarrão*, she added more hot water and gave the *cuia* to her husband.

"So." I clasped my hands together. "Is Leonardo home?"

"Yes," Agnes said. "He's with the others about a mile that way." She pointed her finger to the door, supposedly the direction they were at.

"Near the lake," I said.

"Exactly," she said. "Of course, you probably know this ranch better than we do."

I started for the back door, but João Pedro's words stopped me. "You're going to walk there? They rode their horses. Why don't you take one of our horses?"

Me? Riding a horse? "Hmm, no, thanks. I need the exercise."

I hurried out before they could see the bright red color spread over my face.

I need the exercise? What crap of a response was that?

As I walked the path leading to the lake, I almost regretted saying 'no' to a horse. The sun was baking my head—I had left my hat in my car—and I was pretty sure my tank top had a sweat blotch on the back.

Peachy.

I pulled my hair up in a ponytail and kept on marching. The last three hundred yards were easier, though, as it was slightly downhill.

After twenty minutes of this nonsense, I saw them and halted, my mouth open.

Their horses were tied to a tree to my right, and they were driving trucks—monster trucks—in a race of sorts. I resumed walking, getting closer to their improvised race field, and observed the game.

Guilherme drove an orange and white truck, with Pedro in the passenger seat. Every few seconds, Pedro put his arm out, tapped hard on the door, and yelled, as if to taunt the others. Ricardo drove a blue truck with white and black lines. He also yelled a couple of times, but he mostly just laughed. Leo drove a black and red truck, with Bia seated beside him. From what I could see, he had a cowboy hat on, but no shirt. And that was confirmed when he put his head out through the window and howled, showing off his bare shoulders, while Bia bumped her hands on the door, her grin spreading from ear to ear.

Gosh, they were crazy.

Good crazy. But crazy.

And apparently, they knew how to have fun.

Ricardo hit the brakes and honked the horn three times. It must have been some sort of signal, because the other two trucks came to a stop right after. He pointed to me, and all heads turned my way.

Leo's eyes widened, and a slow smile spread

over his mouth. He started the truck again and drove it close to the edge of the field, skidding to a stop a couple of yards from where I stood.

My heartbeat skyrocket as he got out of the truck and removed his hat. He was shirtless, and his chiseled chest and abs glistened with a thin layer of sweat. I couldn't help but ogle his body, down to the small patch of dark hair poking from under the waist of his fitted jeans.

Lord, help me!

"Hey, *guria!*" Bia shouted. She was seated with half of her body out of the truck's window. "What are you doing here?"

"I ... I ..."

"Don't bother her, Bia." Leo jogged to me, his hair damp, framing the sharp lines of his face, and emphasizing the green-blue shade of his eyes. I was doomed. "Hey! What are you doing here?"

"I ... I ..."

"Hey." He stood right in front of me, his lean body looming too close to mine. I could actually *feel* the heat coming from him. "I didn't mean it as a bad thing. I'm surprised but glad you're here."

Well, I was here on a mission and wouldn't fall for his charms.

I looked around, searching for any goddamn topic to distract me.

I gestured toward the field. "You're destroying it." Before their little game, the grass was like a shiny carpet for the horses to exercise. Now, the grass was mostly gone, and mud took over.

"Yeah, but there are lots of acres on this property, and we only keep a dozen horses at this ranch." He looked around me. "How did you get here?"

"I walked."

His eyes widened. "You walked? From your ranch ...?"

"Of course not. I parked my car at your house. Your father offered me a horse, but I preferred the walk."

"First, you prefer walking than riding a horse? Then you like horses less than I thought you did. Second"—he closed his mouth for a second, and his jaw ticked—"you talked to my father?"

"Yes. Your parents told me you were out here."

He took a step closer and I held my ground, tilting my head up to stare into his eyes. "So, you *were* looking for me." The gleam in his eyes changed from surprised to curious.

I was about to play a dangerous game. "Yes. I need your—"

A loud honk startled me, and I lost my words. I looked to the source, but only saw Guilherme and Ricardo exiting their trucks, which they parked flanking Leo's. They greeted me as if I was a regular guest in their house. I waved back.

"Come on." With his hand on my back, Leo led me closer to his truck. It was huge, with the wheels probably around five feet in diameter.

Leo climbed over the wheel and opened the passenger door. "*Vai com o* Ricardo," he said to Bia.

With a wicked grin, she jumped off the truck. "Have fun," she whispered and winked, before racing to her older brother's truck.

"She's in!" Leo shouted to his brothers, jumping down. They nodded before driving away.

"What?" I turned to Leo, my eyes wide.

He offered me the same wicked grin Bia had just showed me and beckoned me to enter his truck. "Come on. It'll be fun. I promise."

His hand gently wrapped around my waist—I suppressed a shiver—and slightly pushed me toward his truck. I hesitated and turned my back to the truck.

My gaze went directly to his mouth. I shook my head and forced myself to look into his eyes.

With his boyish grin back on, he tugged me at the waist and nodded to the truck's door. "Try it for thirty seconds. If you don't like it, tell me and I'll let you out. Okay?"

"Okay."

Leo brought his other hand to my waist and helped me up, instructing me where to put my feet to climb this monster. He climbed up behind me. Remaining outside the truck, he grabbed the belt and leaned over to buckle the seat belt. I sucked in a deep breath when his arm brushed against my breasts, and regretted it half a second later as his delicious spicy wooden scent mixed with sweat flooded my senses. His head snapped to mine. Too close. Too, too close. My gaze shifted to his mouth again.

We stayed there for what seemed like an eternity, our breathing growing louder, our eyes flickering from our mouths to our eyes and back again. I saw his hands reaching over, but he pulled away before touching me.

Cursing in Portuguese, he jumped down, jogged around the truck, climbed to his seat behind the wheel, and put on his seat belt.

With a lopsided grin, he said, "Are you ready?"

Before I could answer, he turned the keys and the engine roared to life. The truck vibrated and hummed, and adrenaline began working in my system.

Okay, this can be fun.

"Now, for the right soundtrack." He turned on the stereo to *Truck Yeah* by Tim McGraw, and I smiled.

He hit the gas and we were off. I slapped my hand over the door and held on tight as he sped up, going directly into Ricardo's path. I tensed with each yard he drove.

"What are you doing?" I asked, recoiling into the seat.

"Wait," Leo whispered.

They were a few yards away when both turned their trucks to opposite sides. I was yanked to the side and actually laughed as the tension bubble was gone.

"*Galinha*," Leo cried out of his window.

Ricardo yelled something back, but with the music, the engines, and the language barrier, I couldn't make out a syllable.

Then we were in Guilherme's path. This time, Leo held on. I watched his profile as he stared at his cousin, defiance in his expression, a sense of power in his features. It was hot. My gaze traveled down to his shirtless torso, to his taut muscles and six-pack abs. He was incredibly hot.

I fanned myself, wishing I could jump into the lake to cool off.

I couldn't deny it anymore. I had admitted to myself I didn't love Eric anymore, that I needed to break things off between us, and I needed to be honest right now too.

I was into Leo. I was into him way too much. Maybe it was because he was the most gorgeous and hottest guy I had ever laid eyes on, or maybe it was because he cared about horses as much as I did, or maybe it was because he came into my life during a bad moment and made things a little better. Or maybe it was all of the above and more. I didn't care about the reason, I just cared that I now could breathe again, that I could actually think about him, about his body, about his mouth, about his smile, without feeling guilty, without telling myself it was a fleeting crush.

It wasn't.

However, things weren't that simple. Even if Leo still wanted me, I had to solve heap loads of problems I had with Eric first. In my mind, Eric wasn't my boyfriend anymore. He hadn't been since I first realized I didn't love him anymore, and it only got worse after he hit me. But in Eric's mind, I was still his girlfriend.

My attention was brought back to the present when Leo said, "Watch this."

He was focused on the game and kept on driving straight to Guilherme's truck.

I sank into the seat, regretting my decision to have entered the truck.

"Don't worry. He'll back out. He always does." Leo quickly glanced at me, then past me, and he frowned. "*Droga*." I was about to look to the side, to whatever he had seen, when he reached over with his right hand and clasped my leg just above my knee. I held my breath. "Hold on."

And I did. He probably didn't mean it like it sounded, but I grabbed his arm for dear life, bringing his hand up my leg a little without really meaning to. His skin was hot, and his muscles were hard under my palm.

He hissed. "I hate to say this, but we're gonna crash if I don't have my hand back."

I let go quickly. "Sorry."

"Don't be sorry." With a lopsided grin, he turned the truck ninety degrees to the left, and, after ten seconds, he turned one hundred and twenty degrees to the right.

That was when I saw Ricardo's truck coming from the right, flying past Guilherme's truck and shaving inches off it. If Leo hadn't seen Ricardo coming, he would have hit us, right on my side.

"*Veado*," Ricardo yelled from the open window

of his truck. One more Portuguese word I didn't know.

Slowing down, Leo drove his truck to the edge of the field. He turned to me, his eyes shining. "Don't ever be sorry for touching me, *morena*. For letting me touch you." My breath hitched. Oh crap.

He cursed under his breath and accelerated.

I watched over my shoulder and saw Guilherme coming at us. He missed us by a few inches, and that brought a whole new level of worry.

"Do you guys ever crash?"

Leo stepped on the gas and drove away from Guilherme. "Yup. All the time."

"Do you ever get *really* hurt?"

"Not really. Just a few scratches here and there." He shot me a devilish grin, and my heart rate went up. "Don't worry. I won't let you get hurt."

His words should have brought assurance to me, but instead, I flinched, remembering similar words Eric said to me not long ago. *You know I would never hurt you.*

What if all men were like Eric? Charming, lying, deceiving, abusing?

When I noticed, I had recoiled from Leo, my side glued to the door.

He turned the truck to the right, avoiding Guilherme's maneuver and causing me to move closer. Once the truck was straight, I hurried to the corner again.

"What's wrong?" Leo asked, his tone laced with worry.

"Nothing."

"I don't think so." Leo glanced at me, his eyes pleading. "Talk to me. You know you can tell me anything."

I couldn't. If I told him, he would make me go to the police, and I couldn't do that. Not because I was afraid Eric would be more enraged and come after me. No. I actually thought that would stop him and make him stay away. But it would ruin the lives and careers and businesses of everyone around us. The club, the ranch, the breeding farm, Eric's family business, even the United States Polo Association would be tainted in this mess. I couldn't bring myself to be the cause of all that. No. I had to find a way to deal with it quietly.

"It's nothing," I whispered.

Leo jerked the wheel to the right, missing Ricardo's truck by a few inches, then he turned to me. "Talk to me, *morena*." Those eyes were mesmerizing, and his voice, with its alluring accent, wrapped around me, cradling me almost like his arms had done before. "I can see something is wrong. Please, *morena*, tell me."

No. Leo wasn't like Eric and would never be like Eric, but I still couldn't tell him anything.

"I can't—"

It all happened too fast. The truck was shaken out of its path. A loud smashing and grinding sound rang in my ears. My body jarred to the side, and the back of my head bumped the door frame.

Then it went quiet for about twenty seconds.

"*Meu Deus*," someone said.

"Leo! Hannah!" someone else shouted.

I heard metal scraping against metal, and felt a hand on my cheek. "Hannah. Wake up."

I tried opening my eyes, but my head spun and my chest hurt.

Leo's voice came next. "Hannah, are you okay?"

"We should take her to the hospital," Bia suggested.

I fought against the dizziness and fluttered my eyes open. "I'm fine."

Bia stood by the open door with Ricardo, while Guilherme and Pedro waited on the ground.

Leo was perched over the seat on my side, his features etched with apprehension, but otherwise no injuries.

"Are you okay?" I asked.

A smile tugged the corner of his lips up. "I'm okay. How about you?"

I rubbed the back of my head. I could feel a bump coming to life already, but other than that and the place where the seat belt had tightened against my chest, I was okay.

"Me too."

"Are you sure?" Bia asked.

I tried turning to her, but dizziness assaulted me. "I am." I took a deep breath and sat straighter. "What happened?"

"Sorry," Leo muttered. "I was paying more attention to our conversation than to the game and didn't see Gui coming at us from the side."

"I totally expected you to turn!" Guilherme shouted from the ground.

"I know," Leo shouted back. He took my hand in his. "I'm sorry."

On purpose, Bia cleared her throat before jumping down and pulling Ricardo with her. I would have flipped her off or rolled my eyes at her, but my head spun thinking about it. However, with Leo so close and staring at me like he needed to pull me onto his lap and take care of me, my head would've spun anyway.

I averted my eyes. "How bad is the truck?"

"I didn't go out yet, but it doesn't look like anything major. It's not easy to put a dent on a monster truck."

"That's good, I guess."

He scooted back to his seat, his eyes clouded. "So the game is over. You can finally tell me why you came here."

His tone was ... annoyed? I couldn't tell exactly, but it was off.

All of a sudden, I felt too self-conscious and stupid. Self-doubt joined the party, and I wasn't sure I could ask him for help.

"I ... I ... never mind," I whispered, turning my back to him and getting ready to jump down.

"Where's the boyfriend?"

That stopped me. I ended up scooting back to my seat and facing him—which, with his goddamn looks and no shirt, was hard to accomplish without drooling. "First, I think you know where he is. Second, I don't consider him my boyfriend anymore."

The meaning wasn't lost to him. "But he still considers you his girlfriend."

"Well, I haven't tried to break things off yet. Once he's back from Switzerland, I'll find a way to end it."

"Why?"

Fear crawled in my chest. Had he seen too much in my eyes? "Why what?"

"Why are you breaking things off with him?"

I swallowed. "Things aren't working anymore. They haven't been for the longest time, but now I can see it more clearly."

I didn't wait for more questions or insinuations. I turned and jumped out. The others were nowhere to be seen, their trucks parked on the edge of the field, their horses gone. Only one horse remained. Minuano.

I didn't know what else to say or do, so I just started walking away—until his hand closed around my elbow and he pulled me to him. I squealed as my chest crashed against his, my hands over his naked, dear Lord, pecs.

With wide eyes, I pulled my hands away. "For goodness sake, put on a shirt!"

He threw his head back and laughed out loud. His laughter was hearty and filled warmth to my core. When he was done, he leaned his head down toward mine, his eyes on mine. "Why? Can't handle it?" I gulped, trying and failing to think of an answer. Once again, I started walking away. "So you came here to tease me?" Leo asked.

"No."

"Then what for?"

I stopped walking and looked at him. "I need your help. Again." I sighed. "I have two or three weeks to make Argus noticeably better before animal control comes to check on him again, but he withdrew from me and nothing I do works. Though he seemed to have a soft spot for you."

He offered me his boyish grin, and my heart soared. "I know someone else who has a soft spot for me."

I rolled my eyes. "What? You're crazy."

"Maybe I am." His eyes shone with mischief. "So, do you want my help or not."

I sighed in defeat. "Yes, I want your help."

He extended his hand to me and I took it. We shook on it.

"When do we start?" he asked in a teasing tone.

Shaking my head, I resumed my long walk back to where my car was parked. "Please, put a shirt on."

He laughed out loud, and I knew I was doomed.

26

"WHAT'S THAT SMILE FOR?"

I stopped humming one of Carrie Underwood's songs and glanced over my shoulder. Jimmy had entered the stable. I shrugged and kept on humming and brushing Dakota's shiny coat. She liked being brushed, and I hadn't done that myself in a long time.

"Wait." Jimmy halted outside her stall. "It's way too early, you're smiling, and you're brushing a horse." He squinted at me. "What happened?"

"Nothing," I muttered.

In truth, I didn't know why I had slept so well and woken up feeling even better. My father was in the hospital, Eric was away but I could feel the shackles on my ankles, I hadn't called Mr. Clarkson to discuss my father's farm, though I received a call from Mr. Nash about selling the ranch, and Argus hadn't accepted the strawberries I brought him this morning. Nothing good there. Except for the previous day and the ride my feelings took on a roller coaster. I couldn't stop thinking about the adrenaline of riding with Leo in his monster truck, the way he looked at me, the way he touched me.

Shaking my head, I dropped my arm and stepped out of Dakota's stall.

Two and a half years ago, I had felt somewhat like this with Eric. I had felt almost as attracted and intoxicated by Eric as I felt for Leo now. Almost. I could feel the difference. I had been an easily impressed teenager with Eric, and I was now a battered, knowing woman with Leo. Still, my natural defense system was alert, and I felt stupid—and damn good—for finally admitting my feelings for Leo to myself.

"What?" Jimmy asked as I walked past him. "What did I say?"

"Nothing," I repeated, realizing it was not even seven in the morning yet. "What are you doing here so early?"

Jimmy reached for a pair of bridle and reins

hanging over Chip's stall door. "Couldn't sleep so I thought I should come in and start early."

I nodded, knowing all too well how he felt. Right after grandma's and Hercules' death and my move to the ranch, I couldn't sleep either. Each noise, each crack, each neigh woke me up. At first, I recoiled under my covers, but after a couple of weeks, I just shot up and went to the stables to work. With time, I got used to the noises and the dark and slept through. That didn't mean I was completely unafraid of being alone here, though.

Jimmy opened the door, put the halter around Chip's face, and led him out to the arena.

I settled the brush in its place on a shelf along the wall, then picked Belle to take her out with Chip to exercise. At the arena, I let her run free, trusting Jimmy would take care of both of them. Back inside, I looked around, wondering what I should do next.

My gaze fell on the last stall in the corridor. Argus's stall. As usual, he was curled up in a corner.

Gathering my patience and determination, I grabbed the brush from the shelf and approached him.

With him, slow was the way to go, so I halted before the door of his stall. "Hey, boy." I waited for him to acknowledge me before making any other move.

It took him over ten minutes to turn his muzzle and look at me.

"Can I come in?" I shook my head. Asking can I come in to a horse? I was clearly going nuts.

His gaze never wandered off mine as I opened the door, stepped in, and closed the door again. I leaned against the wooden railing and waited.

Once again, the pain and mistrust in his eyes brought a painful squeeze to my heart. But, behind it all, I could see he was fighting his own demons. By our history, I knew he wanted to trust me. He just didn't know how.

My cell phone began ringing, and he curled up again, snorting.

"Sorry, sorry," I said, exiting the stall. I fished my phone from my pocket and stared at the screen.

Eric. Calling at 7:20 a.m. As if I would answer him.

I pressed the end button and stuffed the phone back into my pocket.

It ranged again and Argus neighed.

I reached for my phone, turned it off, and gave up the idea of entering Argus's stall in the next hour.

This early and so much trouble. Coffee. I needed more coffee.

I threw the brush back on the shelf and marched out of the stable just as a black horse and a rider trotted up the road, coming right at me.

My heart stopped.

Matching his horse, Leo was dressed in a black shirt and dark jeans. His hair was swept back with the wind, and he smiled when he saw me.

I couldn't help but smile back. For just a second. Then I remembered he was here on business and I needed to keep my distance from him.

He brought Minuano to a stop by my side.

"Hey," he said, slipping off his horse.

"Hi," I muttered, looking at my feet. "I was about to make coffee. Want some?"

"Sure. Can I put Minuano inside?"

"Of course."

He walked a couple of steps backward, his eyes steady on mine, making my heart beat faster. When he turned to the stable, I took a deep, relieving breath and dashed inside the house.

I mumbled things like "get a grip," "settle down, girl," and "control your heart" while putting water in the coffee machine.

Like a girly girl, I looked at my reflection on

the back glass door. I seemed okay in my tank top, jeans, and boots. Didn't I?

I realized how stupid I was acting and cursed myself for being this far gone. The same chant—" get a grip," "settle down, girl," and "control your heart"—came back to my mind. It wouldn't be easy.

I heard the front door opening and closing, and then his footsteps as he crossed the hallway.

When Leo entered the kitchen, I thought my skin would melt with anticipation. He halted past the doorway, and his eyes locked on mine. And, as if we had turned on a switch, the kitchen felt alight, charged with too much energy, ready to blow. The room was quickly filling with raw desire and want and longing, and I would drown in it.

He took two long strides and stopped again in front of the island. It was the only thing between us, and it felt as if there wasn't *and* there was too much space between us.

The coffee maker beeped, and, clearing my throat, I stripped my gaze from his and turned to it. I busied myself by serving two mugs of coffee and cutting two pieces of chocolate chip cake. Without looking at him, I set everything on the table and sat down.

I gestured to the chair across the table, and a couple of seconds later, Leo sat down.

"You're here early. Fell off your bed?" I asked, trying to break the ice. Or, better, to cool down the heat. I regretted the moment I raised my eyes to his and was knocked out with his intense stare.

"Something like that." He sipped from his mug. "I didn't think you would be up yet."

"And you came even so?"

He nodded. "I planned on starting with Argus. More like just staying by his side and letting him get used to me again until you woke up."

My heart fluttered. First, because he admitted that he thought about me when I wasn't with him. Second, because he really wanted to help me with Argus.

I averted my eyes and picked at the cake with my fork.

We talked a little bit more. He asked about my father, and I told him my father was hanging in there. He asked if I had baked the cake, and I told him that I had bought it at a bakery in town. He asked if I knew how to cook, I said yes. I asked him if he knew how to cook, he said yes. Then I pressed my mouth closed so I wouldn't ask him to cook for me sometime.

After we ate and drank, we took our plates to

the sink, and I refilled my mug while he loaded the dishwasher. Besides the charged air, it flowed as if we did this kind of thing every day. The way our movements looked like puzzle pieces, completing each other. The way we almost touched each other when reaching for things. The way my body turned to his whenever he was too close.

I took a deep breath when I realized Jimmy was right. We were acting just like he had said we did.

In that synchrony, Leo and I walked out of the house and into the stable.

Minuano was in the stall beside Argus's. Belle and Chip were back inside, and Jimmy was in Black Jack's stall, brushing his coat.

"Mr. Fernandes." Jimmy smiled. "Good to see you here."

Leo nodded. "Hey, Jimmy."

We walked all the way to the end and stood in front of Argus's stall. The horse was in his usual corner, but this time he was standing up.

"What has he eaten today?" Leo asked.

I glanced over the rail. The strawberries were still in the bucket on the lazy Susan. "Nothing."

He tilted his head my way and looked into my eyes. "We're gonna help him, and he'll be better in no time." He touched my arm with his warm hand

—I shivered—and at that moment, I totally believed him.

Watching Leo as he entered and stood tall inside Argus's stall—his chest puffed, his shoulders squared, his stance sure and proud—I realized once more how incredibly hot he was, and how much I was into him.

This feeling was different, whatever it was. Love? No, not yet. But, if it kept growing at this rate, it soon would be. When I was a teenager and fell for Eric, I remembered being in over my head. He was a man; I was a young, silly girl. It was overwhelming in an I-went-to-the-30-Seconds-to-Mars-concert-and-touched-Jared-Leto kind of way.

With Leo, it was a conscious thing. The overwhelming feeling was controlled in some ways. It was allowed, and so much more powerful because of that.

I sighed, not sure how long I could stay beside him and not surrender.

Like me, Leo knew Argus needed time. His patience amazed me.

Over fifteen minutes passed before Argus spied over and snorted at Leo.

After another ten minutes, the horse turned his body toward Leo.

After another fifteen minutes or so, when I was

about to sit down on a bench because my legs were starting to hurt, Argus took one step in Leo's direction. The next step came faster, after only seven minutes. The third didn't take four.

Argus was standing two feet from Leo.

Without turning, Leo reached back and beckoned me to come to him with his hand.

"What?" I asked in a low tone, afraid of disrupting their progress.

He glanced over his shoulder and mouthed, "Come."

Okay. I was deliberate with my steps as I entered the stall and stood beside Leo. Snorting, Argus retreated a step. I was about to retreat too, but Leo's hand on my back stopped me.

He pointed to the lazy Susan. "Take the strawberries."

Careful with my movements, I did as he said, and stood beside him again. His hand snaked around my waist, and he pulled me in front of him, my back flush with his chest, my butt pressing right under his hips. Not the best place and time to feel a heat low in my belly, but I couldn't really control it.

"Don't move," he whispered in my ear, and I shivered.

One of his hands remained around my waist,

while the other clasped my arm and extended it forward, offering the strawberries to Argus.

I gulped.

Snorting, Argus trotted in a circle in the little open space, stomping his hooves loudly against the ground.

I shrunk into Leo.

"I'm here, *morena*," he whispered, his hot breath brushing against my skin. I wanted to melt into him, to pull his arms tighter around me, to—

Argus stopped right in front of me, his ears alert and his body tense.

Painfully slow, the horse bowed down and took a few strawberries from my hand. He swallowed them, then took the rest, but he didn't raise his muzzle this time. Instead, he nudged my hand. I gasped.

He nudged it again, and I slid my hand under his chin, feeling his silky coat for the first time. Tears clouded my vision as I reached to him with my other hand and caressed his cheek.

As if waking up from a dream, Argus pulled back, snorting.

I stared as the horse recoiled to his corner. What had I done wrong?

Leo shook me from my daze when his hand pressed against my side.

With a closed-mouth smile, he held my hand and pulled me out of Argus's stall.

Jimmy stood right there, with a smile of his own. "That was incredible," he said. "After the past three days, this was incredible. And he let you touch him, Miss Taylor. He never lets me touch him. Only the vet touches him, and that's by force, not because he lets him."

It was incredible, and it wasn't. I felt great that he had let me touch him, and that he had asked for it, but now that it was gone, I … missed it. I glanced over my shoulder. Argus lay on the ground, his head low.

"Hey," Leo said, and I brought my attention back to him. "It was progress. A great progress."

I nodded. Yes, it was progress and it was larger than the baby steps I thought we would experience right away. However, baby steps didn't seem enough anymore.

I KNEW THINGS WOULDN'T GET EASIER WITH ARGUS just because he had touched me, because he allowed me to touch him, but deep down, I hoped it would.

Leo came early the next day, and it took us two hours to get Argus into the arena. After the exercise, the horse ate half a bucket of grain. I was eager to touch him again, but each time I approached him within three feet, he dashed away.

"Don't worry, *morena*," Leo said. "He'll come to you again."

I hoped Argus would do it soon. We had only a week more, maybe ten days to work it out before Eric came back. Not that I knew what difference having Argus well would make. Eric had made it clear he wanted the horse out of here, well or not. However, I told myself I was more worried about animal control coming to check on him and finding out Argus was regressing instead of improving.

On Monday, Leo came early in the morning, before his practice started. We tried the waiting game again, but Argus didn't eat and didn't allow me to get too close.

After Leo was gone, I stayed with Argus a little longer, but he didn't pay any attention to me. Frustrated, I went to the hospital and had lunch with my mother and Hilary. My father had had another surgery and was breathing on his own again. He had woken once or twice but didn't stay like that for long. The prospect was good, though the doctor had no idea when he would be able to go home.

I came back to the ranch before three and at around six, Jimmy was gone and I was out in the arena with Argus. Clouds appeared on the horizon, threatening to disrupt the nice, sunny days we had been having. I hoped it wasn't a big thunderstorm, because that wouldn't help with Argus's progress.

My heart sped up when I saw Leo driving into the ranch. He parked his SUV beside the stable and jogged to where I was, sitting over the wooden fence. His hair was damp, fresh out of a shower, and he wore his team's shirt and blue jeans.

"How is it going?" he asked, coming up the fence and sitting beside me.

"The same. He gets tired and lies down. Drinks lots of water, eats only enough not to pass out."

"At least he's exercising and eating, even if a little."

I sighed, my eyes on Argus as he galloped past us. "I know."

"Did you try touching again?"

I nodded. "But I used the old trick. Just stand there and wait for him to come. We played that game for over an hour this afternoon. He came close to me but didn't touch me. When I raised my hand, he trotted away."

Leo put his hand over my knee and squeezed it. "Give him time."

I raised my eyes to him, and his stare took my breath away. When would I *not* be this breathless around him?

"How was practice?" I asked, in need of something to distract me from his hand and his heart-wrenching stare.

"Good," he said, pulling his hand away. I had to restrain myself not to grab it and put it on my knee again. "Gui fell off his pony when he tried to steal the ball from me."

I gasped. "Is he okay?"

Leo laughed. "Oh yeah. We teased he's gonna be even more cuckoo after hitting his head, but he's fine."

"You guys are crazy."

"We're also fun."

"Yes, you are," I whispered, remembering the monster truck game.

For the next few minutes, we watched Argus as he ran along the arena. The silence between us was comfortable, and I actually felt like I wasn't alone.

When Argus stopped to drink some water, Leo turned to me. "So, my mother is making a Brazilian dish for dinner and she told me that I'm not allowed to eat at home if I don't bring you with me."

I gaped. "What?"

"She knows you're here alone and she wants to feed you, because according to her, you probably don't eat well."

I chuckled, my heart warming. Then my face fell as a thought came into my mind. "Leo, what did you tell your parents about me? I mean, they think I'm still Eric's girlfriend. They probably think the worst of me."

"*Pois então*." Leo ran his hand over his hair. "I kinda told my mom you're not dating that jackass anymore."

"What?"

"Why that face?"

"What face?"

"As if it was a lie."

I averted my eyes. "It's not a lie, but ... nobody else knows. I don't want people talking about it behind our backs. I need to solve this with Eric first, before everyone else finds out."

"My mother would never tell anyone," he said, his tone tight and a little disappointed. "In fact, my entire family would never tell anyone. I trust them."

"Sorry." I returned my eyes to his. "I didn't mean any disrespect." A small smile spread on my lips. "I think your family is pretty cool, actually."

His eyes lit up. "Does that mean you're coming?"

As much as I wanted to try a nice Brazilian dish, and see more of his life with his family, it wasn't right. He might have told his parents that I wasn't dating Eric anymore, but I would feel out of place and as if they were asking "what is she doing here" behind my back.

I jumped off the fence. "No." Dismayed with myself, I walked toward Argus along the fence. He stopped trotting when he sensed my approach. I slowed down, my hands to my sides, showing him I had good intentions.

A few moments later, Leo appeared by my side.

"I thought you were gone," I said, my eyes on Argus.

"I was calling my mother, letting her know you and I won't be having dinner with them."

I halted and stared at him. "What?"

He seemed disappointed. "Why do you sound so mad?"

"Because ..." I shut my mouth.

He took a step toward me, and his body loomed over mine. "Because you like when I spend more time with you, even though you don't want to admit it."

"Oh, I've admitted, all right, but I—"

His eyes bugged and he interrupted me. "You've admitted it? That you like me? When?" I walked around him, shaking my head. He gently clasped his hand around my arm and pulled me toward him. "*Morena*, tell me. Please." I averted my eyes, and he tilted his head toward me. "Don't make me beg."

I raised my chin and looked into his eyes, suddenly aware that I couldn't escape him. Even if I wanted to. And I wasn't sure I wanted to. "To myself. I've admitted it to myself. But—"

"No buts," he interrupted me. His hands snaked around my waist, pressing me against him. "I can't think of any reason not to kiss you right now."

Without giving me time to form a coherent sentence in my jumbled mind, Leo erased the last three inches separating his mouth from mine. His lips touched mine, tentatively at first, testing me, giving me time to back away, but I, too, couldn't think of any reason not to kiss him back. I *wanted* to kiss him, to taste him, to touch him.

He pulled away slightly and his eyes searched mine. To show him I wouldn't back out, I stood on tiptoes, sliding my hands up his arms, and licked his lower lip. He groaned before capturing my mouth with his and taking it all. And I willingly gave it to him.

His lips were soft and demanding, moving with mine in a perfect rhythm, and his taste was delicious. When I kissed him harder, stroking his tongue with mine, he groaned again. Then his hands slid down my legs, to my thighs, and tugged them up, around his waist. Without breaking the kiss, he backed us up, pinning me against the dirty fence. But dirt was the last thing on my mind as he pressed his hips against mine, and I could *feel* how much he wanted me. I whimpered, the heat in me increasing.

I almost died when his lips left mine, but I sighed in relief when he traced his tongue along my jaw and down my neck. I sunk my nails into his shoulders, pulling him closer, if that was even possible.

I had never felt like this. Eric never made me feel this hot, this needy, this wanted. Kissing Eric had been good, but this ... this was magical.

"*Delícia*," he whispered against my skin before gently biting the soft spot where my shoulder and my neck met.

I tugged his earlobe between my teeth, then ran my tongue behind it. He shivered.

Then his mouth was over my ear, but he didn't really touch it. He provoked me with his elaborate breath brushing against my skin. It made me crazy, just as I suspected he wanted. His hands slipped under my tank top, his skin hot on mine. His fingers teased the edge of my bra.

"I want you," he breathed out in a husky tone,

and to prove his point, he thrust his hips against mine once more, making me gasp.

I wanted him too. Right here, right now.

But I didn't feel free yet.

I tried to get through the heavy lust cloud in my head to tell him that, but his mouth was back on mine before I could utter a single letter, and I was lost once again. His kiss was ... perfect. The right equilibrium between hard and soft, demanding and asking, giving and taking. It was intoxicating and I was already becoming addicted to it. And to his touch, and to his scent, and to his body ...

I was taken. But I couldn't be. Not yet.

It took all the inner strength I had, but I lowered my legs, put my hands over his shoulders, and managed to push him away. Thinking I was probably playing, he pushed against me, but I held my arms between us.

Leo looked at me, confused. "What? I thought you were enjoying this."

"I-I was." More than I thought possible. Avoiding his inquisitive eyes, I looked past his shoulder to Argus. "But this isn't right."

He stepped in my way, making my eyes meet his. "Why not? You said you're not that guy's girlfriend anymore."

"I'm not. But he doesn't know that yet, and until he does, I don't think I'll feel ... free."

He frowned. "Free? You sound like you're his slave." If only he knew. "*Morena*, is there something you're not telling me?"

"No," I said too quickly. "No. Everything is fine." I watched him, the concern written across his expression. "I knew asking your help again would be a bad idea."

He took a long breath, stuffing his chest. "I respect you and that means I respect what you want too. If you want me to pretend we don't desire each other, I will try to." I squinted at him. "I promise I won't touch you, I won't kiss you, I won't say anything that suggests it, unless ... you make the first move."

"I won't make the first move."

One corner of his lips tugged up, and his eyes shone with mischief. "We'll see."

I crossed my arms. "Now what?"

With loving eyes, he reached to my arms, unknotted them, and took my hand in his. "Now, we work on Argus."

28

———

TRUE TO HIS WORDS, LEO DIDN'T TRY ANYTHING during the next two days. We spent the entire weekend together. We worked on Argus, we helped Jimmy, we got the riding classes ready, and we helped them when they were back.

Jimmy barbecued for us on Saturday evening —Leo insisted on putting a fillet on the grill.

"It's a *gaúcho* thing," he said.

Jimmy made a face at Leo, and he explained people who are born in the south of Brazil are called *gaúcho*.

I got a dose of my whiskey on the rocks to go with the barbecue, and offered them drinks. Jimmy had a beer, and Leo refused them all and grabbed a soda. I found it odd that a guy his age was refusing alcohol, but I didn't dwell on it.

The next day, Leo made us lunch—something called *carreteiro*—in which he used the leftover fillet from the barbecue, and it was delicious. We gazed at the stars while closing the stable doors, and he would leave with a frown, worried that I was alone on a ranch that had already been set on fire. We walked around the property, and I showed him where the waterfall was. He tried to push me in the water, but I dodged him. At that moment, his arm locked around my waist, and that was the only awkward moment of the entire weekend.

More importantly, Argus was responding well to the exercises. He even ate a full bucket of grain and a couple of strawberries from my hand on Sunday.

It was perfect.

On Monday, Leo came early, before his practice, and then in the evening.

Jimmy had just left when Leo brought Argus to the round pen and gave me his reins.

"What do I do?" I asked, taking the reins.

He leaned on the fence, and I tried to focus on his instructions, not on the fact that his gray polo shirt hugged his shoulders and arms like they were breathing him in, or that his dark jeans were fitted in the right places. I loved the fact that he always wore his black hat and matching black boots—like a true cowboy.

I shook my head and cursed myself for being this weak around him.

"Hold on to the reins and walk around with him," he said, as if that were the most normal thing in the world, especially with a mistreated horse. I raised my eyebrows at him and he smiled, taking my breath away. "Walk at different speeds. Pause. Retreat. He should remain half a foot behind you and do what you do."

"That's it?"

He nodded. "That's it."

It seemed simple enough.

I turned to Argus and looked into his eyes. "We're going for a stroll, okay, boy?" My fingers itched to reach up and touch him, but I held on. This was not the time and place. Maybe after we were done practicing, not before when I could spoil everything.

Argus didn't snort, didn't whine, and didn't blink.

Great.

I took a deep breath and tugged on the reins, giving the first step. He didn't come.

I looked at Leo with a now-what expression.

"Relax the reins and keep going," he explained. "If he doesn't go, then you stop after a few steps, but remember to keep the reins relaxed."

I tried again. With relax-the-reins in my mind, I gave the first step. And the second. And the third. I was about to stop on the fourth, but Argus moved, following me.

A smile threatened to burst on my face, but I shooed it away, lest I disrupt Argus's collaborative mood. I kept my lips straight, my mind calm, my posture firm but not imposing, and the reins relaxed. And I kept moving.

I increased my speed and Argus matched my steps, always half a step behind. I stopped. It took him a second to do it, but he stopped. When I walked slowly, Argus waited for two or three of my steps before giving one of his own, but he was coming. He was following me.

I halted once more, and this time he did it half a second later. I retreated—and that he didn't do. He actually snorted and stomped his foot.

Leo pushed away from the fence and started toward us, but I raised my hand, stopping him.

I turned to Argus and looked into his eyes. The urge to touch him grew within me. "What is it, boy? Hmm? Don't like walking backward? Me neither. It's strange and you never know where you're going, right? You can't see if there's any obstacle to trip over. I totally understand. But you know," I whispered, leaning closer. "I'm here and I'm taking care of you. I won't let you go through any obstacles you don't want to, okay?"

Argus nickered and my eyes widened. Had he really understood me and agreed with me? I glanced over my shoulder to where Leo was, and his proud smile was enough to make my pride rejoice.

I got ready and returned to the exercise. I pulled Argus forward first, on a speedy walk, and he came with me. I stopped, he stopped. I went forward again, walking normally, and he kept up with me. Without halting first, I started walking backward. Argus instantly stopped.

"Come on, boy, you can do it." I gently tugged on the reins.

He made a loud noise like a sigh and then, slowly, he moved backward.

I had to lock my body not to jump up and down, and held on to my hand before it stroked his white coat.

Calm, Hannah. He feels what you feel. Stay calm.

Argus and I played that game for over forty minutes, until he didn't hesitate stopping or retreating when I did.

"Good job, boy," I said, pulling the reins over his neck, so he could trot around the round pen without having them hanging and bothering him.

Whirling on my feet, I walked to where Leo was leaning against the fence and noticed Argus was coming with me. Leo raised one eyebrow at me, and I smiled.

I took two more steps before stopping. Argus stopped too.

I put a hand over my mouth to help me suppress the happy laughter trying to come out. Oh damn, the horse was following me *without* any reins or ropes!

I walked in a circle, and Argus followed my every step. I sped up, and he caught up with me. I stopped again, and he did too. I retreated and he did too.

With a big grin, I strolled to Leo with Argus in tow.

"Impressive," he said, his face alight.

"I'm impressed too," I whispered, afraid of scaring Argus. I turned to the horse again. "You can go exercise, boy." Instead of trotting away, he advanced a step. "What is it, boy?" I extended my arms to my sides, wary of moving too much, too sudden. Argus took another step toward me and nudged my forearm with his muzzle. I froze.

Slowly, Leo stood behind me, closer than necessary, clasped his hand around my elbow, and guided my hand to Argus's neck.

I held my breath.

Until my cell phone started ringing. Argus neighed and trotted away, and Leo closed his arms around me and pulled me back, probably trying to get me out of the way, in case Argus advanced on me.

"No, no, no." I cursed with some nasty words in my mind as I reached for my phone in my pocket. Eric's name flashed on the screen, and I only pressed the end button.

Leo offered me a knowing look. "Have you accepted any of his calls lately?"

I averted my eyes and shook my head. Deep down, I knew this action would make Eric even more upset than he already was, but I didn't know what to say to him, I didn't know what to tell him. I didn't *want* to tell him anything. Hi, how are you? Are you winning? I didn't care about that anymore.

Leo ran the back of his hand down my arm, and I shivered. "How about we finish for today?"

I checked the hour on my phone. It was almost eight and we hadn't dined yet. Would he stay for dinner? I hoped so.

"Sounds good," I said.

I picked up the ropes and whip from the floor while Leo grabbed Argus.

We walked across the arena in silence. I looked up, hoping to find some stars, but the sun hadn't set yet. When lowering my eyes, my gaze fell on Leo. I could stare at him forever, it seemed. So handsome, so alive, so sure of himself, so simple, so kind, and so caring about Argus ... and me.

Leo saw me staring. "What?"

I looked down as heat crept up on my face. "Nothing."

He put Argus in his stall with a bucketful of grain, and helped me check the other horses and to close up.

We exited the stable, and I worked up the nerve to invite him to stay longer, to have dinner with me and talk a little.

I opened my mouth, but he spoke first.

"I should get going," he said, his tone low.

My heart sank. "Oh. Okay."

He turned to the path leading to the parking lot, and I caught up with him.

He showed me a lopsided grin. "Are you doing the guy thing? Walking me to my car?"

I shrugged. "It's my house. I can do whatever I want."

His smile was gone, and his eyes were serious. "And you want to walk me to my car?"

I returned the stare. "I want to," I said, not sure where this bold feeling was coming from.

As we approached his car, butterflies assaulted my stomach. What was I doing? I was encouraging him. Perhaps I should stay behind and say goodbye from the path.

I couldn't make up my mind, and then we were standing by his SUV's door.

Every nerve in my body came alive when he turned around and stepped too close to me, his body hovering inches from mine, his intense eyes on mine. His eyes flicked down to my mouth, and I inhaled a sharp breath.

Groaning, Leo put his hands on my waist, whirled me around, pushed his hard body on mine, and pressed me against his car.

"You said you wouldn't try anything."

"I tried to resist," he said, his voice breathless. "I told you. It's hard. Especially when I notice you don't want me to resist. I *cannot* resist it."

I put my hands on his chest with every intention of pushing him away, but the muscles of his pecs under my palms caught my breath, and I melted. I was melting, and there was nothing I could do.

"You have no idea how much I want to kiss you right now," he said, his breath brushing against my lips, and I shivered.

"I think I do," I whispered.

"Please, *morena*, tell me I can kiss you." His hand clasped around my nape. "I *need* to kiss you."

Intoxicated, I wrapped my arms around his neck and pulled him down to me. *I* kissed him. Without wasting one millisecond, Leo kissed me back. I felt him relaxing in my arms, as if he had finally won a fight and now could celebrate the victory. He moaned when I entangled my tongue with his. His hand on my neck slid up, his finger entwining in my hair, and his other hand slipped under my tank top and clutched my waist. He took control and changed the rhythm of the kiss, his soft lips slowing down against mine, but his tongue going deeper. It was erotic, and my body was on fire, screaming for his.

My hands traveled south, and, almost without realizing what I was doing, I clasped his butt. Holy crap, what a butt! He moaned again and, as if my hands had triggered it, he grounded his hips forward, brushing his hardness against my pelvis. I gasped against his lips.

Suddenly, he pulled back and rested his forehead on mine, without loosening his grip on me.

"You're gonna kill me like that," he whispered, sounding more breathless than before.

"I'm sorry." I let my arms fall to my sides as shame invaded me. "Crap, now it's all ruined."

He reached for my hands. "What?"

"You and me, working together to help Argus. I made you agreed not to try anything, and now look at us."

"I said I wouldn't do anything unless you began it, and you did begin it."

I buried my face in my palms. "Damn it, what have I done?"

Leo's breath tickled over my ear. "You kissed me, and let me tell you, it was one hot kiss."

I punched his shoulder in a teasing way and instantly felt bad about it. A playful punch still reminded me of Eric's violence.

"I'm sorry," I muttered.

Leo held my hands and tilted his head so I would look at him. "Stop apologizing. It was great, why apologize?"

"Because we said we would keep distant from each other, and now it'll be even more awkward being around you when you come to help me with Argus. *If* you come help me with Argus again."

A minute passed, and I saw the change in his

expressions. He dropped my hands. "I'll keep my distance from you if that's what you want."

I stared into his eyes, putting as much confidence in my words as I could. "That's what I want," I lied.

There was too much going on, and I couldn't keep up. I would give anything to be free of Eric right now so Leo could take me wherever he wanted. But I wasn't free. That thought made me sick to my stomach. I wasn't free. As if slaves were still common things.

Leo looked to the side, to the darkness, his jaw tight. "Okay."

I stepped to the side, and he opened the door of his car. He was about to say something when my cell phone rang again.

Sighing, I pulled it up and saw it was Eric. Again.

Leo frowned at me, one of his fingers stroking the black ring. "You should pick that up."

He slipped inside his SUV and, without saying goodbye or waving or looking back, Leo drove away.

I stood in the same spot until I couldn't see him anymore. Then I pressed the end button of my phone and raced into the house, eager to get me a glass of whiskey.

29

I SHOULD HAVE EXPECTED IT, BUT I WAS SURPRISED when two days went by without seeing or hearing from Leo. When he left the ranch that night, he looked upset.

Putting on a pretty face when nothing in my life felt good was pretty challenging, but I had no choice other than to keep going. I worked on Argus, I ignored Eric's calls, I visited my father at the hospital, and I did my chores at the ranch.

One thing was better though. Hilary and I talked about her designs now, and she told me her dreams about going to fashion school and working her butt off—which was definitely a good surprise.

Friday morning, I had just taken Argus to exercise in the arena when Jimmy approached me.

"Is everything all right?" he asked.

I looked at him as if he had gone gaga. "Of course."

He took his hat off and ran his hand over his hair. "That ain't the truth, 'cause you're crankier than usual."

I snorted. "What?"

He went on about being stressful, my father in the hospital, having to run the ranch, and thinking about the breeding farm, my noticeable problems with Eric, my feelings for Leo ... I tuned him out, not in the mood to argue.

"You didn't hear a word I said," Jimmy complained.

I was about to tell him it wasn't true, that I had listened to plenty of it, but preferred to tune the rest out before I was rude to him, when my cell phone rang.

An unexpected name flashed on the screen.

"Hey, Megan," I said, walking along the arena's fence, away from Jimmy.

"Hi. How are you? How's your father?"

"He's doing better. At least, that's what the doctor tells us."

"Good. I'm glad. I hope he can go home soon."

Me too, however, at this point, we didn't know if he would come home or not.

I bit my tongue, eager to ask her why she was calling, but not wanting to sound rude.

"I wanted to check on you," she continued. "I kinda miss you at our teas. It's odd not seeing you and your mother there."

Stunned, I stopped walking. "Wow, Megan, thanks." I cleared my throat and decided to be a little polite. "So, how are you?"

"Same thing," she said, her chipper tone back on. "A little disappointed with Leonardo. After that kiss, he never got back to me. He doesn't even look at me at the club and he dodges any of my attempts of talking to him. I don't know what I did wrong."

Crap. "Maybe you didn't do anything wrong. Maybe you two just didn't click. Or maybe he realized he's into someone else. Or ... maybe he has a girlfriend back in Brazil."

"You know, I never stop to think about it." She sounded as if I had just given her the formula for making money grow on trees. "He's too gorgeous to be girlfriend-less. He must have a girl in Brazil, waiting for him."

Did he? No ... he would have told me the other day, wouldn't he?

She told me a bit more about her latest shopping spree and her plan of spending one week in the Bahamas with her family's yacht by the end of summer. She had been nice enough to call and ask if everything was okay with my father and me, the least I could do was actually pay attention to her and comment here and there, as a good friend would do.

Later that morning, I took Hilary and my mother to have lunch at a nice restaurant close to the hospital. Only God knew how much cafeteria food was in their system, and they needed something better to keep strong. It was a nice change, though my mother kept looking at her phone. If she was checking the time or expecting a call from the doctor, it didn't make a difference. She was eager to go back to my father's room, and that was nice, actually. I hadn't seen her this dedicated and worried about him in years. Perhaps once he was well, their relationship would improve too.

I was back to the ranch by two. There was a new riding group starting, and I wanted to be there to meet them and tell them the rules myself. They seemed like a good bunch and listened carefully to all I said.

By five, Paul was done with his classes, and by six, Jimmy was finished with his chores. I was tired and disappointed and thought about going in, taking my boots off, putting my feet up, and drinking a nice glass of whiskey. But I couldn't give up now. Eric would be back soon and ... I don't know. I just felt that if Argus was better, if he was stronger by the time my *dear* ex-boyfriend was back, I would be stronger too. And I needed all the strength—physical and emotional—I could get.

Argus was in his usual corner when I entered his stall.

"Hey, boy." I sat down with my back against the closed door. Who cared if the ground was dirty? Not my shorts, for sure.

Argus's ears perked up and he peeked at me for a moment, but then he went back to ignoring me.

"I wish you would let me touch you again," I whispered.

"Me too."

I shot up to my feet. Leo entered the stable, pulling Minuano by his side, his expression solemn.

Had he meant us or Argus? I wasn't sure and I wouldn't ask.

I tried to recover from the shock of seeing him here. "I thought you were mad at me or something."

"Not mad," he said, tying Minuano's reins to a stall's pillar. "Just frustrated, I guess."

"Sorry."

Leo walked up to Argus's stall, but he kept his distance. "I know I said I would behave and I'm sorry I kept pushing you. I can't help it." He glanced at the floor for a second. "I told you before, Hannah, I'm not a good guy, but I'm trying to be, and when you pull and push like that, the lines blur and I lose control."

"I don't mean to push and pull."

"I know. And that's something that frustrates me too." He took two steps forward, halting two inches from the door that separated us. "My motto is *be true to yourself*, and it's hard for me to see you acting exactly the opposite of it. You want me, I know you do, and when things start getting interesting, you push me away. I accept your decisions, believe me, I do. But I'm not sure I can keep playing this game."

As if a magnet pulled me, I leaned over the door to him. "What do you want from me?"

He brushed my hair back and placed the Douglas Iris around my ear, before cupping my cheek. I shivered with the contact of his warm skin. "You. Simple that."

That was still a mystery to me. He could have chosen any girl at the club, any girl from town. "Why me?"

He pulled his hand away and an instant chill settled over me. "They say we don't choose who we fall in love with, and for the first time in my life, I'm ready to believe a popular saying." He sighed. "But that's not entirely true. I may have accepted helping you with Argus the first time because I was curious and physically attracted to you and I wanted to know more about you, but things and feelings increased too much, too fast. I'm more attracted to you than I have ever been to anyone, more than I thought could be possible. We're good together, we work well together, and even our kisses are like explosives."

My mouth fell open. What the heck was he saying? "Leo ..."

"I apologize for taking two days to come here and tell you in person that I can't do this anymore." He retreated, his eyes still on mine. "I don't want to be the other guy. I don't want to sit and wait. I don't want to be the second choice. Unfortunately, I feel like all of these things when I'm around you, so ... I'm out."

Faster than I could wrap my mind around what was happening, Leo untied Minuano's reins, hopped over him, and galloped away.

Suddenly, more whiskey on the rocks seemed like an urgent need.

I DID DRINK MY WHISKEY ON THE ROCKS FRIDAY night. And Saturday night. And Sunday night. By Monday morning, I felt like I lived in a cycle: happy buzz at night, dreadful hangover the next day.

In his own right, Jimmy was furious with me. He worked on his chores and didn't speak to me all morning. He didn't even glance in my direction. I knew that if I asked what his problem was, or if I huffed or put myself in his path, he would burst and he would say all the things bottled inside him. Things like, what was I thinking, drinking as if the world were ending? What about Argus? What have you done to send Leonardo away? And why was I still dating Eric?

He never liked Eric, and I was sure the only good thing about this discussion would be when I told him I was ready to end things with Eric.

But I avoided him, because I wanted to avoid an argument.

It was late morning when I called my mother and canceled our lunch plans. With my headache, there was no way I could drive to town and sit through a loud cafeteria. Instead, I went into the house and lay in my bed, with boots and all.

Next thing I knew, someone was holding my elbow and shaking me awake.

I opened my mouth to send Jimmy to hell, but when I rolled to my back and saw who was seated by my side, I yelped and scooted as far as I could.

"Hi, baby," Eric said with a smile. "Aren't you happy I'm back?"

Fear clawed through my insides and clutched my heart. "I didn't know you were coming back today."

"Well, you would have known if you answered my calls." The smile was gone, and I recognized the new shine in his eyes. "What's going on? Why didn't you answer my calls? You didn't behave?"

I slid out of the bed and stood beside the window—it was dark out. I must have slept for hours.

"Eric, we need to talk."

"We sure do." He stood. His appearance always amazed me. Nobody would ever guess this handsome and elegant man could hit a woman as easily as he could ride his horse. "Have you behaved, baby?"

I straightened my back, willing the shaking of my body to go away. It was now or never. "I'm not your possession, Eric. In fact, I'm not your anything."

"No, baby. You're my everything."

"Eric, I don't want this anymore."

He narrowed his eyes. "I don't think I heard you right."

I took a deep breath. "We are over, Eric. Over. Please, leave my house."

Rage flooded his features as he marched to me and pinned me to the wall, his fingers digging painfully on my shoulders.

He leaned into me, his face hovering close to mine. "Baby, you don't have a choice. You're mine and that's the end of it."

With my hands on his chest, I shoved him back. "I'm not yours! Listen to yourself, Eric. You sound crazy."

I didn't even see his fist coming.

With the force of his punch, I fell over the dresser, knocking my jewelry box down, and slipped on the floor, over the glass pieces of the broken jewelry box. Pain erupted from under my cheek and spread like scalding water through my face and down my neck.

He grabbed my elbows and hoisted me up with a jerk, making my brain rattle inside my head. He sniffed me, his nose in my hair, and I turned my face away.

"You. Don't. Have. A. Choice," he barked, his teeth gritted.

A sob raked through me. I opened my mouth to protest, but it hurt. Everything hurt.

He half-carried, half-dragged me down the stairs, to the rarely used dining table. I whimpered with each step, fighting back screams and tears.

The table was set with the best china, lit candlesticks, and Eric had brought food from a local restaurant.

"I wanted to have a good night to celebrate since I won the tournament in Switzerland," he said, pushing me down into a chair. "And that's what we're going to do." He sat down on the chair at the head of the table and began uncorking the wine.

Oh ... God.

I felt like I was walking in a heavy fog, and each way I turned, I bumped headfirst into a concrete wall. My head throbbed, my neck stung, my shoulder screamed. I brushed my cheek, hoping my jaw wasn't broken, and touched several pieces of glass that seemed encrusted in my skin. I pulled one out and yelped. Blood stained my fingers.

"You brought that upon yourself," Eric said, serving wine to the flute set in front of me. "I don't want to hurt you, but each time you misbehave, each time you oppose what I tell you to do, I'll have to hurt you."

Tears sprung to my eyes.

This was the worst nightmare I had ever had. And the longest. Because Eric, that wonderful man I fell in love with years ago, who was a great polo player, who was friends with everyone, couldn't turn into this creepy, violent man.

He took my plate and served me a slice of steak and a portion of the side dishes. He set my plate back in front of me, served himself, and raised his wine glass to me.

"To my victory," he said, smiling.

Shit. This was not a nightmare.

A tear rolled down my cheek.

Reaching over the table, Eric shoved my fork in my hand. "Eat." I wouldn't, even if it got me killed. Ceremoniously, he cut his steak, put it in his mouth, and chewed it several times. When he swallowed it, he turned his evil eyes to me. "EAT!"

I flinched as his rage spilled over me.

Okay, enough was enough.

Drawing the rest of my courage and strength, I grabbed the table for support and lifted myself up.

I was able to limp two steps from the table before he was on me. His hand clasped around my throat, pressing the cuts and scratches, and he threw me over the table. My back slammed against the plates and glasses, and my head hit one of the pots. I screamed, trying to push him, to hit him, to kick him away.

He pushed my legs aside and leaned over me, his eyes in rage, his teeth bared, the muscles in his neck tense.

"Eric," I breathed. He would strangle me if he didn't ease his grip soon. "Please, stop this. Just ... let me go. Please."

"How many times do I have to say it?" His voice carried menace weaved in each syllable. "You're mine. Forever."

I didn't want to use this card, and I wasn't even sure I would really do it, but it was the only thing I had to say. "Let me go, or I'll call the police."

He threw his head back and laughed, releasing me. Relieved but shocked, I gasped for air and pushed myself up with my elbows. Still laughing, Eric took his phone from his pocket and thrust it into my chest.

"Go ahead. Call the police." I grabbed the phone before it slid to the floor and stared at him. What game was he playing? His smile changed, and he looked like a borderline lunatic. "You can call the cops in Santa Barbara and tell them every-thing. They won't believe a single word you say.

They were good friends with my father, and they really like me. In fact, they worship me."

My chest deflated. He could be bluffing, of course, but I believed him. I really believed him. Like everyone else, the cops were under his charms.

Eric approached me with deliberate steps. I recoiled, thinking about crawling over the table to the other side. But what good would that do? He would catch up with me, and throw me at something, hurting me more in the process.

He ran his hands over my arms, his predatory gaze back on, and I suppressed a shudder.

"I hoped you would behave, and it wouldn't come to this," he said, before kissing my cheek. I pressed my lips together, hoping the sob coming up my throat would be contained. With his mouth hovering in my face, he said, "Let me try to be clearer. You are mine. Period. You can't escape me. Each time you turn and try to run will be only that. A try. Because I'll catch you and I'll make you regret ever trying to run from me." He licked my cheek, and on instinct, I turned my face away. He grabbed my chin with too much force and snapped my face back to him. "Isn't that enough? I'll give you more, then."

I expected another punch or a kick in the gut.

Instead, he let go of me and stood there, his crazed eyes on mine, his evil smile over his lips. "Hilary is turning out to be a beautiful young lady, isn't she?" The realization of his words hit me stronger than any punch in my face could. I gasped. "How old is she now? Sixteen, seventeen? Do you think she would turn out to be such a nice girl as you if I lay my hand on her?"

I was becoming seriously sick to my stomach. "Eric, please ..."

"I wonder if she will fight me, or if it'll be easy to break her."

I repressed a sob. "Please ..."

"Please, what?" He put his hands on the table, right beside my thighs, and faced me down. "Please, what?"

"Leave her alone," I whispered.

"If you behave, I will. If you behave, if you do everything I tell you, if you don't fight me, I will leave Hilary alone. But if you don't"—he tsked—"I won't have a choice. Hilary will suffer. And you'll watch it." His fingertip traced my jaw, my neck, and down my breast. "Are you going to behave?"

A tear dripped down my face. "Yes."

"Good." He placed a kiss on my burning cheek. "Now, clean up this mess and cook us a new dinner. Meanwhile, I'm gonna take a shower."

He just turned and left, as if it had been a normal conversation, in a normal situation, with a normal couple and a normal life.

Emotionally and physically drained, I curled over the table and cried.

30

KEEPING MY EYES CLOSED AND MY BREATHING DEEP, I pretended to be asleep as Eric woke up early in the morning and left for the club.

Last night, I ended up cooking a simple dinner for us, which he complained about, then sat with him in the family room, where we watched a baseball game. My mind kept an it's-for-Hilary chant, otherwise I would have tried to escape. Again. When we went to bed, he tried to kiss me, with clear intentions of going further, but I couldn't. I ended up crying and he stopped.

"You'll be a good girl from now on," he said, "and our relationship will be perfect again. You'll want me soon. I'll wait for it." He planted a peck on my lips, turned to his side of the bed, and dozed off in a matter of minutes.

It took me hours to sleep, mostly because I didn't want to sleep beside him, but I couldn't get away either. Exhaustion won though, and I ended up falling asleep late into the night. But it was an agitated sleep, with unclear nightmares.

I was thankful that in the morning he went on like normal. I was afraid he would ditch practice that day to stay with me and make my life even more miserable.

Once I heard his car driving away, I dragged myself to the bathroom, took three ibuprofen, crawled back into bed, hugged my pillow, and cried.

I cried for having ever been naive and fallen in love with him. I cried for having found out what a lunatic he was. I cried for not being strong enough and able to defend myself each time he raised his hand to hit me. I cried for his threats—especially the ones about Hilary.

God, please, leave Hilary out of this mess.

Mostly, I cried because I couldn't see a solution for this shit.

A loud banging brought me back from the world of the happy-forget-everything-that-was-bad sleep. And the pain came back with me.

"What the …?"

Dizzy, I climbed out of bed, then stopped. What if it was Eric? It couldn't be. He had just left. Besides, he had keys. If he wanted to get in, he wouldn't knock.

I reached for my phone on the nightstand and saw it was past noon. Gosh, I had gone back to sleep!

It was probably Jimmy, worried that I hadn't shown my face at the stables yet. I went down the stairs, flinching as each stepped jarred my head and sent pangs of pain within my face and neck. In my mind, I rehearsed what I would say so he would leave, and I wouldn't need to open the door for him.

"Hey, Jimmy, I think—"

"Hannah." I almost tripped on the last step, and then froze. It was Leo. "I know you're behind the door, Hannah. I heard your footsteps coming down the stairs. Open the door, please."

I held my breath and didn't move.

What the hell was he doing here? He had made it clear he didn't want to be around me anymore. Moreover, he should be at the club, practicing.

"*Morena*, please."

I pressed a hand to my mouth as a sob threatened to come out. No, no, no. I wouldn't cry now.

"I would rather say all this to your face instead of the door." He groaned. "I know I said I was out, but ... I saw Eric this morning at the club and, I don't know, I was jealous, I guess. He looked happy. Very happy. And I realized that he couldn't possibly be happy if you had broken up with him, because I know any guy had to be out of his mind if he was happy after breaking up with you. I'm afraid you changed your mind, that you didn't break up with him. Please, tell me you broke up with him."

I sat down on the second to last step and waited, shaking and allowing only a few gasps of air in. *Stay quiet, Hannah. Stay very quiet.*

After a long time, I finally heard a loud sigh followed by retreating steps. Then, I sighed too and allowed my breathing to come out normal again. Or almost normal.

The tears fell freely, and I shook hard as the memories and the threats of the previous night came back with a vengeance, bringing back the pain. I still hadn't taken a shower and cleaned the cuts and scratches. I probably looked like shit. I felt like shit.

But first, ibuprofen. I needed more ibuprofen before I passed out from the pain.

Believing I had some in the kitchen, I pushed myself up from the stairs and inched down the hallway.

I found the medicine inside my junk drawer and popped two inside my mouth. I opened the fridge, grabbed a water bottle, and drank half of it in a big gulp.

I inhaled deeply, taking in as much of the permanent vanilla scent as I could, hoping it could comfort me.

My stomach growled, and I realized I hadn't eaten for over twenty-four hours, if I didn't count last night's dinner, because I only picked at my food.

I surveyed the contents of the fridge and browsed the cabinets. There was nothing I wanted to eat. My stomach was asking for food, but I didn't think I could eat anything. I gave up and turned to my coffee machine. In no time, I had a large steaming cup of dark, strong coffee. I held the mug to my face and inhaled deeply, savoring the yummy and comforting scent.

My mind betrayed me, going back to what I wanted to deny.

There had to be a way out of this mess; I just

had to think hard and find it. And I had to be quick too, because Eric's practice would go on for only two or three more hours, then he would be back. I shuddered. Shit, I was so not ready to face him again.

A hinging sound came from the living room, and I almost dropped the mug on my feet. I set the mug down and held my breath.

Shit. Eric was here early, and I hadn't had time to think. I had no idea how to confront him and I probably only had a few seconds before he barged in. I hoped he had a good practice this morning, because then his mood would be a little better. If he hadn't … I was doomed.

I laced my fingers behind my back to control my shaking and decided I should go to him. Unafraid. Strong.

I stepped into the corridor that led back to the front of the house and bumped into him. I jumped back, alarmed as soft hands held my hands and pulled me closer.

Leo. In his polo clothes and boots and damp hair and wide eyes.

"How did you get in?" I croaked.

"*O que é isso?*" He pushed me back into the kitchen and turned me to the sunlight streaming in through the large window. His gaze traveled my face, down my arms. He turned my shoulders a little and stared at my neck too. Then, his eyes narrowed and he growled, "I'm gonna kill him."

He marched to the door, probably intent on driving to the club and punching Eric—which would have been nice—but I couldn't let that happen. I dashed after him and held his arms, pulling him back.

"It's not what you think," I said, panic rising inside of me.

He faced me; his expression was incredulous. "You're gonna deny it?"

"Actual—"

"*Por favor*, don't tell me you fell down the stairs or tripped and hit your face on the doorknob, because, whatever you say, I know what happened here." He raised his hand, and it hovered over my cheek and my neck. He picked a shard from my shoulder, and I winced in pain. "*Filho duma puta*, I can't believe he did this."

My eyes watered instantly. "Please ..."

"Please, what?" His hand dropped to his side, his fist clenched. "Please go after that bastard and kick the life out of him. With pleasure!"

"No!" I sobbed, feeling too weak, too drained to keep breathing. I leaned against the island. "No, please. You ... you don't understand."

"Then explain it to me," he said, his tone harsh. I lowered my gaze and shook my head. Then Leo was right in front of me, his gentle hands on my arms. "Was this the first time?"

"Leo, forget about this."

"Hannah, answer my questions, or I'll have to interrogate the bastard before kicking his ass." He put a finger under my chin and raised my face to his. "How long has this been happening?" I glanced at the wall above his shoulder, but he shifted to the side, putting his face in my line of sight. "Talk to me, *morena*. I can already tell this wasn't the first time. I want to know for how long."

I remained quiet. I wanted to tell him everything, I really did, but that would sound like I couldn't take care of myself and needed him to save me. Not that I could take care of myself, but I hated the idea of looking helpless and broken. Although, I was sure that was exactly how he saw me right now. I didn't want to be the poor princess in the tower, waiting to be rescued by the handsome prince. I wanted to do my own rescuing, though I couldn't see how. All the ways I saw to escape—going to the police, leaving the ranch—opened problem-door X or Y, and I couldn't afford that.

"All right." Leo sighed, looking around. He released me and started opening and closing drawers and cabinets.

"What are you doing?"

"Looking for your first aid kit." He looked up from a drawer. "Wait, no. Maybe it's better if we take you to the police station like that."

"No, no. I can't—"

"The blood and the shards will make quite an impression," he continued. "Though, does it still hurt? We could clean up a bit, where it hurts the most. How about pain medicine, do you have some?"

"Stop!" I yelled.

Leo turned his worried eyes to me. "What?"

I took a deep breath. "I'm not going to the police."

Frustration replaced the worry on his features. "What?"

"I ... can't. I'm sorry, but I can't." I didn't know what else to do, what else to say. "I think you better go before he comes back."

Leo halted in front of me. "Do you hear yourself?"

"Please, don't make it worse than it is."

"Worse? If it's bad, why don't you want to go to the police with me?" He took one of my hands and held it in a cocoon within his. "At least, come with me. We can talk more about going to the police later. Come with me."

My heart hurt more than my face and my cuts. If Eric came back and I wasn't here, he would go after Hilary. "I can't."

"I don't understand." He raised my hand to his lips and kissed my moon-shaped scar, ever so softly. It would have been a perfect sensual moment, if I weren't so broken. "What did he do to you? How come you're defending him?"

I pulled my hand away. "I'm not defending him. I ... I can't."

"He's threatening you." Leo cursed under his breath in Portuguese. "What are his threats? Tell me, *morena*. I want to help you. Tell me what he's threatening you with, and we can find a solution for it together."

Could we?

I stared into his eyes, into his beautiful green-blue eyes, into the strength and hope and worry in them, and I suddenly wondered, why not? I trusted him, so why not tell him everything, every little detail. He would probably hate me for being weak, but I had to take this chance. I wasn't coming up with any new ideas on my own, so maybe he would understand my side and help me think of other ways, other solutions. Besides, if I didn't let him help me, who would?

Once more, I was struck by how much I was into him. Not just his looks or his skill with horses, but because of the way he looked at me, because he cared about me.

"Eric was always jealous, since the first day he showed interest in me. With time, his jealousy grew." I paused. Confessing what had been right in front of me all of these years was harder than I expected. "He also—"

"WHAT THE HELL IS HE DOING HERE?" Eric's voice boomed from the kitchen doorway.

A second later, his fist was on Leo's jaw. Leo staggered back, but he deflected Eric's next hit, and gave one of his own, punching Eric's stomach.

Eric doubled over and glared at Leo.

"Bastard!" Leo shouted. "You're gonna pay for what you did to her." He raised his fist to come at Eric again.

But Eric, being the gentleman he was, grabbed my arm and pulled me in the way. With wide eyes, Leo pulled back as much as he could with the momentum he had gained, and was able to change the course of his fist in the last second.

Eric laughed, sounding demented, and I tried squirming out of his hold. His arm tightened around my waist. "Stop fighting," he whispered in my ear.

I flinched.

With fists clenched, Leo hovered close to us, unsure how to advance. "Get your hands off her!"

"Why?" Eric tilted his head to the side. "She's mine. I can do whatever I want with her. You're the one interrupting us and you should leave before I have to hurt you."

Leo snarled. "I'm the one who's gonna hurt you and make you regret ever being born."

Leo grabbed my arm and pulled me to him, while Eric held me even tighter. I felt like I was being ripped in two. Trying to gain some advantage, Leo used his long legs and kicked Eric's hip, missing me by less than an inch.

The grip around me loosened, and I pried myself from it. Leo's arms found me and held me to him, his touch gentle and worried.

He slipped his hand in mine and beckoned me to the door. "Let's go."

I started running with him. Across the kitchen. Out the door. Past the porch.

"Baby, aren't you forgetting something?" Eric's voice was filled with superiority. And threats.

My heart dove to the depths of despair, and I skidded to a stop.

Leo tugged my hand. "Come on."

I glanced over my shoulder, to Eric's evil eyes. He mouthed "Hilary," and my blood turned cold. Oh shit.

"I can't," I whispered, letting go of Leo's hand.

"What are you doing?" He reached for me and I retreated. "*Morena*?"

A sob shook my body. "I can't go. I'm sorry." I took a couple of steps back, and Eric met me halfway.

He put his hand around my waist possessively, his smug winning expression on his face. "You should leave," he said, his eyes intent on Leo.

"Hannah." Leo gave a step toward me, and I stepped the opposite way. He stopped, his expression puzzled. "You can't stay here, Hannah."

I lowered my head because I couldn't keep staring at him. "I can."

"But it doesn't mak—"

"Didn't you hear her?" Eric interrupted him, his voice rising. "Leave now before I make you leave."

"You can't make me leave," Leo retorted. "I won't leave."

I took a deep breath. "Please, Leonardo, leave."

Even with my eyes on the ground, I saw his

flinch and I could imagine the shock in his beautiful features.

"You can't be serious," he whispered.

"I am." I swallowed the tears threatening to make their way out. "I want you to leave, and please, do not return."

"No, you can't—"

Eric's fingers clasped my skin like a claw. "Leave!" I yelled as the tears clouded my vision. "Please, leave now." He didn't move, and Eric's fingertips dug into my flesh. "Leave now!"

With slow movements, Leo did leave. He stopped several times, and I thought it was to give me the chance to change my mind, but I couldn't.

Eric and I stood there, like statues, watching as Leo's SUV left the property. When he was long gone, Eric placed a gentle kiss on my temple.

"You've been a very, very bad girl, baby. Very bad." He placed his other hand around my waist and turned me to him. He leaned over, and I did my best not to shudder, cry, yell, or run. "Very bad," he whispered against my lips. His hand snaked up to my hair, his fingers weaving with the strands. I was about to get sick, thinking he wanted me to kiss him back, or worse, but instead, he grabbed a handful of my hair in his fist and turned me around. Like a caveman, he pulled me to the house.

I yelped. "Eric." I paused. I almost said *you're hurting me,* but maybe he would only put more force into it then. "What are you doing?"

He didn't answer right away. He took me inside, closed the door behind us, and turned me around to face him, without releasing his grip from my hair.

The glint on his eyes made me shudder. "Time for your punishment."

EVEN KNOWING THERE WASN'T MUCH I COULD DO, I kept on running down possibilities in my mind.

Going to the police in another town. Leaving, hiding at my parents' house. Or running away and hiding from everyone for a while. Or use my grandma's old rifle as a defense weapon. However, I doubted I could really shoot a person, or that there were any bullets left in the house.

Either way, all these options exposed Hilary to Eric's claws, and for that, I pushed them away just as quickly as they came.

Once again, I was relieved when I woke up and Eric was gone. After beating the hell out of me the previous night, the last thing I wanted was to see his face first thing in the morning. This time, he was smarter, though. He didn't hit my face, where it was hard to hide, but he hit everywhere else. My belly, my chest, my hips, my back. I was covered in purple marks, and just getting up from my bed and going to the bathroom was like walking a tight corridor covered in knives.

That day, Jimmy came in looking for me.

"I'm not feeling well," I said, from behind the bathroom door. "I don't think I'll be out today."

"It ain't right, Miss Taylor." His voice sounded a little distant, as if he were standing outside my bedroom. "You've been feeling unwell too often. Perhaps you should see a doctor."

I assured him it was nothing and, if it persisted, I would go to the doctor. I heard his heavy steps as he raced down the stairs and left the house. From my bedroom window, I watched him walk down the path to the main stable, shaking his head.

Around noon, the text messages started.

Leo: *How are you?*

After a few seconds, he texted again. *Stupid question. The real question is, why the hell did you stay?*

I didn't answer and he kept on texting.

We need to talk. I need to understand.

No. I don't need to understand. You do. Please, come to me. Or let me come pick you up.

Please, morena. You can't stay there.

I tried not reading the messages, but my will was too weak. I did erase all of them though, in case Eric snatched my phone at some point and searched for reasons to hit me more.

Jimmy left around 5:30 p.m. and I went to the stable, surprised Eric hadn't come yet. I was actually hoping he wouldn't show up.

First, I checked the other horses. Belle, Dakota, Chip, Black Jack, Dale, Duchess, Zeus, and Abacus. They looked fine and happy and well fed. Then, I stopped by the last stall and peered inside.

Standing in his preferred corner, Argus looked sadder and weaker than the last time I had seen him.

"Hey, boy," I called him, and his ears perked up.

He turned his muzzle to me and snorted.

"I know I haven't been around lately. I'm sorry." I sighed. "Things have been complicated around here, you know."

He snorted again and I smiled, translating it to ha-and-you-think-my-life-is-paradise? Poor horse.

Just when we both started letting our walls down, I had to run away.

My eyes surveyed his body. Even when this thin, Argus's white coat still looked smooth, though I had seen it shinier before. I wanted to bring the shine back. I wanted to bring his strength back. I wanted to bring him back.

Damn it. Eric couldn't keep me away from him. Even if he broke every bone in my body, I wouldn't give up on Argus.

"I have a proposition," I said to Argus, my hands opening the lazy Susan. I placed some grain in the bucket and closed the latch. "How about I work on you when he isn't around, huh? Even if I have to limp my way here with a bruise on my face and all. Would you like that?"

Argus stomped a hoof on the ground, and I thought he would ignore me, until he turned his body and took a couple of deliberate steps toward me.

I smiled.

"I'm glad to see you're well," Eric said, entering the stable and making me lose my smile.

I tensed and Argus neighed, retreating to his corner.

Eric halted beside me, putting his arm around me. He pulled me close and kissed my cheek. I did my best not to breathe because if I did, he would notice the tension in me, the disgust in my gut, and I would suffer for it.

His eyes flickered to Argus. "I forgot all about this horse." His nose scrunched as if Argus smelled. Well, the stables did smell most of the time, but not Argus particularly. "Look at him. What an abomination. I'll make some calls tomorrow. Soon, he'll be out of here.

Terror gripped my chest. No, no, no. Argus wouldn't leave. If he did, then he would remain broken. And so would I.

I didn't protest though. I prayed he forgot about it again, and when he remembered, the calls and arrangements took more time than he expected, giving me more days with Argus.

Eric's hand applied some pressure on my waist, right where a big purple bruise was screaming, and guided me out of the stable.

"How about you cook us some homemade chicken pot pie for dinner?" he said, with a haunting smile.

I slapped a plastic grin on my face and went along with his fakeness.

31

OVER THE NEXT FOUR DAYS, A NEW ROUTINE developed.

Eric woke up early and left for practice. I got out of bed right after he was gone, whipped up a large mug of coffee and went to Argus.

I stayed with him most of the day, just leaving to have lunch with my mother and my sister. Then, I went back to the ranch, helped Jimmy with chores—and he insisted something wasn't right, which bothered me to no end—helped Paul with the setting up and cleaning up from each class, and when they were gone, went back to Argus until Eric came back. I cooked us dinner, we talked about things like his polo career and his plans of taking the first place in the world rank back, and I listened to him talk about our glorious future together—the one where I stayed home, primping his house and taking care of his three children. It disgusted me.

Meanwhile, I tried to behave as much as I could, so his rage would be in control. Which meant ignoring and deleting the thirty-forty messages Leo sent me every day.

Of course, I read most of them.

I'm worried about you.

Please, answer. Anything.

He's a sick man, you know that, right? I saw him today at the club. He goes on as if he is the star of the world. That is so wrong.

Please, morena, tell me you're not on his side.

I can't take this silence anymore.

I've been one button away from calling the police for four days, but I figured you must have a reason for not doing so yourself.

Please, morena, you're killing me.

His messages broke my heart every time.

"How's your father?" Jimmy asked, bringing my mind to the moment. He took the bridle from me.

With a tiny smile, I unbuckled the saddle from Belle and handed it to Jimmy. "Well, my dad is finally recovering, so I guess I do feel better." It wasn't a lie. My father had finally woken up, and if he kept recovering at this rate, he would be home next week or so. However, he didn't remember much of the incident. He had been walking from the elevator to his car when two hooded men showed up and shot him. The end. I still had my doubts about Mr. O'Neill and his hand in all of this.

I guided Belle to her stall and approached Chip to take the gear off him. Paul had just finished a class, and as usual, he dropped the horses and things in the stable and left for his lunch break. If there were other instructors around, I would fire him without hesitation. Alas, there was none and I was stuck with his manners.

"I'm glad he's doing well," Jimmy said as he turned to work on Black Jack. "I hope he remembers more details soon, otherwise the police will have no clue how to start the investigation."

"Me too," I whispered.

I had asked my mother many times if she had any idea who could want Dad dead, but she swore he had no enemies. Not publicly at least. The only recent discussions she remembered were with Mr. O'Neill, but the man had his lawyer responding to it already. I wanted to ask my dad about it, but the police had already interrogated him enough. He didn't need me to interrogate him too.

In a comfortable silence, Jimmy and I took the saddles and bridles off the horses, put them in their stalls, and filled their buckets with grain and water. Then, Jimmy excused himself and went to his house for lunch.

My stomach growled, but I ignored it, knowing it could wait a few more minutes.

First, I wanted to try something.

For the past two days, Argus was responding a little better to me. He ate all the strawberries I brought him and, when out in the arena, he got close several times, but I refrained from reaching to him and scaring him away.

Instead of filling Argus's bucket with grain, I dropped a few peaches in it. From his corner, he watched me and I wished I could read his mind.

I leaned over the wooden rail as he approached the bucket with slow steps. He sniffed the contents of the bucket then raised his muzzle toward me as if asking me what the hell was in there.

I smiled. "Try it. I know you'll like it."

He sniffed the peaches some more. I chanted the patience mantra in my mind as he took over eight minutes to snatch a peach into his mouth. He ate it quickly, snorted, and grabbed another.

"Told ya," I said, a satisfied feeling growing in me. I extended my hand toward him, then, realizing what I was doing, I pulled back. "You'll be okay, you know. I'll make sure of it."

Argus stopped munching and looked at me. The depth of his stare, the insecurity in his eyes, was enough to break my heart. Poor horse. I wish I could scoop his past away with my hands and throw it in the never-happened trash can.

The sound of a car arriving had my pulse speeding up. Eric at this time of the day? Well, not that he ever missed practice to come surprise—or hit—me.

I walked to the stable's entrance and saw a UPS truck in the parking lot. A guy, dressed in a UPS uniform, exited the truck with a small package in his hands. He saw me and walked toward me.

"Can I help you?" I asked when he was close enough to hear me.

He halted a few yards from me. "Hey. I'm here to deliver this parcel to Miss Hannah Taylor."

"I'm Hannah Taylor."

"Oh. Here you go." He handed me the package and dashed away.

"Thank you," I yelled as he hopped in the truck.

What ... I turned the package in my hands. A plain yellow envelope with my name scribbled on one side, a handwriting I didn't know. The truck zipped down the road, and I took a few steps into the stable. A little wary, I ripped the corner of the envelope and took a magazine out. A gossip magazine.

"What the hell?"

The cover highlighted scandals with Kim Kardashian, Lindsay Lohan, and Britney Spears. But there was a green Post-It sticking from the middle. I opened the magazine on the page it was marking, and it took me a minute to realize what I was staring at.

"Oh my God ..." I fell on a bench.

I flipped the page. The article continued for over six pages. Six freaking pages!

Ignoring all the pictures, I read the text first.

LIVING BEHIND LIES

YOU MIGHT HAVE SEEN HIM ON THE COVER OF THE Polo World *magazine, and even illustrating some pages of Vanity Fair's polo stars issue, but you don't really know him.*

Facts you may know:

—Currently ranked number one in the world, Leonardo Fernandes, 20, was born into a family of polo players and is the third son of polo legend João Pedro Fernandes. His siblings, Ricardo and Pedro, and his cousin, Guilherme, are part of his star team, Montenegro.

—His career started when he was 10 years old and won the Copa dos Potros with the Montenegro Jr. Team, which was a subsidiary team for the Montenegro Club founded by his father.

—He was promoted to 10-goal handicap at the age of 18, replacing American Polo star Eric Bennett as the youngest 10-goal polo player in the world.

As nice as his achievements sound, his life isn't a fairy tale.

Due to the intense traveling to attend polo tournaments around the world, Leonardo flunked his senior year of high school and didn't graduate. His father wasn't happy about having a son who didn't finish school, and after a heated argument in which a witness said, "They almost hit each other," Leonardo left his family's house and left his team. He quit polo and indulged in a life of parties, heavy drinking (in Brazil, the legal drinking age is 18), and drugs. Girls flocked after him, and Leonardo was seen with a new "girlfriend" every week.

After a long year, his father interfered in his Casanova lifestyle and put him into a rehabilitation center against his will. According to our source, father and son had many arguments during that time, and still do. "They can't stand each other."

Convinced by his brothers, Leonardo complied with the rehab program and came back to the team.

However, Brazilian media and paparazzi were making the routine of the Montenegro Club a real hell on Earth. It is said that other Brazilian teams had lost their respect for Leonardo and his family, making it difficult to maintain the tournaments' peace.

Some say the opportunity to move and play for a club from the United States knocked on Montenegro's door. Others say it was the other way around, and a bit more, "They totally forced it," our source said. Regardless of how it came to be, Leonardo insisted on coming because he would be able to have a clean slate. Here, the polo fans would only know about his ranking and championship titles history, not about his slips and dark past.

We did a quick search on Google, and at a first look, all we could find about Leonardo was in fact his ranking and championship titles history, and his association with Montenegro Club. Digging a bit deeper, we found dozens if not hundreds of news and articles from the period in which he was living la vida loca.

"Leonardo is a bad boy through and through," our source said. "It's just a matter of time before he slips again and brings the team down with him."

Though this time they won't have anywhere to run and hide.

THE WORDS ENDED AND I SEARCHED FOR MORE. It couldn't be. There had to be more to that story, like "Aha, got ya! Happy April's Fool in July!" but there were none. However, there were pictures. Lots of them.

Leo at age ten, receiving his first trophy.

Leo at age sixteen, training younger kids with his father at the Montenegro Club.

Leo being sandwiched by three girls at a party, his shirt gone.

Leo, completely wasted, being carried out of a party by Ricardo and Guilherme.

Leo driving a convertible, with a bottle of whiskey in one of his hands.

Leo arguing with his father in front of the gate of the Montenegro Club. They really looked like they would hit each other.

Leo at age twenty, leaving the rehab center.

Leo, with his team uniform, punching a paparazzi outside what looked like a restaurant.

Leo standing in the middle of a field during a match with his polo pony behind him, arguing with another player.

My stomach twisted into knots.

Oh. My. God.

Several questions surged in my mind. Was this true? How did this magazine find out about it? Who was this damned source? And why the hell did Leo never tell me about all of this?

It was like I didn't know him. At all.

He lied to me. Or better, he didn't tell me.

I thought he was better than Eric, that he would never hurt me, that whatever we had was special, when in fact he was probably laughing his ass off right now, or skipping practice and partying. Apparently, he was another guy behind my back.

Oh crap. I didn't know what to make of this, and I had to stop my mind from imagining all the possible and terrible scenarios behind his story.

Argus snorted, his head over his stall's door.

"Oh, just ... more drama," I told him, as if he could actually act as my therapist and help me out.

Then my phone rang, and Leo's codename flashed on the screen.

I considered not answering. Well, we weren't exactly on speaking terms anyway, so why did I care about this article? I shouldn't care. I shouldn't want to talk to him.

Ugh, stop being a wimp, Hannah.

"Hi."

He exhaled. "I thought you weren't going to answer me." I kept quiet and he cursed in Portuguese. "I'm guessing you saw the magazine."

"You're guessing right."

"*Merda!*" The sound of some metal being hit echoed through the call. "We were on the field when dozens of reporters barged into the club. Pedro suggested one of the guys had hit second in the world ranking, and the reporters were here for an interview or something. Then, they circled us and started firing questions about my past. I was shocked. The club security guards escorted us to a locker room, and we've been in here for over an hour while they handle the reporters. Meanwhile, Gui did research on his phone and found out about the article in the magazine that came out this morning." He sighed. "I don't know how they found out. I don't know what happened."

How they found out ... I held my breath. "So it's true?"

"Yes, but—"

"Oh shit."

"—they made it all sound bad. Well, it was bad, but there were more bits that they didn't mention."

"More bad things?"

"No, no. No bad things. Just some events that would explain a lot of what happened. Look, I can't lie about it—"

"Not anymore."

He groaned. "I never lied to you."

"But you didn't tell me the truth either." And that was hurting me. He hid things from me because he didn't trust me enough with the truth.

"I thought you would hate me if you found out. I wanted to tell you. I really did, but I was so scared you would stop talking to me, stop seeing me, and I'm so into you that I can't bear the thought of you not speaking to me."

A lump formed in my throat. "Well, you better get used to it."

"What? *Morena*, no, please. Let me explain."

"I don't know if I want an explanation."

"*Por favor.* Once I can get out of here, I'm coming over."

"No. No. You know you can't. Besides, I need some time to process all of this."

He stayed quiet for a few seconds. "I understand," he finally said, his tone dejected. "Just remember there's more to it, and I'm begging you for a chance to explain."

He had confessed there was more to it, and he still thought I could cope with everything just like that? More of what by the way? He said it wasn't more bad things, but what could it be? I couldn't see one good thing coming from what I had read.

"Bye," I whispered before pressing the end button.

Tears burst from my eyes. Sobbing, I pulled my legs up and hugged them, resting my cheek on my knees. I was turning into such a weak girly girl who cried all the time and I hated it. I hated everything that was happening to me and around me.

That evening, Eric seemed in a good mood, and I wondered if he had anything to do with the article. Not because of me, but because Leo had snatched the number one from him, and Eric, being the sore loser he was, had to do something about it.

However, he didn't mention any word about Leo and the article, and I sure wouldn't talk about it.

MY MOTHER, HILARY, AND I HUDDLED AROUND MY father's bed. The doctor had just checked him and said he might go home in a couple of days. He still looked pale and thin, but at least he was awake and recovering.

The moment I had been waiting for came when my mother went out of the room to answer her phone and Hilary decided to make a coffee run.

I sat on the edge of the bed, careful not to jar it too much as he was still in pain.

"Hey, Dad, can I ask you a question?"

He caught the remote and pressed the button to raise the top of his bed. "Sure."

"What exactly happened?"

His eyes flickered to the door behind me, then the window, before settling on me. "You already know, Hannah. I told the police everything I remember. I got out of the elevator and was walking across the parking garage toward my car when two guys jumped out and shot me. Next thing I knew, I was waking up here, six weeks later."

"It's ... it looks like it was a premeditated incident. I mean, they didn't take anything from you, and as you say, they came right at you and aimed at your chest." I paused, a little nervous about getting to the point. What the hell? I swallowed and continued. "Do you have any enemies of any kind? Like, I don't know, a rival or someone to whom you owe money, or maybe Mom's ex-boyfriend still sore that you stole her from him?"

He threw his head back and laughed. Then he groaned, his hand over his chest. "You know well enough that we're friends with the other breeding farms in the region and that we have too much money, and I can't even begin to imagine how I could get into any debt I couldn't pay for, and your mom's ex-boyfriend. Hmm, the last time I heard from him was about his wedding, over fifteen years ago." He sighed. "The only person I was having trouble with was Mr. O'Neill, but I don't believe he had the guts to shoot anyone."

"But then, who? And why?"

He rested his hand over mine. "I don't know, Hannah. I can't stop thinking about it, trying to find a moment where I must have upset someone enough for them to want me dead." He shuddered and I squeezed his hand. "But I can't find any. Yes, I had arguments with lawyers, buyers, friends, your mom. Mr. O'Neill. But who doesn't argue every now and then?"

"I know. I wish I could do something." He arched his brows at me. "I don't know. This time though, I won't let the police abandon this case like they did to grandma."

He nodded. "Me neither."

My mother entered the room, her phone in hand. Her eyes found our hands clasped together, and she smiled. "Am I interrupting something?"

I gasped. My mother just joked! The world was ending.

My father smiled at her and patted the other side of the bed. "Come sit with us."

I glanced from him to my mom and back to him. I hadn't seen this look in their eyes—this enamored, and thankful look—in ... forever. This incident had been a terrible thing, but perhaps, it would bring us closer together.

I left the hospital with a lighter heart and an almost smile on my lips.

At least one side of my life was looking up, and I had to hold on to it with both hands because, if I was gonna get through the other fifteen bad sides, I was gonna need it.

I stopped at a gas station right outside town and began fueling my car.

I leaned against my car, and my mind wandered to Leo and the magazine article. I still couldn't believe it. He had told me he was a bad boy; I just didn't know he meant it. And what a bad boy. According to the article, he flunked school, he partied hard, he slept with every girl that crossed his path, he drank until alcohol became his blood, and he did drugs. He had been in a rehab center, for goodness sake! I didn't think I knew anyone who had gone to rehab. Until now.

He just wasn't worse than Eric, because there was no evidence that he had hit a woman. Yet.

Oh shit.

How could I think that? How could I compare him to Eric?

I didn't know what to think.

My cell phone chimed, and I pulled it out of my pocket.

A message from Leo. *Will you let me explain?*

The real question was: should I let him explain? Before I thought too much about the subject and changed my mind, I sent him a message.

Me: *Yes.*

Leo: *See you at your ranch in thirty.*

Me: *No. About twelve miles into route 154, you'll see a camp. They have a huge parking lot. Meet me there.*

Leo: *OMW.*

32

BUTTERFLIES SOARED IN MY STOMACH, AND MY hands turned a little damp. I felt like the teenage daughter of the town's minister about to sneak out with the bad boy. It wasn't much of a different scenario really, though I wasn't going there to make out with him.

Not really.

Although, my heart hoped his explanation sounded like a miracle, and that afterward he kissed me senseless.

It took me ten minutes to drive to the camp. I parked my car under the shade of a big tree, in the farthest corner of the parking lot, distant from any other car. The minutes passed and there were moments when I almost turned the wheel and drove away, but I realized I would regret not sticking around and listening to his explanations. I would go home and always wonder, what if it wasn't as bad as the article made it sound? What if he really had a reason for all the crap he did? So, I stayed there, biting my nails and trying to calm down my racing heart.

An old car with rusty red paint entered the parking lot and headed my way. I tensed. Uh-oh. I slid down my seat a little, afraid it was someone I knew and could tell Eric they had seen me here.

The car parked right beside mine. I peeked up and saw Leo, wearing a baseball cap and dark gray hoodie, behind the wheel.

After looking around, he slipped out of that car and into mine. As he settled on the passenger seat, it was like the AC had stopped working and the heat from outside had burst inside my car. The tension was almost tangible, brushing against my skin and making me shiver.

The way my body responded to just being close to him always amazed me.

I shook my head, pushing away those thoughts. "Whose car is that?"

"Freddy's. He's the handyman at our ranch." He pulled the hood off but kept the baseball cap. It was incredible how boyish he looked with the cap, and still perfectly hot. And kissable. And lickable.

Once more, I shook my head. *Focus, Hannah.*

"Why are you driving someone's else car?"

"Because my house is surrounded by paparazzi and reporters. It's hell."

"How did you get out?"

The corner of his lip turned up. *Oh, Lord, help me.* "Ri and Pedro went to the front of the house and pretended they were getting my car ready for me to leave. All the reporters followed them. Meanwhile, I sneaked out the back and borrowed Freddy's car. I had to take a huge detour inside the ranch, but by the time the reporters realized what had happened, it was too late."

I nodded, lowering my gaze. I didn't know what to say and I didn't know what to think. Closing my eyes for a second, I reminded myself of all the reasons to be mad and stay away from him. He omitted his past, and what a past! He had even used drugs. Drugs! He had punched people out of rage, and he went to a rehab. Not to mention his playboy lifestyle and all the women he took to his bed. I shuddered, suddenly wishing I could punch all those women myself.

Crap. Even when mad and disappointed, the

jealousy didn't leave me, and neither did the desire.

The silence extended for a couple of minutes until he broke it.

"I'm glad you answered my text," he said, his voice low. "I was worried about you."

I shook my head. "No, don't turn this to me. We're here because you want to explain that article."

"True, but I want to know about you too. You owe me an explanation as much as I owe you one. I'm worried about you, Hannah. Like going crazy worried."

I closed my eyes for a second. He was right. That day in my kitchen, I almost told him what happened. And I still wanted to, even though I was hurt that, after all, we had been through, he had hidden such a big part of his life from me.

"All right. I'll explain my reasons after you explain yours."

He glanced at the line of trees limiting the parking lot. The muscles in his neck tensed, and his jaw popped. "I'm not sure reasons is the best word. I think of it more like catalysts for certain actions."

"I see."

He looked back at me and pulled his left leg

over the seat, turning his whole body to me. "I'm not saying they will make sense, or that you'll understand them, or that you'll forgive me after knowing everything. I omitted my past from you once, saw where that took us, and I'm not willing to go through that again."

His words rattled me, and I leaned my back on my door to keep myself as far from him as I could inside a car. "Just ... tell me."

He took a deep breath. "I was already a good player when I was in my senior year of high school, and my brothers wanted me on their team, even though they were older and had already graduated. Ri went to college, but he took like two classes per semester so that it was easier to keep up. My father said he would allow me to join them because I was talented. So I did, and it was great. We traveled once a month, and sometimes we were gone for two weeks. When possible, I flew home, went to school for a couple of days, then flew back to the tournament for my next game. It was exhausting, but I never told anyone because I loved the game more than anything else in my life. I couldn't imagine not playing ever again. However, with so many missed classes, I lagged behind. I missed important material and quizzes and exams. Some teachers were considerate of my position and helped me out, but others didn't care. At the end of that year, we had won every tournament we had attended, I got my 10-goal handicap, but I failed most of my classes. My father ... he was furious. We had a huge argument about it. He said that he had made a mistake by letting me join the team, that my first responsibility was high school, and things like that. The worst was when he said that I should go back to school, repeat my senior year, and not play for an entire year. He said that it was just one year. Nine months, actually. I would survive. The team would too, with a replacement. Do you have any idea how much that hurt? He was cutting me off from what I loved most in life and he was *replacing* me with someone else. Like I was a disposable object. Like I wasn't his son."

He paused and I held back from reaching to him and taking his hand in mine. "I'm sorry," I whispered.

Taking another deep breath, he nodded. "So, I did as he told me to. After all, he is my father and I had no choice. Even if I challenged him, I was off the team. I went back to school and ended up mocked for repeating a year almost every single day. But what was worse was seeing my brothers and Gui going to the tournaments without me. And they didn't win all of them. That made me pretty pissed. I mean, not that I knew I could help them win, but we had won all of those tournaments the previous year. Anyway, I had to find a way of letting go of my stress and rage. That's when parties and alcohol made their way into my life." He glanced at his hands as he said, "And girls."

Once more, I held back from hugging him. I didn't want to get to any conclusions before listening to everything he had to say. "Go on."

He cleared his throat, and his eyes met mine again. They shone with regret and frustration. "As you can predict, I failed my senior year way before the end of classes. Before my father unleashed his righteousness on me, I left home. That's when things really went downhill. Without my mother and my father to keep me on my toes, I drank all day long. And partied all night. Soon, I was doing marijuana. A couple of months later, I was into all kinds of drugs. I could come up with several excuses for my behavior, but the real reason isn't an excuse. I was mad, really mad, and I was drowning in self-pity." He took off his cap and ran his hand over his hair. "All of those pictures in the magazine are real. None of them are photoshopped. And I'm immensely ashamed of them. I'm immensely ashamed of it all. Unfortunately, I can't erase the past. Because, believe me, if I could, I would."

I crossed my arms, determined not to let him —his side of the story—get to me just yet. "What happened then?"

"The guys and Bia came to me. They stepped into my mess and didn't let me do anything else. I even punched Pedro and Ri a couple of times. I was rude to Bia ... I don't know how she forgave me. Anyway, they boarded my bedroom window and locked me in my room until I was begging for help. So they did help me. They took me to a rehab clinic and checked on me every day."

I smiled, though it was a tiny one. "I had the impression they were nice, but now they sound like really great people."

"They're the best. I don't know what would have happened to me if they hadn't done something. Wait. I know. I would have overdosed by now."

"Don't say that."

"But it's true." He shook his head. "I'm not trying to excuse myself, but can you imagine being forbidden from doing what you love the most while everyone around you, close to you, is still doing it? During dinner, polo was all everyone talked about, and I had nothing to say anymore. In fact, it hurt to listen. And they were gone most of the time. Since I was still in school and Bia was going to college, we were the only ones left behind. But Bia had her own life. Sure, Dad forced her to travel with them a little, and that made me even more alone. I was literally left behind."

I didn't want to, but I began to understand his side of the story.

Polo was his life, and all of a sudden, it was taken from him. Yeah, I would have probably fallen into an unending spiral too, and probably hid it from everyone around me if I could.

"How long did you stay in the rehab clinic?"

"Four months," he answered, his tone heavy. He played with his ring again. "It was hell. I admit I still have a really hard time refraining from alcohol and cigars when I see them, but ... I need to remember how bad it was at rehab and it's gone."

So, that was why he didn't drink during the ball and Jimmy's barbecue. He didn't drink alcohol. Period.

I gestured to his hand. "What does the ring mean?"

"Bia gave it to me once I was out of the rehab. She said it was to remind me of the dark days every time I felt like succumbing again."

I smiled on the inside. So thoughtful. "You touch it all the time."

"Yeah, so everyone tells me." He looked at it. "I guess it became like a relaxation technique. A support or something."

I nodded. I knew the story wasn't over yet. "What happened then?"

"The guys went to my father, who still wasn't talking to me, and protested. They told him they were done if I didn't make the team. He thought they were bluffing and ignored it. The next day, they didn't show up for practice, even though I argued with them about it. They didn't go to practice or tournaments for over two months, until my father gave in and let me in. That"—a sad smile took over his lips—"was one of the best days of my life. Then, the first tournament was one of the worst. Reporters were there, and people whispered when I walked by, looking at me with disgusted faces. It was ... horrible. I wanted to punch them all. And I did. I punched a guy from another team and I punched a paparazzi." He sighed. "I wish I could take those moments back. I didn't want to hit them, but ... they didn't know what they were talking about, you know. Just like now. Everyone is talking about what they read in the article, drawing their own conclusions about it, which are usually much worse than the truth. I don't actually care that they are talking or what they are saying, only that it affects my life. I mean, the club obviously cares about it, otherwise, I wouldn't be suspended right now, and everyone thinks my brothers and Gui are bad people too because I am, and—"

"You're not a bad person." I clamped my mouth, but it was too late. The words had flown out before I could think about it. His eyes widened for a second, and I quickly added, "What then?"

"Right. Hmm, then my father found out the club here was looking to assemble another A team. He was careful to hide my past when he made the proposal, and I think the club really didn't know anything."

"So ... how are things between you and your father now?"

"Tense. We only talk to each other when necessary, and most of the time the talking becomes arguing and even shouting." I now understood what I had seen the day his father and he were arguing at the club, minutes before I asked for his help with Argus. Leo pressed his lips together. "I really try not to, but I still resent him a lot for putting me on the bench while strolling with the others right under my nose. I understand his reasons. As a father, he was trying to do what was right for me and my education, but he doesn't have any idea how he ripped my heart out when he forbade me to play. The resentment is hard to let go."

In a sense, Leo was like Argus. They had gone through rough patches and they had to bring their defenses up. Argus became scared and rude and jumpy to the point of charging someone who got too close. Leo ended up slipping lower and, to numb his suffering, he threw himself into a life without control, and now he omitted his past to anyone, including me.

Officer Michael had been the first to interfere in Argus's suffering. Then I came into the picture, and even Leo helped me bring the horse back from the darkness. We weren't done, but Argus had come a long way from where he was before.

Like Ricardo, Pedro, Bia, and Guilherme did for Leo. Like he said, he couldn't erase his past, but he was trying to be better now. He *was* better now.

Right then, I realized I didn't have any reason to be mad at him. A little disappointed, yes, but not mad. The past was the past. It was done and wouldn't change. What mattered was the now. And right now, he was here with me, asking me to understand him and his reasons.

I finally reached over and caressed the back of his hand with mine.

After a second of shock, he pulled his hand away. "I told you once, Hannah, I'm not a good guy, and I tried hiding this fact even from myself, but it doesn't matter. The past always catches up."

It sure did. But ... I understood him. At least, I thought I did. He had gone through a war zone and was still living with its ghost.

It couldn't be easy.

But here he was, telling me everything from his side, and it really wasn't easy. I couldn't imagine being in his situation.

When I lost grandma and Hercules, I had Eric, who still seemed like a good guy back then, to keep me strong. Besides, I had the ranch to take care of. Even so, I had my ways of protesting, like not riding another horse ever again, or not getting attached to them.

If I didn't have that, I would probably have sunk deeper, just like Leo did.

"We came to start over and my past found us," he continued. "The club suspended me, and they mentioned breaking the team's contract and sending us back to Brazil. We don't want that, but it's not our choice anymore. And because of me, the entire team is paying the price." He closed his eyes for a moment. His inner struggle was visible, and I couldn't help but feel a little sympathy toward him and what he went through. "Right after I rejoined the team and we ran into our first problems, I asked to get out. My father was happy to oblige, but the others wouldn't let me. Once more, they threatened to stop playing if I did. Then, when the opportunity to come here looked real, I mentioned not coming with them, because deep down I knew we couldn't hide my past from the world for long. I knew and yet, I ignored it, especially when they seemed so intent on not letting me go. So we came. And now here we are." He pointed to the car behind him and the cap on his head. "I really should ignore their threats and leave the team. They could find a better replacement and go on with it."

"I honestly think they understand the consequences of their own choices. Besides, I don't think they would let you quit. Even if they did, what would you do with your life?"

He shrugged and something like frustration flashed in his eyes. "Without them, without polo, and without you? I don't know. I don't want to think about it."

My heart skipped a beat. Without *me*?

A lump clogged my throat, and I hastily

pushed it down. "Do you think you would go back to the way it was before?" He looked away and didn't answer me. I scooted closer to the edge of my seat, closer to him. "Hey, Leo, talk to me." I offered him an encouraging smile. "Isn't that what you always asked me to do? Now I'm asking you the same. Talk to me."

His gaze met mine again. There was pure fear swimming freely in his blue-green ocean, and I wanted to jump in and save him from drowning.

"My rage and my disappointment would probably take over, and I would let myself go back to that life. And trust me, this time I wouldn't want to wake up from it, because the shame would be too great. I would rather die from an overdose."

I shuddered. "You don't mean it."

"Oh, I do. I really do." He frowned, his jaw even tighter than before. "Now, it's your turn. Why didn't you leave that bastard yet?"

The change of subject caught me off guard and it took me a minute to answer. "Long story short, Eric is jealous to the point of violence. He also doesn't like when people don't agree with him. And I don't agree with him. So, the years passed and he got more and more violent, until he hit me for the first time a few weeks ago. I was determined to end things with him right then but—"

"Wait." Leo raised his finger. "That day at my house, when we rode the monster truck, he had already hit you then?" I lowered my gaze and nodded. "*Filho duma puta*, how come I didn't see it?"

"Because I waited for the bruises to go away before driving to your house."

"I can't believe it," he muttered in harsh tones.

"He's much stronger than I am. I can't stop him from hitting me when he wants to."

Leo's jaw popped, his neck tense, his hands closed in fists. "*Tche*, this isn't happening."

"At first, I wanted to keep it quiet because I didn't want a scandal. I still don't. Can you imagine how many lives something like this would affect? My parents, the club's reputation. I can't be the cause of that. Especially because the majority of them would believe Eric and whatever lie he told them, not me."

"A little too late to think of the club's reputation now," he said in a sad voice. "Believe me when I say this, you shouldn't care what the truth will bring, because even when you think you're doing everything right, there is always someone there to spoil it."

I understood his statement. It was true for him, but I shook my head. "It isn't that simple. If the problem was only with me, don't you think I would have just left? Hidden in my parents' house or gone for a mini-vacation in Europe to recover from this all? I tried leaving. I tried threatening him." The tears burned behind my eyes. "When I told him I would go to the police, he threatened to go after my sister and hurt her. Really hurt her."

A sob lodged in my throat.

Leo cursed in Portuguese before turning to me with worried eyes. "Do you really think he would go after your sister?"

I opened my arms. "Look at me? About a month ago, I bet you would never think Eric could hit a woman. Neither did I. Well, guess what? He does. Only God knows what else he does." I paused. "I have this theory that he uses his charms and social skills to use other people too." I pointed to myself. "Not at hitting level, but I mean it. And perhaps most people don't even notice what is happening because they are so glad they can help him, they can be around him, or whatever."

"It makes sense. It's sick, but makes sense."

"So, do you really think he wouldn't go after my sister?" Leo didn't answer me, but I saw on his tight expression, on his coiled body, that he knew Eric would go after Hilary. "I can't risk it," I whispered.

"Now what? You stay with him and let him beat the crap out of you?"

"When I do what he wants me to do, he doesn't beat me."

Leo's eyes widened. "*Meu Deus*, did he rape you?"

"No, no." I looked away. "He says I'll accept my new life and he'll wait for me to want him back."

Leo let out a relieved breath. "At least he's not a rapist."

"Yet."

He tensed again. "All right, that's it. You're not going back there. I don't care what you say. You have to stay away from him. Very, very far from him. Don't go back there. Come with me. I'll help you out, and then you can walk away and go back to your life."

"What do you mean?"

He sighed. "If I'm honest with myself, I would tell you to stay away from me too. I tried staying away from you, Hannah. I really did ... but I can't. So I'm telling you, you have to stay away from me too."

It took me a minute to understand his words. "Wait. You begged me to meet you, to call you and let you explain, and now you're sending me away?"

He lowered his gaze to his hands on his lap. "It's for the best."

I shook my head. What was wrong with him?

Suddenly, it all made sense. I never believed in coincidences, and now I knew why Argus and Leo had come into my life. Argus was broken, just like Leo. Just like I was broken. We had been brought together to heal each other ... together. They were my strength, the same way I was theirs.

I wouldn't let him drown in the ocean.

"Leo, look at me," I said, trying to keep my voice soft. When he didn't, I took it up a notch. "Leo, please, look at me." Slowly, he raised his eyes to mine. They shone with unshed tears. My heart lurched. "Now tell me, looking at me, that you meant it. That you want me to stay away from you. That you have no feelings for me." He snorted and averted his gaze once again. "Please, tell me."

When his eyes found mine, I could *feel* the fight in him. I could see it. "Don't ask me that."

"Why?"

"Because I don't want to lie to you."

"Then don't lie."

After an entire minute staring at each other without any other movement, he groaned. "Fine. I can't stand the thought of you away from me. I want you. Too much. All of you. But you shouldn—"

I put my finger over his lips to cut him off, because my heart had just exploded with relief and hope, and I didn't want him to ruin it with words he didn't mean.

More importantly, my heart was filled with courage.

I crawled onto his lap, and as he readjusted himself in the seat, lowering his leg and turning to the front, I straddled him. My hands curled over his shoulders, and his hands rested on my waist. I looked down at him, at his beautiful, surprised face, in delight. In turn, he looked up, his eyes wide, his mouth slightly open.

"Was it that bad?" I asked in a whisper. "To admit that?"

"*Morena ...*"

"Say it again." I lowered my face to his, but held it an inch from his. He straightened, trying to touch his lips to mine, but I retreated a bit. "If you mean it, say it again."

His intense gaze took my breath away. "No. I'll do better." He slid his hands from my waist to my shoulder blades, and he pulled me down, against his chest. I gasped. The movement brought my face lower, and he brushed his lips on mine. A shuddering breath escaped my mouth. Then he pulled back a little and stared into my eyes. "I love you."

I froze.

What? I gawked at him, and he watched me with half a smile.

From the pocket of his hoodie, he fished a purple Douglas Iris out and placed it over my ear, like he always did. He had that flower there the whole time?

"I bet I had this same expression when you crawled onto my lap a few seconds ago," he said, still smiling.

I shook my head once, trying to order my thoughts. "What did you say?"

His smile widened as he wound his arms around my waist. "I. Love. You," he whispered without taking his eyes from mine. I fought against the new tears. "Hey, now. I didn't want to make you cry."

I chuckled, touching the flower. "Yeah, right."

"I was hoping for something a little more cheery."

I wiped away the tears before they could fall. "These are happy tears."

He kissed my chin and I shivered. "Oh yeah?"

I tilted my head to his until our mouths were touching. "Yeah," I whispered against his lips.

Without any hesitation, Leo buried his hand in my hair and pulled my mouth down to him. His lips closed over mine, and I was transported instantly to cloud nine.

I had no idea how I could go from an oppressed and frustrated girl to a loving and horny woman in a matter of seconds. Wait. I knew how. When I was with Eric, I was someone else. I lived in a world I didn't want to, did things I didn't want to. It wasn't my life, and in my mind, I knew I wouldn't live forever like that, even though I didn't see how to break free from that life yet.

When I was with Leo, I was my real self. I was much more like the girl who started dating Eric over two years ago, but I was more mature and surer of myself. And ... I thought I was in love with Leo. And I was sure I was horny, being that I was on celibate mode for almost two months. Or more. The thing was, I was also sure that sleeping with Leo would be magical just because it would be him, and I couldn't stop thinking about it.

I shuddered when his mouth trailed down my neck. My hands found the zipper of his hoodie. I opened it and quickly took it off. Leo raised his back from the seat to help me, his breath warm and rapid over my skin, making the heat building in my stomach travel lower.

His hands glided down to my hips and he pressed me down, against his hips. I moaned as his erection brushed against my pelvis. I shimmied my hips, increasing the contact area and the friction, and Leo groaned, biting the soft spot between my neck and shoulder.

"*Meu Deus, morena.*" He pressed a lingering kiss on my skin, and I bit his earlobe, making him groan again. "Keep that up and you're gonna make me come."

I deliberately hovered my lips over his ear, provoking him with my erratic breathing. "You say it like it would be a bad thing."

"Oh, I would rather be inside you when that happens," he said, and I shivered. "Damn, I want to be inside you so bad."

His hand moved. One went up, under my top. His fingers caressed my skin, and the contact was earth-shattering. I wanted to take off our shirts and embraced him, feel every inch of his skin against mine. The other hand went down to the inside of my thigh.

I shivered once more. "I want that too."

His tongue trailed up my neck. "I feel like a

horny teenager right now." He pulled back and stared into my eyes. "But this is more than just a quick fling. I love you, Hannah, and when I make love to you, it's gonna be in a nice place and it's gonna be beautiful. Perfect. And once won't be enough. Or twice, or three times. I just ... know that once I have you, I won't be able to let you go. And I want that, Hannah. I want you for myself only, forever." He brushed a strand of my hair away from my face. "I can't guarantee we won't argue, and I can't guarantee you won't be mad at my stubbornness and cockiness every now and then. I know you probably heard this and it meant nothing then, but I promise you with all my heart and soul, I won't ever hurt you. Not on purpose. And never with my hands."

To my dismay, my eyes filled with tears again. "What are you saying?"

"I'm saying come with me. Please, for all that is holy in this world, don't go back to him. Come with me."

I held on to his shoulders and shook my head. "I can't."

"You can." He traced under my eyes with his fingertips, taking away the tears. "We can. I'm already in too deep in quite the scandal. One more won't damage my career much more than it already has. And Eric deserves to have his career destroyed."

He was right about that.

"But what about Hilary? I can't do that to her."

He thought about it for a moment. "You tell her the truth."

"I thought about that." I sighed. "It took all the courage I had to tell you about this, Leo. I can't seem to find the courage to tell her."

"You're not alone in this. I'm here with you and I won't let go. I'll help you talk to her. We'll tell her the truth and that she should stay away from him because he'll try to take revenge through her."

I snorted. "She thinks she's superior and strong. Even if she believes it, she'll never do anything about it."

"She's your sister, Hannah. If I know one thing, it is that family matters. Explain to her the best you can. Prove it to her. She'll do what you tell her to."

"Even so ... she'll know the truth, but he'll come after her. She won't know how to defend herself."

"Then she can stay with us. Our house has eleven bedrooms. Eleven! It's more than enough for you and her to come spend a few days with us, or until all of this mess is solved."

"But ... what will your parents think of that?"

"My mother loves you, and I'm sure she'll be glad to take care of Hilary too. My father ... well, I don't care what he thinks right now."

"I don't want to go against your father, Leo. I don't want to be something else he blames for the problems you two have."

"You won't. I promise. If you allow me, I'll tell my parents everything and I'm sure my father will take your side. He'll think of Bia in the same situation and he'll see we're doing the best we can."

I caressed his neck with my fingertips, and he shivered. "Are you sure?"

He took a deep breath. "Ninety percent sure. But let's say he doesn't agree and complicates things? We leave. Hilary, you, and me. We leave and go to a hotel, an apartment, whatever." He cupped my face. "The important thing now is for you to come with me."

I couldn't deny that his plan looked plausible, much more than the other times I considered warning Hilary. I guess that when thinking about a similar solution before, I was alone. I *felt* alone. And weak. This time, I had Leo with me, pushing me, supporting me. I didn't need him to be Prince Charming, but I needed his encouragement to save myself. To save Hilary and me.

"Okay," I whispered.

His eyes widened. "For real?"

"Didn't you ask me to come with you?"

"Yes, but I thought you would say no and I would have to argue about it for another hour."

I smiled. "Well, I really do want to be with you." I kissed the corner of his lips.

His hands slid down my arms. "You have no idea how happy that makes me, *morena*."

I kissed the other corner of his lips. "If it's anything like what I'm feeling, I do."

He hissed and stretched his back, capturing my mouth on his before I could keep teasing him. His lips fit mine perfectly, moving in a slow, sensual rhythm that made me crazy and my head spin. I moaned as his tongue caressed mine. I slid my hand over the bulge in his jeans and Leo jerked, shivering.

"*Ai, meu Deus*," he whispered. "You're not making this easy."

With a wicked smile, I tugged on the zipper of his jeans. He grabbed my hands and placed them on his chest, which with all those muscles was welcomed too.

"What?" I asked, before licking his lower lip.

He groaned. "We should go. The sooner we

leave, the sooner we'll be at my house, and the sooner I can throw you on my bed."

His bed. Under his sheets. With him. I couldn't think of any better place in the world.

The cheer left my body as I realized something. "First, I need to stop by the ranch."

He tensed under me. "No, no."

"I have to go there. To tell Jimmy I'll be gone for a few days, to grab some of my stuff, and to do something with Argus. I need to. Eric said he would call someone to take Argus away. If I'm not there, nothing will stop him from doing that. Or worse, put Argus down."

"But what if he's there?"

"He shouldn't be. He should be at practice for ..." I reached for my cell phone and checked the time. It was 3:10 p.m. "For another two hours. I should be able to find Jimmy there and pack a suitcase during that time. Though I'm not sure what to do with Argus. Maybe I should take him to my parents' house. Then I can pick Hilary up."

"Or we can take him too."

I gawked at him. "You will take me, my sister, and Argus?"

He shrugged. "Why not? If they're important to you, then they are important to me. Besides, you already know I have a soft spot for Argus."

I placed a quick, happy peck on his lips. "How are we gonna take him? He doesn't like being touched. It's not like I can ride him out of there."

Well, it was not like I could ride him. Or ride any horse. Period.

Unfortunately, I wasn't over riding another horse yet.

"How about you drive the trailer to my house?"

"That could work."

"Okay. I'm coming with you. I won't leave you alone there."

He leaned to me, and I was ready to meet him halfway when his cell phone rang. "*Merda.*"

He picked it up and stared at the screen. He cursed in Portuguese before answering.

"Dad," he said, his tone curt. I heard muffled Portuguese words and saw Leo tensing by my side.

After a few seconds and without saying a single word, he turned the phone off.

I reached to him and squeezed his hand in mine. "Want to talk about it?"

Leo squeezed my hand back. "My father didn't know I left and he just found out. He is ... pissed to say the least. He wants me to come back right this instant before he throws me off the team for good."

I frowned. "Maybe it's not a good idea for me to come to your house."

"Of course it is! And if he complicates it, I told you, we leave. Together."

I shook my head. "Leo ..."

He pulled me closer to him. "*Morena*, say whatever you want to say, but I'm not letting you go again."

My heart flipped with comfort. "All right. But you should go home now."

"I won't leave you alone."

"Leo, I won't be alone. Jimmy will be there, and Paul will probably be too. I'll ask Jimmy to take Argus to the trailer while I pack a bag, then I'm out of there."

His jaw tensed for the hundredth time in the past thirty minutes. "I don't like it."

"I know, but it's going to be okay. And I want you to go home. Your father sounded pissed and he'll probably be more pissed when I show up there, so please, go there and prepare him."

He let out a long, strained breath. "Promise me you'll be quick and that you'll call me if anything happens."

I leaned into him and kissed his cheek. "I promise."

He cupped my face in his hands and turned his

mouth to mine. It was a quick, but deep and meaningful kiss, and for a second I forgot what I had to do after.

"Be quick," he said. "Seriously. Otherwise I'm coming after you with my infantry."

I laughed. "All right."

He put on his hoodie and kissed me again before exiting my car and entering his borrowed one.

He waved as he drove away, and soon I followed him out of that parking lot with a smile on my face and hope in my heart.

33

I DROVE BACK TO THE RANCH LIKE A MAD WOMAN. A happy mad woman.

My chest was bursting with excitement and anticipation. I couldn't wait to get to the ranch, do whatever I had to do, and leave.

Leo's plan probably wasn't the best, but it was all we had, and honestly, I didn't know if I could wait any longer for a better one. I couldn't even look at Eric anymore. I had to break free now or I would be the one drowning.

I stopped my car in the parking lot and ran out, leaving the keys in the ignition and the door open. As I jogged to the stable, I looked around. Even though I wouldn't be gone for more than a week or so—at least, I hoped I wouldn't. One week was enough to dissuade Eric and tell the club or the police about who he really was, right?—I knew I would miss this place.

I rushed into the stable. "Jimmy?" He didn't answer, but Argus did. He came to the door of his stall and spied over it. "Hey, boy." I walked up to him and got as close as I thought he would allow me. "I need you to trust me, okay?" He snorted and I chuckled. He was too smart for his own good. "We're taking a short vacation. You and me. I promise you, you'll like the place we're going."

He snorted once more but didn't back away.

The same feeling as when I was with Leo came back. The three of us were connected, I was sure of it. One saving the other.

I took a deep breath and stepped forward. He retreated. I opened the door and entered his stall, expecting him to retreat to his corner. But he didn't. He stood his ground only two feet from me.

I peeked at his bucket. It was filled with grain.

"You didn't eat anything today?" I scooped a handful of grain and extended my arm to him. "Come on, boy, you have to eat something." I took a step in his direction and I almost cried in relief when he didn't recoil. "If you eat, I'll bring strawberries and peaches for you. Deal?"

For a long while, he stared at me. Then he

stretched his neck and ate from my hand. When the grain was gone, he didn't back away. Instead, he nudged my hand. Holding my breath, I ran my palm from under his chin to his cheek. He leaned against my touch, closing his eyes. A bubbly laugh escaped me, and a single fat tear ran down my face. I took a step forward and placed my cheek against him. He sighed, as if in relief, and I felt his muscles relaxing as I ran my hand over his beautiful coat. Poor horse. All he needed was care and love and understanding, and I wanted to give it all to him. Leo and I would give it all to him.

"I'm gonna take care of you," I whispered. Then he tensed, and I pulled back a little to look at him. "What is it?"

"How touching," Eric said.

I tensed right along with Argus.

My heart pounded as I whirled to face him. He still wore his dirty practice uniform.

"Eric, what are you doing here so early?"

An evil grin appeared on his mouth. "Well, let me see." He approached the stall's door, and Argus retreated to his corner, snorting and stomping his hooves. "I had this feeling that my woman might be misbehaving."

"What?"

He lunged forward and grabbed my arm. "Don't play games with me."

I jerked against his death grip. "Eric, release me."

Argus neighed and charged him. He raised his front hooves, trying to make Eric retreat, but Eric brought his hand forward, showing a whip he had been holding behind his back. He swatted the whip at Argus hard, harder than the other time he used it against the horse. He slashed Argus's neck.

"No!" I jerked free of Eric's grasp.

With enraged eyes, Argus came at Eric again, but Eric dodged one of Argus's kicks and hit the horse again with the whip, this time on his left thigh. Once, twice, three times. Nickering, Argus's knees trembled and he stuttered back.

"No!" I ran to Argus and knelt beside him.

Using the whip, Eric advanced on Argus. The horse stepped back, entering his stall, and Eric closed the door. He grabbed my elbow and hoisted me up and out of the stall.

"Bastard!" I pushed him away, but his grip only tightened. I tried kicking him, clawing him, but without letting go of the whip, he turned me around, pressed my back against his chest, and held my hands together. "Let me go!"

"Never," he whispered in my ear. I shuddered

as desperate tears made their way to my eyes. Holding me tight, he walked us out of the stable. "I want to talk about your misbehavior and your punishment."

"Eric ... Argus needs help. He's bleeding. Please, let me help him." I didn't even know why I bothered asking him that, but I couldn't help myself. I had to ask. To beg. "Please, let me go to him."

"Why would I do that? I'm hoping that horse will bleed to death."

I clamped my mouth as a sob assaulted me.

Thirty minutes ago. I wanted to go back to thirty minutes ago. Everything was perfect, or looked like it could be perfect thirty minutes ago.

My phone chimed.

Holding both my wrists in one hand, Eric fished my phone out of my pocket with the other. He stared at the screen and then turned his enraged eyes to me. He showed me the phone. It was a message from Leo: *What's taking you so long?*

"See? You misbehaved." He threw the phone on the ground with all he had and then stomped on it to finish the job. My phone was gone. "I won't lie. I'll enjoy punishing you."

I whimpered as he pushed me up the porch steps.

"Hey! What's happening here?" It was Jimmy.

With a growl, Eric threw me to the ground just like he did with the cell phone, and I banged my head on the foot of a swing chair.

Dizzy, I lost a few seconds of what occurred, but when I recovered, I sat up.

Eric brandished the whip high and brought it down on Jimmy.

"No! Eric! Stop!" I wobbled to my feet, but had to kneel when the world whirled around me. "Eric …"

Jimmy's raised arms took most of the hit. Blood quickly soaked his sleeves. Staggering, he tried to punch Eric, but Eric stepped out of the way and whipped Jimmy on the back. The old man fell on his hands and knees and screamed. I screamed too.

Eric unleashed the whip on Jimmy a handful of times more, until the old man was lying on the ground, motionless.

I crawled down the steps. "No, no, no."

Ignoring me, Eric grabbed Jimmy's hand and pulled him to the stable. I forced myself to my feet and wobbled to them. I followed Eric as he dragged Jimmy to a stall full of hay. He dropped Jimmy's limp body—at least I could see he was still breathing as his chest moved slowly up and down—behind a wall of hay, and tied him to one of the wooden posts. Then he put another piece of rope around Jimmy's mouth.

"Oh my God, please, Eric."

Another sob made its way up my throat. This couldn't be happening. No, no. Eric hit me. Okay. I mean, as okay as it could be. Some men hit women, unfortunately, and Eric was one of them. I could deal with that. I had been dealing with that. Hating every minute of it, but I handled it. Eventually, I would get out of it. But ... this? Slashing someone with horse whips and tying a person and leaving him to bleed? And he did the same to Argus.

Eric was a monster. A pure evil monster.

He turned to me with enraged eyes. He had some rope in his hands, and I knew what he wanted to do with it.

I ran out of the stall and out the stable. Still a little dizzy, I lost my footing on a loose stone and fell on the ground. I heard his footsteps approaching and quickly shot up. I raced to my car, and as I touched the open door, it closed with a bang when Eric pushed it.

He tsked and I whimpered.

"You're still misbehaving," he said, his tone too cold.

"Please. You don't want to do this," I whispered, leaning against the door and away from him. But he stepped closer, putting himself right in front of me and any possible exit.

"Who says I don't?" He reached for my hands, and I pulled them away. Desperate, I charged him, pushing him back with my shoulder, but he laughed and put his weight against me, pinning me to the car again.

I screamed and raised my hand to claw him. Once more, he laughed and held my wrist before my nails could touch his face. Then I kneed him. Unfortunately, he saw it coming and twisted to the side, and I kneed his thigh.

With renewed anger in his gaze, Eric slapped me with the back of his hand, sending me to the ground.

Before I could recover, he was sitting over me and tying my hands together.

I jerked against him, but it was too late. "No! Please, Eric, don't."

He lifted me from the dirty ground. "If you don't stop complaining, I'll tie your mouth too."

Would screaming get me anywhere? Nobody would hear me anyway. Not right now at least.

"I won't complain anymore," I muttered as tears rolled down my cheeks.

He wound his arm around my waist. "Good girl." He kissed my cheek and I flinched.

I scoured my mind for a quick plan, a way out, but nothing came to me, and I was too exhausted and broken to try anything. The best thing at this moment was to go along with what he said. Hopefully, I would feel less dizzy and stronger soon, and would be able to come up with a plan.

So I didn't fight when he led me to the house.

As we climbed up the front steps, I glanced over my shoulder to the stable. Tears blurred my vision and I suppressed a sob. I prayed Argus and Jimmy were strong enough to hang on until ... I didn't know.

34

Eric threw me down on an armchair in the living room, untied my hands, and then tied my wrists to the arms of the chair. He excused himself, as if he were actually polite, and went to the kitchen to make some calls.

I couldn't make out the exact words, but I did hear his tone and it didn't sound pleasant.

He stayed on the phone for over twenty minutes. If it was one call or several, I had no idea, and I didn't really care because my mind was trying to come up with a plan. Any plan. Any idea. Any spark of an idea. Anything.

Other than to wait for someone—more specifically Leo—to notice something was wrong, I had nothing.

I heard a car approaching and my heartbeat sped up. I held my tongue so I would not scream for help until I was sure whoever it was could help me, but my hopes dwindled when Eric strolled into the living room and opened the front door.

I heard heels clicking on the stone path leading from the parking lot to the house.

"Where were you?" he asked.

"Don't complain, Eric," the woman said, and I gasped. His mother! "I was downtown meeting with friends. If I were home, it would have taken me longer to arrive." Chloe walked past him and into the living room. Her conflicted eyes settled on me. "Oh, Eric, what have you done?"

He hissed. "Don't. Just don't."

She approached me. "Are you okay, dear? I mean, are you in pain? Can I get you anything?"

Hmm, what? "Freedom," I said.

She patted my hand and turned to her son. "This isn't really necessary."

Eric ignored her. "I need to go ... somewhere. Keep an eye on her." He pointed at me with his chin. "Bring her water, food, whatever, but *don't* untie her." With her gaze to the floor, Chloe nodded. "Okay, then." He quickly approached me, kissed my cheek—and I flinched again. "Be right back."

He left the house, and I exhaled as if fresh air had invaded my lungs after weeks under a dense fog.

But the fog settled back around me when Chloe sat down on the couch beside my armchair, avoiding looking me in the eyes.

"What's happening?" I asked, unable to hide the surprise and disgust from my voice. "Can't you see what he is doing?" I jerked my arms, but they barely moved. "He's insane. Literally. And you're helping him?"

Oh crap, what if she was insane too?

She didn't answer me right away, and I thought she wouldn't, until she finally whispered, "I don't have a choice."

"What? Of course you do. Cut these ropes and let me go. There's your choice."

She lifted her face and stared at me, her eyes brimming with tears. "I can't go against him. I won't go against him." She brushed her fingertips under her eyes, but one drop rolled down, leaving a streak of mascara on her pale cheek. "There's no easy way of saying this, so I'm just gonna go ahead and say it. Eric isn't right in the head, Hannah."

I gaped at her. "What?"

"I mean, *really* not right in the head. There's something wrong with him. Of course, he would actually have to want to be examined and diagnosed, and he would never do that. I actually never said this out loud until now, but I've talked to specialists about him and read many books about mental health and ..." She sighed. "He can't be normal. It would explain his behaviors, his moods, his anger, his lack of regret over the things he does."

I gulped. "What else does he do?"

She looked down at her hands and picked at her nails. "Oh, Hannah, I don't think you want to know."

"Actually, I do. I want to know everything."

With a practiced smile, she stood. "I need some water. While I'm in the kitchen, can I get you anything?"

"What? No, Chloe, answer me. Tell me what you know."

She waved at me as if I had told her an unfunny joke. "All right, then. I'll be right back." She whirled around and disappeared through the hallway.

What the hell?

On instinct, I jerked against the ropes until they bit into my skin and I whimpered in pain. "Shit." My gaze didn't stop darting around, trying to find a solution, a way out, as if it would pop from the wall or from under the couch. Anywhere.

Then the house telephone rang.

I froze.

I stared at it, so lonely sitting on the shelf along the wall between the staircase and the hallway door. Oh, how I wanted to know who it was. I hoped it was someone who knew me, not a salesperson who wouldn't give a damn if the phone was answered or not.

The telephone stopped ringing and I wanted to scream. Maybe if I screamed too loudly, the person calling would listen. Crap, I was already thinking of impossible solutions, since there was no possible one.

With her perfect makeup redone, Chloe came into the living room. She had a tray with water, juice, a bowl of fruit, a loaf of bread, butter, jelly, and some of my favorite cookies and crackers.

"I don't know exactly what you want, so I brought what I found," she said, placing the tray over the coffee table. She sat back on the couch and smiled at me, as if this was a normal situation.

I pressed my lips tight, but the words came out anyway. "I'm starting to wonder if you're insane too."

She shook her head, her smile faltering. "I assure you I'm not. I do the things I do so Eric won't unleash his rage on me. Besides, he's my son. Even if he is what as unstable as I think he is ... I can't seem to imagine him thrown in jail."

Jail? Well, hitting a woman could be reason enough to be thrown in jail, but something told me there was more.

I took a deep breath. "What else did he do? Please, tell me."

She averted her eyes. "I can't decide if telling you everything might actually help or not. Perhaps, if you know, you'll see the real danger and stop going against him."

Real danger? Wasn't I already in real danger?

I was shaking. "What do you mean?"

When her eyes returned to me, the tears were there once more. "A person like him only thinks about himself and how he can be richer, more successful, more handsome. It's always about him, and always about more. The problem is, he has have no regrets. None." She took a grape from the bowl and stared at it as if it were a diamond or something equally precious. "Eric was a selfish and rude kid. He didn't care about his so called friends. He took advantage of them. Of all of us. I never understood why, until I started connecting the dots."

I was afraid to ask, but I had to know. "What dots?"

The telephone started ringing again, and my heart skipped a beat. Chloe tensed and the two of us stared at it in silence until it stopped.

I closed my eyes for a second and wished with all my heart it was Leo or someone else who would find it odd that I wasn't answering my cell or house phone, and called the police. I didn't care if the police were friends with Eric, because really, would they defend him after seeing me tied to a chair? And Jimmy and Argus bleeding outside?

I took a deep, shuddering breath. For now, I had to know more. "What dots?" I repeated the question.

"The night before the car accident that killed my husband and my oldest son, and put me in a deep depression, Eric had a big fight with his father. At that time, Eric was already playing polo, and Nolan didn't approve of it. He thought it was a waste of time, and that Eric was playing with the family's wealth. Nolan told him he was a disappointment of a son, and that Ian would inherit everything and become the head of the company, while Eric would be his employee out of pity.

"Then he started dating you, and he became obsessed with you. In his mind, you could help him be better, be richer, be more famous, be more known. The night before the ranch caught fire, Eric and you had an argument too. He didn't want you to go to college, and he hated the fact that you were living on campus. But he hated more the fact that you spent most of your weekends here, with your grandma and your horse, instead of with him. He would come here to visit you for a few hours, when in fact he wanted all of your attention.

"The day before your father's latest incident, didn't you have an argument with Eric too? He was sure he had convinced your father that selling the ranch was for the best. He was sure your father could convince you of that. Then you tell him your father approved and supported your choices.

"When Leonardo Fernandes came into the picture, Eric noticed right away that this new boy couldn't take his eyes off you, and that you seemed at least curious about him too. Then he takes the title from Eric. A couple of weeks later, this boy's past explodes into the media. Not to mention your new horse, Argus. Eric still doesn't know what to do about him."

Fear gripped my heart. My hands trembled. My mind spun.

"Wait ... wait." I took a long breath and shook

my head. No, it couldn't be. "What are you saying?"

She popped the grape into her mouth and took her time chewing and swallowing it. If I were free, I would be at her throat by now.

"The obvious," she said. "Eric hired someone to cause the accident that killed his father and his brother. Eric hired someone to set fire to this ranch, killing your grandma and your horse. Eric hired two men to shoot your father, and he killed them himself for not having succeeded. Eric hired someone to find out anything about Leonardo that would destroy his career and hopefully make you hate him, because killing him would raise suspicions, though I think he would consider it again if that boy and you got closer."

Got closer? Acid churned in my stomach. "H-how does he know about Leo?"

"Sometimes he sends Pete to follow you," she said, her tone indicating that having me followed was routine. "And Eric plans on doing something about your new horse."

"He just did," I croaked. My stomach flipped, and I felt like I would throw up everything I ever ate in my entire life. "It can't be."

Chloe nodded. "The same thing I used to say

when I first found out about what he was capable of."

I looked at her, at this woman who seemed so poised, so elegant, so right, and yet harbored a murderer in her house. Looks were indeed deceiving.

"How exactly did you find out?" I asked, my voice trembling as much as I was.

"The police said the car accident was just that, an accident, but I didn't want to let it go. Nolan was such a careful driver, and I knew there was more to it. So, I started researching on my own. That's when Eric came to me and told me to stop looking for answers I didn't want to find. I asked him what he wasn't telling me, and he didn't say anything. But I began paying attention. Most of the time, my son is charming, elegant, a real gentleman, but underneath, when he thinks nobody is watching, he's cruel, rude, violent, selfish, evil. Soon after, I connected the first dots." She put her hand over the scar on her neck. "He told you this was from the car accident, right? It wasn't. This was him, Hannah. This was the first one, after I told him he needed psychological help, and I've plenty of other scars on my back and ... everywhere. He did these. He cut me. He said it was my punishment. I've learned to behave the way he wants me to.

Now, he doesn't even hide his crimes from me any-more." She rested her hand over mine. I would have pulled it away if I could. "I don't want that to happen to you."

She wanted me to be like her? To accept that her sicko son would rule my life, and cut me every time I looked in the opposite direction he wanted me to? She was even more of a sicko than he was. I would rather die right now than live the rest of my life under Eric's influence.

I looked at her, hoping my eyes had enough begging in them. "Then cut my ropes, please. Let me go."

"I can't," she whispered. "You shouldn't want to leave too."

"Excuse me?" How could she say that?

"Hannah, there's no way of escaping him. Even if you run, he'll hunt you forever. I know he threat-ened your sister. Don't think for a second he won't do it, because he will. Keep confronting him, and he'll go after her in no time." She shook her head. "It can be so much worse, Hannah. He can turn you into his slave. Literally. You'll never leave the house."

I looked out the window to the stable. It seemed peaceful, like it usually was, and for a second I wondered if I had dreamed everything that happened. If it was all a nightmare, soon I would wake up in my bed, Eric would be gone, because he had listened to me and accepted our break up, Jimmy would be taking Argus out to the arena to exercise, and Paul would be preparing one of his classes.

The perfection bubble burst when I remembered Jimmy and Argus were somewhere inside the stable, bleeding and suffering.

Tears brimmed in my eyes.

I tilted my head to Chloe and peered at her. "Why did you tell me all this?"

"To show you he'll act against you if you don't do whatever he asks."

"He already acted against me!" I choked. He had killed my grandma and Hercules. He had hurt my father, and now Jimmy and Argus. And he did hurt Leo too—not physically but I had felt his pain as if it were a real cut.

"That's what I'm telling you, Hannah. That's nothing compared to what he can actually do."

It didn't make any sense. How could there be anything worse than killing, planning to kill, plotting against family, or imprisoning the person he said he loved?

I couldn't quite grasp why she was helping him, protecting him. I mean, he was sick. Crazy. A lunatic! But I wasn't a mother. Even so, I couldn't imagine defending a son of mine to this extent. More and more, I believed she was sick too.

Anyhow, she was my only way out of here. At least, the only one I could see right now. If I could appeal to her guilt or shame, I could convince her to loosen my ropes, of letting me use the bathroom alone, or something.

"Chloe—"

The front door opened and Eric stepped in, followed by Pete, his chauffeur. He still wore his practice clothes, but now he had a gun tucked in the waist of his pants.

He smiled at me, his award-winning grin. "Did you miss me?"

35

PETE WATCHED ME FROM THE DOOR, IN A TRAINED bodyguard pose, while Eric and his mother whispered in the hallway. I couldn't make out the words, but they sounded harsh.

After quite some time, Chloe approached me with a tight smile. She bowed close to me and patted my hand. "I'll see you soon," she said.

My eyes widened. "What? Where are you going?"

Eric strolled into the room like a king. "Home. She's going to start dinner for us."

Like a true mother, Chloe kissed her son's cheek, waved at me, and left.

At once, the air around me became dense and

my breathing sped up. Without her here, how would I escape?

Eric gestured to the door. "You can wait outside, Pete."

With a curt nod, Pete turned and walked out.

That left him and me alone.

Fear built up inside me, and my hand shook harder.

He sat down by my side, in the same spot his mother had taken before. "We'll be gone soon too," he said. He smiled at me, as if this were the most normal setting ever.

I swallowed down an ounce of my fear. "What are we waiting for?"

"Mr. Nash is on his way to sign the sales agreement."

"Sales agreement?"

"Yes. You're selling this piece of crap to him, and you'll sign the sales agreement tonight. In about a week, we should meet at his lawyer's office to sign the actual sales contract."

I gaped at him.

First, how the hell could he do this to me? He said he loved me—which now I had my doubts. He was confused between love and obsession—but wanted me to sell what I loved most in this life? Second, how the hell could he ask Mr. Nash to come here? Here! Where a man and a horse were hidden in the stable, bleeding to death. Wasn't he the least bit worried that Mr. Nash would see them?

Perhaps the no-worry went along with the no-regret from being truly insane.

Though I hoped Mr. Nash came. Even if I didn't like the man, he would see the things going on around him and he wouldn't just wave them off, would he? No. I hoped not. I hoped he came and called 9-1-1 right away.

I shook my head. Shit, it was still hard to believe, even though everything pointed his direction. After his first freak out, I was worried about his temper and his jealousy. If only I knew there was much more to it. I'd dated and kissed and slept in the same bed as a crazy person for over two years without ever realizing it. Oh, he had already killed his father and his brother, and threatened his mother when he started courting me. My stomach revolved.

He took my hand in his. "Are you okay?"

I jerked against the ropes on my wrists and shot him what I hoped was a furious look. "Is this okay, Eric?"

"It's for your own good, baby?"

"You're insane."

He closed his hand over mine and pressed it. Hard. I yelped. "Don't fight me. Don't argue with me. Don't say things that I don't want to hear. I love you, baby, but I can and I will make your life miserable if you don't behave."

The loud ring of the house telephone made him let go of my hand and shoot up to his feet, his hand over the gun at his waist.

Pain rippled from my fingers, past my wrists, to my elbows, and fear crawled up my spine.

"Fuck," he muttered. He rushed to the telephone and pulled the wires from the wall. "There. Now it won't bother us anymore." He turned to me with his charming smile. Lucky me, I didn't fall for that anymore. "Where were we?"

He took a step toward me, but a knock on the door made him halt.

"Mr. Bennett, there's a car entering the property," Pete said through the closed door.

"Is it Mr. Nash?"

"I don't think so," Pete answered.

Someone? Not Mr. Nash? My heart thumped against my chest so rapidly, I thought Eric would hear it and hit me for being this hopeful.

Cursing, Eric opened the door and spied out. Then he turned to me with an evil smile. "Oh, my luck."

The fear returned, squashing any grain of hope I could have.

With the front door open, it was easy to hear the car parking, the door opening, and the heels clicking on the stone path. Heels?

Eric walked out, pulling the door closed behind him, to meet whoever was approaching.

"Hello there," he said.

"Hi, Eric."

My blood went cold and my heart stopped.

"Good to see you," Eric said.

"Yeah, you too," Hilary said, sounding bored. "Where's Hannah?"

"Inside. Do you want to come in?"

"No!" I yelled.

"What was that?" Hilary asked. "Is she playing some game? I'm gonna skin her alive if she is."

"Come in, you'll see," Eric said.

"No, Hil! Don't!" I screamed.

"Hannah?"

The door opened and Hilary stepped in, followed closely by Eric.

All primped up in a cute summer dress and four-inch sandals, Hilary had just walked into my latest nightmare.

"No, Hil. Oh, God," I cried as Eric locked the door.

Hilary turned in my direction and froze. "What's ... what's happening?"

Eric put a hand on his waist, purposely beside his gun, so Hilary would see it. "We're playing a game, like you guessed. Want to join us?"

Hilary's wide gaze went from his face to his gun, and back to his face. "What?"

"Leave her alone, Eric!" I jerked against the armchair. Crap, if this was a simple kitchen chair, I would be able to fall back and break it or loosen the ropes.

Hilary took a step away from Eric. "What's happening?"

Eric brushed his fingers over the gun on his waist. "How about we start by having Hilary sit down so I can explain the rules?"

She glanced at me, unsure and scared. Fighting back the tears and the panic attack that was brewing in my chest, I nodded. She clambered back until she fell on the couch, her eyes always flickering between Eric's lunatic expression and his gun.

"I don't understand," she whispered.

Oh, I didn't fully understand it either. The only thing I understood was not wanting to get shot, or Hilary too. And, if right now I needed to kiss the floor that Eric stepped on, I would do it. Somehow,

I would make sure this wouldn't end this way. However, each time I realized I had no idea how and if it would end, desperation gripped my heart, and all I wanted to do was curl into myself and cry.

"You know, we can make this work." Eric paced across the coffee table from us, his evil smile wide. "Hilary will join us in our happily ever after, and it'll be perfect."

I felt sick.

"What's he talking about?" Hilary whispered to me.

"I'm talking about you two behaving and doing exactly what I tell you to." Eric halted. "Or I won't have any other choice than to hurt you."

Hilary glanced at me, millions of questions in her eyes. "What's wrong with him?"

I shook my head, hoping she would shut up, but it was too late. Eric jumped over the coffee table and leaned over her, one of his hands on her shoulder, the gun under her chin.

She whimpered.

"Eric, please." My voice broke. "Leave her alone. She's confused and scared." Not that I wasn't, but I had a bit more experience dealing with him. "Please."

He pulled the gun down, but leaned closer to her and licked her cheek. "She tastes good," he whispered as Hilary flinched away from him, a disgusted look in her eyes. Eric raised his hand and slapped her. Her head whipped to the side, and she fell on the couch.

"No! Stop!" I cried.

Eric grabbed a handful of her hair and pulled her up to face him again. Hilary was crying.

I fought against the ropes, not caring that I was only hurting my wrists more. Damn it! "Eric, oh my God. Please, Eric."

"She has to learn," he said, his mouth hovering over her red cheek. "You'll learn."

A loud sob shook her body, making me cry too. I wanted to hug her, to take her out of here, to send her somewhere safe.

Eric knelt in front of her, trailing the gun down her neck, her shoulder, slowly along the strap of her dress. He momentarily stopped by her cleavage, and his eyes shone with something I knew too well.

"Eric." I kicked my foot in the air, but he was one or two inches out of reach. "What are you doing?"

He smiled at me. "I wonder if her body is as perfect as yours." With deliberate movements, he placed a hand over her knee and slowly moved up her leg.

Oh, Lord …

"Stop!" I yelled. "Please, stop!"

Hilary tried moving away, by jerking her legs and scooting to the side, but he pressed the gun to her chest and she stopped, whimpering.

His hand continued sliding under her dress.

A tear rolled down my cheek. "You don't want to do this, Eric. Please, you're only trying to get back at me. I'm here. I'll be good. I promise. Please, don't do this."

He licked his lower lip. "I don't believe you. I think you too need a lesson. Besides, who says I don't want to do this?"

He leaned over her and her sobs became louder. He buried his face in her neck, and Hilary turned her face as far away from him as she could. Still holding the gun, he grabbed her hips and pulled her to the edge of the couch. Oh, Lord, no, no, no. I tugged against the ropes, against the chair. I kicked my legs. I screamed. I had to do something. Anything.

Eric sniffed her hair and moaned, thrusting his hips on hers. She screamed.

"You like it, don't you?" he asked, settling the gun beside them on the couch. His hand moved quickly over the waist of his pants.

"Eric, please, I beg you, don't do this," I asked, my voice breaking with every word.

He turned to me, the glint of mad desire burning his eyes. "Don't be such a bitch." He licked his lips again. "You'll have your turn. Right after I'm done with this sweet girl."

As he was pulling his pants down, his phone rang.

Cursing, he pulled back and reached for his phone and the gun on the couch. He looked at the screen, cursed some more, and stood, pulling his pants back up.

"Hello," he said into the phone, walking to the opposite side of the room.

Hilary lay limply on the couch, her head down and her blond hair over her face. She was crying and trembling.

"Hilary," I whispered. She lifted her face to me, her hair still like a curtain over her. I wanted to tell her I was sorry, that I loved her, and that everything would be all right, but we didn't have much time. "Hil, grab the knife." She brushed the hair from over her damp eyes. "The butter knife on the tray. Get it."

Like she had been injected with adrenaline, she straightened her back and, spying over to Eric, who had paced around the other corner of the living room, she grabbed the knife.

"I'm not sure this will work," she whispered, bringing the knife to my ropes. With shaking hands, she started working on it. "This knife is too dull. This is going to take forever." She stole glances at Eric every two seconds.

"Keep going," I said, my voice low. "Probably not the right time to ask, but what are you doing here?"

"A guy named Leonardo called Mom, saying he had been calling you and you weren't picking up and that something was wrong. He said something about not coming here alone; he said to call the police to come check on you. Of course, he made Mom worried, so she called you and got the same thing. By then, she was pulling her hair out. So, I offered to come check on you."

I shook my head. "Leo said not to come alone. You shouldn't be here."

She struggled against the knife, and it almost fell from her hand, scratching me in the process. "Sorry," she whispered.

We spied over at Eric.

"I understand," he said to whoever was talking to him. "We have time."

Hilary's hands stopped moving—not shaking

—as she stared at him. "I can't … I can't believe it's the same guy."

I slapped her hand, but it was more like my fingers brushing over her palms. "Hey!"

"Sorry," she muttered before working on the rope again. "This will take forever."

"Then you better keep at it!" I hissed.

She had cut half the width of the rope when we heard Eric saying goodbye on the phone. Quickly, she hid the knife under me and returned to the corner of the couch.

"I'm sorry about that," Eric said, turning back to us. "Mr. Nash will be a little late, which means" —he strolled closer, and I tensed as his eyes fluttered from Hilary to me, back to Hilary, then back to me—"we have a lot of time for ourselves."

36

INSTEAD OF FORCING HIS WAY WITH HILARY RIGHT away, Eric went to the kitchen—two minutes that Hilary and I worked more on the ropes—and brought back a bottle of wine and three glasses.

He pushed the tray away and sat on the other side of the coffee table, diagonal between Hilary and me.

She was still trembling, and I didn't blame her. I was trembling too; I just was more focused on cutting my ropes, kicking him in the gut, and running away.

With his perpetual *charming* smile, Eric filled the glasses with red wine and offered them to us.

"Ah, I guess I'll need to cut one of your arms free," he said. He set my glass down and pulled a penknife from his pocket. My eyes widened, and I prayed he chose to cut the ropes Hilary hadn't touched.

She stared at me, her eyes as wide as mine.

I held my breath as Eric reached for my left arm. The arm with the rope half cut.

"What the fuck?" he asked, twisting my arm to have a better look at it.

A scream rang in my ears as Hilary grabbed the wine bottle and broke it over Eric's head. Red liquid splashed everywhere as he tumbled to the floor. She took the penknife and cut me free.

My heart racing, I picked up a plate from the tray and broke it over Eric's head. Just to make sure. Then, I grabbed Hilary's hand and we raced out of the house.

We skidded to a halt when we saw Pete on the farthest corner of the porch, a gun apparent on his waist, and another man standing by the cars in the parking lot.

"Shit," I muttered.

I tightened my grip around Hilary's hand and pulled her forward, rushing to the stable. With her heels, she tripped over the stones, but I held her up and we continued running.

"Jimmy!" I cried once we crossed the doorway. "Argus!"

Nothing. My heart died a little. I wanted to stop and help them, but I had to get Hilary out of here first. Get *us* out of here first.

I let go of Hilary and took a bridle and reins from the wall.

"They're coming," Hilary said, her voice a high pitch.

I pushed the bridle and reins into her hands. "Go. The fourth stall to your right. It's Belle. She's easy and gallops fast. Just ... hop on her, get her going, then put on the harness."

She looked at me confused. "What?"

"Just go." I pushed her again and turned to the wall, grabbing another bridle and reins for me.

She retreated. "I don't understand."

"They probably run faster than us, but they won't run faster than a horse," I explained, walking to Chip's stall. "Now go!"

She whirled on her heels, and I turned to Chip's door.

From the corner of my eyes, I saw both bodyguards a few feet from the stable.

"Shit," I muttered. "Argus!" I opened Chip's door.

Argus whimpered and I froze. Oh, Lord. He was still awake, maybe conscious. Without thinking, I ran to his stall. He was on the floor, blood smeared everywhere. I pressed a hand over my mouth as a sob racked my body.

Pete entered the stable, and the other man was fast approaching. I glanced over to Belle's stall and saw Hilary pulling her out. She would make it, but I wouldn't have time to mount and gallop away.

I turned to the wall again and grabbed a whip, much like the one Eric used to hurt Argus and Jimmy. Nausea settled in my stomach. I didn't want to be like Eric. I wasn't. However, I had to fight my way out of here.

Pete halted a few yards from me, his gun trained at me. "Don't move!"

I froze.

Behind me, Hilary froze.

I shook my head and raised the whip. "Go, Hil." I ducked, in case Pete shot, stepped aside, and brought the whip down on his arm.

"Aaah!" The gun fell to the ground and he cradled his arm, a thin red line emerging from under his shirt.

Shit. What had I done? Before I could feel bad about it, the other man stepped into the stable.

"Go, Hil," I repeated, as the second man drew his gun from its holder.

"But—"

"NOW!" I screamed, interrupting her protest.

"Stop!" the man yelled. I didn't know who he wanted to shoot, or if he would shoot at all, but I stepped into his line of sight, hoping Hilary's wasn't too high above my head.

Moments later, the sound of Belle's hooves stomping the ground grew distant, and that simple fact brought such a relief to me.

From behind Pete and the other bodyguard, I saw Eric stumbling out of the house. His clothes were stained from the wine, and I thought I saw a small trail of blood running down his head. That gave me a tiny bit of satisfaction—bet he never saw that coming!

I focused my attention on both bodyguards. Pete was already on his feet, his gun back in his hands. Shit. Three against one.

Argus's high-pitched nickering sounded from somewhere behind me, and my heart swelled. Even hurt, he was still trying to get to me.

The bodyguards spied around me, and I could only guess Argus was trying to get out of his stall.

"Don't hurt her!" Eric's voice boomed from the distance as he climbed down the front steps of the porch.

The bodyguards didn't lower their guns, but at least I was more relieved that they wouldn't shoot me in case I decided to run, which was exactly what I was thinking about doing. I doubted I could outrun them, but if I had a cell phone or something, I could call 9-1-1 while running. I hoped Hilary had her cell phone on her and called someone. Or, maybe I could trick them and reach my car. The keys were still in the ignition ... I hoped.

Eric reached the halfway point in the path to the stable.

All right. Now or never.

I inhaled all I could.

Five.

Four.

Three.

Two.

Tires squealed and my heart skipped a beat. Mr. Nash wouldn't enter the property on a bootleg turn.

The bodyguards glanced over their shoulders as Eric's eyes widened. A second later, he ran, really ran, out of the way as an SUV drove by right where he had been a second ago.

With the same hoodie and cap as before, Leo opened the door of his Grand Cherokee and stepped out, his baseball bat in his hand.

His eyes found mine, and I could see and feel the relief in them once he found me intact.

My chest felt tight with so much hope.

And love.

Leo shifted his gaze to Eric. "I'm so ready to kick your ass."

With a growl, Eric turned his hand toward Leo. I yelped, but Leo swung the bat, hitting Eric's hand and sending the gun flying. The bodyguard I didn't know dashed to them, while Pete lowered his gun briefly and advanced to me.

Still in a daze, it took me a precious second to react and run from him, a second he used to catch up with me and wrap his arm around me, tight, pulling my back to his chest and his gun to my neck.

"Stop fighting," he said through gritted teeth.

I did stop fighting, but only because I had to think for a minute.

Somehow, Leo knew how to fight, and it was kind of entrancing to see him dodging and parrying and landing blows with or without the bat, like a professional boxer. I shook my head, remembering his past and realizing he probably learned how to fight during his rebellious years.

"She'll never be yours," Eric said, preparing a hook. But Leo ducked, slamming the bat on Eric's back.

Eric fell on his knees on the ground.

"She's a person and she belongs to herself alone," Leo said, letting the bat go down again.

Eric screamed as it struck his side.

Then, the second bodyguard raised his gun and pointed it at Leo.

Desperation gripped my heart. "Leo!" I cried.

He jumped to the side just as the shot boomed through the air, and I gasped. Surprising everyone, even me, Leo whirled around, bringing the bat to the bodyguard's head. The man fell on the ground.

Before I could react—hit Pete in the groin, bite his hand, elbow his stomach, or something—Argus neighed behind us. Pete glanced over his shoulder and I took advantage to reach to Argus' stall and unlatch the door. The horse came barreling out toward Pete. The bodyguard stepped to the side, causing his grip to loosen around me and putting him in a perfect place. With all the strength I had, I kicked Pete past the door behind him, inside the tack room. He staggered back and almost fell to the ground. I quickly closed the door, thankful the keys were on this side of the door. I locked it and threw the key away.

Pete banged against the wall. "Let me out!"

I tuned him out as I turned to Argus.

His white coat was stained by blood flowing

from the thin cuts on his neck and leg, and he looked jittery.

I raised my hands. "Hey, boy, it's me." Carefully, I approached him and gently ran my hand over his muzzle. "You're gonna get through it."

The sound of a shot made me jump, and I whirled around.

Leo fell on his knees, his hands over the side of his abdomen.

"No!" I cried, giving a couple of steps in his direction. Until Eric turned to me, the gun in his hand and a wicked smile on his lips. "No," I muttered.

Shaking, I grabbed Argus's mane and pulled him to run by my side. He didn't move, just poked me with his muzzle. Understanding what he wanted, I held on tighter to his mane and pulled myself up, without saddle, without bridle, without reins.

His first step was wobbly, and I questioned the stupidity behind mounting him to escape. But he regained his footing and started trotting away.

Without resisting it, I glanced over my shoulder. Eric was skidding to a stop, the gun ready, and Leo was on the ground, the bodyguard hovering over him like a predator. What the guard didn't see was Leo's hand, reaching for the bat a few inches away.

I patted Argus's neck and he sped up. We crossed the back gates in no time and kept accelerating. Until another shot exploded from inside the stable.

Argus's knees caved in and we went tumbling down. For a couple of seconds, we were one single mess. Then his chest fell over my legs, and we lay sprawled on the ground. Pain shot from where my side had taken the brunt of the fall.

Argus snorted, trying to get up, but couldn't. Dizzy, I pushed up on my elbows and watched Argus falling over me for a second, still trying to understand what happened. When things clicked, I sat up the rest of the way, gasping.

Blood sputtered from Argus's side like someone had opened a faucet of water.

"No, no," I muttered, pulling my feet from under him. "Argus, boy, please. Hang on."

He inhaled, a wheezing noise that sent fear rolling down my spine.

I glanced to the side—Leo brawled with the bodyguard, blood trickling down the side of his hoodie, and Eric approached us—wishing a cell phone would pop into my hands, and I could call

Dr. Bohm to come and take Argus to the hospital right away. I couldn't lose him.

Eric stood by us, his gun pointed at Argus. "I should have killed him a long time ago."

"No," I croaked, putting myself between his gun and Argus.

Eric glared at me. "I don't see any reason to keep him alive, baby. Besides, he is losing a lot of blood. I don't think he'll recover anytime soon."

Movement behind Eric caught my eyes, but I refused to look. Instead, I kept my eyes on his, begging him not to do it.

A leaf crunched under a sole, and Eric turned to the noise. Leo swung his bat and hit Eric's face, making him stagger to the side. Recovering, Eric raised his gun to Leo, but I ducked under his arm and raised it up, making the bullet fly to the sky.

Leo took advantage of that and swung his bat toward Eric again. Eric pushed me toward it, and Leo barely had time to stop it before it hit me in the chest. Gasping for air, I fell on my knees beside Argus. The horse jerked, visibly trying to get up, and Leo glared at Eric.

"I'm gonna kill you," Leo said, his teeth gritted.

"No, I'm gonna kill you!" Eric pressed the trigger, and the bullet hit the baseball bat, causing Leo to lose his grip on it. The bat fell at his feet, broken in two.

"No!" I cried, trying to get up.

Eric was about to shoot Leo again, but Argus jerked up, kicking his hind legs at Eric and making him stumble back.

Leo charged Eric, punching him in the face. Eric fell on the ground, but he hooked my ankle and pulled me with him. I fell back, hitting my head on a rock. It all went dark for a second, but then I found myself by Eric's side, his gun at my neck.

"Try anything, and I'll kill her," he said, pressing the cold metal against my skin.

I yelped.

Leo was frozen, his eyes wide. Slowly, he raised his hands. "All right. I'll do whatever you want me to. Just don't hurt her."

Eric sat up, pulling me with him. He turned his face to me, inhaling deeply. I winced. "Stand there. Very still. Your arms at the side."

Leo's eyes met mine, and I saw the conflict in them. He wanted to save me, but dead, he wouldn't be able to.

I felt movement behind us but wasn't sure what it was. Eric's gun pointed to Leo caught my attention, and I forgot about all of it.

"Any last words," Eric asked.

Leo nodded, without taking his eyes from mine. "I love you," he whispered. Then he glared at Eric. "And you're a sick bastard who deserves to rot in hell." Leo's tone rose. "Even so, that wouldn't be enough. Motherfuckers like you should feel on their own skin what they have done to others." Leo's voice kept on getting louder. "I just wish I somehow had a hand in your demise, because you'll have one and it's going to be sooner than you think."

Leo smirked and I gaped at him. What was happening?

All of a sudden, Argus's hooves fell over Eric's back, and Leo reached forward, grabbing my arm and pulling me away. He embraced me tightly as Argus reared, letting his hooves come down over Eric again, making him scream. As if trying to avenge everything he had ever done to anyone, Argus stomped Eric's body.

I clamped my ears, not wanting to hear Eric's screams, and buried my face in Leo's neck, inhaling his familiar scent, allowing myself to drown in him.

His arms wound around me, and he kissed the top of my head. "You're okay now. Everything is okay now."

Sirens sounded in the distance.

Over Leo's shoulder, I saw Hilary—with her phone in her hand—and Belle making their way back. I turned my head behind me and saw Argus as he collapsed to the ground, Eric by his side, immobile.

37

MY PARKING LOT LOOKED LIKE A CIRCUS. A TRAGIC circus.

Five police cars, three ambulances, my mother's car, and two other cars with Leo's family. Not to mention the reporters trying to get past the police line.

I was seated on the back of an ambulance; a paramedic tried to examine me while I glanced around.

After arresting Pete and the second bodyguard, and loading Jimmy and Eric into ambulances and dispatching them to the hospital, the police officers walked around the ranch, collecting evidence and such.

Still shaking, Hilary sat by another ambulance

with my crying mother beside her. My mother had already embraced and kissed me thousands of times since she arrived. She also apologized repeatedly for not noticing anything weird about Eric before. But it wasn't her fault. It was nobody's fault.

Leo was huddled in a circle with his family a couple of feet from where I was. He kept looking over his shoulder at me, his eyes and sad smile saying more than words could. He had his palm over the bandage on his side where the bullet had grazed him. Thank God, it hadn't been worse.

On the other hand, Argus didn't seem quite well.

After stomping on Eric, he collapsed. Leo called the vet right away, and while he was on his way, I wouldn't allow a paramedic to touch me before doing something about Argus. There was nothing they could do because they weren't permitted to, but I felt a little better for trying.

Soon, Dr. Bohm and his assistant arrived and started working on Argus. Both of them looked worried while they moved around Argus, doing only God knew what.

I took a step toward them, and the paramedic gently pushed me back. He turned my face and checked my cheek under a lantern kind of thing.

"You'll be fine," he said. "Perhaps just a minor concussion from hitting your head, but other than that, fine." He settled the lantern down. "But take it easy. And stay awake for a couple of hours more, if you can. If in the morning you're feeling dizzy or in pain, have someone drive you to the hospital for further exams."

I nodded and he turned to his clipboard.

I glanced to Hilary and my mother, then to Leo and his family. They seemed well, as well as they could be, and I didn't feel like joining their conversations. I had already told them what I remembered of the events, and everything else I knew, at least three times. To the police, to my mother, to Leo's family. And each time, I felt more exhausted and drained than before.

I approached Argus just as Dr. Bohm stood up.

He glanced at me. "I was able to stop the bleeding for now, but he'll need surgery to take the bullet out. I also need to evaluate the internal damage and repair it if I can."

If I can ...

I knelt beside Argus. He looked unconscious, but maybe he was sleepy from the sedative I saw Dr. Bohm giving him. I brushed my fingers over his soft white coat, afraid of hurting him.

A sob lodged in my throat. He had ignored his injuries to save me, more than once.

A hand clutched my shoulder, and I knew who was it without having to look. I rested my hand over Leo's.

Dr. Bohm moved around Argus. "We need to take him to the animal hospital right away," he said.

Moments later, his truck was parked beside Argus, and Leo, João Pedro, Ricardo, Pedro, and Guilherme helped Dr. Bohm and his assistant drag Argus inside it. The assistant hopped on the back with Argus as I caressed his hind leg one more time. Leo stood by my side and put his arm around my shoulders.

Dr. Bohm paused in front of us. "I'll do the best I can to save him." Then he shut the doors and ran to the driver seat.

I rested my head on Leo's shoulder as the truck drove away, carrying one of the things I loved most in this life.

A tear rolled down my cheek.

"He'll be all right," Leo said, pulling me against his chest. I slid my arms around his waist and buried my face in his shirt. "He went through rougher patches, didn't he? And now he has you. He will fight and he'll make it."

I hoped so. I really, really hoped so, because ... I couldn't lose him now.

I tilted my head up and stared into Leo's eyes. "I think I'll go to the animal hospital, stay there until ..."

"I know you're worried, *morena*. I am too. But you need to rest. You need to take a nice shower, eat some comfort food, and go to bed, even if you can't sleep. Unfortunately, staying up in a waiting room all night won't help in any way." He ran his fingers over my cheek, brushing a strand of my hair away from my face. "I'm sure Dr. Bohm won't hesitate in calling you if he needs to."

I couldn't imagine staying here, waiting for news, but I knew Leo was right. I felt like I would collapse in a couple of seconds. Collapsing in the waiting room of an animal hospital wouldn't be the best.

I stood on tiptoes and lightly grazed his lips with mine. "You're right."

Ricardo cleared his throat, and we turned to him, without actually letting go of each other.

"The police are asking everyone to leave, so, hmm, we're going," he said.

I turned my head toward the house, and sure enough, the police were putting up those yellow tapes around it. Another cop grabbed a roll of tape and marched to the stable.

"Shit," I muttered.

Bia walked up to us, her expression forlorn and so unlike her usual self. "You're welcome to stay with us," she said. "You can borrow my clothes if you want."

I tried smiling at her generosity, but I didn't feel like it. "Thanks." I wanted to stay with them, with Leo, but there were other people who needed me at this moment. Surveying the place, I found Hilary and my mother stepping out of the ambulance, a cop talking to them. I could see from here that Hilary was still shaking. "Thanks, really, but I think I should stay with my family tonight."

Ricardo and Bia nodded. "I understand," she said.

Her expression changed to something like confusion, until she stepped forward, pulled me from Leo, and gave me the fastest and most awkward hug of all times. Then she turned and walked away.

"I'm glad you're okay," Ricardo said before following his sister.

I watched them go as a comfortable feeling poked amid all the bad stuff in me.

"So," Leo said, clasping my hand and pulling

me to him again. "I'm not going to lie. I wanted to be by your side tonight, to hold you myself, to lull you to sleep, but ... I understand why you want to be with your mother and sister."

I ran my hands up his arm. "I wanted that too." I wound my arms around his neck as his hands snaked around me. "But they need me. My mother is freaking out, and Hilary ... well, I don't really know how she is. I think I should be by her side tonight."

Leo stared into my eyes, a frown twisting his brows. "I'll miss you."

I knotted my fingers into his hair and pulled his head down to me. "I'll miss you too," I whispered before taking his lips into mine. He opened his mouth to me, sighing, his muscles relaxing. Our lips moved slowly, gently, quietly, but that didn't prevent the heat from building up south of my stomach, especially when he stroked my tongue with his.

I pulled back before I let myself dive into the moment. All I wanted was to dive into the moment, but I couldn't. Not yet.

I gave him another quick peck and turned away. He held on to my hand until my steps took me too far from him.

Without looking back, I rushed to catch up

with my mother and Hilary as they walked from the ambulance to the parking lot.

"There you are," my mother said. She had an arm around Hilary's shoulder. "I was beginning to wonder if you would come with us or not."

"I'm here and I'm coming with you," I said.

I stepped closer, and she draped her other arm around me too. "Good, because I don't plan on letting you both out of my sight ever again."

AFTER MY MOTHER DROVE US TO HER HOUSE, WE SAT on a couch in the living room, hugged, and cried. Hours must have passed by the time we finally stood up and went upstairs.

I cried again once I was in the shower. I cried over the girl I had been when Eric swept me off my feet. I cried over the years wasted with him. I cried for all the terrible things he did. I still couldn't grasp the fact that he had a hand in my grandma's and Hercules's death, in my father's incident, in Leo's scandal, but then I saw him hurting Argus and Jimmy, and ready to abuse Hilary.

I cried for Jimmy. I cried for Argus. Poor, dear Argus. I cried for Hilary. Gosh, how I hoped she wouldn't be too traumatized by this. I cried over me. Over my injuries, over my pride, over my feelings.

I wasn't sure what would become of Eric—he had been in bad shape when he was taken to the hospital, but he had enough on his back to rot in jail. And there was his mother too. Once I told the police everything, they sent a cop to her house. She was probably at a police department right now, being interrogated.

Which reminded me of the upcoming scandal. With the number of reporters that were at the ranch, who had probably come from Leo's ranch, I didn't doubt several magazines and newspapers would sport this tragic event on their covers by tomorrow.

However, right now, I didn't care about scandals.

When I was finally able to leave the shower, I put on comfy PJs and tiptoed to my mother's bedroom. She was waiting for us, seated on her bed. She pointed to the table in front of the window, flanked by two fancy armchairs, where there was a tray with lots of yummy food.

My stomach growled.

Hilary soon joined us and we ate in silence.

Then, without any invitation, Hilary and I

climbed onto Mom's king-size bed. With a small smile, she joined us, lying in the middle.

In the dark, we three held hands.

Mom sighed. "I don't think any of us wants to talk about what happened just yet and I believe we'll have a hard time falling asleep. But, when you're rolling from side to side, remember that you made it through it." She squeezed our hands. "Soon, your father will be home, and we'll be all together again and we'll make it through whatever ghosts are left together." She squeezed our hands. "I love you both so much." Her voice broke, and Hilary and I scooted closer to her.

38

"WE SHOULD BE LEAVING IN ABOUT HALF AN HOUR," my mother said.

She was seated on a lounge chair in the sunroom, already dressed and ready to go. Hilary and I were seated on the matching rattan love seat, still in our PJs.

"Okay," I said, getting up. "I'm gonna get ready."

Hilary stood up by my side. "Me too."

As we walked out of the sunroom, she reached for me and, holding hands like two lost five-year-old girls, we walked across the hallway and into the foyer.

I had just set foot on the first step of the stairs when the bell rang.

With a frown, I turned to the door.

"Holy shit, haven't they bothered us enough this morning?" Hilary said.

"Apparently not," I said, walking to the front door. Rosa stepped out from the hallway, but I waved her off. "I've got it. No worries."

She withdrew back to the kitchen as I unlocked the door and opened it.

My heart skipped a beat. Or four.

Leo stood there, in dark jeans, a fitted dark green polo, his cowboy boots, and huge Starbucks packets in his arms.

"*Bom dia*," he said with a tight smile. "Technically, it's almost eleven in the morning, but hey, it's still morning. I thought you might have overslept and not had breakfast yet because, you know, last night ..." he wandered off. His eyes left mine and went south, widening, before running me up and down, each inch making me aware of the skimpy material of the shorts and tee, and the fact that I wore no bra. However, the shine in his eyes told me he approved of it. "And you're even in your pajamas. Perfect." His gaze shifted to the stairs. "Oh, good morning."

Hilary waved at him before rushing up the stairs.

I crossed my arms over my breasts. "What are you doing here?"

He lifted his shoulders an inch, indicating the packets he held. "I brought brunch, for you three. And me."

I smiled and stepped aside. "How did you dodge the reporters?"

"Oh, I have my ways." He entered the house, deliberately taking his time while walking past me, his eyes on mine.

Without pausing completely, he placed a Douglas Iris around my ear. My heart squeezed in contentment. I took a sharp inhale and, turning to the side, closed the door behind him.

I grabbed one of the packets from him and gestured ahead. "Over this way." I showed him to the dining room, placed the packet on the table, and held up a finger. "Be right back." I dashed to the kitchen and informed Rosa about the visitor. "Please, bring plates and whatnots."

She looked at me, stunned. "But you already ate."

"Yes, well, he doesn't have to know about that."

Laughing, she shook her head, and I rushed back to the dining room.

Leo had taken a seat close to the head of the table. "Is this place all right?" he asked.

"Yeah," I said, walking to the chair right beside his. I sat down, suddenly nervous. "Thank you for this."

He turned to me with his cocky grin. "I hope you're hungry."

"Starving," I said.

A second later, Rosa came by the dining room and set it for brunch for us.

"Won't your mother and Hilary join us?" Leo asked.

"I can call Mrs. Taylor," Rosa said, leaving the dining room before I could come up with some excuse.

Leo reached for the packets and began working on them. I helped. There was a ton of food to feed three moms, four Hilarys, and maybe three Hannahs too. He had brought plain, dark coffee, several kinds of scones, cake slices, and sweet bread, and even wraps.

My mother walked into the dining room. "Hello, Leonardo."

"Good morning, Mrs. Taylor," Leo responded, sounding a little nervous.

"Hmm, what's happening here?" she asked, a wide smile on her lips.

"Leo brought brunch," I said, trying to emphasize the hidden don't-say-anything message with my eyes and tone.

She didn't get the hint. "But you already ate. Twice. And we have lunch plans."

Leo's head whipped to me. "What?"

"I'm sorry," I whispered.

"Why didn't you say anything?"

"Why would I? I mean, you came here, all prettied up and bringing me food. It was so sweet, I didn't want to ruin it."

He leaned back in his chair. "Well, it's sorta ruined now." He glanced over his shoulder, but my mom was gone. "You ate twice already?"

"Yeah, well ..." I sighed. "We had a pretty crappy night and around 5 a.m. we decided to stop lying in bed without purpose. Since then, we barely stopped. First, the three of us talked about the previous night, mostly to judge how much it affected Hilary."

"How is she?"

"A little shaken, but fine. She'll be fine."

"What else?"

"Then the police came early." Thank goodness, I had a robe handy when they knocked on the door. "They made me tell them everything again." I suppressed a shudder. "They said Chloe Bennett confessed everything."

I didn't want to tell him about Eric, though I hadn't been the one going after information. Apparently, he had listed me as his emergency contact with his health insurance, and someone called me to let me know his state. Which wasn't good. Argus had broken too many bones and ruptured too many ligaments and tendons. The probability of Eric ever walking again was low, and there was a chance he wouldn't be able to move his arms. Even knowing I shouldn't wish that on anyone, I couldn't help feeling like he got what he deserved, because really, death would be an easy way out.

"I've talked to Jimmy too," I continued. "He's in the hospital recovering. Other than blood loss and a few whip marks on his back, he'll be fine."

"I know."

My eyes widened. "You know. How?"

He shook his head. "Not important. Keep going."

"Well, if you know that, maybe you know that he's also working through his phone now, because he got someone to go over to the ranch and transfer the horses to the stable in the back. This friend of his will watch over them until we can go back."

"I didn't know that." Leo reached over the table and rested his hand over mine. "I can stop by once a day and make sure they are okay too." I glanced at our hands, and he quickly pulled his away. I frowned. What was that? Before I could ask, he continued, "I know about Argus too."

"You do?"

He ran his hand over his hair. "Yeah. I stopped at the animal hospital before coming here."

"You did?"

"I wanted to know how he was, and, if possible, to see him, see him well, so I could tell you that myself."

My eyes watered. I had spoken with Dr. Bohm earlier, but still, I wanted to hear this from Leo. "And?"

"He needs to go into a second surgery soon, but he's holding on. Dr. Bohm thinks his chances of making it through this are good."

I nodded, a tear rolling down my face.

Leo's fingertip stopped the tear halfway down. His touch sizzled my skin and I shivered. His eyes found mine as he pulled his hand away, but I didn't let him. I caught his hand and pulled it back to me.

"You're acting weird," I said. "Like ... you're shy."

He splayed his fingers over my cheek, cupping my face. "Not shy. Just a little precautious."

"And why is that?"

He leaned closer, and I held my breath. "Because, after last night and all the other events, I'm afraid of looking like I'm coming on too strong and scaring you away. You have no idea how frustrating it was to wake up at 7 a.m. and try to convince myself not to come here right away. So, I did things I thought you would like to busy my mind. I visited Jimmy and Argus, and then stopped by Starbucks because I know you love coffee."

New tears brimmed in my eyes. "You're so good to me."

He used his thumb to brush my tears away. "No, *morena*, you're so good to me." I fisted his shirt and pulled him closer, glad that he didn't resist it. "I was so afraid you would push me away."

I was afraid of that too. The entire morning, I wondered what would happen to us. I wondered if he would call me, but then I remembered my phone had been smashed to pieces. I wondered if I should go to him. And say what? For some reason, since last night, my insecurity was on high alert. I had been trying to come around it, and plant in my mind the idea of going to his house after I visited my father and Argus, hoping that, by the end of the day, I wasn't feeling so unworthy.

But here he was, coming to me with a sweet

brunch I would eat in spite of feeling full, just because he had brought it to me. Just because he showed me he cared.

I stared into his eyes. "I think we established the status of ... *us* in my car yesterday afternoon."

He flicked his gaze to my lips, then back to my eyes. "Is there a 'we'?"

I leaned in his direction, just a tiny bit. "I don't know. You tell me."

On purpose, I licked my lower lip, enjoying when his eyes followed the movement.

He took a deep breath. "Yes, there's definitely a 'we,'" he whispered, using his hand on my face to bring me closer.

His lips brushed against mine, and I let out something like a half-sigh, half-moan. He groaned, taking my mouth on his. His tongue dipped deep and made me moan again. With one of my hands still clutching his shirt, I pulled him closer, as close as we could be while seated on these chairs. Crawling on his lap did cross my mind, but I didn't think my mother would appreciate that.

His hand slid up my thigh, sending all thoughts of my mom away. Heat spread through me as he deepened the kiss, moving his lips like it was a sensual dance.

The sound of heels clicking on the hardwood

floor broke us apart, though I held his hand on my thigh, desperate to remain in contact with him.

My mother entered the dining room seconds later. "Hannah, I've talked to your father. He said he'll forgive you for skipping lunch if you promise to come later. He wants to see you himself and make sure you're okay." Her gaze shifted to Leo. "And you're welcome to come too, Leonardo."

I smiled. "Thanks, Mom."

"Thank you, Mrs. Taylor."

"I do have a name, you know," Mom said.

"Ah—" Leo opened his mouth and glanced at me with wide eyes.

"It's Joyce," I whispered, laughing.

"Yes, thank you Mrs. Tay—Joyce."

She nodded, with a grin. "Better." She narrowed her eyes at me. "Hannah, where did you get that flower?"

Heat crept on my cheeks. "Leo brought it to me."

"It's beautiful," she said, smiling. She checked her cell phone. "All right. Hilary and I are off. We'll see you two later."

"Bye," Leo and I said as she walked out.

Turning back to Leo, I touched the flower around my ear. "I never told you this. I know it's a common flower around here, but this is my favorite flower."

He smiled. "If you had told me that sooner, I would have given you one every single time I saw you."

Not wasting time, I snaked my arm around his neck and pulled him to me. "Hmm, where were we?" I asked, my mouth against his. He parted his lips to kiss me, but I pulled away. "Come on," I said, taking his hand in mine and standing up.

"Where are we going?" he asked, but I didn't answer.

I pulled him with me as I rushed to the foyer and up the stairs; paused at the top and looked out to the driveway through the window, just in time to see Mom's car leaving the property; and walked down the corridor on the second floor and into a heavy white door.

"Whoa." Leo whistled, whirling around.

I let my eyes survey my bedroom too.

Three of the walls were dark beige, while the fourth was a dark brown. And it was against that wall that my queen size bed stood. The headboard was painted the same color as the wall, and the frame had carvings all over it. Horses. Above the bed, a huge picture of Hercules and me adorned the wall, offsetting the brown with its bronze frame. I was turned to him, laughing, his black muzzle buried in my chest. For the past few months, it had hurt to come in here and look at the picture, but I never had the courage to take it down. Now, I wanted a similar picture by its side. Same size, same frame, but with Argus.

"You like it?" I asked.

"Wow, your bedroom is awesome." He ran his fingers over the dresser, which had the same carvings as the bed. "Has it always been like this?"

"Oh no." I chuckled. "Until I was eight years old or so, it was pink and had plenty of princesses and ballerinas everywhere."

He paused before a tall shelf between the two floor-to-ceiling windows. "All of these are yours?"

I walked up to him, but halted a foot behind, my eyes on the trophies and medals decorating every inch of the shelves. "Yes."

He read the labels on the trophies, probably checking out the name of the jumping competitions. "You're good!"

"Was," I corrected him. I took the flower from around my ear and placed it on my nightstand.

Leo whirled to me. "I bet you still are."

I shrugged. "That doesn't matter now. I don't want to go back to it. Really." I sighed. "I just want to go back to the ranch and take care of it. Soon my classes will start again, so that will keep me busy too."

"Are you sure that's what you want?"

I stepped into him and lifted my chin to face him. "I know what I want right now," I whispered, sliding my hands under his shirt.

With his eyes fixed on mine, Leo let out a loud sigh. "We don't have to do this today, you know that, right?"

"I know, but I want to."

"Are you sure?"

I placed a soft peck under his jaw, and he shivered. I smiled. "You don't sound like you want it."

He groaned. "*Meu Deus*, I want it. I want you. But I need to be sure you are sure, *morena*, because, if you say yes now and we start, I'm not sure I'll be able to stop it." He ran his hand over my arms. "I know I'll be instantly addicted to you."

I stood on tiptoes and licked his lower lip. He closed his eyes and inhaled.

"Just the way I want you to be," I whispered. "Now, Leonardo, show me how much you want me."

Immediately, his mouth claimed mine, and he walked me back, until my legs hit my bed. Without breaking the kiss, I sat down and he knelt before me, his hands sliding up my legs. I tugged on his shirt, and we stopped kissing only long enough for me to pull it over his head. Then his lips were on mine again, and his hands resumed their perusing. I did some perusing of my own, fingering and running my nails over his biceps and triceps and shoulders, amazed at how ripped and perfect he was.

I expected him to reach for my shorts, but he kept moving his hands up until they were under my tee, his fingers splayed against my stomach.

"I love feeling your skin," he whispered, trailing kisses down my neck, sending ripples of pleasure through my body. Then he pulled my tee over my head. His eyes shone as he examined me. I felt my cheeks heating, but I wasn't sure it was from embarrassment.

Without taking his eyes from mine, Leo pushed me back on the bed by the shoulders and pulled my shorts off. Next, his jeans slid to the floor, and I couldn't help but stare at the bulge inside his black boxers. Oh my God ...

He crawled over me and kept his body above mine, just one or two inches, but close enough for me to feel the heat from his body and ache for it, for touching him, for feeling him.

"*Perfeita*," he whispered, lowering his face to mine and brushing a soft kiss over my lips. "So beautiful." He made to tease me again, but I couldn't take it anymore. I reached up, wrapping my legs around his waist and placing a hand behind his neck, and pulled him to me. I gasped when his weight pressed me down, and I felt his hardness against my pelvis. The heat of his skin burned me, and I moaned, feeling that heat growing within me.

"I need you," I whispered in his ear. Leo groaned, his face buried into my neck. He nipped at my skin, thrusting his hips against mine. I gasped. "Oh, God, please."

I reached down and slipped my hands under his boxers, with intentions of taking it off, but he moved, trailing kisses from my neck to my chest. He cupped one of my breasts and flicked his tongue on the hard nub. I cried, arching against his touch.

His other hand slid lower and into my panties.

He raised his eyes to me and held my gaze while he flickered his tongue over my nipple again, and rubbed his fingers around my entrance. I squirmed, not because I didn't want it, but because it was too much, and I felt like I would fall into pieces at any second.

He closed his mouth over my breast and sucked hard, just as his finger slipped inside me. I cried, arching to his touch and knotting my hands into his hair.

Leo kept on teasing my breast with his tongue as he slipped a second finger inside me. I moved my hips to meet this touch, the pressure increasing, the heat building.

He sucked on my breast harder and pushed his fingers deeper, making me delirious.

A second later, the world around me exploded. "Leo!" I cried, trembling against him.

With a naughty smile, Leo repositioned himself, bringing his face to mine again. "Deus, *morena*, that was so hot, and you're so freaking hot."

"That *was* hot," I said, out of breath.

He kissed me. Deeply. Hungrily. Lovingly. For a moment, I was lost in the seductive world of his lips, but I wanted more of him. I needed more of him.

I pushed him up, breaking the kiss. He arched a brow at me, but I just smiled. I flipped him to my side, pressing him to lie on his back. I grabbed a condom from the nightstand and worked my panties and his boxers off. With the foil package between my teeth, I straddled him, but kept my hips high enough so that we weren't touching yet. He groaned, closing his hands on my waist and pulling me down. I swatted his hand away, before closing mine around his shaft.

His head rolled back and he groaned. "You're gonna kill me, *morena*."

"If it's in pleasure, I'm glad to oblige," I said, running my hand up and down his length.

Leo clutched the sheets beside him as I continued to stroke him. His breathing went up several notches, and his face contorted in pleasure. It satisfied me to no end.

"*Morena*, I can't ... no ... please," he muttered.

Understanding the message, I stopped caressing him and ripped the foil package. He reached for the condom, but I shook my head. I bit my lip as I rolled the condom over him.

Leo groaned. "*Deus do céu*, that's so fucking hot."

"Oh yeah. Let's see what you think about this."

I lowered myself to him slowly. His hands clutched my hips as I slid down. He moved his hips. "Shhh," I said, teasing. "This is my game."

"*Meu Deus.*"

Surprising him, I lowered myself hard on the rest of his length, and he moaned. I moaned too, amazed at how well he fit me, how deep he went, how hard he was.

I rocked up and down, enjoying the view of his

rippled chest. I traced my nails over his six-pack, and then over his pecs, playing with his nipples. Staring into my eyes, Leo held my wrists there, my palms over his chest. I could feel the rapid thump-thump of his heart. He began moving his hips, matching my strokes beat by beat. Slowly, he pulled me closer, and in a silent consent, we moved faster. He slid his arms from my wrists to my elbows, then to my back, holding me close and filling me up. The heat was increasing; the pressure was building.

"Oh, God, Leo ..." I whispered. "I'm ..."

Without warning, he flipped us. He carefully settled my head on my pillow, propped himself with his hand, and began pumping into me, deeper, faster.

"Like that?" he asked.

"Yeah. Oh yeah," I whispered.

I felt him tensing, and suddenly his thrusts became even more rapid and deep.

My eyes rolled inside my head, and I screamed as I climaxed. One stroke later, Leo joined me. He buried his face in my neck as his body thrashed against mine.

After a couple of seconds, he rolled to his sides, still breathing hard, and pulled me to him. I rested my head on his shoulder, and he caressed my back with his fingertips.

I gently placed my hand over the bandage on his side. "Didn't this hurt?"

"I felt it a few times, but nothing that would make me stop." He kissed my forehead. "By the way, that was—"

"Amazing," I finished for him.

"Hell, yeah, totally amazing." Leo put his hand under my chin and turned my face to his. "It's official. I'm addicted." He gave me a quick peck before staring into my eyes. "I love you, Hannah."

"I l—"

"No," he interrupted. "Please, don't say it if you don't mean it. I don't mind not hearing it back. For now." He smiled.

I propped myself on my elbow and scooted closer to him, my face directly above his. "I want to say it because I mean it. I love you, Leonardo."

His hand found my neck and he pulled me to him, his mouth capturing mine. I melted into him, and without really thinking about it, moved over him.

He sucked on my lower lip. "*Deus*, I confess I enjoyed hearing that more than I thought I would."

"I love you," I whispered.

He kissed me again; his lips melded perfectly into mine. Then, he groaned and pulled away. "I hate to do this, but I don't want your mother to dislike me on the first day we're officially together. We should get ready and go."

"Hmm, you're right," I muttered, leaning down to kiss him again.

He surrendered instantly. His hands traveled down my back, and I wiggled against his hips.

He half-groaned, half-laughed, breaking the kiss. "You're sneaky."

"Hmm, perhaps." I smiled at him.

He shook his head and scooted from under me. "*Morena*, I love you, and for that it would be really bad if your mother hated me."

I sighed. "Okay, but one condition." I sat up on the bed. "We repeat this tonight."

With a smile and a naughty gleam in his eye, Leo embraced me, pulling me to him. "Oh, *morena*, we're not going to repeat it." He gave me a quick peck and moved his lips over my ear. "We're going to do better."

I shivered. "I can't wait."

EIGHT MONTHS LATER

The wind whipped my hair and I smiled.

It was a beautiful spring morning, still chilly, but radiant.

I leaned forward and brushed my hand over Argus's neck. He nickered, but kept on galloping through the field, the muscles of his powerful body contracting and expanding with each move.

It had taken him three surgeries and about four months to recover from the shot, but after that, he progressed almost daily. His jumpy and scared self was left behind, and he became this beautiful, strong horse I always knew he could be. He was also a fast runner. I had gotten many offers on him, but I refused them all. He was *my* horse ...

my friend. There wasn't any money in the world that could take him from me.

I pulled on the reins and directed him back to the stable.

He neighed in protest, and I laughed.

"It's time, boy. I have a bunch of stuff to do," I said.

We approached the arena, but he didn't slow down and stop so I could open the gate.

Instead, he sped up.

"Argus ..." I muttered, knowing exactly what he wanted to do. I pulled the reins tighter and pressed my legs to his sides, preparing myself.

Making me chuckle, he accelerated even more, as if that were possible. The fence was closer and closer. I leaned forward and, two seconds later, he jumped over it.

We soared into the air, and I inhaled deeply, loving the two-second flight.

His hooves hit the ground inside the arena, and I laughed. He was just ... amazing.

Argus slowed to a trot and brought us to the stable, just as another amazing someone stepped out of the stable, wearing low-riding jeans. And nothing else.

My goodness.

I jumped off Argus and turned to Leo. With a

will of its own, my gaze ran over him, taking in his perfect form inch by inch, especially his rippled chest and his gorgeous face.

"That was an incredible jump," he said, running his hand over his disheveled hair. I loved that look on him.

"It was." I bit my lip. "*Bom dia.*"

"*Bom dia.*" He smiled, reaching his hands to me. "I love it when you speak Portuguese."

I stepped into his embrace and placed a soft kiss under his jaw. He sighed. "When I *try* speaking Portuguese. *Try* being the important word here."

Since he basically moved to the ranch with me about five months ago, he had been teaching me words and expressions in Portuguese. It was confusing, and most of the time I only ended up twisting my tongue, but I loved it.

I ran my hand over his naked chest, remembering what we had done last night, and every night for that matter. I slid my hand lower, and he groaned.

"*Morena ...*"

"What?" I nipped the soft spot under his ear. "You come out of bed with no shirt, and it's not even that hot out here. It's all your fault."

His hand splayed on my back, and he teased

me with his hot breath over my neck. "And what are you doing out of bed so early?"

"Well, I had to hide the Easter eggs, but I was done faster than I thought I would be, so I decided to take Argus out for a stroll."

"Oh yeah. I forgot about that." He tilted his mouth to mine. "Happy Easter."

"*Feliz Páscoa*," I whispered, proud of myself for remembering how to say it in Portuguese.

His lips parted to take mine, and Argus nudged Leo's arms with his muzzle, making him stagger two steps to the side.

He chuckled. "A jealous horse. I'll never get used to it."

With a smile, I patted Argus's neck and grabbed his reins. "Come on, boy."

I walked past Leo, purposely brushing my body on his. His hand stroked my waist and my smile widened. While I took Argus's saddle and halter off, Leo brought him water and grain.

Minuano neighed from the next stall.

I snorted. "Hmm, my horse is jealous? And what about yours?"

Shaking his head, Leo turned to Minuano and caressed his cheek. He muttered something to the horse—in Portuguese.

"Hey, you two!" I took the saddle in my arms.

"No gossiping in the stable. Especially when I can't understand it."

"Ha, another reason to do it!" Leo teased.

He took the saddle from me, I picked up the halter from the ground, and we put them away in the tack room. I was placing the bridle on the wall when Leo's hands came around me, his chest pressing my back.

"So, what else do we need to do before our families come for lunch?" he whispered, his mouth trailing a hot path on my shoulder.

I moaned. "I need to finish preparing lunch, but that shouldn't take long. What time is it?"

"A little past nine." He pulled my hair to the side, and I tilted my head along with his touch. He grazed his teeth on my neck, his hot breath bringing a welcomed ache between my legs. "We told them to come at eleven, right?"

"Yes," I gasped as his hand snaked under my top.

He groaned over my ear, provoking me, while his hand traveled up my belly and under my bra. "I think I should help you to the shower before they come, *morena*."

"I had plans of working on a project for my econ class," I said, out of breath.

"How can I persuade you to work on your project another time?"

I reached behind my back and cupped the bulge in the front of his jeans. He groaned.

"Hmm, if you promise to scrub every inch of me clean," I whispered.

"With my tongue," he responded, as breathless as I was.

I shivered. "Yes, please."

Without warning, he turned me around and pulled me into his arms, making me laugh.

He turned his boyish, cocky smile at me, and my breath caught. I loved these moments when I looked at him, and even after eight months, I was still struck by how gorgeous and delicious he was, and by how much he cared about me.

And I knew this feeling would never lessen.

He walked out of the tack room, his arms tight around me, but halted when we heard the sound of a car approaching.

He dropped me to my feet. "What the hell?"

I shrugged and exited the stable, Leo on my heels, to see who it could be. My father's car came to a stop in the parking area, and a second later, my father, my mother, and Hilary stepped out.

"I swear I told them to come around eleven," I muttered.

Leo knotted his fingers with mine and pulled me to the arriving guests.

My father walked slowly, his arm looped around my mother's. He looked well and healthy again, but since his incident, it was like a fraction of his strength had left him and didn't want to come back. Nevertheless, he kept on working and riding and working some more. Twice a week, I spent my afternoons with him, learning the business involved in a breeding farm. When he could, Leo came along with me, since he knew a lot about breeding from his family's farm in Brazil.

My mother smiled at my father, and I was reminded of how much their relationship had improved in the last few months. It was like they were a young couple again. My mother had changed a little too. She was less uptight and didn't become upset with me when I skipped teas at the club. Much to my surprise, she joined a nonprofit organization that helped women and children living or running from domestic violence. Every now and then, when the memories didn't hurt much, I went with her.

So did Hilary.

I glanced at her. As usual, she was incredibly beautiful in jeans, a blouse, and high heels. Her golden hair fell in waves behind her back, and she looked more like an angel than a real girl.

Looking at her, nobody could tell what she felt on the inside. Unfortunately, she had rough times after the day Eric showed his real claws. She had nightmares and didn't like being alone with men —any men, except for my father and Leo. She was going to therapy, and apparently, it was working, but slowly.

But she was young, and I was sure she would recover fully. Someday.

A little uncomfortable about being shirtless, Leo crossed his arms.

"Sorry we came so early," my father said, embracing me. "But your mother insisted."

She slapped his arm in a playful way. "I thought she could use some help with cooking, cleaning, hiding the eggs."

I opened my mouth to tell them the eggs were already hidden, but then Hilary stepped in front of me with a basketful of colored eggs, and I shut my lips.

"Good thinking," I said, taking the basket from Hilary. "Well, come on in."

We turned toward the house, but stopped when we heard a new sound of cars driving down the road. Two cars. Leo's family.

He looked at me, his eyes wide, and I chuckled. Oh well.

His father and mother walked up to us with bright smiles.

After Leo's suspension and Eric's arrest, João Pedro and Leo seemed to be working out their problems. After a day-long meeting and an open interview with the press where Leo told his version of his past—or what he felt comfortable talking about—the club allowed Leo to come back to the team, and a couple of weeks later, offered them a new contract—of three years. And, according to them, chances were that the contract would be renewed for another three years. But I wasn't worried about that now.

Ri, Pedro, Bia, and Gui slid out of the second car. Ri had broken up with his girlfriend-almost-fiancée after finding out she had been the witness who told the press about the insides of Leo's past, after Eric ratted him out. She tried defending herself, saying she was upset by being left behind because of Leo, but Ri couldn't forgive her. Pedro and Gui continued single and partying, not too hard though. And Bia had a fight with her parents and applied to colleges all over the country. Soon, she should be receiving acceptance or rejections letter, though João Pedro already told her that if she insisted on going to college, she could go to Santa Barbara—he wouldn't allow her to go anywhere else. However, she had told me that she would just leave when the time came, with or without his blessing.

João Pedro held a thermal bottle but slapped Leo's chest with his free hand. "Go put on a shirt, boy!"

Leo groaned and tightened his arms over his chest.

"*Bom dia*," Agnes said with a *chimarrão* in her hand. "We thought about coming early to help you two, but I'm guessing we weren't the only ones with that idea."

My mother laughed. "Isn't that nice? We can prepare everything together now."

Bia rolled her eyes. "Awesome. And my bed already misses me." She stopped by my side and bumped her shoulder on mine. "Hey, do you think the bed in your guest room would want me?"

I chuckled.

"How about we start, then?" Leo asked. Everyone agreed, and he gestured to the house.

"Good idea," Bia said, jumping in front of everyone. "The guest bedroom is mine!"

We watched as our early guests walked the

path leading up the porch steps, chatting like a big happy family.

"I don't know if I'm glad they are here early or not," Leo said.

I smiled. "I'm trying to be glad." I pulled him to me, putting my arms around his neck. "Think about this, it's a good thing our families get along. And"—I brushed my lips on his—"we still have the entire night to enjoy each other."

With a smile, Leo snaked his arms around my waist. "I like the way you think, *morena*. In fact, I'm pretty sure I *love* everything about you."

I clasped my hand on his nape and pulled him to me. "Good. Because I *love* everything about you too."

***

READ BIA'S STORY NEXT ON *BREAKING AWAY*!

THANK YOU

If you want to see exclusive teasers, help me decide on covers, read excerpts, talk about books, etc, join my reader group on Facebook: Juliana's Club!

ABOUT THE AUTHOR

While USA Today Bestselling Author Juliana Haygert dreams of being Wonder Woman, Buffy, or a blood elf shadow priest, she settles for the less exciting—but equally gratifying—life as a wife, a mother, and an author. She resides in North Carolina and spends her days writing about kick-ass heroines and the heroes who drive them crazy.

Subscribe to her mailing list to receive emails of announcement, events, and other fun stuff related to her writing and her books: www.bit.ly/JuHNL

For more information:
www.julianahaygert.com

facebook.com/julianahaygert

twitter.com/juliana_haygert

instagram.com/juliana.haygert

goodreads.com/juliana_haygert

pinterest.com/julianahaygert

bookbub.com/authors/juliana-haygert

ALSO BY JULIANA HAYGERT

To find links and more info, go to:

www.julianahaygert.com/books/

Shorts

Into the Darkest Fire

Tested

Standalones

Daughter of Darkness

Rite World: Blackthorn Hunters Academy

The Demon Kiss (Book 1)

The Hunter Secret (Book 2)

The Soul Bond (Book 3)

The Shadow Trials (Book 4)

The Infernal Curse (Book 5)

Rite World

The Vampire Heir (Book 1)

The Witch Queen (Book 2)

The Immortal Vow (Book 3)

The Warlock Lord (Book 4)

The Wolf Consort (Book 5)

The Crystal Rose (Book 6)

The Wolf Forsaken (Book 7)

The Fae Bound (Book 8)

The Blood Pact (Book 9)

The Wyth Courts

Winter King (Book 1)

Spring Warrior (Book 2)

Summer Prince (Book 3)

Autumn Rebel (Book 4)

The Fire Heart Chronicles

Heart Seeker (Book 1)

Flame Caster (Book 2)

Sorrow Bringer (Book 3)

Earth Shaker (Novella)

Soul Wanderer (Book 4)

Fate Summoner (Book 5)

War Maiden (Book 6)

www.ingramcontent.com/pod-product-compliance
Lightning Source LLC
Chambersburg PA
CBHW061336190726
48288CB00005B/1471